A PALAZZO IN
THE STARS

ALSO BY PAUL DI FILIPPO

A PALAZZO IN THE STARS

PAUL DI FILIPPO

East Baton Rouge Parish Library
Baton Rouge, Louisiana

WILDSIDE PRESS

To Deborah, who makes any home a celestial palace.

Published by Wildside Press LLC.
www.wildsidebooks.com

CONTENTS

INTRODUCTION

I seem to write stories more slowly than I used to. Oh, the individual sentences still come at roughly the same pace, accumulating steadily at a rate of 500 or 1000 good words per day, and thus any distinct tale gets completed about as fast as it did thirty years ago, when I began my career. But the days available for fiction seem to shrink. My job as a reviewer means much of my time is spent reading the books of others, then cudgeling my brains for the best way to convey annoyance, delight and insightful literary wisdom—such as I may possess.

But nonetheless, stories do still emerge, since that first sale in 1977 (fortieth anniversary, here I come!), and they have a way of piling up. This collection represents the output of about two-and-a-half years, and, while I might have filled such a book in one year's writing time circa 1990, there's nonetheless another collection's worth of newer stuff awaiting curation, beyond this volume. I guess by now I should realize that, for me at least, the process is inevitable, rather like another process I am all too familiar with: acquiring extra pounds. Pleasurable, stealthy and yet eventually noticeable to all.

I hope you enjoy these stories of recent vintage.

ABOUT GALAXY OF MIRRORS

If this story recalls to you the work of Jack Vance, the resonance is deliberate. I've tried emulating my hero only once or twice, with mixed results. I hope the pastiche is not too distracting here.

This was my first attempt to explain Fermi's Paradox—why does the universe seem empty?—for an anthology devoted to that theme, edited by Pete Crowther. My second attempt will appear in my next collection. Until then, the logic given here must be considered definitive!

GALAXY OF MIRRORS

Silent and observant, Fayard Avouris clustered with his fellow chattering tourists at the enormous bow-bellied windows constituting the observation deck of the luxury starliner *Melungeon Bride*. Their lazy, leisurely, loafers' ship had just taken up orbit around the uninhabited wilderness world dubbed Youth Regained. Soon the cosseted and high-paying visitors would be ferried down to enjoy such unspoiled natural attractions as the Scintillating Firefalls, the Roving Islands of Lake Vervet, and the Coral Warrens of the Drunken Monkey-mites. Then, before boredom could set in, off to the next stop: the hedonistic casino planet of Rowl.

Contemplating the lovely, patchwork, impasto orb hung against a backdrop of gemlike stars flaring amber, magenta and violet, Fayard Avouris sighed. This trip had failed, so far, either to re-stimulate his sense of wonder or replenish his intellectual pep.

A fellow of medium height and pudgy girth, Avouris did not necessarily resemble the stereotypical professor of anthropology, but neither did he entirely defy such a status. He looked rather too louche and proletarian to be employed as an instructor by such a famous university as the Alavoine Academy of Durwood IV. His style of dress was humble and careless, and his rubicund countenance marked him as a fan more of various weathers than library interiors. But a certain pedantic twist to his lips, and a tendency to drop the most abstruse and aberrant allusions into mundane conversation betrayed his affiliation with the independently thinking classes.

A proud affiliation of many years, which he had routinely cherished up until his nervous breakdown some six months ago.

The unanticipated mental spasm had overtaken Avouris as he lectured a classroom full of graduate students, his remarks also being streamed onto the astromesh for galactic consumption. His theme that day was the explicable exoticism of the several dozen cultures dominant on Hrnd, ranging from the Whitesouls and their recondite taxonomy of sin to the Gongoras and their puzzling paraphilias. As he recounted a particularly spicy anecdote from his field studies among the Gongoras, involving an orgy featuring the massive "walking birds" of the Faraway

Steppes, an anecdote that could always be counted on to hold the audience spellbound, he suddenly felt his own savor for the tale evaporate.

And then his hard-won mental topography of galactic culture instantly flattened.

Ever since his own undergraduate days, Fayard Avouris had painstakingly built up a multidimensional mental map of the hundreds of thousands of human societies and their quirks. Useful as an aide-mémoire, this metaphorical model of the Milky Way's myriad ethnographical topoi resembled a mountain range of human diversity, a splendid chart of mankind's outre customs.

But all of a sudden, his laboriously honed virtual creation deflated to a thin pancake of dull homogeneity.

Whereas previous to this moment Avouris had always seen humans, the only sentients in all the vast galaxy, as creatures exhibiting a practically infinite range of behaviors, suddenly his species seemed to resemble paramecia in their limited repertoire. Like some star collapsing into a black hole and losing all its unique complexion in darkness, all the manifold variations of human behavior born of chance, circumstance and free will now imploded into a kernel of mere instinctual responses to stimuli. Humanity seemed no more than hardwired automatons. Sentience itself, so precious and unique amidst all the organisms in a life-teeming galaxy, appeared more like a curse than a gift. All of humanity's long variegated history appeared bland and predictable.

Avouris slammed to a stop in mid-sentence, and froze in place, hands clamped on the podium. A hastily summoned EMT crew had been required to remove him from behind the lectern.

* * * *

Alavoine Academy had been very understanding and sympathetic. The tenured holder of the Stridor Chair of Anthropology simply needed a sabbatical; he had been working too hard. A university-sponsored ticket for the next cruise of the *Melungeon Bride* would solve everything. He'd return invigorated and in top-notch mental health.

But now, three planets into the cruise, as Fayard Avouris contemplated more sight-seeing—this time, thankfully, on a world devoid of humans—any such recovery seemed increasingly problematical. The matter of how he could ever reawaken his quondam fascination with the antics of his race plagued him. Moreover, he had begun to suspect that his own dalliance with neurosis was not unique—that this affliction was becoming widespread, and that his own anticipatory bout with it reflected merely a greater sensitivity to the zeitgeist.

On this cruise, Avouris had discreetly probed his fellow passengers, seeking to ascertain their level of excitement regarding their itinerary. The first three stops had occurred at worlds that boasted supremely exotic cultures that deviated far from the galactic norm, a consensual baseline of behaviors continually updated by astromesh polling.

On the world known as Karoshi, people vied to perform the most odious jobs possible in order to attain the highest social status. The most admired and rewarded citizens, virtual royalty, were those who applied medicinal salves to the sores of plague victims via their tongues.

On Weebo III, exogamy was enforced to the exact degree that no two citizens could enjoy intercourse unless a different stranger was invited into the affair each time.

And on Tugnath, a booming trade in afterlife communications involved the perilous enactment of near-death experiences among the interlocutors.

And here they were now at the edenic Youth Regained, afterwards to be visiting Rowl, Lyrely, Ahab's Folly, Zizzofizz and Port Canker. Surely, an itinerary to feed a lifetime of vibrant memories.

And yet Avouris's companions manifested little real excitement. They seemed bored or apathetic, no matter how bizarre their encounters with oddball races. Why? Not because they were all jaded cosmopolites; many of the travelers aboard the *Melungeon Bride* were entirely new to starfaring. No, the only explanation that Avouris could sustain involved immunization to the limited ideational space of human customs and beliefs.

No matter how strange a culture looked initially, upon closer contemplation it became merely one more predictable example of a general class of human behaviors. Death, sex, piety, hedonism, sports, procreative ardor, fashion sense, artistic accomplishment—these few motivators, along with a couple of others, constituted the entire range of determinants for human culture. True, the factors could be combined and permuted in a large number of ways. But in the end, a discerning or even a naïve eye could always unriddle the basic forces at work.

This sense of a limited ideational space constraining the potentials of the species was what had brought Avouris down with a crash. And he suspected that some of the same malaise was beginning to afflict the general populace as well, a millennia into the complete expansion of humanity into the peerless galaxy.

If only other modalities of sentience had presented themselves! Mankind could have had various educational windows to look through, rather than an endless hall of mirrors. But galactic evolution had been cruel and parsimonious with regards to intelligence...

Flatscreens across the observation deck and on various personal devices came to life with the voice and face of Slick Willywacker, the ship's obnoxious tummler. Fayard Avouris experienced a crawling dislike for the clownish fellow.

"Hey-nonny-nay, sirs and sirettes! Prepare to embark for a glamorous groundling's go-round! We'll be loading the lighters with the guests from cabins A100 through A500 first. Meanwhile, have a gander at these little imps cavorting in realtime down below!"

The screens filled with Drunken Monkey-mites at play in the surf. The tiny agile beings seemed beguilingly human, but Avouris knew that they were in reality no smarter than a terrestrial gecko.

Sighing deeply, Avouris turned toward the exit. Perhaps he'd just sit at the bar and drink all day…

Startled exclamations and shrieks caused the anthropologist to whirl around and face the windows again.

In the moment of turning his back upon Youth Regained, the planet had changed radically.

Where before empty plains and coasts and mountain ranges had loomed, there now reared vast conurbations, plainly artificial in nature. From this low-orbit vantage, Avouris could even make out extensive agricultural patternings.

Avouris inquired of a stranger. "What happened?"

The elderly woman replied in a dazed fashion. "I don't know. I just blinked, and life was altered!"

The screens had gone blank during this inexplicable and impossible transition. But now they flared back to life.

A single Drunken Monkey-mite face dominated each display. But this creature resembled the little imps of a minute past only insofar as a lemur resembled a human. This evolved being wore clothing, and stood in a room full of alien devices.

The Monkey-mite spoke in perfect astromesh-standard Galglot.

"Hello, ship in orbit. Who are you? Where do you come from? We have never had visitors before!"

Fayard Avouris felt a big smile crease his face.

Life had suddenly become vitally interesting again.

* * * *

The stark and cheerless offices of the Okhranka on Muntjac in the Al'queem system had not been designed to coddle visitors. Generally speaking, the only types who visited the Okhranka willingly and via the public entrance were vendors of spyware and concealed weaponry; informers either vengeful or altruistic; errant politicians being called out to correct their views; and kooks with sundry theories regarding infernal dangers and utopian opportunities.

Fayard Avouris knew without a doubt that the officials of the galactic security apparatus would certainly place him in the last-named category. An academic from a small institution, however respectable, purporting to hold unique insights regarding the biggest conundrum of recorded history, a puzzle which had kept all the best minds of the galaxy stymied for the past six months— Well, how else could he appear to them, other than as one of those eccentric amateurs who claimed to hold the answer to the fabled disappearance of the *Pitchforth Lady*, or the key to the unbreakable ciphers of the Neo-Essenes?

Knowing how he must appear to these bureaucrats, who were probably observing him in secret even now, Avouris strove to maintain his dignity, composure and respectability, even as he tallied his third excruciating hour of waiting in this uncomfortable chair. For the twentieth time he paged through a hardcopy leaflet entitled *A Field Agent's Best Practices for Intra-urban Rumor Quelling* without seeing a word of the text, all the while revolving in his mind the most compelling way to deliver his pitch.

Ever since making his discovery some five weeks ago, Avouris had striven to reach someone in the government who would pay heed to his findings. After many futile entreaties, this appointment with a mid-level apparatchik had been the best meeting he could secure. He wondered now what I. G. Narozhylenko would look like, how receptive he would be. Avouris had tried searching the astromesh for details of the man, but as an Okhranka functionary, the fellow was almost nonexistent so far as public records went. Avouris hoped he would be neither too apathetic nor too closed-minded to listen to an unconventional theory.

Just as the anthropologist was about to peruse the old leaflet for the twenty-third time an inner door opened, and Narozhylenko's personal assistant appeared. Avouris instinctively admired the young woman's grace and shape and modest yet stylish fashion sense. Short hair the color of a raven's wing, arrayed in bangs across an intelligent forehead, nicely framed alert, inquisitive features.

"You may enter now, Professor Avouris."

Inside the office, Avouris dropped down into a guest chair microscopically more comfortable than his previous seat. To his astonishment, the woman took up a desk chair on the far side of a nameplate scribed AGENT I. G. NAROZHYLENKO.

"You are I. G. Narozhylenko?"

"Yes, Ina Glinka Narozhylenko." The woman smiled wryly. "You had a pre-formed conception of me at variance with reality?"

"No, of course not! That is, I—" Avouris gave up apologies and explanations as a waste of time. Luckily, Narozhylenko did not seem put out, or inclined to pursue the embarrassing matter. Indeed, Avouris seemed to detect a small smile threatening to escape bureaucratic suppression.

"Let's get right to your business then, Professor. I won't apologize for keeping you waiting so long. As you might imagine, our agency has been stressed beyond belief in dealing with the advent of these non-human sophonts. Not only must we manage the pressing practical issues involved in fitting them into galactic culture, but the implications of their instant creation carry even more disturbing challenges. The past six months have overturned so many paradigms that we can barely get our heads above the wreckage. Galactic culture is churning like a Standeven milkmaid on the eve of the springtime butter-sculpting festival."

Avouris appreciated the clever metaphor. It seemed to bespeak learning, humor and broad-mindedness: three qualities he could appeal to in his pitch.

"I agree absolutely. Out of nowhere, our age has become a revolutionary era."

The miraculous and instantaneous transformation of Youth Regained from a wilderness planet into the seemingly long-established homeworld of the first non-human civilization ever encountered had been merely the opening note in a bizarre symphony of spontaneous generation.

Shortly thereafter, the world known as Pronk-Kissle had instantly flipped from uninhabited desert wastes to the thriving techno-hives of giant talking sand fleas.

Voynet VII suddenly sported a global culture of stratospheric sentient gasbags.

Spaethmire now hosted a single group intelligence distributed across billions of individuals resembling both sessile and mobile slime molds.

Los Caminos now featured continental-spanning burrows populated by sensitive and poetical beings who resembled naked mole-rats crossbred with whales, each one large as a subway car.

And so on, for another two dozen transformed worlds scattered across the formerly humans-only galaxy, with fresh instances occuring at regular intervals.

All these new alien civilizations had just two things in common.

They all claimed to have arisen naturally over geological timespans on their native planets.

None of them had ever encountered humans before.

These mutually exclusive assertions—each tenet impossible in its own way, given humanity's long acquaintance with these worlds—had engendered scores of theories, none of which had yet been proven to represent the truth of the matter.

Ina Glinka Narozhylenko regarded Avouris sternly. "You're not here to tell me you have the answer to these manifestations, are you, Professor? Because I do not believe that your field of expertise—anthropology, is it not?—could feature insights unavailable to our best quantum physicists and plectic fabulists."

Momentarily distracted by the deep grey eyes of the attractive Okhranka agent, Fayard Avouris hesitated a moment before saying, "Oh, no, Agent Narozhylenko, I don't pretend to know the origins of these aliens. However, I do believe that I can predict with some degree of accuracy where the next such outbreak will occur."

Narozhylenko leaned forward intently. "You have exactly fifteen minutes to justify this bold assertion, Professor."

"I have here a memory stick. If you would be so kind as to plug it into your system, Agent Narozhylenko...."

The woman did so.

On a large screen popped up a navigable simulucrum of the galaxy. Avouris rose to stand beside the screen where he could interact with the display.

"Here are the recorded outbreaks." The map zoomed and shrank across several scales, as Avouris called up the locations of the alien worlds as he had plotted them earlier. "Do you see any pattern to their distribution?"

"No. And neither did any of several thousand experts."

"Ah, but that is because you do not have a solid theory that would allow you to examine and compare the relevant data sets."

Avouris went on to explain about his personal disllusionment, his dismal anti-epiphany regarding human limitations and sameness, and how he believed that such a malaise was now a general, albeit unrecognized condition across the galaxy.

"I call this spiritual ailment 'Mirror Sickness.' Perhaps you've seen symptoms of it around you, or even in yourself...?"

Agent Narozhylenko sat pensive. "Yes...yes... I recognize the feeling. Proceed with your presentation."

"I have spent hundreds of hours since the first alien incursion performing astromesh polling across thousands of worlds on the phenomenon of Mirror Sickness." The screen came alive with animated histograms. "Sifting the results involved the employment of a number of expert machine systems, or I would not have finished for years. In any case, here is a map of the neurosis, graded by severity of symptoms."

Avouris overlaid his findings atop the display of alien outbreaks.

Agent Narozhylenko rose slowly to her feet. "They match... They match exactly! Aliens are appearing at equidistant loci relative to those humans worlds most despairing of the limitations of our species."

"Let's call them 'the loneliest worlds,' for convenience's sake. And you'll note that the manifestations are precisely encoding the severity gradient of Mirror Sickness, from worst case downward."

Narozhylenko approached the screen and magnified a sector of the galactic map. "Wustner's Weatherbolt should display the next outbreak then. In just a week's time." She turned to Avouris. "Are you currently free from teaching duties, Professor Avouris."

"Now, and perhaps for the rest of my life!"

* * * *

Agent Ina Glinka Narozhylenko manifested superior piloting abilities at the helm of her little space clipper, the Okhranka-supplied *Whispering Shade*. Fayard Avouris felt utterly safe in her hands, although her extremely speedy and cavalier passage through the Oort Cloud on the extremes of the Sockeye star system where the world called Wustner's Weatherbolt revolved had induced a little transient anxiety in the anthropologist.

But now, as the homely little ship floated serenely and safely above the rondure of the planet where—if Avouris's theory and calculations were correct—a miraculous transformation from nescient virgin mudball to home of another unprecedented alien civilization was about to occur, Avouris could not fully relax. Unable to quell a griping sense of injustice, he felt compelled to speak.

"I still can't believe that you and I were deputed alone to affirm my theory. Are your superiors insane or merely mingy, that they could not devote more resources than this to such a potentially lucrative information-gathering expedition? Where is the vast armada of research vessels that should have accompanied us?"

Across the cabin from where Avouris sat, Agent Narozhylenko fussed with the craft's small food reconstituter, preparing a meal. Avouris admired her efficient, graceful movements. He only wished the woman would open up and discuss personal matters with him. The social ambiance during their journey of three days had been rather more arid and formalistic than Avouris could have wished. But so far, Agent Ina Glinka Narozhylenko had maintained a scrupulously business-like demeanor. After his one attempt to call her by her given names and to probe into her familial background had been met with silence and a frosty stare and the subliminal threat of esoteric martial-arts dissuasions, he had refrained from any further pleasantries. So now all he could do by way of conversation was complain.

"The Okhranka Directorate," said the agent in response to his gripe, "are not fools or gamblers. And their resources are always limited, never more so than at present. Oftentimes only a single agent is tasked with a complex assignment. We are highly competent and trained across a broad number of surprising disciplines. The *Whispering Shade* boasts all the sensors of a larger craft, so more vessels would be superfluous. And the satellites I've launched give us complete telemetric coverage of the planet. Believe me, if we witness the fulfillment of your prediction, the next such occasion will merit a fuller contingent."

Avouris grumped before responding. "Well, I suppose you people know what you're doing."

Narozhylenko cocked one eyebrow. "A very generous allowance on your part, Professor Avouris. Now, would you care for some shabara fillets?"

After eating they rested in their separate berths, under a programmed bout of artificial sleep. The guardian machines triggered wakefulness well in advance of the projected time for the planetary transition. Then commenced the nerve-wracking waiting.

"What do you see as the probable cause of these eruptions of nonhuman sentience, Professor?" Narozhylenko asked, while she fiddled with the satellites' feed. "Of the theories so far proposed, I place Planck-level punctuated equilibrium first, global de-masking of long-established hidden worlds second, and mass mind-tampering third."

Avouris shook his head thoughtfully. "No, no, none of those explanations appeal to me as sufficiently comprehensive. Whatever the answer, it will be more complex than any scenario so far advanced. And then we have the question of motive. I can't believe this is a natural phenomenon. A prime mover is implied. Who, and why? And why now?"

"Perhaps your own theories about the spatial distribution of the changes will contribute to an ultimate solution, Professor."

"So I hope. Now, let us focus on these screens. The change is imminent, I believe."

Agent Narozhylenko moved to magnify the image of Wustner's Weatherbolt on one display, but even as she did so the planet vanished, to be replaced by an edgeless curving wall bristling with dangerous-looking protrusions.

Avouris could merely gasp, and say, "What the—?" before Narozhylenko had moved to step down the scale of the display.

Interposed between the *Whispering Shade* and the altered planet was a space-going vessel that had appeared from nowhere. So enormous as to render the Okhranka ship a pea next to a prize-winning pumpkin, the alien craft radiated martial prowess and a defiant hostility.

Narozhylenko's frantic fingers found an active communications channel.

A separate panel showed a being that resembled a bipedal lobster colored fungal white. Its stubby midriff legs wiggled angrily. It occupied a command center bustling with others of its kind.

Avouris had time only to say, "That's plainly an evolved form of the Ghost Crawdad of Miravalle Caverns." Then the lobster was speaking.

"You are friends of the World Thinker, or enemies?"

"Who is the World Thinker?" asked Narozhylenko.

"Wrong answer. Now you must die."

A coruscating sphere of blue-gold energy bloomed from the ship of the Ghost Crawdads, but the *Whispering Shade* was already curving and jinking away. The ball of destruction missed them and decohered violently but uselessly, flooding space with radiation. On the communications channel, the lobster captain gestured silently with his antennae, audio transmissions temporarily suspended at Narozhylenko's behest.

Sweating yet composed, Narozhylenko said, "We have to get well beyond the mass of the planet before I dare kick in the superposition drive! Even then it's extremely dangerous. Stall these angry arthropods somehow! Go!"

She flicked the audio back on, and Avouris began to babble.

"Sweet saltworms to you, my hardshell friends! May all your mates molt most enticingly! You mistake us for enemies! We are not! This World Thinker you mention is unknown to us. Please enlighten us poor, exsoskeleton-bereft, leg-deficient beings."

The lobster captain made no reply, but evidently shut off his own audio to consult with his officers. Narozhylenko evoked a tithe of additional power from the *Shade*'s engines. Avouris felt his own shirt pasted to his wet armpits.

"That's it, keep it up! Just another five minutes...."

The lobster's idiosyncratic but intelligible Galglot resumed. "You must know the World Thinker, source of all intelligence. His gift is a poisoned one, though. Admit it! Don't you wish his destruction, impossible as that might be?"

"Oh, of course! Death to all World Thinkers! Free the sentients!"

The lobster captain performed what could only be interpreted as a disdainful arthropodic glare. "Your protestations are insufficiently sincere. Goodbye."

Several more deadly rosettes of energy bloomed, converging rapidly and ineluctably on the human ship, just as Narozhylenko shouted, "Now!"

The *Whispering Shade* juddered, leaped, its metal bones ringing with one tremendous *bong!*, then settled down into easy superposition travel outside the relativistic universe.

Agent Narozhylenko jumped up from the controls and flung herself at Fayard Avouris. He hardly knew how to react, half-expecting chastising corporal punishment for his diplomatic incompetence. But the agent's kisses and caresses soon allayed that fear. Avouris returned them heartily.

In the interstices, the anthropologist whispered, "Oh, Ina Glinka...."

"No," she whispered lusciously, "call me Rosy...."

* * * *

The armada amassed around Wangba-Szypyt IX would have caused the Ghost Crawdads to shed their tails and flee. The Okhranka Directorate were taking no chances on the arrival of another belligerent spacefaring set of aliens. The human ships were porcupined with weaponry.

On the command deck of the lead cruiser, Rosy and Fayard occupied a rare position of civilian perquisite. Agent Narozhylenko was discussing tactics with a dour silver-haired soldier named Admiral Leppo Brice, while Avouris speculated with a team of academics about which species native to Wangba-Szypyt IX would be the candidate for uplift by the mysterious World Thinker.

"I like the odds on the Golden Dog-Snails. They already exhibit complex herd behaviors...."

After their safe return from the Sockeye system, Rosy and Fayard had been throughly debriefed by the Okhranka. The telemetric records of their encounter with the Ghost Crawdads and the transformation of their planet had proven illuminating. Physicists were still analyzing the instantaneous phase-change the planet had undergone, but no final theories about the methodologies or technics employed by the enigmatic prime mover referenced by the Ghost Crawdads was forthcoming as yet. Of course, researches among the other, more placid alien races also continued apace.

The success of Fayard's prediction and the strategic resourcefulness of Agent Narozhylenko naturally ensured that both would be invited to witness the next eruption of sentience.

As for their personal affairs—well, Fayard often caught himself whistling tunelessly and wearing the broadest of grins. All his old anomie derived from Mirror Sickness had been disspelled like mist before a tornado. Such was the power of Rosy's affections.

Additionally, Mirror Sickness itself seemed to be abating as a cultural wavefront. The arrival of these new sophonts into the formerly homogenous galactic milieu was having a stimulating positive effect.

Avouris had taken this change into account in his calculations, redoing his astromesh polling to reflect the changed gradients of Mirror Sickness. His old predictions, in fact, had nominated the world of Bricklebank as the next candidate for change after Wustner's Weatherbolt. But the new dynamics had brought them here instead.

And now the predicted moment was nearly at hand.

Hemmed in by taut-nerved military personnel, Fayard and Rosy intently observed the big screen dominated by a view of the mottled sapphire that was Wangba-Szypyt IX.

The anticipated moment came—

—passed—

—and passed again, with no evident change.

Admiral Brice demanded, "Status groundside!"

"No alterations, sir!"

Avouris began to feel sick. "What of Bricklebank?"

The communications officer reported no relevant news from that world, then hesitated at fresh data.

"Admiral Brice, a mining colony in the Furbini system reports an uplift outbreak there!"

"Belligerents?"

"No, sir. The new aliens appear to be vegetative in origin."

A grim-faced Rosy clasped the hand of her lover in support. His voice weakly solicitous, Fayard Avouris contributed: "That would probably be the Hardaway Pitcher Plants. They already employ their vines like tentacles...."

Admiral Brice glared at the hapless anthropologist. "Luckily, Professor, your incompetence has resulted in no harm to any innocents."

"I assure you, Admiral, the next time—"

But the next predicted occurrence likewise failed to meet Avouris's specifications.

And after that, his services were no longer valued at a premium.

* * * *

What damnable factor had thrown off his careful plot of the contingent uplift instances? Avouris sensed that the errors were down to a faulty map of the Mirror Sickness. But his polling techniques and data-mining were watertight, as evidenced by his success at Wustner's Weatherbolt.

Therefore, he must be getting bad inputs. Could some cultural force manifesting only in the portion of the galaxy currently under examination be responsible?

Avouris began a mental tour of his restored virtual topography of human culture.

The Leatherheads of Xyella would speak truth only to fellow clansmen, but his polling of them had enlisted such informers.

The Mudmen of Bitterfields offered the reverse of what they believed. A transparent fix.

The Pingpanks of Stellwagen V radically modified all their speech with a complex vocabulary of mudras. Trivial to interpolate those gestures.

The Perciasepians of Troutfalls—

Some trained intuition made Avouris re-examine what he knew about this culture.

Six months ago, unknown to an otherwise preoccupied Avouris, a prophet named Hardesty had manifested among the Perciasepians. Hardesty's rubric? Simplicity itself!

Optimism triumphed reality!

Archived news reports revealed that the faddish ethos had spread like a plague, to the point that no Perciasepian nowadays would ever admit to any despair.

Here was the blot in his calculations! The Perciasepians had denied any Mirror Sickness among them.

Hastily, Avouris took his Perciasepian datapoints from half a year ago, prior to Hardesty's advent, added in some compensatory factors, and reformulated his maps.

Eureka!

The office of Ina Glinka Narozhylenko had never witnessed such an intemperate visitor. Bursting into Rosy's inner sanctum, Avouris found the agent occupied with the minor and semi-humiliating tasks she had been assigned since the debacle of sponsoring Avouris.

"Bofoellesskaber! Bofoelleskaber!"

"Fayard, please. What does that nonsense mean?"

"It's the place where the next uplift outbreak will happen! You've got to tell the Directorate!"

"They want no part of you or me."

"Then we'll just have to go alone to prove we're right."

"I cannot secure a ship from the Okhranka this time."

"We'll rent one! What good are my savings now? Are you with me?"

Rosy sighed. "Who would take care of you otherwise?"

* * * *

Once more, Rosy kicked at a plant resembling a green hassock. The vegetable furniture emitted a squeak from its punctured bladders, and collapsed fractionally into itself.

"Damn that cheating shipyard! And damn me for trusting them!"

Sitting on another living ottoman, Fayard nursed his contusions and sighed. "Please, Rosy, no more self-recriminations. Your skills are the only reason we are still alive."

Some yards distant, the crumpled hulk of an old Pryton's Nebula-skimmer still exuded vital fluids into the lush turf of Bofoellesskaber, at the terminus of a mile-long gouge in the planet's rich soil. The rental craft would never journey from star to star again.

Rosy plopped down beside Fayard. "Granted. But I should have done a better pre-flight inspection. It's just that we were in such a hurry—"

"My fault entirely. But look at the bright side. We're unharmed for the moment. When the uplift happens, chances are good that the new aliens will be benevolent. Their presence will register on the Director-ate's desktop, an expedition will arrive, and we'll soon be safely home."

"I suppose...."

"Let's brace ourselves now. We can expect the change soon."

Fayard and Rosy hugged each other as they tried to anticipate what the uplift experience would feel like from planetside. Would the un-known phenomenon have any effect on their own constitutions? Might they be mutated in fast-forward fashion?

A subliminal shiver like the kiss of a ghost resonated through them. The moment must have come! But outwardly, nothing had changed.

"We must be distant from any new alien settlement on this world...," ventured Avouris.

"Fayard, look!"

Rosy was pointing skyward.

Bofoellesskaber's single sun had been replaced by three.

A voice spoke in their heads: *Welcome to your future. I am the World Thinker, humanity's final heir.*

* * * *

As the World Thinker patiently explained things to his accidental visitors, his work was practically child's play, here in a period some two billion years removed from Fayard and Rosy's time.

Viewing the past and selecting a planet with the best potential for uplift, and in a galactic location where it would subsequently do the most good to mitigate Mirror Sickness, this demiurge would abstract the world entire from its native era. Brought forward to the far future and in-stalled in this artificial star system whose three suns could be modulated to provide just the right spectrum that would mimic the original stellar environment, the world was ready for development.

The World Thinker next approached the species chosen for uplift treatment, tinkered with its genome to foster sentience, and then simply allowed Darwinian evolution to take its course over a few hundred or thousand millennia. No acceleration necessary. The alien culture would develop naturally in situ. When judged ripe, the whole world would be translated back to Fayard and Rosy's era without more than a single unit of Planck time having ticked by in the eyes of the human observers in the past, thus making a whole race appear to arise instantaneously out of nowhere.

"But why?" asked Avouris. Despite receiving no visible sign of the World Thinker, Fayard had conceived an image of the being from its mental projections, an image which consorted nicely with a fussy old neurotic and knowledge-heavy librarian from his own undergraduate days.

A note of resigned sadness filtered into the World Thinker's speech. *To render myself non-existent.*

The native timeline known to the World Thinker had never exhibited any sentience save humanity. The cosmic human civilization had succumbed to wave after wave of Mirror Sickness, resulting in myriad ugly apocalyptic crashes and warped resurgences, an endless cycle of inbred frustration and soul miasma that had culminated in the World Thinker's own lonely damaged birth at the end of human history.

I am an imperfect thing, half mad and so much less than I could have been. I bear within me the entire record of humanity's bitter isolation. But it occurred to me that I could remake the past, to engender a better scenario. So I chose your era as the pivotal moment to install change, and began to seed it with alien sentience.

Rosy interrupted. "But if you still exist, then your plan did not work. Your seeding occurred two billion years ago, and yet you remain. You should have vanished instantly upon first conceiving of your scheme."

A faint sense of laughter seemed to permeate the next words of the World Thinker.

But then how would the scheme ever have been carried out to result in my vanishing? No, the chronal paradoxes are unresolved. Am I operating across multiple timelines, living in one and tinkering with another, or do all my actions occur only in one strand of the multiverse? Maybe I am improving the continuum nextdoor to mine. Is that yours, or not? In any case, I have no choice but to continue. Humanity cannot develop in a healthy manner without alien peers. I am testament to that premise.

The three suns of Bofoellesskaber were now setting, and the air grew chill. Fayard and Rosy held each other more tightly.

"What's to become of us?" Avouris asked.

Your presence will allow me to fulfill one last seeding, the most crucial of all. Don't worry: I will visit you from time to time with aid.

Realization struck Avouris like a blow. "Surely such a sophisticated entity as yourself will not endorse such a cliché!"

No reply was forthcoming. Instantly their surroundings had altered.

The air, the light, the smells, the sounds—all possessed a primeval rightness, an ancestral gravity.

Rosy laughed with a touch of grimness. "Earth! Would you care to guess the date?"

Avouris sighed, then chuckled. "Far enough back, my dear, that there will be no constraints on our family size whatsoever, I imagine."

ABOUT GUARDING STELLA

My pal Chris Reilly died on June 10, 2014, at a youngish age, of a drug overdose. A fellow Rhode Islander, Chris was a "real piece of work," as the cliché goes. Manic, opinionated, heedless of conventionality or his own best interests, Chris loved comics and media and books with a mad passion. In short, he was the quintessential fanboy. And as such, he really wanted to have a story appear in one of the professional SF magazines. I agreed to co-author one with him, and you'll see the result below. But, despite thinking it pretty swell, we could never sell it, and eventually quit trying.

I did not see Chris much after the comics store where we used to congregate closed, and his midnight phone calls stopped coming. Mutual friends tell of some troubled years at the end of his life. I wish we could have sold this tale while he yet lived. But I am firmly convinced he's looking down from Asgard, while rollicking with Thor and Company, and relishing its appearance now.

GUARDING STELLA

[WRITTEN WITH CHRIS REILLY]

Whoever Stella Maris might be, she used the most expensive stationery Winter Quinn had ever seen. A thick bond the parchment color of an old white millionaire's pampered hide, the sheet of rag paper looked fit to print currency on. Quinn held it up to the light streaming in through his office windows and saw the woman's initials watermarked into the grain. If she were still alive, Quinn's mother would have said, "You're dealing with real class here, son." But then again, Quinn's mother had been the kind of status-seeking woman who had named her only child "Hugo Winterhalter," after a middlebrow composer.

Just getting an old-fashioned piece of snail mail was an oddity in Quinn's line of work. Most of his clients came to him through recommendations by other satisfied patrons. In such cases, he'd get a discreet telephone call or visit in person. Some folks found Quinn through his web site, QUINN'S PROTECTION SERVICE, "Every Body Needs a Buddy." In such cases, e-mail served to make the initial arrangements. What the U.S. Postal Service usually brought Quinn were second notices on overdue bills. (Quinn earned decent money regularly, but two alimony checks every month ate up a lot.)

A faint scent wafted from the letter to Quinn's nose. Inhaling deeper, he detected a subtle and elegant floral perfume. The fragrance aroused Quinn, his suspicions and his lusts—the former more than the latter. Why go to all this elaborate—and intimate—formality just to hire a bodyguard? Perhaps Stella Maris was a little loony, a kind of Blanche Dubois figure looking for more personal kinds of attention from a big guy in a suit, other than just interposing himself between her and unwanted or harmful strangers. Lots of Quinn's clients had walked a fine line between eccentric and psychotic. That kind of mental imbalance seemed an occupational disease of the very rich, the only kind of people who could afford Quinn's high per diem rate. In the five years Quinn had been doing this kind of work, ever since blowing out his knees in the service of the New England Patriots, he had run into all types of neurotic behavior.

Elderly hypochondriacs, oversexed teens, egocentric entertainers, self-righteous politicians—Quinn had dealt with them all.

But the contents of Stella Maris's letter were quite rational and reasonable. She was newly relocated to this city, and needed the services that Quinn could provide. She cited the last such agency that she had done business with, Quick and Chase. Quinn recognized their name. They were the ones who had recommended Quinn.

As a loner, Quinn could afford to pick and choose his clients carefully. Generally, he had to be on call 24/7 for the duration of his contract, and only took on one client at a time. Most people needed his services only intermittently in their lives, depending on the level of media attention they were generating at the moment. Traveling from walled residential enclave to exclusive club to guarded resort to private yacht to secure film or recording studio, the rich and famous generally avoided mingling with those who could annoy or damage them. It was only when they were forced to descend into the gutter—to go to court, attend an awards ceremony, campaign for votes—that they called on Quinn and his kind. The longest stretch Quinn had ever served a single client was the eight months it took the cops to catch the guy sending threatening notes to his famous novelist client.

At the moment, Quinn was booked only a week ahead, guarding a film director during Sundance. After that, he was free.

He sniffed delicately once more at the stationery in his hand. Something about this disturbing scent—

Stella Maris had provided a phone number. Quinn took out his cell and punched the digits in.

* * * *

The black limousine radiated an aura of wealth. Wealth and the easy, instinctive will to employ it, either as inducement or threat. A limo driver stood attentively outside the car, ready to open the door for Quinn. The driver, Quinn thought, looked oddly buff, like a Chippendale's dancer in a limo driver's costume.

"Mister Quinn, it's an honor, sir," said the driver as he opened the door for Quinn.

"Honor?" asked Quinn.

"I was at Foxboro Stadium in 'Ninety-three. The team was trailing twenty-two to twenty-one in the fourth quarter; you drove the Patriots sixty-eight yards on eleven plays and hit Vrabel with a one-yard touchdown with two minutes and fifty-one seconds left on the clock."

"That was a life and a half ago, but thanks anyhow."

Quinn felt his knees grind as he climbed into the limo. He had downed a shot of vodka with a handful of oxycontin and Demerol before his appointment to meet Stella Maris, his usual nightly tonic. But the perpetual low-level pain in his joints was still present. Maybe he should rethink his surgical options. He had seen something on the Discovery Channel the other night, about Teflon prosthetics—

Before his eyes had even adjusted to the dark of the limo's interior, he recognized the same faint scent of the unique floral perfume that had wafted from the Stella Maris's letter. The scent aroused strange conflicting sensations in Quinn once more.

Being chauffeured to a meeting with a client was nothing new to Quinn, so why did he feel like a nervous high-school kid going to the prom?

The car wended its way through the city streets and out into the 'burbs. The driver wanted to talk sports, but dropped his chatter for a professional silence after a few desultory grunts from Quinn. Soon they were out in McMansionland, where the garages for the family fleet of SUV's were nicer and larger than the decaying tenements enjoyed by inner-city families.

Through the remote-controlled gates in a high stone wall, down a long and sinuous tree-lined driveway, and up to the doors of an impressive pile of brick and granite, a moonlit chateau like one of the legendary "summer cottages" of Newport's Gilded Age.

A servant met Quinn and led him to a hall off the main entrance, a desert of marble and carpeting, tasteful artwork that still managed to shout its price, and some Empire couches that disinvited actual sitting. Used to the haughty disdain of the rich for keeping timely appointments with their inferiors, Quinn waited patiently for fifteen minutes before Stella Maris deigned to arrive.

Waiflike, seemingly no older than twenty-one, Stella Maris possessed a beauty that forced Quinn to exert an extraordinary level of control over himself. As a pro ballplayer, he had been with gorgeous women aplenty. His two ex-wives had been major-league arm-candy themselves. But seldom had he been affected like this. Stella Maris's signature perfume preceded her, much stronger than its traces in the limo, and Quinn could only attribute his unease to whatever odd associations that scent held for him.

The young woman's skin was almond dusted with gold. Her green eyes resembled fractured chunks of jade, catching the light strangely in harsh facets. Her slender figure possessed entirely adequate curves, shown to best advantage by the red spaghetti-strap slip she wore. A pair of sandals left her feet exposed. Her toes were long, perfectly shaped, the nails painted crimson. She wore one ring on the middle toe of her right foot. The ring appeared to feature a trio of real emeralds. So perfectly formed and unroughened were her feet that Quinn imagined someone must have carried her for her whole life. Yet stunning and innocent as she appeared, he nonetheless felt an urge to check for the comforting presence of the pistol holstered in the small of his back beneath his jacket—an insulting move that he quashed with some effort.

Stella Maris extended her small, delicate hand. "Winter Quinn," she said definitively, in a voice all silk and smoke.

Quinn took her hand. For one brief moment he received the tangible sensory impression of a scaled claw. But then the unlikely delusion—born no doubt of vodka, painkillers, and a moderate fatigue—evaporated, and he was holding a warm womanly hand that offered a firm shake despite its size.

"Ms. Maris. It's a pleasure to meet you. When we spoke a week ago, you seemed to indicate that the demand for my services was somewhat pressing."

Stella Maris captured Quinn's eyes with her own olivine gaze. He found it impossible to look away. "Oh, there's no emergency, Mr. Quinn. May I call you Winter, by the way?" Quinn nodded. "Very good. And let me be Stella to you. I can assure you that no bad guy is out gunning for me at the moment—so far as I know. There have been no threats against my life, no suspicious incidents, no hordes of importunate charity cases showing up at my door. In fact, I feel perfectly at ease here in my new home."

"I don't understand then—Stella. If you feel so well protected already, what do you need me for?"

Stella smiled, and Quinn felt, she could cure cancer with that smile. "It's for my, ah, excursions about town that I'll need your protection. As you know, I'm new to your city. I don't know all its social intricacies yet, its distinctive layers of nuance and custom. Getting out and about, those are the times I'll rely on your survival instincts and composure, skills which I'll pay handsomely for, just as I did for your predecessors. I hope you can begin immediately. I've been so bored the past week, while you were enjoying yourself at Sundance."

Stella's mild teasing caused Quinn to redden out of all proportion to the jest. Still, he began to gain a better understanding of the assignment being offered. Stella Maris was a party girl, one who liked to go slumming, perhaps to experience some of the rougher side of the city's nightlife. In the background, Daddy and Mummsy permitted such activities—activities they could neither fully condone nor effectively stop—so long as their daughter was adequately chaperoned by some attentive muscle.

Quinn tried tactfully to assess whether he was dealing with the proper family member here. "Is there someone else in your family I should be speaking to on this matter as well?"

Stella Maris remained unoffended. "Oh, by no means, Winter. I live here quite alone, aside from the servants. I'm fully into my majority, you see. Complete control of my finances as well. My family—my family resides mostly in the old country."

Quinn tried to imagine what country Stella Maris might possibly hail from. But her accentless English and pan-ethnic good looks failed to provide him with much in the way of clues.

"You'd give me advance notice of the times and dates when I was needed?"

"Insofar as possible. At least a few hours' heads-up. More generally, a whole day's worth."

If he knew Stella's schedule in advance, he could fit other small assignments into his day. Quinn had an arrangement with the Mayor's office to provide supplemental coverage for visiting dignitaries. And there were always other freelance opportunities in this age of Homeland Security concerns. He was tired of devoting himself exclusively to single clients. The setup was like the worst aspects of serial monogamy. His last stint with the egotistical film director at Sundance had worn him down. Saving the man from a beating at the hands of an enraged cinematographer who'd been cheated of his proper credits had just been just the icing on the cake of Quinn's weariness. Shepherding a beautiful spoiled heiress around town once in a while would be a treat—even if it meant listening to loud bad music and witnessing the decadence of the idle rich.

Still, Quinn didn't want such a plum assignment all that desperately. Something about Stella Maris and the prospect of being by her side for long stretches of time both disgusted and fascinated him, a mix of emotions he found unfamiliar and uncomfortable. So he named a figure to Stella that was twice his usual rate.

She never blinked, but merely nodded and said, "Let me write you a check for a month's retainer, Winter."

In light of her casual acceptance, Quinn had no graceful way out—if escape was something he even desired. He tried one last jab though, venturing into the most sensitive territory connected with the rich that he knew of. "Fine. But where exactly does your money come from, Stella?"

Such a blunt inquiry failed to rouse the woman's ire. "Oh, it's all very, very old money, Winter. It's a vast and ancient fortune distributed everywhere, which nowadays compounds itself effortlessly, without any legatees having to get our hands dirty. There's no contemporary indus-trial rivalries behind it, no tedious dirty-dealings, if that's what you're worried about. No vile, reprehensible, or illegal transactions that would bring enemies crawling out of the woodwork. Those days are all in the past for my family. Nowadays, my fortune leads a very mild-mannered and genteel life of its own."

As if unconsciously illustrating her point, Stella Maris, smiling that entrancing smile, slipped her right foot from her sandal and rubbed it against the back of her bare left calf, burnishing the gemstones in her toe-ring like a miser buffing his first gold coin.

* * * *

The limo stopped in front of the club called L.A.S., joining a caval-cade of cars and people more suitable for a Hollywood premiere than an unexceptional Wednesday night in an often dowdy New England city. Through the tinted car windows, Winter Quinn spotted Leland Aurin-Staros, the owner himself, working the door of the club, seeing himself as cross between Alen Rubel back in the day, and Peter at the gates. Quinn had guarded Aurin-Staros and his guests on several occasions. But that didn't mean he necessarily endorsed the man's sleazy chicanery or bloated ego. In fact, he had turned down recent assignments from Aurin-Staros, disliking the way the club-owner used people up and threw them away like soiled tissues.

Stella Maris had slid from the limo's leather embrace almost before Quinn could register her movement. He hastened to join her on the pave-ment. Once outside the car's anonymous protection, Quinn expected to be blasted by the paparazzi's cameras. But oddly enough, the normally voracious photographers gave her only a quick glance and moved onto the next limo.

"One of the benefits of being a mystery, Winter," said Stella Maris.

Winter smiled with one eye squinted. "How do you remain an enig-ma, Stella? I've done some research. Your family name is fairly well-known in Europe at least, yet you never get your picture in the tabloids."

Stella Maris linked arms with Winter so he would appear an escort, not hired muscle. She flashed him a coy smile, and they walked past the velvet ropes, toward the club's main entrance.

"Discretion and instinct, Winter."

"I understand the former. But instinct?"

"It's something my parents passed onto me. A gift. The ability to know whom you can trust."

Winter made no immediate comment. Did Stella Maris trust him? She must, to have hired him so readily. But was that trust an honor or a burden?

"That still doesn't explain the paparazzi. You can't disarm those hyenas with discretion and instinct."

"What about magic then? Do you believe in magic, Winter?"

Winter paused for a moment. He had seen some odd things in his life, but nothing overtly supernatural. "No. Do you?"

Stella's laugh was temple bells and lapping wavelets. "Not really. But how else can you explain it?"

Closer to the door, they attracted the attention of Aurin-Staros himself. "Her!" shouted the owner to one of the doormen. "Bring me the beautiful blond—the one with the pet ape."

The doorman guided Winter and Stella Maris to the door.

Quinn was surprised when Stella kissed Aurin-Staros on the cheek, in a familiar way.

"Hello, Lee," she said.

Aurin-Staros smiled triumphantly at Quinn as he hugged Stella, sliding his hands with the pride of ownership to the small of her back. "You are a vision my dear. You look even younger than the last time I saw you."

Stella broke away from the embrace, seeming neither pleased nor disconcerted by the attention. She tugged Winter by the hand, pulling him towards her.

"Lee, I want you to meet—"

"Winter Quinn," Aurin-Staros interrupted.

"Leland." Quinn was as polite as he could be to a man who had done the kinds of things he knew Aurin-Staros had done.

If Stella detected hostility between the two men, she made nothing of it. "C'mon, Winter. I want a drink"

Quinn gave Aurin-Staros a hard look as he passed, but the man only grinned, radiating shameless pride in his sordid reputation.

Every club with any pretension to trendiness that Quinn ever visited had been an uncomfortable sinkhole of smoke and noise and aggressive pheromones, and L.A.S. was no exception. Before they had been inside more than thirty seconds, a bare-bellied cocktail waitress approached Stella and handed her a martini. The waitress said something to Stella which Quinn couldn't hear, but the import of the message was supplemented with a head gesture. A guy at the bar had bought Stella a drink. The grinning jerk had coke dealer practically stamped on his head, white guy gangsta wannabe with more gold than brains. Pure trash.

When Trash Boy lifted his glass to Stella Maris, flashing teeth wrapped in knobby gold wire, Quinn half expected Stella to freeze him dead.

But to Winter's amazement, Stella raised her glass in return. "He's pretty," she remarked, "in a tasteless way." Leaving Quinn, she walked toward the bar; stopping occasionally to dance a few flirtatious steps with every other man she passed.

Without speaking a word with Trash Boy, Stella began to dance with him. If Winter had learned anything in his years in night clubs, it was that the essence of dance is sexual attraction, the art of assuming positions that would not be tolerated in polite company. Stella Maris's dance was the total abandonment of restraint. Winter was amazed at how, given Stella's raw sexuality, worthy of Salome, Trash Boy's steps were about as cool as Guy Lombardo on 'ludes.

Quinn took up a watchful position against the bar, never taking his eyes off Stella. The duty was tedious, despite Stella's show, but it was what Quinn was getting paid for.

After several numbers, Stella led her completely bedazzled partner across the floor, towards a door with a sign above it that read THE RAB-BIT HOLE: PRIVATE. Stella opened the door, and she and Trash Boy entered.

Quinn was on the point of following them when he felt a hand on his shoulder. He turned to confront Aurin-Staros, keeping three-quarters of an eye on the Rabbit Hole door.

Leering, Aurin-Staros said, "Don't take it so hard Quinn. You don't have what she wants. You're a protector, a knight in shining armor. You're not the sort of man a woman like her can drink like a can of beer, and once you're empty, crush you and toss you over her shoulder. Men like you aren't disposable playthings; they're useful tools whose edges must remain unblunted. Sex is reserved for the helpless, hapless, yet al-luring weaklings."

"This isn't about sex, Leland. Stella and I are strictly client and guardian. Anyway, who is that scumbag she's with?"

"He calls himself 'Boot.' Utter garbage. He fancies himself a coke dealer, but ingests more of his product than he sells. I only let him in because—"

Leland was interrupted by a scream from the Rabbit Hole that was louder than the house PA. Oddly androgynous, the guttural yawp could have issued from either Boot or Stella. Without a second's hesitation, Winter ran towards the door. As he got closer to the private room, push-ing patrons aside, the continued screams were accompanied by several loud thuds, and crashes.

Quinn kicked the door open, gun drawn, as he shouted, "Stella, are you—"

Winter found himself in a moderate-sized room empty of any human souls, illuminated by red bulbs in several wall fixtures. Several stained velvet couches huddled like survivors of a train wreck. A coffee-table held an ashtray and some empty drinking glasses. An open inner door led to a bathroom. Neither the Rabbit Hole nor bathroom possessed any exits or windows.

"—all right?" said Quinn uselessly. Then he inhaled his first breath of the room's cloistered air and nearly gagged. A pungent floral aroma, not unlike Stella Maris's perfume, but carrying grace notes of rot and as strong and concentrated as a skunk's spray, filled his nostrils. He noticed then a veil of what appeared to be charcoal dust in the air, the motes settling as the finest ash on the floor.

Before he could make any sense of the unpeopled room or its sparse contents, his cell phone rang. The caller ID window displayed the name STELLA MARIS.

Aurin-Staros entered the room with several members of his security staff. "Is everything all right, Winter?"

Ignoring the club owner, Winter took the call on his cell phone.

The unmistakable voice of Stella Maris slithered into Quinn's ear.

"Tell him everything is fine, Winter. There's no need to worry about me."

The connection died. Quinn noted that Stella had not included Boot's health in her reassurances.

* * * *

The strange altercation at L.A.S. and its aftermath was never explained over the next few weeks to Quinn's satisfaction. Stella had tossed off a few glib, dispassionate phrases about Boot groping her, some vicious physical payback on her part, then a hurried flight out the door of the Rabbit Hole and into the street, followed a second or two later by a chagrined Boot, all supposedly occurring while Quinn had been chatting with Aurin-Staros at the bar. Of course the tale was an arrant lie, an utter fabrication. Quinn, in full professional mode, had never taken his gaze completely off the Rabbit Hole door, nor had there been time enough between the screams and his reaction to permit such a sequence of events. Yet plainly the matter was of no concern to either Stella or Aurin-Staros, a dead non-issue, and Quinn became disinclined to pursue it.

Boot's views on the matter were not forthcoming. Some desultory yet fairly thorough inquiries on Quinn's part failed to turn up the drug dealer. The man seemed to have abandoned all his old haunts, perhaps unnecessarily fearing rape charges from Stella.

So in the end Quinn simply shrugged off the mystery and continued to perform his duties at those unpredictable intervals when Stella Maris summoned him.

Accompanying the heiress, Quinn got to make an intimate yet unpleasant survey of various nightspots up and down a fairly extensive stretch of the East Coast. Most of the clubs had the same ambiance of sleazy pleasures and desperate fun that L.A.S. had exuded, an atmosphere utterly unsophisticated and banal, in Quinn's view, yet one which Stella seemed to bask in. It was a blur of expensive drinks (not that Quinn was paying, but still, something inside him protested on principle), tortured notes from synthesizers and drum machines and turntables, Stella's endless repertoire of foxy dance floor moves, a Felliniesque parade of wanton, wanting faces—all capped by long drowsy rides home in the limo driven by the ever-present hunky chauffeur, Stella in the fullness of her employment having taken to using Quinn as an expensive pillow, her unique and perturbing scent wrapped around him like coils of the Medusa's hair.

There was never a repetition of the scene at L.A.S., nor was that anomalous event ever referred to.

Occasionally Stella would choose to conduct long and somewhat probing dialogues with Quinn as they rode from mansion to club or back again, conversations whose ultimate import was hazy.

"Do you believe, Winter, in the notion of an elite? A class of people who by birth and heritage and certain qualities exist above the common herd?"

"Yeah... Of course I believe that elites exist. Any fool with one ear, a half open eye and the math skill to add one plus one and come up with two can see that."

"So do you also believe that those above are more deserving than others?"

"I don't think that's true. I don't think that just because someone is born into affluence they actually possess qualities that set them apart from people born into less fortunate circumstances. No, I actually think people with nothing have more of a drive to become something. How many oil tycoons have had a kid grow up to write an opera, or paint a portrait you'd hang on one of your mansion's walls?"

"True, but who was the last pauper who birthed a poet laureate that took up residence at 1600 Pennsylvania Avenue?"

"It takes an MBA to run this country, in this century. That's a diploma, not a brain. Look at that Tookie Williams guy. He was nominated for the Nobel Peace prize sitting on death row. Talk about from nothing to something. Does privilege mean that you are intellectually doomed? No. Does poverty mean that you'll be the next Plato? No, but it sure ups the odds."

Stella smiled in a fashion that left Quinn recalling a meat-sated alligator he had once seen when the Patriots played down in Florida. "So you're a believer in the My Fair Lady theory? Our fates are all mutable. Why, you're a regular Henry Higgins, although with more impressive biceps, Winter! Every Cockney flower girl a duchess—given the right training, then—according to you? No natural distinctions between individuals, no great chain of being—or even food chain—with some the top and other at the bottom?"

Stella's blithe certanty of her views left Quinn a little uneasy.

"Well, of course different people have different talents, different abilities—"

Suddenly Stella became as engaged and passionate as Quinn had ever seen her. Gone was her usual unflappable sang-froid and ennui. She laid a hand on his arm, and her grip was surprisingly strong. Her signature scent seemed to strengthen.

"I'm not talking about piddling little matters like perfect pitch or a painter's eye or the ability to throw a football accurately, you fool! I'm talking about an innate superiority of spirit, of soul! A molten core deep in your gut that informs every cell of your being. An ancient, unnamable force that animates your appetites and sharpens your senses. An unassailable, unimpeachable voice that tells you that you are special, raised by destiny to reign, orders of magnitude above your distant animal cousins masquerading as humans. Haven't you ever felt anything like that?"

Under the force of Stella's demands, Quinn checked his own past, dug out moments when he had known the feelings she sought to name without naming. If he were to be absolutely truthful, he could recall fleeting moments, mostly in the barbaric scrum of the playing field, when he had exulted in just such a sensation of superiority. And if his honesty were to extend even further, he would have to admit missing such moments since his forced retirement.

The admission must have been plain to read in his features because Stella released his arm and sat back contentedly.

"No need to answer me outright, Winter. You know what I'm talking about. That's the main reason I hired you, you see. This is not the time for further discussion, but you can be sure that I'll bring this topic up again soon."

* * * *

That night they had driven to the Berkshires and back, just to attend a gallery opening and an exclusive party afterwards. The hour was even later than Stella generally indulged in, and Quinn was feeling all his years. Oh, to be as young as Stella again, but wishing wouldn't make it so. As the big car pulled up to the mansion's front steps, Quinn tried to regather his faculties, wary as ever of possible ambushes on his client at transitional moments. Winter got out of the limo with Stella, and walked her to the front door. He punched in the security code. As the door opened he felt an electric jolt from the handle shoot up his spine and back down his legs. It was just a quick jolt, perhaps attributable to some old nerve injury, and so he shrugged it off and went through the door, preceding Stella in the manner of a diligent bodyguard.

He was not in the mansion's vestibule. Contrary to all the rules of logic and laws of physics, he now stood in what looked to be a cave, a cave straight from the Arabian Nights, a cavity in the heart of the world, where the blood of life is composed of frozen torrents of jewels and gold.

Of Stella, there was no sign.

A pale, mutable, barely sufficient radiance flickered from several of the larger jewels, a polychromatic aurora. Quinn thought to detect a figure standing in the flickering shadows.

"Who's there? Where am I?"

A gaunt, pale man wearing a black trench coat stepped forward. "Hello. You are Winter Quinn, yes?" The man's accent was unplaceable.

Quinn's knees throbbed, felt close in fact to buckling, and not solely from the aftermath of old injuries. He felt as if his entire body, nerves, muscles and bones, were being plucked by some sadistic harpist. Quinn struggled to focus on getting some answers that would explain his bizarre shift in space and time.

"I asked you, where am I? And where's Ms. Maris?"

The gaunt man smiled, and pointed to the treasure behind him, as if those mounds of wealth explained everything. "I am called Toil, yes. Just one of her many servants, as are you. You have discovered her lair. But you have further, deeper questions, yes?"

Winter pressed his index finger to his wrist, checking his pulse, fearing he was having a heart attack.

Toil regarded Quinn with evident pity. "Ask yourself this, Mr. Quinn. How could a chasm the size of the earth's belly be here? Did you open a door that normally lead to such landscapes, or perhaps trigger magical growth in a metamorphic building? No, of course you did not. I brought you here, to my mistress' secret recesses, for a little talk, yes"

Winter's back used the cave's cold stone wall to support his weight, preventing his trembling knees from cracking like thin glass beneath him.

"I just opened a door," said Winter. "And I find a geek talking like Jim Morrison. What's happening?"

"William Blake, actually. 'If the doors of perception were cleansed everything would appear to man as it is, infinite.' Artists are thieves, Mr. Quinn, yes."

Winter reached around to the small of his back for his pistol, but found only an empty holster.

"Blake met one of Stella's kind, and it intoxicated him. It is their scent, you see. That sublime chemistry did not so much open up a world of visions, but rather bent the proper world that he already faced daily. The perceived universe became no more real than a notion, relatively unimportant."

Winter was trembling like a child, and sweat stippled his face. "Their scent?"

"Yes, their scent. Like a sublime floral perfume. It is said that Poe kept rotting apples in his writing desk to stimulate his imagination. The scent aroused images that abstracted his own reality. This was not just imagination. The scent you see, can open the doors of perception, yes"

"If you're really one of the hired help, then you'll explain all this and help me get back to where I belong."

Toil smiled in a half-embarrassed fashion. "I am indeed one of Stella's creatures. But I am not entirely loyal, Mr. Quinn. You see, it is hard and unceasing labor to cater to the base needs of such a beast, to stroke its hide and stoke its ego and catalog its riches. And after a few lifetimes, one begins to grow weary of one's servitude, and to contemplate any rebellion that might lead to release. Not overthrow of the mistress in order to take her place, but simply as an end to pointless laboring. This vast treasure you see around you, a horde spanning centuries, holds no attraction for me or my fellows, for whom I act as spokesman." Toil reached down to his feet and picked up a modern-looking medallion. Quinn swore he could see the name "Boot" engraved in it. "Instead, we have dared to intercept you for a frozen moment to beg you to kill she who employs us, thereby set us free, yes. You are our only hope for release, since you have somehow gained the trust of Stella Maris and are in a position to end her life. After this boon, if you so desire, you may claim her treasure as your own."

"What the hell are you talking about? Stella's not some kind of monster—"

"But she is, Mr. Quinn, yes. And not just any kind of monster, but a very specific one. Found in almost every culture's mythology, yes. She is a fierce fighter who seeks to destroy. She has attacked castles both ancient and modern, and will continue to do so until she is defeated by a warrior. For you see she is a dragon, yes. Their life span is hard to judge. Some have been known to live over a thousand years. None have died from old age though. They were often killed by humans, until one day, they all vanished. Overnight, the dragons were all gone along with their treasure. It was their final and most masterful trick. They learned how to masquerade as humans you see, to hide among their victims, yes."

Quinn's heart galloped, and his joints and skeleton continued to vibrate to some obscure chthonic beat. He felt like a mass of wet clay under the rough shaping hands of a potter, as if he were being remade. Forcing himself to ignore his distress, he tried to make sense of what he had just heard. Toil's story was a coherent, even plausible tapestry. Yet it was a picture that contradicted everything Quinn had ever assumed to be true.

Toil seemed to take pity at last on Quinn. "I can see you need time to assimilate the reality of your situation, so I shall return you to your typical existence. But we really dare not risk contacting you again. A dragon's senses and intuition are formidably acute. None of us wish to experience the excruciations she can devise. So you are on your own from now on, Mr. Quinn. Do as you think best, for yourself and for others. And act quickly, while you still may. Farewell."

The floor of the vestibule of the Maris mansion felt cold and implacable against Winter Quinn's cheek. He became aware of Stella shaking him and urging him to get up. Quinn found that his body was no longer entranced by the forces he had experienced in the treasure cave, and that he was slowly able to climb to his feet.

Stella seemed genuinely concerned. "Winter, what happened? You just collapsed!"

Quinn nearly divulged the whole odd experience, but at the last moment some innate caution led him to hold back. Instead, he confessed a different, distracting truth.

"I've been mixing pills and booze for a while now, to deal with some old pains. I must've popped a few too many tonight, and they brought me down. But I swear it won't happen again."

Stella instantly switched from concerned acquaintance to stern boss. "Please see that it doesn't. This is not the kind of behavior I expected of you. And I'm certainly not paying for such slovenly conduct. You're dismissed for tonight, Mr. Quinn."

In his own car, heading home, Winter Quinn experienced a peculiar fleeting hallucination. His car turned into a snorting, mailed war steed, his clothing into armor, as he surged a greensward clotted with the blood of all the warriors who had gone before him.

* * * *

Quinn thought long and hard about what Toil had revealed and the bizarre circumstances under which he had done so. He was convinced of the reality—on some level—of that experience. The intense physical pain he had felt while talking with Toil could not have been manufactured solely by his imagination. Upon regaining awareness in the mansion's vestibule, he had been weak as water.

As for the revelations about Stella's nature—well, Quinn had already begun to see her as a bit of a dragon, although he might not have chosen that particular term until it was supplied. It was not that she breathed fire or terrorized villages. Those were merely a dragon's more obvious and ultimately inconsequential characteristics. Trademarks, but not essential, like, Einstein's hair. In any tale Quinn had ever heard, the core of a dragon was its lust for whatever caught its fancy, its disdain for the herd of men, its reveling in sheer possession, its intensity of feeling. These attributes Stella had exhibited in spades and clover. Any man she saw and coveted, she took. Any hedonistic experience she desired, she plunged into deeply. And her contempt for the human race was palpable.

But did these characteristics constitute sufficient sins to condemn a person to death? Many people exhibited such traits, and many such had gone on to do good deeds for the human race. Some brilliant artists were arrogant bastards. Some beneficent statesmen privately reviled their constituents. Who was Quinn—who was the mysterious Toil?—to pass judgment on someone just because they did not conform to a moral code so stringent that it carried the Ed Asner seal of approval? Nominated a knight, Quinn could not see himself in such an avenger's role. He had too much empathy with the creature on the pointy end of the lance. And who was Stella hurting after all? Surely her playmates were equally complicit in whatever decadent shenanigans she had inveigled them into.

One thing nagged at Winter though, and that was the medallion engraved with the name of "Boot" that Toil had flourished—flourished quite calculatingly, Quinn now realized. Recalling the guttural yawp that had issued from the Rabbit Hole, Quinn wondered what Boot would have had to say about Stella's role in his disappearance.

For several days after his vision, Quinn wrestled with these enigmas and their attendant questions. Stella Maris did not contact him during this period. If he had seen her, he might've confessed his doubts to her and sought her reaction to the charges Toil had leveled against her. That surely would've had decided the matter one way or another. But she did not summon him, so he stewed alone.

When, on a Thursday, she finally called and informed him to be ready to accompany her the next night, Quinn felt a paradoxical flood of both relief and repugnance.

These emotions were still with him on Friday when he parked his car at the mansion and climbed the front steps. The setting sun, nearly blocked by the tall trees of the estate, cloaked the steps in dusk. Quinn did not let himself in, but rang the bell and waited.

Stella soon answered the door herself, dressed very informally, in jeans and a plain blouse. Quinn experienced a moment of fear at the absence of the anonymous servant who had first greeted him months earlier. Had the man been discovered as a pawn in Toil's treachery against their dragon mistress, leading to his death?

As if sensing his unease, Stella said, "I've dismissed the staff for tonight. I'm holding a small soiree here, and wanted some privacy."

"We're not going out?"

"No, not at all. I'm just having a few very old and dear friends over."

"What could you possibly need me for then?"

"Do we have to argue on the front steps, Winter?"

Quinn entered the house. Immediately, Stella's scent enveloped him, a heady, musky bouquet both carnal and metallic, vegetal and chtonic.

"I need you tonight because such a concentration of wealthy souls as I am going to assemble here is never safe from assault. What if gangsters caught wind of this event and decided to kidnap us all for ransom? Who would I rely on then for help?"

"Oh, come on, Stella! If any such grab was made, it would have to amount to a large terrorist strike. I'd be less than useless against such odds."

Stella laid a warm, small hand on his bicep. "Very well, then, just say I've come to enjoy your company. You wouldn't deny me the pleasure of that, would you? And what difference does it make? You're getting paid, after all." Stella smiled, and Quinn felt the radiance of her expression all the way to the soles of his feet. "Please, say you'll stay..."

Flattered despite his determination to remain aloof, Quinn shrugged. "Sure. Why not? You're the boss."

"Must you cast me in such sterile terms, Winter? I think we have much more in common than otherwise."

Quinn made no reply.

Before they had been dismissed, the staff had laid out a large buffet. In Stella's absence—she had gone to get properly dressed—Quinn nibbled at some olives. He tried to resolve the varied conflicting emotions and theories he had regarding Stella and her world, but failed to cut through the knot of enigmas she represented. Part of his concentration was stolen by the pain in his knees. They ached worse than most nights, making Quinn recall the agonies he had endured in the treasure cave.

Stella's guests began to arrive around nine. Some seemed as young as Stella, part of her generation, while others boasted a more mature mien. But in all cases the guests exuded an almost tangible confidence and prosperity. It seemed as if they had been rich for so long, and gotten their way so invariably, that they could not conceive of a world where they did not sit atop the very throne of creation.

By ten the last guest seemed to have arrived, bringing the number of partygoers to a modest dozen or so. Quinn had been introduced to all of them, but retained none of their names. His usual fine faculties for cataloguing relevant faces and personal data seemed to have been disturbed by something. It was only after some time that Quinn realized what the disconcerting factor was.

All the newcomers possessed the same scent as Stella. In the men, the odd bodily odor held less floral notes, more of a briny accent. But the shared odor was definitely a familial quality. Could all these people be Stella's blood relatives?

The room where the buffet had been established was truly enormous. Quinn had seen smaller gymnasiums. The concentrated musk of the partygoers was potent enough to cloud the vast space, yet no one else seemed to be affected by the scent. They chatted gaily over the muted strains of medieval music issuing from the mansion's sound system.

The outer wall of the big room consisted of a series of curtained French doors. By eleven Quinn was feeling dizzy enough to take some fresh air. He had his hand on the ornate door handle when, to his sudden surprise, it turned and the door was yanked outward from his grip.

Men poured into the room, masked men carrying automatic weapons. In seconds, nearly fifteen assailants had surrounded Stella and her guests.

One thug had been delegated just to watch Quinn. Already familiar with Quinn's habits, the man gruffly ordered, "Unless you wanna' get stove-piped, dig out that gun you got at your back real slow, and drop it on the floor."

Quinn did as demanded. There was no way he could deal with such a team of evident killers alone. He directed his attention toward Stella.

Stella and her peers seemed in no way disconcerted by the arrival of the thugs. Some were even smiling. Recalling Stella's earlier comments, Quinn realized that this whole affair must be a charade; a performance arranged by Stella and designed to add some thrills to the bored lives of the idle rich. Perhaps certain partygoers were in on the act.

The man who appeared to be the leader of the gang aimed a burst of automatic rifle fire ceilingward. His bullets brought down a chandelier which crashed almost atop one of the guests.

"All right!" yelled the man. "That was just to get your attention. My men are going to be tying you up. Any trouble, and you're dead meat."

Equipped with plastic ties, the thugs began to cuff the guests. They met no resistance, and soon Stella and her friends were all secured. Quinn was excluded from the procedure, which he knew in his gut meant he was doomed to be executed.

When the men had finished, Stella looked calmly at the leader and said, "I think you've had enough fun for now. We've allowed it because a certain sense of deluded satisfaction seasons the meat."

"Shut up!" yelled the man in charge, and raised his weapon as if to strike Stella with the stock.

Quinn tensed his muscles for a useless lunge.

The air around Stella hazed and coruscated, crackling with bolts of prismatic energy. And she was gone.

In her place reared a dragon.

Whiskers like barbed wire, glittering chest scales broad as hubcaps, fangs like the prongs of a steam shovel bucket, claws curved as scimitars, tail heavy as a battleship's hawsers. The dragon steamed waves of cloying fragrance, thick as spume off a storm-tossed sea. Some idiot-savant part of Quinn's astonished mind registered the scent as identical to that in the Rabbit Hole after Boot's disappearance.

Within seconds, the other guests had enacted their own transformations.

The room was barely big enough to contain all the armored flesh. But the dragons were graceful. Graceful in their killing.

Quinn could not remember falling to the floor. But that was where he huddled during the noisy slaughter. From time to time a spray of blood drenched him. Strangely enough, although he wanted to vomit, he found himself accepting the copper-smelling bath, almost as if it were his natural medium. Curious urges pulsed within him.

Before too long, the massacre had ended. The assailants had all been rendered down to unrecognizable shreds, save for one man clutched in the claw of a dragon. Unconscious, this victim was plainly still alive.

The dragon bearing this last survivor thumped three-leggedly over to Quinn. The dragon used its head to nudge Quinn. It was like being slammed with a keg of beer. Then the dragon laughed.

Quinn had once thought that Stella's laughter resembled temple bells and lapping wavelets. In dragon form, her amusement registered as discordant brass gongs and crashing surf on a boulder-strewn shore. Her speaking voice was a wind from the depths of the galaxy, where human concerns held no sway.

"Winter, dearest, I have brought you your first taste of your endless future. I've saved the yummiest one for you."

"What— I don't understand… I'm a knight, your foe."

The dragon's eyes were each as big as Quinn's head, baleful jade orbs with slit pupils that seemed to reflect the cave of treasures, not the gore strewn ballroom. Her eyes were half concealed by pebbly lids as the dragon squinted in pleasure and laughed once more.

"A knight! How amusing! Who told you that? Winter, you're a dragon, born to inherit the earth but never educated to your status."

"My mother…" muttered Quinn "My mother was…"

"Human? Yes. Yes she was." Replied the beast that had been Stella Maris.

"Your father was a dragon of the promiscuous nature, and you are the fruit of one of his brief affairs.

"I recognized you as such from the moment we met. All this has been your initiation. All you need to do is swallow a small morsel of human flesh, and you'll change like us. You've maintained your human form far too long, which is why your body is failing. One taste and all your aches and pains and foolish mortal restraint will become things of the past. A past you'll forget, you'll live the Present, and know the Future. Can't you feel the transformation aborning already, thanks to the sacred blood on your lips? The only thing nearly as potent is masses of sweet treasure."

To be reborn better than new. To become immortal. To have Stella in his arms as an equal. And at such a reasonable cost…

Stella pricked her insensate yet living victim with a single claw and gouged out a gobbet of thigh meat. She held it out to Quinn.

"Come, Winter, bite and chew and swallow. These men merited such an end, or they would never have been swayed by my anonymous appeal to their greed. Don't let their sacrifice be in vain. I've done it all for you, my mate."

Quinn contemplated the gruesome hunk of flesh being tendered to him. It should have been the dragon's guts on the end of his lance, shouldn't it?

Closing his eyes, Quinn inhaled deeply, the smell of blood masked almost entirely by the dragon's omnipotent musk.

ABOUT A SCIENCE FICTION FANTASY

Stanislaw Lem taught me everything I know about reviewing imaginary books. I think he might have even invented this particular mode. It's a lot of fun, especially if the book comes from an imaginary world.

This little piece earned me a fan letter from Gregory Benford, an accolade I cherish.

A SCIENCE FICTION FANTASY

Making a Case for Morrisian Fiction: Why Heroic Epic Fantasy is So Rare, by Professor L. McCafferty, University of Syrtis Major Press, 2011.
Reviewed by Thomas Brightwork for *The PMLA*.

*

Some academics have nothing better to do with their time than fruitlessly to argue "What if?" Of course, as any literate person knows, this mode of thought experiment is perfectly suited to science fiction, and is in fact one of the main tools of that all-encompassing literature that so dominates today's bookstores, cinemas, classrooms and canonical journals. But professors seeking seriously to examine matters of literary history should restrict themselves to more scholarly tools and approaches, and avoid speculative avenues. We scholars cannot, after all, compete with the likes of such living masters as Bester, Sterling, Atwood, and Weinbaum.

For the first half of his book, however, Professor McCafferty does hew to the straight and narrow, in impeccable fashion. This portion of his study forms a useful primer on the roots and brief effloresence of a minor genre of fiction which nowadays is as dead as the epistolary novel.

Professor McCafferty traces the birth of what he terms "Heroic Epic Fantasy" or "Morrisian Fiction" back to the late Victorian period, specifically the "prose romances" of William Morris. He follows its haphazard development in the works of such forgotten authors as George MacDonald, William Hope Hodgson, and Lord Dunsany. McCafferty's analysis of the themes, tropes and styles of this kind of fiction are cogent and exhibit a keen intellect. He makes a particularly telling point when he focuses on the fact that the majority of these fictions took place in invented worlds, "secondary creations" with no apparent ties to our own continuum. It was this tragic flaw, we learn, that would ultimately doom the genre.

In the twentieth century, during the era of the pulp magazines, there were minor eruptions of such fiction, most notably in the magazine *Weird Tales*. For instance, in 1932, the famous writer Robert E. Howard published his one and only story concerning a barbarian named Conan: "The Phoenix on the Sword." But this abortive foray into what McCafferty labels "blades and black magic" fiction was not to be repeated. Howard—who died just last year at the lamentably early age of 105 on his Texas ranch—was tapped to pen the exploits of the pulp science hero Doc Savage, and turned all his energies in that direction. And *Weird Tales*, under the inexpert editorship of H. P. Lovecraft, went bankrupt the next year, sending Lovecraft himself into a non-literary career. (Yes, that beloved national institution, Lovecraft's Yankee Ice Cream Company, was founded by the same fellow.)

The subsequent several decades saw sporadic and limited incursions of such fiction, cropping up like occasional cuckoo eggs in the pages of various science fiction pulps: works by de Camp and Pratt, Hubbard, Leiber, and Brackett. But without a committed editor or dedicated venue to serve as center for their efforts, Morrisian writers did not prosper.

Then, of course, World War II intervened. The dire events of that global calamity—can anyone forget such atrocities as the Nazi fire-bombing of Oxford, which wiped out so many promising scholars, C. Lewis, J. Tolkien and a visiting Jos. Campbell among them?—concentrated the minds of both writers and readers on hard reality. Tales set in "secondary creations" held no allure: they seemed to smell of shirking one's duty, of a willful, unpatriotic refusal to face tough facts and deal with them. "Escapism" became a taunt and slur. Technology and science fiction, however, went hand-in-hand, the literature serving as a playful and entertaining, utopian laboratory to explicate and inspire the modern, scientific path of progress—admittedly, with no little allegiance to the military-industrial complex.

With the end of WWII, and the advent of the Western-Soviet détente, conditions became even less hospitable for the Morrisian writers. During the post-conflagration Renaissance, all the world's attention was concentrated on such shared human enterprises as space exploration, undersea mining, macro-engineering and the construction of nuclear fusion powerplants. Science education flourished at all levels, with competitive Knowledge Bowls—both domestic and between friendly rival countries—coming to overwhelm professional sports. International polls revealed that the majority of citizens experienced utmost satisfaction and zest with their daily lives, their careers and civic challenges. The Age of the New Frontiers had dawned, and science fiction was the perfect embodiment of it, eventually coming to dominate the literary world as it still does to this day.

It is at this point in his narrative that Professor McCafferty goes off the rails of history and into a speculative terra incognita. He spins out an improbable scenario by which Morrisian fantasy—an unlikely and repugnant blend of megalomaniacal delusions, crude bipolar divisions of the world into good and evil, infantile narcissistic Messianic beliefs, contravention of the laws of physics and cosmology, retrogressive privileging of monarchies and feudalism, deliberate ignorance and supression of the harsh crudity of pre-technological living conditions, and a reliance on cliched supernatural entities—could have become a best-selling mode of fiction. So morbidly and upsettingly vivid is McCafferty's portrayal of this ridiculous scenario—a world in which readers stick their heads, ostrich-like, into overblown and endlessly protracted multivolume tales of schools for wizards, omnipotent rings, and battles between vampires and werewolves, rather than creatively face the real issues of the day and solve them—that one almost suspects the good professor has gained illicit access to the Large Hadron Collider's Multiversal Viewing Scanner, and actually seen a warped timeline where such a sordid state of affairs is the hideous norm.

ABOUT FARMEARTH

Sometimes I think that a "bright teenager" might be the quintessential, default protagonist for all SF stories. This does not mean, precisely, that tales with such characters at their centers must emerge as Young Adult fiction. But just as "The Golden Age of SF is thirteen," so too is the smart adolescent a perfect vehicle for depicting a future or alien world, since they can be expected to be change-oriented, inquisitive, daring and naïve, traits which the author can exploit to deliver his portrait of a world.

In any case, here's the story of how a bunch of future kids nearly destroyed the ecosphere. All from their bedrooms!

FARMEARTH

I couldn't wait until I turned thirteen, so I could play FarmEarth. I kept pestering all three of my parents every day to let me download the FarmEarth app into my memtax. What a little makulit I must have been! I see it now, from the grownup vantage of sixteen, and after all the trouble I eventually caused. Every minute with whines like "What difference does six months make?" And "But didn't I get high marks in all my omics classes?" And what I thought was the irrefutable clincher, "But Benno got to play when he was only eleven!"

"Look now, please, Crispian," my egg-Mom Darla would calmly answer, "six months makes a big difference when you're just twelve-point-five. That's four percent of your life up to this date. You can mature a lot in six months."

Darla worked as an osteo-engineer, hyper-tweaking fab files for living prosthetics, as if you couldn't tell.

"But Crispian," my mito-Mom Kianna would imperturbably answer, "you also came close to failing integral social plectics, and you know that's nearly as important for playing FarmEarth as your omics."

Kianna worked as a hostess for the local NASDAQ Casino. She had hustled more drinks than the next two hostesses combined, and been number one in tips for the past three years.

"But Crispian," my lone dad Marcelo Tanjuatco would irrefutably reply (I had taken "Tanjuatco," his last name, as mine, which is why I mention it here), "Benno has a different mito-Mom than you. And you know how special and respected Zoysia is, and how long and hard even she had to petition to get Benno early acceptance."

Dad didn't work, at least not for anyone but the polybond. He stayed home, cooking meals, optimizing the house dynamics, and of course playing FarmEarth, just like every other person over thirteen who wasn't a maximal grebnard.

The way Dad—and everyone else—pronounced Zoysia's name—all smug, reverential and dreamy—just denatured my proteome, and I had to protest.

"But Benno and I still share your genes and Darla's! That's ninety percent right there! Zoysia's only ten percent."

"And you share ninety-five percent of your genes with any random chimp," said Darla. "And they can't play FarmEarth either. At least not maybe until that new generation of kymes come online."

I knew when I was beaten, so I mumbled and grumbled and retreated to the room I shared with Benno.

Of course, at an hour before suppertime he just had to be there, and playing FarmEarth.

My big brother Benno was a default-amp kid. His resting brain state had been permanently overclocked in the womb, so even when he wasn't consciously "thinking" he was processing information faster than you or me. And when he really focused on something, you could smell the neurons burning.

But no good fairy ever gave a gift without a catch. Benno's outward affect was, well, "interiorized." He always seemed to be listening to some silent voice, even when he was having a conversation with someone. And I'm not talking about the way all of us sometimes pay more attention to our auricular implants and the scenes displayed on our memtax than we do to the person facing us.

Needless to say, puffy-faced Benno didn't have much of social life, even at age sixteen. Not that he seemed to care.

Lying on his back on the lower bunk of our sleeping pod, Benno stared at some unknown landscape in his memtax, working his haptic finger bling faster than the Mandarin's grandson trying to take down Tony Stark's clone in *Iron Man 10*.

I tried to tap into his FarmEarth feed with my own memtax, even though I knew the dataflow was encrypted. But all that happened was that I got bounced to Benno's public CitizenSpace.

I sat down on the edge of the mattress beside him, and poked him in the ribs. He didn't even flinch.

"Hey, B-man, whatcha doing?"

Benno's voice was a monotone even when he was excited about something, and dealing with his noodgy little brother was low on his list of thrills.

"I'm grooming the desert-treeline ecotone in Mali. Now go away."

"Wow! That is so stellar! Are you planting new trees?"

"No, I'm upgrading rhizome production on the existing ones."

"What kind of effectuators are you using?"

"ST5000 Micromites. Now. Go. Away!"

I shoved Benno hard. "Jerk! Why don't you ever share with me! I just wanna play too!"

I jumped up and stalked off before he could retaliate, but he didn't even bother to respond.

So there you have typical day in the latter half of my thirteenth year. Desperate pleas on my part to graduate to adulthood, followed by admonitions from my parents to be patient, then by jealousy and inattention from my big brother.

As you can well imagine, the six similar months till I turned thirteen passed by like a Plutonian year (just checked via memtax: 248 Earth years). But finally—finally!—I turned thirteen and got my very own log-on to FarmEarth.

And that's when the real frustration started!

* * * *

Kicking a living hackysack is a lot more fun in meatspace than it is via memtax. You can feel muscles other than those in your fingers getting a workout. Your bare toes dig into the grass. You smell sweat and soil. You get sprayed with salt water on a hot day. You get to congratulatorily hug warm girls afterwards if any are in the circle with you. So even though all the kids gripe about having to leave their houses every day for two whole shared hours of meatspace schooling at the nearest Greenpatch, I guess that, underneath all our complaints, we really like being face to face with our peers once in a while.

That fateful day when we first decided to hack FarmEarth, there were six of us kicking around the sack. Me, Mallory, Cheo, Vernice, Anuta, and Williedell—my best friends.

The sack was an old one, and didn't have much life left in it. A splice of ctenophore, siphonophore, and a few other marine creatures, including bladder kelp, the soft warty green globe could barely jet enough salt water to change its mid-air course erratically as intended. Kicking it got too predictable pretty fast.

Sensing what we were all feeling and acting first, Cheo, tall and quick, grabbed the sack on one of its feeble arcs and tossed it like a basketball into the nearby aquarium—splash!—where it sank listlessly to the bottom of the tank. Poor old sponge.

"Two points!" said Vernice. Vernice loved basketball more than anything, and was convinced she was going to play for the Havana Ocelotes some day. She hugged Cheo, and that triggered a round of mutal embraces. I squeezed Anuta's slim brown body—she wore just short-shorts and a belly shirt—a little extra, trying to convey some of the special feelings I had for her, but I couldn't tell if any of my emotions got communicated. Girls are hard to figure sometime.

Williedell ambled slow and easy in his usual way over to the solar-butane fridge and snagged six Cokes. We dropped to the grass under the shade of the big tulip-banyan at the edge of the Greenpatch and sucked down the cold soda greedily. Life was good.

And then our FarmEarth teacher had to show up.

Now, I know you're saying, "Huh? I thought Crispian Tanjuatco was that guy who could hardly wait to turn thirteen so he could play FarmEarth. Isn't that parity?"

Well, that was how I felt before I actually got FarmEarth beginner privileges, and came up against all the rules and restrictions and duties that went with our lowly ranking. True to form, the adults had managed to suck all the excitement and fun and thrills out of what should have been sweet as planoforming—at least at the entry level for thirteen-year-olds, who were always getting the dirty end of the control rod.

"Hi, kids! Who's ready to shoulder-surf some pseudomonads?"

The minutely flexing, faintly flickering OLED circuitry of my memtax, powered off my bioelectricity, painted my retinas with the grinning translucent face of Purvis Mumphrey. Past his ghostlike augie-real appearance, I could still see all my friends and their reactions.

Round as a moonpie, framed by wispy blonde hair, Mumphrey's face revealed, we all agreed, a deep sadness beneath his bayou bonhomie. His sadness related, in fact, to the assignment before us.

Everyone groaned, and that made our teacher look even sadder.

"Aw, Mr. Mumphrey, do we hafta?" "We're too tired now from our game." "Can't we do it later?"

"Students, please. How will you ever get good enough at FarmEarth to move up to master level, unless you practice now?"

Master level. That was the lure, the tease, the hook, the far-off pinnacle of freedom and responsibility that we all aspired to. Being in charge of a big mammal, or a whole forest, say. Who wouldn't want that? Acting to help Gaia in her crippled condition, to make up for the shitty way our species had treated the planet, stewarding important things actually large enough to see.

But for now, six months into our novice status, all we had in front of us was riding herd on a zillion hungry bacteria. That was all the adults trusted us to handle. The prospect was about as exciting as watching your navel lint accumulate.

At this moment, Mr. Mumphrey looked about ready to cry. This assignment meant a lot to him.

Our teacher had been born in Louisiana, prior to the Deepwater Horizon blowout. He had been just our age, son of a shrimper, when that drilling rig went down and the big spew filled the Gulf with oil for too many months. Now, twenty years later, we were still cleaning up that mess.

So rather than see our teacher break down and weep, which would have been yotta-yucky, we groaned some more just to show we weren't utterly buying his sales pitch, got into comfortable positions around the shade tree (I wished I could have put my head into Anuta's lap, but I didn't dare), and booted up our FarmEarth apps.

Mr. Mumphrey had access to our feeds, so he could monitor what we did. That just added an extra layer of insult to the way we were treated like babies.

Instantly, we were out of augie overlays and into full virt.

I was point-of-view embedded deep in the dark waters of the Gulf, in the middle of a swarm of oil-eating bacteria, thanks to the audiovideo feed from a host of macro-effectuators that hovered on their impellors, awaiting our orders. The cloud of otherwise invisible bugs around us glowed with fabricated luminescence. Fish swam into and out of the radiance, which was supplemented by spotlights onboard the effectuators.

Many of the fish showed yotta-yucky birth defects.

The scene in my memtax also displayed a bunch of useful supplementary data: our GPS location, thumbnails of other people running FarmEarth in our neighborhood, a window showing a view of the surface above our location, weather reports—common stuff like that. If I wanted to, I could bring up the individual unique ID numbers on the fish, and even for each single bacteria.

I got ahold of the effectuator assigned to me, feeling its controls through my haptic finger bling, and made it swerve at the machine being run by Anuta.

"Hey, Crispy Critter, watch it!" she said with that sexy Bollywood accent of hers.

Mumphs was not pleased. "Mr. Tanjuatco, you will please concentrate on the task at hand. Now, students, last week's Hurricane Norbert churned up a swath of relatively shallow sediment north of our present site, revealing a lode of undigested hydrocarbons. It's up to us to clean them up. Let's drive these hungry bugs to the site."

Williedell and Cheo and I made cowboy whoops, while the girls just clucked their tongues and got busy. Pretty soon, using water jets and shaped sonics aboard the effectuators, we had created a big invisible water bubble full of bugs that we could move at will. We headed north, over anemones and octopi, coral and brittle stars. Things looked pretty good, I had to say, considering all the crap the Gulf had been through. That's what made FarmEarth so rewarding and addictive, seeing how you could improve on these old tragedies.

But herding bugs underwater was hardly high-profile or awesome, no matter how real the resulting upgrades were. It was basically like spinning the composter at your home: a useful duty that stunk.

We soon got the bugs to the site and mooshed them into the tarry glop where they could start remediating.

"Nom, nom, nom," said Mallory. Mallory had the best sense of humor for a girl I had ever seen.

"Nom, nom, nom," I answered back. Then all six of us were nom-nom-noming away, while Mumphs pretended not to find it funny.

But even that joke wore out after a while, and our task of keeping the bugs centered on their meal, rotating fresh stock in to replace sated ones, got so boring I was practically falling asleep.

Eventually, Mumphs said, "Okay, we have a quorum of replacement Farmers lined up, so you can all log out."

I came out of FarmEarth a little disoriented, like people always do, especially when you've been stewarding in a really unusual environment. I didn't know how my brother Benno kept any sense of reality after he spent so much time in so many exotic FarmEarth settings. The familiar Greenpatch itself looked odd to me, like my friends should have been fishes or something, instead of people. I could tell the others were feeling the same way, and so we broke up for the day with some quiet goodbyes.

By the time I got home, to find my fave supper of goat empanadas and cassava-leaf stew laid on by Dad, with both Moms able to be there too, I had already forgotten how bored and disappointed playing FarmEarth had left me.

But apparently, Cheo had not.

* * * *

The vertical playsurface at Gecko Guy's Climbzone was made out of MEMs, just like a pair of memtax. To the naked eye, the climbing surface looked like a grey plastic wall studded with permanent handholds and footholds, little grippable irregular nubbins. But the composition of near-nanoscopic addressable scales meant that the wall was instantly and infinitely configurable.

Which is why, halfway up the six-meter climb, I suddenly felt the hold under my right hand, which was supporting all my weight, evaporate, sending me scrabbling wildly for another.

But every square centimeter within my reach was flat.

The floor, even though padded, was a long way off, and of course I had no safety line.

So even though I was reluctant to grebnard out, I activated the artificial setae in my gloves and booties, and slammed them against the wall.

One glove and one bootie stuck, slowing me enough to position my second hand and foot. I clung flat to the wall, catching my breath, then began to scuttle like a crab to the nearest projecting holds, the setae making ripping sounds as they pulled away each time.

A few meters to my left, Williedell laughed and called out, "Ha-ha, Crispy had to go gecko!"

"Yeah, like you never did three times last week! Race you to the top!"

Starting to scramble upward as fast as I could, I risked a glance at Anuta to see if she were laughing at my lameness. But she wasn't even looking my way, just hanging in place and gossiping with Mallory and Vernice.

Sometimes I think girls have no real sense of competition.

But then I remember how much attention they pay to their stupid clothes.

Williedell and I reached the top of the wall at roughly the same time, and gave each other a fistbump.

Down on the floor, Cheo hailed us. "Hey, Crispian, almost got you that time, didn't I!"

Cheo's parents owned the Climbzone, and so the five of us got to play for free in the slowest hours—like now, eight AM on a Sunday. Cheo had to work a few hours on the weekends—mainly just handing out gloves and booties and instructing newbies—so he couldn't climb with us. Of course, he had access via his memtax to the wall controls, and had disappeared my handhold on purpose.

I yelled back, "Next time we're eating underwater goo, you're getting a faceful!"

For some reason, my silly remark made Cheo look sober and thoughtful. "Hey, guys, c'mon down! I want to talk about something with you."

The girls must have been paying some attention to our antics, because they responded to Cheo's request and began lowering themselve to the floor. Pretty soon, all five of us were gathered around Cheo.

There were no other paying customers at the moment.

"Let me just close up the place for a few minutes."

Cheo locked the entrance doors and posted a public augie sign saying BACK IN FIFTEEN MINUTES. Then we all went and sat at the snackbar. As always, Williedell made sure we were all supplied with drinks. We joked that he was going to grow up to be flight attendant on a Amazonian aerostat—but we didn't make the joke too often, since he flared up sensitive about always instinctively acting the host. (I think he got those hospitality habits because he was the oldest in his semi-dysfunctional family and always taking care of his sibs.)

Cheo looked us up and down and then said, "Who's happy with our sludge-eating FarmEarth assignments? Anyone?"

"Nope." "Not me." "I swear I can taste oil and sardines after every run."

That last from Mallory.

"And you know we've got at least another six months of this kind of drudgery until we ramp up maybe half a level, right?"

Groans all around.

"Well, what would you say if I could get us playing at a higher level right away? Maybe even at master status!"

Vernice said, "Oh, sure, and how're you gonna do that? I could see if Crispy here maybe said he had a way to bribe his Aunt Zoysia. She's got real enchufe."

"Yeah, well, I know someone with real enchufe too. My brother."

Everyone fell silent. Then Anuta said quietly, "But Cheo, your brother is in prison."

As far as we all knew, this was true. Cheo's big brother Adán had got five years for subverting FarmEarth. He had misused effectuators to cultivate a few hectares of chiba in the middle of the Pantanal reserve. The charges against him, however, had nothing to do with the actual dope, because of course chiba was legal as chewing gum. But he had misappropriated public resources, avoided excise taxes on his crop, and indirectly caused the death of a colony of protected capybaras by diverting the effectuators that might have been used to save them from some bushmeat poachers. Net punishment: five years hospitality from the federales.

Cheo looked a bit ashamed at his brother's misdeeds. "He's not in prison anymore. He got out a year early. He racked up some good time for helping administer FarmEarth among the jail population. You think we got shitty assignments! How would you like to steward gigundo manure lagoons! Anyhow, he's a free man now, and he's looking for some help with a certain project. In return, the people he takes on get master status. It may not be strictly aboveboard, but it's really just a kind of shortcut to where we're heading already."

I instantly had my doubts about Adán and his schemes. If only I had listened to my gut, we could have avoided a lot of grief. But I asked, "What is this mysterious project?"

"In jail, Adán hooked up with Los Braceros Últimos. You know about them, right?"

"No. What's their story?"

"They think FarmEarth is being run too conservatively. The planet is still at the tipping point. We need to do bigger things faster. No more tip-toeing around with little fixes. No more being over-cautious. Get everybody working on making Gaia completely self-sustaining again. And the Braceros want to free up humanity from being Earth's thermostat and immune system and liver."

"Yeah!" said Williedell, pumping his fist in the air. Mallory and Vernice were nodding their heads in agreement. Anuta looked with calm concern to me, as if to see what I thought.

Four to two.

I didn't want to drag everyone else down. And I *was* pretty sick of the boring, trivial assignments we were limited to in FarmEarth. All I could suddenly picture was all the fun that Benno had every day. My own brother! Ninety percent my own brother anyhow. I felt a wave of jealousy and greed that swept away any doubts. The feelings made me bold enough to take Anuta's hand and say, "Count us in too!"

And after that, it was way too late to back out.

* * * *

We met Adán in the flesh just once. The seven of us foursquared a rendezvous at the NASDAQ Casino where my Mom Kianna worked. The venue was cheap and handy. Because we weren't adults, we couldn't go out onto the gaming floor, where the Bundled Mortgages Craps Table and Junk Bond Roulette Wheels and all the other games of investa-chance were. But the exclusion was good, because that was where Mom hustled drinks, so we wouldn't bump into her.

But the Casino also featured an all-ages café with live music, and I said, "We shouldn't try to sneak around with this scheme. That'll just attract suspicion. We've hung out at the Casino before, so no one will think twice to see us there."

Everyone instantly agreed, and I felt a glow of pride.

So one Friday night, while we listened to some neo-Baithak Gana by Limekiller and the Manatees (the woman playing dholak was yotta-sexy) and sipped delicious melano-rambutan smoothies, we got the lowdown from Cheo's brother.

Adán resembled Cheo in a brotherly way, except with more muscles, a scraggly mustache, and a bad fashion sense that encouraged a sparkly vest of unicorn hair over a bare chest painted with an e-ink display screen showing cycling porn snippets. Grebnard! Did he imagine this place was some kind of craigslist meat market?

The porn scenes on Adán's chest—soundless, thank god—were very distracting, and I felt embarrassed for the girls—although they really didn't seem too hassled. Now, in hindsight, I figure maybe Adán was trying to unfocus our thinking on purpose.

Luckily the café was fairly dark, and the e-ink display wasn't back-lit, so most of the scenes were just squirming blobs that I could ignore while Adán talked.

After he sized us up with some casual chat, he said, "You kids are getting in on the ground floor of something truly great. In the future, you'll be remembered as the greatest generation, the people who had the foresight to take bold moves to bring the planet back from the brink. All this tentative shit FarmEarth authorizes now, half-measures and fallback options and minor tweaks, is gonna take forever to put Gaia back on her feet. But Los Braceros Últimos is all about kickass rejuvenation treatment, big results fast!"

"What exactly would we have to do?" Anuta asked.

"Just steward some effectuators where and how we tell you. Nothing more than you're doing now at school. You won't necessarily get to know the ultimate goal of your work right from the start—we have to keep some things secret—but when it's over, I can guarantee you'll be mega-stoked."

We all snickered at Adán's archaic slang.

"And what do we get in return?" I said.

Adán practically leered. "FarmEarth Master status, under untraceable proxies, to use however you want—in your spare time."

Williedell said, "I don't know. We'll have to keep up our regular FarmEarth assignments, plus yours… When will we ever *have* any spare time?"

Adán shrugged. "Not my problem. If you really want Master status, you'll give up something else and manage to carve out some time. If not—well, I've got plenty of other potential stewards lined up. I'm only doing this as a favor to my little bro' after all…"

"No, no, we want to sign up!" "Yeah, I'm in!" "Me too!"

Adán smiled. "All right. In the next day or two, you'll find a FarmEarth key in your CitizenSpace. When you use it, you'll get instructions on your assignment. Good luck. I gotta go now."

After Adán left, we all looked at each other a little sheepishly, wondering what we had gotten ourselves into. But then Mallory raised her glass and said, "To the Secret Masters of FarmEarth!"

We clinked rims, sipped, and imagined what we could do with our new powers.

* * * *

The mystery project the six of us were given was called "Angry Sister," and it proved to be just as boring as our regular FarmEarth tasks.

Three years later, I think this qualifies as some kind of yotta-ironic joke. But none of us found it too funny at the time.

We were tasked with running rugged subterranean effectuators— John Deere Molebots—somewhere in the world, carving out a largish tubular tunnel from Point A to Point B. We didn't know where we were, because the GPS feed from the molebots had been deactivated. We guided our cutting route instead by triangulation via encrypted signals from some surface radio beacons and reference to an engineering schematic. The molebots were small and slow: the six of us barely managed to chew up two cubic meters of stone in a three-hour shift. A lot of time was spent ferrying the detritus back to the surface and disposing of it in the nearby anonymous ocean.

The mental strain of stewarding the machines grew very tiresome.

"Why can't these stupid machines run themselves?" Vernice complained over our secure communications channel. "Isn't that why weak AI was invented?"

Cheo answered, "You know that AI is forbidden in FarmEarth. Don't you remember the lesson Mumphs gave us about Detroit?"

"Oh, right."

A flock of macro-effectuators had been set loose demolishing smart-tagged derelict buildings in that city. But then Detroit's Highwaymen motorcycle outlaws, having a grudge against the mayor, had cracked the tags and affixed them to Manoogian Mansion, the official mayoral residence.

Once the pajama-clad mayor and his half-naked shrieking family were removed from their perch on a teetering fragment of Manoogian Mansion roof, it took only twenty-four hours for both houses of Congress to forbid use of AI in FarmEarth.

"Besides," Mallory chimed in, "with nine billion people on the planet, human intelligence is the cheapest commodity."

"And," said Anuta, "having people steward the effectuators encourages responsible behavior, social bonding, repentance and contrition for mankind's sins."

Williedell made a rude noise at this bit of righteous FarmEarth catechism, and I felt compelled to stand up for Anuta by banging my drill bit into Williedell's machine.

Vernice said, "All right, all right, I give up! We're stuck here, so let's just do it. And you two, quit your pissing contest!"

The six of us went back to moodily chewing up strata.

After a month of this, our little set had begun to unravel a tad. Each day, when our secret shift of moonlighting was over, none of us wanted to hang together. We were all sick of each other, and just wanted to get away to play with our Master status.

And that supreme privilege did indeed almost make up for all the boredom and tedium of the scutwork.

Maybe you've played FarmEarth as a Master yourself. (But I bet you didn't have to worry, like us six fakes did, about giving yourself away to the real Masters with some misplaced comment. The paranoia was mild but constant.) If so, you know what I'm talking about.

You've guided a flock of aerostatic effectuators through gaudy polar stratospheric clouds, sequestering CFCs.

You've guarded nesting mama Kemp's Ridley turtles from feral dogs.

You've quarried the Great Pacific Garbage Patch for materials that artists riding ships have turned on the spot into found sculptures that sell for muy plata.

You've draped skyscrapers with vertical farms.

You've channeled freshets into the nearly dead Aral Sea, and re-stocked those reborn waters.

You've midwifed at the birth of a hundred species of animals: tranked mamas in the wild whose embryos were mis-positioned for easy birth, and would have otherwise died.

That last item reminds me of something kinda embarrassing.

Playing FarmEarth with big mammals can be tricky, as I found out one day. They're too much like humans.

I was out in Winnemucca, Nevada, among a herd of wild horses. The FarmEarth assignment I had picked off a duty roster was to provide the herd with its annual Encephalomyelitis vaccinations. That always happened in the spring, and now it was time.

My effectuator was a little rolligon that barreled across the prairie disguised as tumbleweed. When I got near a horse, I would spring up with my onboard folded legs, grab its mane, give the injection, then drop off quickly.

But after a while, I got bored a little, and so I hung on to this one horse to enjoy the ride. The stallion got real freaky, dashing this way and that, but then it settled down a bit, still galloping. I was having some real thrills.

And that was when my ride encountered a mare.

I hadn't realized that spring was breeding time for the mustangs.

Before I could disengage amidst the excitement and confusion, the stallion was sporting a boner the size of Rhode Island, and was covering the mare.

I noticed now that the mare wore a vaccinating effectuator too.

The haptic feedback, even though it didn't go direct to my crotch, was still having its effect on my own dick. It felt weird and creepy—but too good to give up.

Before I could quite climax in my pants, the titanic horsey sex was over, and the male and female broke apart.

Very cautiously, I pinged the other FarmEarth player. They could always refuse to respond.

Anuta answered.

Back home in my bedroom, my face burned a thousand degrees hot. I was sure hers was burning too. We couldn't even say a word to each other. In another minute, she had broken the communications link.

When we next met in the flesh, we didn't refer to the incident in so many words. But we felt compelled to get away from the others and make out a little.

After a while, by mutual consent, we just sort of dribbled to a stop, without having done much more than snog and grope.

"I guess," said Anuta, "that unless we mean to go all the way, we won't get to where we were the other day."

"Yeah, I suppose. And even then...."

She nodded her head in silent agreement. Regular people sex was going to have to be pretty special to live up to the equine sex we had vicariously experienced in FarmEarth.

I felt at that moment that maybe FarmEarth Master privileges were kept away from us kids for a reason.

And a few weeks later, when everything came crashing down, I was certain of it.

* * * *

My Moms and Dad were all out of the house that fateful late afternoon. I was lying in bed at home, bored and chewing up subsoils with my pals and their effectuators, eking out a conduit which we had been told, by Adán, represented the last few yards of tunnel, in accordance with our schematics, when I felt a poke in my ribs. I disengaged from FarmEarth, coming out of augie space, and saw my dull-faced brother Benno hovering over me.

"Crispian," he said, "do you know where you are?"

"Yeah, sure, I'm eating up hydrocarbons in the Gulf. Nom, nom, nom, good little Crispy Critter."

"Your statement exists in non-compliance with reality."

"Oh, just go away, Benno, and leave me alone."

I dived back into augie space, eager to get this boring "Angry Sister" assignment over with. We were all hoping that the next task Adán gave us would be more glamorous and exciting. We all wanted to feel that we were big, bold cyber-cowboys of the planet, riding Gaia's range, on the lookout for eco-rustlers, repairing broken fences. But of course, even without star-quality assignments, we still had the illicit Master privileges to amuse—and scare—us.

"Hey," said Mallory when I returned to our subterranean workspace, "where'd you go?"

"Yeah," chimed in Vernice, "no slacking off!"

"Oh, it was just my stupid grebnard brother. He wanted to harass me about something."

Cheo said, "That's Benno, right? Isn't his mom Zoysia van Vollenhoven? I heard he's hot stuff in FarmEarth. Inherited all his Mom's chops, plus more. Maybe he had something useful to tell you."

"I doubt it. He's probably just jealous of me now."

Anuta sounded worried. "You don't think he knows anything about what we're doing?"

"No way. I just mean that he sees me playing FarmEarth eagerly all the time now, so he must have some idea I'm enjoying myself, and that pisses him off. He's always been jealous of me."

At that moment, I felt a hand clamp onto my ankle in meatspace, and I was dragged out of bed with a *thump*! I vacated my John Deere and confronted Benno from my humiliating position on the floor.

"What exactly is the matter with you, Ben? Do you have a short-circuit in your strap-on brain?"

Benno's normally impassive face showed as much emotion as it ever did, like say at Christmas, when he got some grebnard present he had always wanted. The massive agitation amounted to some squinted eyes and trembling lower lip.

"If you do not want to admit your ignorance, Crispian, I will simply tell you where you are. You are at these coordinates: sixty-three degrees, thirty-eight minutes north, and nineteen degrees, three minutes west."

I didn't bother using my memtax to look up that latitude and longitude, because I didn't want to give Benno's accusations any weight. So I just sarcastically asked, "And where exactly is that?"

"You and your crew of naïve miscreants are almost directly underneath the Katla volcano in Iceland. How far down you are, I have not yet ascertained. But I would imagine that you are quite close to the magma reservoirs, and in imminent danger of tapping them with your tunnel. Other criminal crews spaced all around the volcano are in similar positions. May I remind you that whenever Katla has gone off in the past—the last time was in 1918—it discharged as much toxic substances per second as the combined fluid discharges of the Amazon, Mississippi, Nile, and Yangtze rivers."

Holy shit! Could he be right? My voice quivered a little, even though I tried to control it. "And why would we be in such a place?"

"Because Los Braceros Últimos plan to unleash the Pinatubo Option."

Now I started to *really* get scared.

Every school kid from first grade on knew about the Pinatubo Option, named after a famous volcanic incident of the last century. It was a geoengineering scheme of the highest magnitude, intended to flood the atmosphere with ash and other aerosols so as to cut global temperatures by a considerable fraction. Consensus wisdom had always figured it was too risky and uncontrollable a proposition.

"I cannot let you and your friends proceed with this. You must tell them to halt immediately."

For a minute, I had almost felt myself on Benno's side. But when he gave me that order in his know-it-all way, I instantly rebelled. All the years of growing up together, with him always the favored one, stuck in my throat.

"Like hell! We're just doing what's good for the planet in the fastest way possible. Los Braceros must have studied everything better than you. You're just a kid like me!"

Benno looked at me calmly with his stoney face. "I am a Master Class Steward, and you are not."

"Well, Mr. Master Class Steward, try and stop me!"

I started to climb to my feet when Benno tackled me and knocked me back down!

We began to wrestle. I expected to pin Benno in a couple of seconds. But that wasn't how things went.

I had always believed my brother was a total lardass from all his FarmEarth physical inactivity. How the heck was I supposed to know that he spent two hours every weekend in some kind of martial arts training? Was I in charge of his frigging schedule? We didn't even share the same mito-Mom!

I found myself snaffled up in about half a minute, with Benno clamping both my wrists together behind my back with just one big strong hand.

And then, with the other hand, he rawly popped out my memtax, being none too gentle.

I felt blinded! Awake, yet separated from augie space for more than the short interval it takes to swap in fresh memtax, I couldn't access the world's knowledge, talk to my friends, or even recall what I had had for breakfast that morning.

Next Benno stripped me of my haptic bling. Then he said, "You wait right here."

He left, locking the bedroom door behind him.

I sat on the bed, feeling empty and broken. I couldn't even tell you now how much time passed.

The door opened and in walked Benno, followed by his mito-Mom, Zoysia van Vollenhoven.

Aunt Zoysia always inspired instant guilt in me. Not because of anything she said or did, or any overbearing, sneering attitude, but only because of the way she looked.

Aunt Zoysia was the sexiest female I knew—and not in any kind of bulimic high-fashion designer-label manner either, like those thorough-breds the Brazillians engineer for the runways of the world. I always thought that if Gaia could have chosen to incarnate herself, she would have looked just like Aunt Zoysia, all overflowing breasts and hips and wild mane of hair, lush wide mouth, proud nose and piercing eyes. She practically radiated exuberant joy and heartiness and sensuality. In her presence, I always got an incipient stiffy, and since she was family— even though she and I shared no genes—the stiffy was always instantly accompanied by guilt.

But this was the one time I didn't react in the usual manner, I felt so miserable.

Aunt Zoysia came over and sat on the mattress beside me and hugged me. Even those intimate circumstances did not stir up any horniness.

"Crispian, dear, Benno has described to me the trouble you've gotten into. It's all right, I completely understand. You just wanted to play with the big boys. But now, I think you'll admit, things have gone too far, and must be brought to a screeching halt. Benno?"

"Yes, mother?"

"Please find a fresh pair of memtax for your brother. We will slave Crispian's to ours, and bring him along for the shutdown of Los Braceros Últimos. It will be highly instructional."

Benno went out and came back with new memtax in their organic blister pack. I wetted them and inserted them, and put on my restored haptic bling. I booted up all my apps, but still found myself a volitionless spectator to the shared augie space feed from Zoysia and Benno.

"All right, son, let's take these sneaky bastards down."

"Ready when you are, Mom."

You know, I thought I was pretty slick with my Master Class privileges, could handle effectuators and the flora and fauna of various biomes pretty deftly. But riding Zoysia's feed, I realized I knew squat.

The first thing she and Benno did was to go into God Mode, with Noclip Option, Maphack, Duping and Smurfing thrown in. That much I could follow—barely.

But after that, I was just along for the dizzying ride.

Zoysia and Benno took down Los Braceros Últimos like a military sonic cannon disabling a pack of kittens. Racing around the globe in augie space, they undercut all the many plans of the Pinatubo-heads, disabling rogue effectuators and even using legal machines in off-label ways, such as to immobilize people in meatspace. I think the wildest maneuver though was when they stampeded a herd of springboks through the remote Windhoek encampment where some of the conspirators were operating from. The eco-agitators never knew what hit them.

The whole roundup lasted barely an hour. I found myself back in my familiar and yet somehow strange-seeming bedroom, actually short of breath and sweaty. Zoysia and brother Benno were unruffled.

"Now, Crispian," said my Aunt sweetly, no sign of the moderate outlaw blood she had spilled evident on her perfect teeth or nails, "I hope you've learned that privileges only come to those who have earned them, and know how to use them."

"Yes'm."

"Perhaps if you hung out a little more with your brother, and consented to allow him to mentor you...."

I turned to glare at Benno, but his homely, unaggressive expression defused my usual impatience and dislike. Plus, I was frankly a little frightened of him now.

"Yes'm."

"Very well. I think then, in a few years, given the rare initiative and skills you've shown—even though you chose to follow an illegal path with them—you should be quite ready to join us in ensuring that people do not abuse FarmEarth."

And of course, as I've often said to Anuta, wise and sexy Aunt Zoysia predicted everything just right.

Which is why I have to say goodbye now.

Something somewhere on FarmEarth is *wrong*!

ABOUT A POCKETFUL OF FACES

This story was commissioned by my friend Lars Schmeink as my contribution to a wildly successful international SF conference he arranged in Hamburg, Germany, in the year 2010. I am eternally grateful for his patronage, and the chance to present this story live before such a hip audience. (My reading was video'd, and it used to be available online—maybe still!)

If there is anything more fun to write than a blend of noir and SF, I don't know about it. It's like the Reese's Peanut Butter Cups of fantastika: two great tastes that go great together!

A POCKETFUL OF FACES

1. THE FACE ON THE KITCHEN FLOOR

We had to break down the door before the suspect could flush the illegal face. But we had to do it quiet. It would take the perp just a few seconds to deface his twist and dispose of the evidence if he heard or even suspected any clumsy incursion. So two of us—me and Teo—stood back on alert while Claudette jammed the home security circuits and sprayed the area around the door lock with metallophages.

In seconds the latch was bug shit and we were slipping in smooth as a steak off a matrix. Me first: biggest and toughest always leads. And I hold the current precinct record for "sheer presence caused suspect to crap his pants."

Out of the corner of one eye I noted Teo squirting the warrant into the perp's phone, making us all nice and legal.

First room was a fashionable parlor with no one present. I figured we'd try the bedroom next. Bedrooms acount for forty percent of face-crime scenes. The law-abiding public might imagine those stats higher, but they don't reckon with the inventive perversities of the average perp. I've arrested offenders in garages, offices, public restrooms and, once, up a tree.

I called up the floorplans of the house on my phone and slick-footed toward the bedroom door. Teo and Claudette, wavers drawn, covered my approach and our backs. Most perpetrators of face crimes are meek as house tigers. But some can become irrationally violent when their kinky fantasies get exposed.

Bedroom came up empty too. That left the kitchen and bathroom of the small house. On a hunch, I nodded toward the kitchen, and we moved toward the swinging door.

I paused a moment, listening: a soft lapping and smacking sound, like cattle at a water hole, accompanied by subdued moans. Here was our guy. I hand-signalled Claudette and Teo, and we bulled in.

"APE raid!" I shouted as the three of us spread wide into the kitchen.

And there they were, perp and twist.

The perp was a dweebish, balding male in his forties, naked and covered with a variety of sloppy foodstuffs: pudding, stew, gravy, noodles. He looked like the newbie at a frat initiation. The edible mess dripped off him and onto the tile floor.

The twist was naked too, save for a frilly apron around its waist. Kneeling on the floor, the sexy female figure was lapping at the slops. I could see the Protein Alley tattoo on its rump: corporate logo and serial number.

Upon our bursting in, the perp—one Lester Holtzclaw, according to the warrant—vented a loud shout, jumped guiltily to his feet, tried to run, slipped in the comestible mess, and whomped down flat on his back, giving his head what must have been a painful whack on the tiles. It was all I could do not to burst out laughing. If the crime hadn't been so serious, I would have.

My partners holstered their wavers. Lester wasn't going to offer us any trouble. They moved to upright him and zip-liana his wrists.

Meanwhile, the confused twist paused in its servile assignment and swivelled its head around to regard me. The blank, stolid expression on the stolen human female face disconcerted me, as it always did no matter how many times I found myself confronting one. I didn't recognize this smeared, greasy face as belonging to any celebrity I knew, licensed or unlicensed—and I knew plenty, thanks to staying current with APE bulletins on most-boosted faces. So it had to be the face of someone with personal significance to Lester. I winced inside. Those cases were always more pathetic, I thought, more ethically problematical. I can barely empathize with wanting to steal some celebrity's face, to possess a piece of cultural mana and glamour. We're all taught and wired to lust after such demigods. But to heist the face of someone you know personally, simply to satisfy your own warped desires—? That's just plain creep city.

Teo and Claudette had Lester on his feet, and were reading him his rights.

"We are registered officers from the Aspect Protection and Enforcement Squad. You have the right to remain silent…."

While my fellow APES processed Lester, I moved over to the twist. "Stand up," I said, reinforcing the verbal command with the haptic code tapped onto the underside of its wrist. The twist stood up. I used my phone to photograph the face and check it against the global APE database—Facebook, we called it, after some extinct antique software. The ID came back in a couple of seconds. I turned to Lester, who was hanging his head in shame.

"Marsha Mueller. What is she to you?"

Lester's voice was weak with defeat. "My boss. For seven hellish years. She blocked all my promotions, fucked with all my projects, slagged me in front of my co-workers. She never let up! I wanted to kill her! But I chose this instead. I'm not a monster, am I? What I did was better than murder, wasn't it?"

"We'll let the courts decide. Now, where's the omics stick?"

"Inside the toilet tank, in a ziploc."

Teo went to retrieve the stick, and soon returned. I looked at the innocuous ten-exabyte storage device that contained all the omics data necessary to grow a stolen face: phenome, proteome, metabolome, mechanome... Reverse-engineered from Marsha Mueller's stolen DNA. Then I stuck it in my pocket.

"Okay, Lester, we've got to take you in now. Let's get you a bath-robe or coat or something. You're gonna ruin our cruiser's upholstery otherwise."

Lester cast a surprisingly tender glance at the patient and immobile twist. The object and focus of his hatred had somehow become dear and precious to him. I had seen it a hundred, hundred times before. But all the emotion flowed in one direction only: the twist's limited brainpower, derived from a multispecies melange of animal neurons, registered no anxiety or interest in the proceedings.

"What—what will become of her?"

"This synthetic human reverts to manufacturer property now. Some-one from Protein Alley will be by shortly to claim it, once we log your arrest. But first, we need to remove the evidence."

I suppose I could have waited till Lester Holtzclaw had been bundled off, before I defaced the twist, but I wasn't really concerned with sparing his feelings. Maybe something inside me even wanted to inflict an extra measure of grief on the perp. Whatever the case, I did the necessary deed, just as I had hundreds of times before today.

I slapped a microneedle decoupling patch onto the stolen face of Marsha Mueller. Chemical signals cascaded through the human flesh and its distributed ganglia. Simultaneously a thousand microscopic points of attachment and command—nerves, muscles, anchors—retracted from the synthetic substrate of the twist's own flesh—a substrate compatible with any human genome, and incapable of immune-system rejection without command.

Seconds ago the aspect had been seamlessly, invisibly bonded. But now Marsha Mueller's face began to detach everwhere at once, and fall off like a soggy washcloth: empty, gaping slots at eyes and nostrils and between the toothless lips.

I caught the wet, pulpy mass, no thicker than the thickness of my hand (but I've got a big hand), in a sterile homeostatic pouch, and sealed up the collapsed aspect.

The slick, pin-pricked, blood-stippled, factory-issued face of the twist was revealed as a generic aspect as vapid as that of a crashtest dummy: a sketch of humanity, gender-neutral, rendering the lush female body below it utterly surreal.

Lester wailed and threatened to crumple, but Teo and Claudette upheld him and hustled him out of the house.

I led the twist back to its sleeping pallet, bedded it down, and ordered it to go offline. On my way out, I secured the ruined door as best as possible, and branded it with smart crime-scene tape that would broadcast a stand-off warning to any phone, and record any trespass.

The time was a little past eleven AM, and we still had two more arrests to make that day.

2. SMALL FACES

You can't control your DNA. I don't care if you're Lark Soule, with all her billions, or some sprocket addict in the gutter. You can't live in an impermeable bubble, although some famous people try. But you're shedding skin cells all the time. A hair comes loose from your head and flies off in the breeze. You sneeze into a tissue and throw it away. The pedicurist sweeps up your toenails. It's the technological equivalent of making a voodoo doll. Anybody from intimate lovers to strangers in the street can lay their hands on your genome with a little effort, and from that cheap and easy acquisition it's a short step to stealing your face.

So aspect protection and enforcement always means trying to plug a dike with myriad leaks. We just can't stop the crime at the lowest level. All we can do is register in Facebook the biometrics of every citizen's face, so that we can make positive IDs; bust the black labs that grow stolen aspects; and nail the perps that buy them.

My duties for the past three years had consisted of solely the last-named task. I was good at it, but it was growing old. Every morning when I arrived at the APE House, I already felt weary and stale and jaded. The prospect of confronting the sordid fantasies of my fellow citizens, as embodied in their twists and stolen faces, had begun to nauseate me. You can imagine how I felt by the end of my shift. So although I was initially reluctant to leave Claudette and Teo—we made a great team, and I didn't know who my new partner might be—I finally put in for reassignment.

Approval came through about three months after the Holtzclaw arrest. That morning I got a note on my phone to report to Major Hewitt

Askeland, instead of to my usual commanding officer. I was excited, but suddenly apprehensive. Upon my arrival at APE House, everything looked strange and unreal to me. I had a sense that my life was branching down some untraceable path, for good or ill.

I had to wait outside Askeland's office. He was seeing a liason from the Aspect Licensing Agency. We interfaced—if you'll forgive the expression—with the ALA frequently. They were the folks who collected royalties and fees from legitimate aspect licensing, and disbursed the monies to the copyright holders.

It was a complicated system: you paid per unit just to grow a famous face, and then additional fees based on public exposure times of any twist wearing that face. Every time you saw what you assumed was your favorite pop star gamely but moronically smiling and waving at the opening of some mall, while two counties away the identical face on a different twist was doing the same thing, the copyright holder was sitting at home raking in the bucks. Every time you trotted out your twist arm candy wearing a famous sexy face, the possessor of the original aspect collected their cut, after agent's slice. The legal face market was huge. We were only called in to arrest blatant violators of these standard arrangements.

Once inside Askeland's office, I wrinkled my nose at his endo-scent. He had chosen a perma-cologne expressed in his sweat that reminded me of a cinnamon plantation crossed with a tobacco farm. Maybe his wife liked it.

"Detective Smoke," Askeland greeted me. He dressed sharper than a lustron dandy, but back in the day he had held that same perp-self-befouling record I currently claimed. He stood to shake my hand, and I felt the undiminished strength of his grip.

"Have a seat, Isham. We're sorry to be losing you from the offender squad. But likewise, the lab raiders are getting a good cop."

"I hope to contribute a lot to the cause, Major."

"I'm sure you will. Let me bring you up to speed on the scene. Have you been following the trend in miniaturization and portability of face-growth tech?"

"No, not really."

"Well, it's alarming, and a huge headache for us. The era of just a few years ago, when you needed large stocks of special nutrient feed, an uninterruptable power source, and a big culture vat are no more. We don't find warehouse labs that resemble pirate versions of the corporate face-growing facilites anymore. Now all you need is a matrix canister the size of a fire extinguisher that runs off a lithium-air battery, a few bags of sugar, and some amino acids from GNC. It's a function of home meat production. You can kludge a George Foreman Junior Make-a-Steak device into a face-growing chamber with minimal smarts. The blueprints are just a download away."

"I get it. Every man his own aspect knockoff artist."

"That's just it. And, I'm sorry to say, the old-timers among our lab raiders don't really know the best tactics to track down these one-person operations. They're still fighting the last war, looking for large-scale crime. That's why we need your skills. And those of your peers on the force."

"That brings up an important question, Major. Who's my new partner?"

Askeland used his phone. "Detective Roy, can you come in now, please?"

Maybe I had seen Velzy Roy around the APE House before, and maybe not. But now, as she walked through the office door, she registered on my alert brain and senses like a terrorist target on a drone's hot mouse cortex.

Nearly six feet tall, long fall of wavy hair with the sheen of a black dahlia in a florist's window, flawless mochachino complexion, a smart bindi in the shape of a blinking eye, curves like the arc of a swallow in flight. A stunner, a looker. With one exception.

Her face was as blank as that of a twist. Oh, all the requisite features for a unique beauty were there. But emotionally, the canvas was empty, frozen. She radiated some kind of suppressed damage, a legacy of hurt, and upon first impression I silently cursed the luck of the draw that had brought us together. Your partner can save your life—or get you dead. You want one who's always one-hundred percent present in the moment, not off nursing some hidden wound in their happy place.

But I let none of my trepidation show as I stood and shook her surprisingly strong hand.

"I've followed your busts, Detective Smoke." Her self-possessed and equable voice matched her formidable and striking looks. "You do good field work."

"Isham, please."

"Velzy's fine then."

"Thanks for the compliments. I'm counting on you to get me up to speed in a new game."

Major Askeland said, "That brings me to a point of tactics, Isham—a matter Detective Roy knows well. I just told you that nowadays the majority of the face cloning is done by individuals. But they're networked into cells. When someone wants an illegal aspect, they go to a face broker, who contracts out the job. These brokers are insulated by several layers of command. Busting the individual growers is good enough, but ultimately futile. There's always another low-level scab ready to take their place. But anytime you can work your way up the network and take out a broker, you immediately undercut a thousand growers, who all lose their orders."

"I understand."

"Good. Now, I'm giving you and Detective Roy the rest of the day off, to get to know each other and talk about your strategies. Then, to-morrow, I'll brief you on some open cases."

Velzy and I thanked the Major and left his office.

"Manny Almeida's?" I said.

"Suits me."

The bar was just a few blocks from the APE House, and attracted its fair share of off-duty cops in the evening. But in the middle of the day it would be semi-vacant and quiet. They offered a limited but hearty menu of Brazilian churrasco and caipirinhas as subtle and deadly as IEDs.

We grabbed an isolated dark booth and ordered food and drinks. While we waited for the grilled meats, we sipped our lime-tinged poison and chatted about nothing much. Velzy was politely friendly and rea-sonably informative, without really ever opening up. When the fragrant, steaming platters arrived, I was gratified to see her dig in with gusto. She certainly wasn't acting like any kind of victim, depressed to the extent of having no appetite. And that big lush body of hers needed calories to stay as fit as it evidently was.

After our third round of drinks, I started telling her about King, my jacksy.

"He's an unusual transgenic mix. Sixty percent jackal, forty percent husky, instead of the reverse ratio. Best corpse-sniffing animal the local FEMA emergency responders ever had. But King's retired now. Burned out his nostrils on a suicide victim he tracked down in the middle of a heavily wooded state park. Guy had swallowed a pint of insecticide, and the poison was leaking out of his pores—"

Actually, King had retired due to hip dysplasia before I had adopted him. But the booze made me want to test Velzy with a typical cop's horror story, to see if I could get her to open up or break down or do something revealing, so that I could guage her mental condition better.

Instead, she calmly set down her fork and regarded me with eyes like steadicams.

"Isham, maybe you're wondering something about me. Wondering what makes me so distant. I try not to lapse into a thousand-yard stare. I socialize as best I can. I don't think I'm overly preoccupied with my past, or damaged to the point of jeopardizing myself or you during the course of our work. All my skill-sets are intact. I'll make a good partner for you, just as I have for others. But I *am* recently recovered from a nervous breakdown, complicated by PTSD. Two years in the past now. Since that time, I've gotten some regulatory wetware installed that keeps me at an even keel. I never get too excited about anything, good or bad. That's my story."

"Okay. Understood."

"Fine. Thank you for your empathy."

But like a fool, I couldn't let the matter go, and after our fifth drink, I said, "Want to talk about what triggered your breakdown?"

Velzy's eyes glittered with an alcoholic sheen, but also with some underlay of pissed-off resentment toward my probing, an emotion kept damped down by her wetware.

"You want to hear my story? Okay. I was on the offender squad, just like you. And then I made what turned out to be my last bust. He was a cannibal. You ever meet one of those kinda perps? Buys stolen aspects not in order to sleeve a twist, but for cooking and eating. Broiled faces, a la carte. But this one was a pedophage. Specialized in kids. The faces of toddlers, small as burgers after they had shrunk from cooking. Do you know what a dishful of those smell like, fresh from the stove? If you don't, count yourself lucky. Because I still smell them every day. Faint and distant, but always at the edge of perception. I came back to APE just to try to make sure no one else ever had to experience what I did."

All words had left me. I stared at the congealed meats on the platter between us.

When at last I found my tongue, I said, "You set 'em up, I'll knock 'em down."

Velzy's lips evinced the thinnest ghost of a smile. "Or vice versa— partner."

3. SKUNK FACED

By two AM, the stakeout had already gone on for twelve hours, and the inside of our unmarked car smelled like durian-flavored potato chips, stale coffee, hot pastrami, horseradish and mustard—all of which we had consumed during that interval. Velzy didn't favor any endo-perfume, but her perspiration was scent-neutral, as was mine. Our methane-suppressing gut flora were working, and we each wore industrial-strength epidermal scrubber bugs. Gone were the days of funky cop sweat and flatulence as background aroma to such assignments.

We were parked in the deep shadows at the mouth of an alley, beneath an extinct street lamp, surveilling the front of a large anonymous building that had once been a server farm. Totally unsuited for today's organic server farms of networked twist brains—or for any other obvious commercial use—the building and its worthless contents had been abandoned in place for years, the district around it going steadily to seed.

No pedestrians passed, and very few vehicles. The air smelled of the city's distant river, beyond which a freeway droned.

Velzy continued to exhibit a loose-limbed infinite patience, the silhouette of her striking face at ease and unperturbed. But I didn't have the benefit of her wetware, and was starting to get antsy.

"Tell me again about this *cara-ladrona* we're waiting for. What makes her so important?"

Velzy's voice was as steady as her statue-like visage. "Rosa Todd. Most people see her as nothing but a party animal. And animal is the operative word, because she's always sporting some beasty mod or other. She lives off her father's reputation and trust fund. But she also happens to be one of the best face counterfeiters around. Her work is meticulous—artistic even. The faces she produces never show any malformations from improper use of growth hormones or morphogen gradients. So all the richest and most powerful brokers use her. If we can nab her with an illegal face, we might be able to get to some really important bad guys. But she's very shifty. Never keeps the matrix containers at home, or with any of her friends. Tracking her here took months."

"And she's going to show up tonight for sure?"

"Word is she's got a ripe face to harvest for an important client."

"Okay, it's worth losing another few hours of sleep then."

Velzy suddenly stiffened from her watchful repose and, *sotto voce*, said, "Won't have to wait much longer. There she is."

Across the street from us a short compact female trotted down the sidewalk. I say trotted, because her bare legs had been reconfigured into non-human articulation, and she sported a large bushy tail. She wore a torso-covering garment with a little frilly skirt.

I had my hand on the car door release, but Velzy stopped me. "Let her get inside. That place is enormous, and we could search all night for the face. We need her to lead us to it, and for her to have it in her possession when we nail her."

We watched as Rosa Todd ducked down the side of the building. I held my phone up toward the old server farm, and the magnified infrared image of her easing in through a side entrance showed clear. We gave her forty-five seconds, and then quickly reached the same door.

Inside the windowless building, perfect blackness reigned. We used our phones to navigate. Fifty yards down the ranks of dead storage cabinets, all their unspinning discs holding yesterday's news, Rosa Todd's heat blur stood out. She must have been using a similar app—unless her eyes themselves had been modded—because she moved without hesitation. But she also never thought to look behind herself.

We silently narrowed the gap between us. Todd turned down an aisle. We quickened our pace.

We came upon her kneeling, lifting a piece of false flooring, where the cables ran. The face-growing unit stood out as a distinct heat source.

"APES," I bellowed, hoping to scare the shit out of her. "Drop it!"

I scared something out of her all right: a burst of skunk juice from implanted glands at the base of her tail. The spray caught me full in the face.

While I tried frantically to regain my sight, I heard scrabbling, crashing, yelling and cursing.

By the time I could see again, the fight was over.

Velzy had Todd in a one-armed chokehold, and was reaching for her liana cuffs with the other. My partner regarded me with no obvious sympathy.

"I stood off to one side, so she couldn't nail us both. She dived down under the false flooring after spritzing you, and we never would have caught her. But I grabbed that idiotic tail and yanked. It's anchored very well. Do you think you can collect the face, while I zip up Stinky…?"

I nodded in mute agreement. My epidermal bugs were already dealing with the stink. Soon I would be back to normal. Humbled, but normal.

4. SMILEY FACE

I would never be able to bring myself to regard Bangor as the nation's true capital, no matter how many politicians and transplanted landmarks the Maine city boasted. Even though I admired the sharp lines of the Stephen King Department of Justice Building, the Washington Monument consorting with Paul Bunyan's statue just rang false to me somehow. But I was part of only a small minority holding that feeling. Most of the nation had transferred their allegiances from broiling, flooded, ruin-strewn DC to the cooler northern city with no compunctions or unease.

Velzy and I had taken mass rail transit from Manhattan and arrived after a pleasant two-hour trip. We talked about the case for the first hour of the journey, and then I dozed for the second.

After a full three days of pleasant and mild-mannered interrogation without benefit of sleep or food, Rosa Todd had ratted out her immediate superior, a mid-level face broker named Claire Layton. But when we raided Layton's last-known address, we came up dry. While an APB went out on Layton, there was little else we could do immediately.

Except investigate the face that Todd had been sculpting.

The face belonged to a dead woman, Joanie Sprawls. Five years ago Joanie had died, apparently of a drug overdose, leaving behind no heirs or immediate family save for sister Wynonie. The dead woman's name would probably have faded totally from consensus memory, except for one thing.

Wynonie Sprawls, the living sister, was married to Winfrey Shifflet, a senator from Texas deemed a frontrunner in the next presidential election. Joanie's tragic death had been a news blip in Senator Shifflet's career, sad but ultimately inconsequential.

Whenever a non-celebrity face was found cloned, we always interviewed the family. The kind of impulses and motivations leading to such an unglamorous counterfeiting were usually very personal. In this case, though, there might also be a political angle.

"You think some opponent is out to smear Shifflet through his dead sister-in-law?" I asked Velzy.

"Hard to see how."

"Let me work at it."

"Knock yourself out."

That was my cue to nap.

At the Bangor train station, Velzy and I looked around for a hired car out to the Shifflet home, just about eight miles south of downtown in the district of Hampden, which had more or less become the Georgetown of Bangor. But on this busy summer Saturday with tourists aplenty, nothing was available except a pricey twist palanquin.

"I hate these," Velzy said.

"Me too. But we've got no other options."

"The Major will kick at our expense account though."

"He needs some token that we're not perfect."

Velzy pulled her almost-smile, and we climbed into the luxurious, well suspensioned, transparent box. We braced ourselves as four intensely muscled twists lofted us off the ground and began to trot south in their special lane of the street. I didn't opaque the cab, as I wanted to see our route. A pack of twists under human supervision were busy excavating the future site of the Lincoln Memorial Reflecting Pool. Their backbreaking labor was perfectly carbon-neutral.

The Shifflet mansion, home to the Texas Senator when Congress was in session, was a Gilded Age Italianate building overlooking a luscious green lawn that ran down to the banks of the Penobscot River. While our blank-faced twists crouched in the driveway, sweating and swallowing great gulps of air, we announced ourselves via phone. A maid let us in, and conducted us to a library full of actual analog books. They must have come with the house, because I couldn't picture a Texas politico holding such a thing.

To give Senator Shifflet and his wife credit, they kept us waiting only about two minutes.

Instantly familiar, the Senator struck me as even more photogenic and charismatic in person than he did in his media appearances. With his trim physique, thick mane of silver hair and boyish face, he combined experience and youthful idealism in one highly electable package. Smiling broadly and a bit automatically, he shook Velzy's hand first, then took my own in a firm clasp. When he spoke, however, his expression modulated to a somberness befitting the topic.

"Welcome, Detective Roy, Detective Smoke. I'm sorry you had to come all this way to our beautiful capital on such a morbid mission. But we'll do all we can to help you. Now, please allow me to introduce my wife, Wynonie."

Like her formerly beautiful dead sister Joanie, Wynonie Sprawls Shifflet had once been a Texas state beauty queen—but that was a long time ago. Now she weighed about seventy-five pounds more than in her prime, with rolls of fat at neck and paunch. Still, dressed in designer finery, she sparkled becomingly, exuding traditional Southern vivacity, dampened only by the melancholy sentiments raised by the nature of our visit.

"I'm very pleased to meet you all. But this awful news—my poor little sister's face—"

Wynonie Shifflet began softly to weep, and her husband cradled her with one arm while patting her broad rump tenderly with genuine affection. "There, there, dear, these officers will soon have the criminal under lock and key, and there will be no further profanation of Joanie's memory."

Regaining control of herself, Wynonie said, "It's only that my poor sister was such an innocent. She was just a troubled soul. The drug use, the unwise choice of partners and friends— Why would anyone want to resurrect her in this vile fashion?"

Velzy stepped in. "That is indeed the crux of our visit, Senator. Can you think of anyone who might wish to do you or your career some kind of harm by impersonating Joanie, or raising her up as some kind of specter? Was there anything more to her death than the details that reached public notice?"

Senator Shifflet cogitated visibly, as if he had been asked to balance the national budget instantly. "No, no, it was simply the unavoidably tawdry death of a drug addict. No whiff of scandal otherwise. I simply can't see why anyone would commission a counterfeit of my deceased sister-in-law's aspect."

"Mrs. Shifflet?"

"No, I—I have no other insights than what my husband offered."

Velzy and I noodled around the matter for another half hour, accepted a cold iced tea from the Senator and his wife, promised laughingly to support any future runs for national office he might make, and then departed.

In the palanquin, I said, "Only finding out who commissioned that aspect of Joanie Sprawls will let us crack this case."

Velzy's calm voice nonetheless managed to contain some hint of foreboding, based on whatever her intuition was whispering to her.

"Let's hope nobody else wants to stop us from finding out."

5. THE MAN OF A THOUSAND FACES

Someone had truly intended to render Claire Layton's corpse evidentially useless to us. They had sown the dead body—at least I hoped Layton had been dead at the time—with fast-growing mycofibril spores. Her remains, in a transparent quarantine bag, resembled an amorphous fallen tree trunk overgrown with bruise-colored bracket fungi.

I didn't believe Layton's death had been coincidental. The matter of Joanie Sprawls' counterfeit aspect had suddenly acquired much larger implications. But I still couldn't figure out how anyone could have planned to use her stolen face against the Shifflets.

I turned away from the disturbing sight and said to Velzy, "What next?"

"We need to crack open the level above Layton. I don't think that whoever ordered the Joanie Sprawls aspect placed the order directly with Layton. She was known for her expertise and contacts downward, among the *cara-ladrones*, not upward, for her client list. Let's go see Todd again."

We got from the city morgue to the cells at APE House just in time to find Rosa Todd making bail. Her rich father's attorneys had finally managed to circumvent the necessary judges.

A week behind bars had not improved her disposition. Like some tantrum-prone child unaware of the seriousness of her offenses, Todd stuck her tongue out at us and feinted with her striped tail. I didn't flinch, because I knew she was still stuffed with jailhouse inhibitors.

"You APEs can suck my dick! If I get even ten hours of community service for this charge, I'll be fucking stunned!"

"You have a dick too?" I said. "Is it as rancid as your ass?"

Todd's face burned solar-bright, and then she said, "Eat shit and die! While you're jerking off at home tonight, I'll be at Club Mitosis with all my beautiful friends!"

She stormed out, insofar as someone weighing about eighty-five pounds and looking like an anorexic chipmunk could storm.

Velzy regarded me with mild curiosity. "Was that juvenile banter strictly necessary?"

I smiled. "It sure was. Now we have ourselves another stakeout. With luck, the bouncers at Club Mitosis will halt people outside in line long enough for us to get a long-range Facebook ID for each one."

* * * *

We ranked the people who had partied at Club Mitosis that night with Rosa Todd in order of interest, and on our third visit we hit paydirt.

Bradford ter Peste was a Dutch national currently resident in the USA. He had been a multi-millionaire from his shipping interests in Rotterdam, before that city drowned and his holdings took major hits. Now, he was merely comfortably well-off.

His apartment overlooked Park Avenue. The doorman probably made more in tips in a month than Velzy or I did in yearly wages. We rode the elevator to the twenty-first floor.

Bradford ter Peste towered six inches above even me, all shaggy blonde hair and ruddy complexion. His English was impeccable, as were his clothes from the trendy new Italian designer, Paola Discepola.

"Please come in, detectives. You mentioned something about a stolen face? I can assure you that none from my collection are missing, nor have any been illegally duped. You are welcome to examine them, as well as my ALA licenses."

He thumb-swiped at his phone and squirted us all the proper documents. I didn't bother studying them that moment, since I was certain he would never have given us forged licenses.

"Yes, we'd like to see your library of faces, Mr. ter Peste. Are any of them currently sleeved on twists?"

Ter Peste regarded us with elite condescension, as if we were Visigoths crapping in a Roman villa. "I do not believe in having dumb brutes model anything as exquisite as a human face. My collection is all contained in homeostatic display units, where their beauty may truly shine. Please follow me."

We marched through a succession of rooms, any one of which loomed twice as big as my whole apartment, before reaching the Dutchman's library of faces.

Subtle low-watt track lighting illuminated a forest of columns; atop any one plinth rested a sealed glass cylinder. Inside the life-support unit an invisible armature supported a living face in anatomically correct configurations, feeding it nutrients through capillaries. Of course, each face lacked eyes and teeth, but otherwise they were utterly lifelike. The effect was haunting, a gallery of mute and blind observers.

Velzy took out her phone. "You don't mind if I ID each one of these, and compare them against your licenses, do you, Mr. ter Peste?"

"No, of course not."

While my partner handled that chore, I sized up ter Peste, looking for some gap in his smug connoisseur's confidence.

"You're obviously a great appreciator of human beauty, Brad. Is there a Mrs. Ter Peste who meets your standards?"

"I regret that so far I have not found the perfect woman."

"Is that why you commissioned a stolen aspect of Joanie Sprawls? She was gorgeous, I'll admit it. At least until the drugs devastated her. Stick her face on the right twist, and you've got a knockout piece of tail."

Ter Peste's expression didn't change much, but I could tell I had rankled him. "I have no idea what you're talking about, detective."

Velzy continued to flash the faces, seemingly focused on that task, but she was paying close attention to our dialogue.

"Maybe it's like you said, you don't ever bother using a twist. Maybe you just have sex with the empty faces. Roll them up into a fleshy tube—"

Ter Peste lost it then, growled and threw a punch. I ducked, but still caught part of his jarring fist on the side of my face. Then he was writhing on the ground under Velzy's waver beam spotlighting his crotch.

I read him his rights as he was recovering, and told him the charge was assault. Now the apartment was a legal crime scene, and we started tossing it.

My phone picked up a hidden heat source behind a wall. A certain bookshelf swung aside. Inside were several more faces of the illegal kind.

One belonged to Wynonie Sprawls Shifflet.

"Bingo," I said.

Velzy replied, "This is very disturbing—and puzzling too."

I turned to ter Peste. "C'mon, pal, it's time for you to take a little ride."

I had a hunch we'd get a name out of the face broker in less time than it had taken to break Rosa Todd.

I was right. But I never guessed what name it would be.

6. THE FACE THAT MUST DIE

Bangor loomed ahead of the slowing train. The weather outside was grey and drizzling. Same inside our compartment. Velzy and I weren't talking to each other. Not a good state for partners to find themselves in.

Finally she broke the silent impasse.

"You know I still don't condone your strategy today. And I could stop you too. I *am* the senior detective here."

"Velzy, listen to me. This is simple social engineering. It's something good cops do all the time. I'll bet you used to do it too. Picking at sore spots until someone explodes. An emotional perp is a careless perp, and that's the way we like them. They practically fall into our laps. You'd agree, if it weren't—"

I stopped. Velzy gave me a hard stare.

"Weren't for my wetware. My blocks. Is that what you were going to say?"

"Yes. Yes, damn it! I've worked with you now for nearly a month. I've seen what a good cop you are, what a smart and capable person you are. But you're like a hobbled thoroughbred—like a racecar stuck in third gear. You can't run full out. Half our job is feeling stuff, and you're swaddled in yards of bubble wrap. You've got to drop the shields and take a chance on getting hurt again."

"And I suppose you'll be there to pick up the pieces when I do?"

Nobody ever called me a touchy-feely type guy. I hadn't had a real lover in two years, just sex partners from hookup services. I didn't want Velzy for a lover now, I told myself.

But without planning to, I pulled her to me and held her tight.

"Yes," I said quietly. "Yes, I'll be there."

She was doing something in my arms, but I didn't realize what her jerky spasms signalled. At first I thought she was trying to break away. But then I realized what was happening.

It was as close as her wetware would allow her to come to sobbing.

When she had finished, I let her go.

Damp eyes contrasted with her usual stolid expression.

"God damn you," she said. "You'd better be!"

The train pulled in, and we got off.

I was carrying the veiled homeostatic unit filled with Wynonie Shif-flet's stolen face.

This time we found a traditional cab. We passed what seemed to be the eternal twists digging the unchanging hole for the Reflecting Pool.

As we pulled up to the front door of the Shifflet mansion, I said, "Remember, this is the only way we can bag our guy today. We've got no hard evidence, no financial transactions or video meetings or tapped phone calls. It's only the word of ter Peste against a respected Senator. You know our case is shit, unless we provoke something."

"I'm onboard."

"Great."

No books had been touched in the library so far as I could see. The senator joined us, alone this time. He glanced at my burden, then looked uneasily away.

"Senator, we need to see your wife too."

"She's feeling unwell, I'm afraid."

Velzy said, "We have to insist."

"Oh, all right. Follow me."

In a sun room and conservatory rendered dreary by the weather, we found Wynonie Shifflet half reclining on a couch. When she saw us, her eyes were drawn like steel balls by a magnet to what I carried. She tried to look me in the face, but couldn't.

"Mrs. Shifflet, we found the man who commissioned the aspect of your dead sister. But he wasn't acting on his own initiative. He was just a broker. Someone placed an order with him. And that person also ordered this at the same time."

I raised the cloth veiling the carrier, and showed Wynonie Shifflet her own stolen face. Velzy's attention was riveted on the woman, while I observed her ashen-faced husband.

But the senator's wife failed to exclaim or break down, simply asking tonelessly, "And who ultimately ordered these two faces?"

"Your husband."

I waited for someone to speak, and finally Wynonie said, "That's not possible."

I started to refute her when Velzy suddenly made a move.

In a blink, she had slapped a decoupling patch to Wynonie's cheek.

The face of the woman began instantly and unstoppably to peel away like the skin off a fruit, until it plopped to the floor.

Underneath was the visage of Joanie Shifflet, Wynonie's dead sister.

The immunosuppressive drugs required for a human to wear an aspect are easy to obtain. They're the same ones that allow beasty mods to be grafted on and prosper. But they do cause decay in the aspect and the need for replacements. And wearing an aspect over your own face around the clock also takes its toll. The thousand piercings of the micro-attachments, the sequestering of the hidden face from sun and air. Joanie Shifflet looked like an exposed grub or woodlouse.

Senator Shifflet began to speak. "You must understand. It was all an accident. I was drunk one night, and Wynonie and I had a fight. She fell, hit her head, and died. Her sister had no real life of her own. She agreed to the masquerade—"

The senator's wife said, "Tell them the truth, Winfrey."

And then I knew.

I hit Joanie's face with a second decoupler.

That aspect sloughed off as well, revealing Wynonie once again. But this doubly buried stratum of the woman resembled a pasty, gaunt-cheeked ghoul more than any living human. When she spoke, the effect was that of a voice issuing from a grave.

"He and Joanie were lovers. And I killed her. And took her place to please him. And then she took mine. He knew—but he didn't know. It was all a fantasy."

The raddled revenant picked up the Joanie face, cupped it gently and crooned, "My sister, myself, my sister, myself—"

ABOUT CANDLE IN A
CHIANTI BOTTLE

For years and years I had the main title of this story in my notebooks as an inspiration. The phrase seemed to capture everything about the long-lost, romantic, beatnik, coffee-house era of the late Fifties, early Sixties. But I had no story to go with it. Then Luis Oritz asked me for a piece for a project, a story that would reflect some kind of quintessential New York ambiance or attitude, and all the elements came together for me.

If I had a time machine, I'd certainly voyage back to this era to hear Miles Davis or Dave Brubeck in some smoky, intimate setting. Forget visting dinosaurs or the Crucifixion or Antietam—Bleecker Street, here I come!

CANDLE IN A CHIANTI BOTTLE

OR, WIGOUT AT THE CORNER OF
BLEECKER AND MILKY WAY

1. AH-LEU-CHA

Why, you query winsomely and whimsically, did I, Nick Champion, forever hassled, overburdened artiste of the thyratron tube control panel, always end up being the sad cat delegated to sweep up the gruesome broken glass after a night of happy rioting by A-Trainers, Birchers, militant pansies, Bronx Bagel Babies and Minor Mafia thugs? Because good ol' Nick Champion, I reply with equal panache and demureness bordering on bile, was the only fucking employee of the Village Gate that a) knew which end of a broom met the pavement; b) was awake and sober at seven AM; and c) was even crazier in love with this wayout dive than its owner Art D'Lugoff, that's why.

You dig?

So there swept I, morning of Thursday September 24, Anode Dominatrix 1959, using a wide-mouthed galvanized dustpan to funnel the shards of the Gate's front windows into a big dented trash barrel. I was fortified mightily by two espressos from the Gaslight Café, personally brewed by owner John Mitchell. I lived above the Gaslight, up on MacDougall just a couple of blocks from the Gate. I could have lived above the Gate itself and saved some berries, if I had been satisfied with flophouse conditions, but that wasn't my bag. I liked my home scene neat and refined: Wollensak reel-to-reel, Heywood-Wakefield couch, bullfight posters on the bedroom wall.

At 6:30 in the morning, Mitchell wasn't up early, he was up super late. Big bill o' fare at the Gaslight yester-eve, with the basket making the rounds a half dozen times. Poets, musicians, dancers, a real happening. The noise of the performances and the finger-snapping response of the kittens and gators in the audience drifted up the airshafts to lull me asleep when I turned in at 1:30. Wednesday was always an early night off for me at the Gate, once I got the simple lighting set up for the perennial closing slot holder, Big Tex Poteet and his Reet Petites. They weren't Monk, but D'Lugoff had nothing against pulling in the squares, and Wednesday was a slow night.

Consequently, I slept like murder and was up five hours later. I never needed much sack time.

So I wander from the street down grease-slippery steps into the empty Gaslight cave through the open service door and find Mitchell in front of his big ancient La Pavoni *Ideale*, which looks like a Little Nemo steam locomotive mated with a samovar, and I say, "Crema me, daddy-o." Red-eyed and sleepy, Mitchell snorts semi-derisively-like, then pulls me a ristretto, and one for himself. We clink cups, then sip.

"Surprised you slept through all the hullaballo," he said.

My stomach elevatored down to my engineer boots. "Not another riot?"

"Just a small one. The cherry-toppers fulla bulls whooped in fast, gotta give 'em that."

"What is it with these jiveass muthafuckers? Can't they all just get along?"

"You know the score as well as me. The local Dagoes who used to run Greenwich Village hate anyone not born here. The spades off the A-Train hate the ofays. The ofays freak when they see white Bronx Bagel Babies hanging with the A-Trainers. The Minor Mafia is out to loot and pillage everyone indiscriminately. The ban-the-bombers hate the my-country-right-or-wrongers. The folkniks hate the rock-n-rollers. And everyone hates the fags—even the fags!"

I winced at Mitchell's last gibe. "A sad scene, man. If only people could learn to hang loose and live together peacefully."

Mitchell slid a second espresso in front of me. "Not likely, my friend. Not in my lifetime or yours. And meanwhile, innocent window glass everywhere is the victim. Makes me glad the Gaslight's totally underground. You guys never should have expanded to the first floor. I hear the Gate took a major hit."

I downed the long black and got to my dogs. "Guess I'll mosey over then. Thanks, John."

Out on MacDougall, I saw that the Kettle of Fish next door sported fresh plywood. Later, I learned that Café Wha?, the Punjab, Rienzi's, the Cock'n'Bull, and the Port of Call had all donned similar wood cheaters. I hustled down Bleecker. Would D'Lugoff have seen fit to spare me some labor, and boarded up any damage already?

Corner of Thompson gave me the answer. Only a mishmash of old thumbtacked posters and hastily frame-stapled tablecloths shielded the gaping windows. Uncool and inutile, to say the least. Teahead architecture. I sighed, then got busy.

By the time I was done getting all the glass up off the pavement and out of the windowframes, I had acquired an appreciative audience of one, out of all the incurious sparse passersby. Chester Kurland, he of the entertaining cosmic spongebrain.

Chester lived above the Gate in the grotty flophouse establishment that had festered there for years, long before the advent of the club. Rooms fifty cents a night, bedbugs no extra charge.

Somewhere north of sixty, Chester was a World War Uno vet. Came out of the trenches with gas-rotted lungs and a lifetime monthly check from Uncle Sugar. For the past forty years he had paid his month's rent in advance, then converted the rest into booze and beans at a ratio of ten to one. Miracle he was still alive. Chester resembled a toothless, withered, sexless apple dumpling wrapped in flannel and wool and an inch-thick, almost visible funk of moldy days of future passed.

Chester always came up short in the mazuma department around this time of the month, so I was suspecting to get hit up for a donation to the "Keep Kurland Katatonic Fund." But the old saucehead surprised me with one of his intermittent gnomic utterances. Rubbing the back of one dirty hand across his whisker-fringed lips, he mumbled, "Sumpin inna cellar, Nicky."

Chester was the only person who ever called me Nicky, aside from my Mom, and even her bellow wouldn't carry all the way from Iowa. "Yeah, Chester, I know there's something in the cellar. A lot of somethings. A stage, my lighting board, booze, the plywood I need for this job—"

Chester got angry then at my goofing on him. That surprised me, since he never usually got peeved. "No, asshole, sumpin *new!*"

"And how would you know, Chester?"

The ancient rummy deflated, all his aggressive certainty gone. "Aw, thahell witchoo… I need my breakfast. So long, Nicky."

He rolled off, and I could hear him muttering something like, "*Felt* 'im show up, know I *did…*"

I trundled the barrel back to outdoor storage, then used my keys to let myself into the Gate.

The darkened, musty, fermentatious club radiated a spooky, throttled-down vibe, as if all the ghosts of the past two years' performers were embedded in the walls, playing silently, sending spectral notes out to pile up in ectoplasmic drifts. I got a little antsy, something that never usually overtakes me here, and I've been in these early-morning-Nick-to-the-rescue circumstances more times than I can count. Goddamn that Chester and his spooky talk!

The basement of this building, Mills House No. 1 it had been named at its erection sixty years ago, was labyrinthine and capacious. Parts of it still weren't wired for electricity, including the room where the plywood sheets were stored against riot and other Acts ob De Lawd. So, lacking a flashlight, I grabbed one of the centerpieces from a table, and fumbled in my pocket for some matches.

The candle in the chianti bottle flared to life, immediately beginning to add more picturesque red wax drippings to the encrusted wicker basket cradling the glass. These faux folksy flambeaux were ubiquitous in Village joints, and I felt like hipster Diogenes looking for an honest fix.

Down in the cellar I made my way to the storage room.

I opened the padlocked door and saw a man sitting on the floor.

At first, in the wavering shadows, I couldn't be sure it *was* a man. I mean, I couldn't be sure once I had unpeeled myself from the ceiling and my nerves stopped quivering like the strings of Milt Hinton's double bass after he was done slapping them. But in the interval from my first glimpse of what appeared to be a formless heap to this moment, the figure had resolved into a veritable person.

The guy was a spade, dressed in a shabby suit and battered brogans. He sat right atop a grating that communicated with the sewers, and whence wafted noxious aromas. Hard to tell his age, anywhere from twenty to fifty. Eyes closed, head slumped.

And then he lifted his head and opened his eyes.

You hear about "animal magnetism" and charisma and suchlike stuff, but until you run smack dab up against a real case of it, you don't believe in such powers. Leastwise, I didn't.

But this guy's gaze, catching the candlelight, held some kind of weird attractiveness, a blend of naivete and knowingness, strength and fragility, openness and depths of mystery.

He began to speak, but seemed to have trouble forming sensible words.

"Ah, ah, ah. Loo-cha! Loo, loo, loo-cha! Ah-loo-cha!"

My own voice was none too steady. I still couldn't figure out how he had gotten in here. I hadn't opened this room in ages, and chances are no one else would have either.

"What's that, man?" I queried nervously. "You into Bird? 'Ah-leu-cha?' I dig, great song…"

He got unsteadily to his feet, and it seemed that his pants cuffs trailed down into the drain, snagged on something. But then he pulled free and advanced on me.

"Ah-loo-cha! Ah-loo-cha!"

Suddenly a thought appeared in my brain as if beamed there. "Whoa, pal, slow down. You trying to tell me your name? Al? Al Luchow?"

My question scored a big hit. He nodded his head violently, and smiled with teeth.

"Okay, Al, how'd you get in here? You been locked in all night? Damp as hell. No matter, you're free now. You may as well beat it."

Al frowned, and shook his head in the negative.

"Nowhere to go, huh? You looking for work? I could use a hand getting these sheets of plywood upstairs. After that—well, we'll see."

Al stayed mute. I had a hunch he'd never say anything but his name—and that hunch proved a dead cert. But he snatched up several big sheets of plywood like they weighed nothing, dashed past me and headed for the sun.

Looked like I had a new helper—at least for today.

2. STRAIGHT, NO CHASER

The Gate was secure again, wooden windows awaiting the glazier. Al Luchow had really helped. Muscles aplenty, despite his skinny build.

Out in the sunny morning, I had been able to size up his looks better. His suit was from nowheresville, some kind of grotty foreign weave like woof of raffia and weft of kelp. His complexion was kinda greenish below the African bronze, jaundiced in a weird way. Although his looks were craggy and ill-assorted, ugly even, he still radiated that raw animal appeal I had sensed in the basement. His speech was nonexistent, but he smiled a lot.

With Al effortlessly holding up the big sheets, I drove the nails home into familiar holes. Many more riots, and the window frames would look like Swiss cheese. We finished by 7:30, and I turned to Al.

"You hungry?"

Grin and nod.

"Okay, c'mon. My treat. Oh, and here's a couple of bucks for your work."

Al took the dough and pocketed it without apparent concern or appreciation. Go figure.

We went over to the T. A. Waters Diner on the northeast corner of Washington Square, and found a booth right away, despite the breakfast crowd of students, suits and second-string Sartres.

"What do you want, Al?" I noticed Al was studying the menu upside-down, and I got embarrassed for him. Probably grew up raggedy-ass barefoot Mississippi sharecropper poor. "Hey, I know what's good. I'll order for us both, okay?"

The waitress was a raven-haired, big-boobed dancer who went by the name Iota Scintilla. Today she was wearing a Mexican shawl over a peasant blouse that put all her assets on display. I had seen her perform at Trude Heller's Versailles club inbetween musical acts. As a dancer, she was an excellent waitress. That was the problem with half the acts on the Village scene: all ambition and enthusiasm and ego and very little talent.

I had Iota bring us dual stacks of pancakes, sausages, eggs over easy, coffee and hash browns. When the food came, Al made a face of vivid distaste at the eggs and sausages, but immediately began to scarf down the pancakes and potatoes, so I traded my portions of the latter for his share of the former.

I found Al's company quite pleasant, despite his silence. That ethereal buzz he radiated soothed and pacified urban-taut nerves. Most people talked too much anyhow. But my good mood shattered with the arrival of Clover Sterbcow.

"Hello, Nick," she crooned like honey over treacle, and I winced.

Clover hailed from the New Orleans Sterbcows. Had a mushmouth accent out of some minor Tennessee Williams play. Dad was a fatcat lawyer-type down there. Clover had come to New York at age nineteen to "find herself." Got a plump monthly check from Papa and Mama Sterbcow. No money worries, nothing to occupy her fine but untethered mind except self-indulgence, trivia, gossip and a network of interpersonal relationships among her intimate circle of thousands that rivalled the complexity of Politburo alliances and enmities.

Today Clover wore a white man's buttondown shirt under a tan windbreaker, and heathery twill pants over her just-too-ample hips. Sandals revealed toenails painted black. An ankh on a leather cord around her neck completed the ensemble. Oh, and pixie-cut and pout.

Cute as a bug, in a sub-Shelly-Winters fashion, Clover really wasn't a bad sort, compared to lots of others in our mutual scene, except for one fatal flaw.

She had convinced herself that she was noggin-over-nookie in love with me. And that bag of hers was most ab-so-tively not mine.

"Clover," I clippedly countenanced. "Haven't seen you since the Miss Beatnik 1959 contest."

That was a jab. Clover had had her heart set on winning that gig, but had lost to Angel, a boss seventeen-year-old chick. Only the immediate funnelling of a half dozen White Russians down the Sterbcow gullet had forestalled a mean catfight.

Clover stuck her tongue out at me. "You're a stinker, Nick. But that's how I like 'em. Who's your new friend?"

I made with the intros. Al beamed at Clover, but didn't seem to dig the practice of shaking hands. Instead, he rummaged in one greasy jacket pocket and came out with a piece of foreign-looking candy wrapped in some kind of dust-colored fuzzy cellophane.

Clover took the candy and stuck it in her own pocket. "Thanks, Al, you're sweet. Not like *some* people I could name. So, Nick, you gonna comp me into the Monk show on Friday?"

"Only if you bring six paying customers with you."

"Can do. Little Clover knows just how to pluck the social strings. I'll see you there. You *too*, Al!"

And then she sashayed out of the T. A. Waters Diner in her wide-hipped sugar-magnolia invitation-to-love way.

I looked at Al and he was still grinning. "You damn fool, she's on-stage like that with everyone. Shallow as a Cuban revolutionary's grave. Oh, well, you'll find out for yourself, I guess."

Clover's mention of seeing Al again later in the week made me think. What was I going to do with him? He obviously had no pad of his own, or he wouldn't have been crashing in the basement of the Gate. (And just how had he gotten into that locked cellar room, which I hadn't opened all day yesterday, and me holding the only key? Did Art have a key too? Probably did, come to think of it. But why would he put Al in there anyhow? Or had the vagrant slipped in unnoticed in some fashion?) And if Al had a home life of any sort, he would also have taken off by now. But plainly, he had no better place to go. I couldn't just turn him loose with a good conscience.

I made up my mind then and there. My duties at the Gate beyond doing the lights had proliferated past all justifiable bounds, simply because I was the most competent employee D'Lugoff had. If all these tasks were going to fall onto my shoulders, I deserved an assistant. Al could be that guy.

"Al, let's go. We're going to get you gainfully employed. Your taxes will be funding Project Mercury before you know it."

By now the hour was nearing nine, and I figured Art D'Lugoff would be in his office, attending to the many matters involved in running the club.

We found the impressario of the Village Gate behind his messy desk, a bundle of barely constrained quivering energy. He was studying liquor distributor invoices and smoking an early morning stick of tea to take his edge off. He exhaled a big lazy fragrant cloud of buzz smoke at us, and said, "Howdy, Nick, have a hit."

"No thanks, Art, you know I don't indulge."

"How about your buddy? Here you go, cat, ride the dragon."

Al Luchow accepted the joint, studied it—then threw it to the floor and crushed it to pieces.

Art jumped up. "Hey, man, that was primo weed! What's your weirdo hangup anyhow?"

Al flashed the expanse of his pearly whites on Art, and handed him a no-name candy. Art tossed the lozenge onto his desk. "Aw, you're nuts, both of you! Too straight to contemplate! What're you doing in here at this godforsaken hour anyhow?"

"Reporting on how we secured your precious establishment from vandals, that's what."

"Oh, yeah, the windows." Art calmed down. "That was one flipping mad scene last night. Man, I wish everyone in the Village would learn to co-exist. Well, thanks, Nick, I appreciate it."

"I couldn't have done it so quick without Al's help. You think we can take him on as a kind of dogsbody?"

"What's it gonna cost me?"

I ran a quick calculation involving weekly rates at the flophouse above the Gate, and some simple vegetarian meals. "Fifteen bucks a week."

"Make it twelve, and you've got a deal."

"Solid, jackson!"

Art sat down again and grabbed a flyer off his pile of papers. "Now that we've signed up your nursemaid, I need your help. I want you to go check out this new joint. On the sly, like. It's an Ivo Marinelli operation."

Ivo Marinelli was a rival impressario. But unlike the general run of Village club owners, he tended to play dirty. Up till now, he had stayed out of our neighborhood, focusing his activities uptown. He liked to keep a low profile. Rumors had him as a silent partner in the Copacabana, the Latin Quarter and the Eden Roc—places where the stuffed-shirt L7 crowd hung out, listening to cornball acts like the De Castro Sisters, Lewis and Martin, and Kurt Maier on the piano. News of his arrival here was a stone downer.

I studied the broadside. "The *Gargoyle Galaxy*? And it's only three blocks from us."

"Yeah, I know, like we need the competition. The Village is over-stocked already with joints. The Café Wha, the Café Bizarre, the Commons, the Roue, the Harlequin, the Blue Angel, Gerde's Folk City, the Vanguard— Just how thin does everyone think we can slice this pie? And now Marinelli barges in with his shark tactics. Go suss him out, Nick, okay?"

I turned to leave in a hurry. Anything that threatened the beautiful thing we had here at the Gate got me worried. The bad news made me momentarily forget about Al. He caught up silently with me outside Art's office.

"Oh, right, let's get you set up with a pad. And then maybe you can help somehow."

Al gave me a candy. I stuck it in the pocket of my jeans.

3. FRAN-DANCE

I cleaned up nice. With construction grime removed, hair slicked down, Ray-ban cheaters, Hugh Beaumont cardigan, chinos and loafers, I looked like any other BMOC out to sample the beatnik scene. Joe College on the prowl for Janey Beret.

I had left Al Luchow in his new quarters above the Gate, with instructions that I'd catch him later. When I departed, he was busy studying the glowing coil of the room's beat hotplate as if he had never seen one before. I just prayed he wouldn't burn Mills House No. 1 to the ground.

It was only noon, and I didn't expect the *Gargoyle Galaxy* to be open yet. I was just intending to size up the façade, try to scope out how much gelt Marinelli was investing. But to my surprise, I found the joint already pulling in eager novelty-seekers, fickle Village habitués bored with their usual hangouts. So in I went, Thyratron Tube Theseus into the Louche Labyrinth, under the deliberately primitive hand-lettered sign that advertised:

VINO, VIXENS AND VERITAS

HOWL AT THE CONEY ISLAND OF YOUR MIND

MORE BOP FOR YOUR VOOT

The interior of the *GG* featured plush couches, artfully mismatched, and low tables (each spiked with the universal candle in a chianti bottle), dim overhead lighting and arty prints: Utrillo, Soutine and Dufy. A big full-service bar occupied one wall of the room, staffed by two cauliflower-eared apes, uncomfortable in striped Apache dancer shirts, who looked about as esthetically inclined as Floyd Patterson. Marinelli's muscle. Bead curtain at the corridor leading to the WC—or, as the sign had it, "Shakers and Sitters." The whole effect was *House & Garden* Bohemian, trendy and "hip," but utterly soulless.

At the end of the large room, perpendicular to the bar, a wide stage dominated. A trio was playing jittery jazz, Eric Dolphy lite, and a woman was dancing. Barefoot, dressed in a green leotard hand-painted with flowers, she had Iota Scintilla's bombshell build, but ten times her talent. Whipping her long blonde hair around and writhing her limbs like an octopus on uppers, she also wailed a song.

"Pull my daisy, tip my cup, all my doors are open. Cut my thoughts for coconuts, all my eggs are broken. Jack my Arden, gate my shades, woe my road is spoken. Silk my garden, rose my days, now my prayers awaken…"

Standing at the bar I bought a beer I barely sipped and watched the performance till it ended. The woman slinked offstage like a wounded leopard in a cloud of musk.

The bass player said, "That was Fran Panagiotis, cats, interpreting 'Pull My Daisy,' from a new film due out soon. Give it up for Fran."

The finger-snapping had barely begun when one of the simian bartenders tapped my shoulder and said, "Mr. Marinelli wants to see youse, chum. Right through there." He jerked a gnarly ear toward the beaded curtain.

I suppose I could have just strolled out. But now that I had been sussed as a spy, I figured confrontation with this intruder onto the Village scene was my best bet.

Marinelli's office door loomed at the dark end of the corridor, beyond the johns. I knocked, then let myself in.

With his coarse pig-iron features and squat barrel body, Ivo Marinelli resembled a fireplug in clothes. And what clothes! Some rube's idea of a beatnik outfit, assembled off the rack at Gimbel's: striped pullover shirt, bandana knotted around his neck, Levi's that looked as if some subordinate had dutifully distressed them for the boss, and a pair of unscuffed Red Wing boots. Marinelli was plainly aware of the ridiculous figure he cut, as he itched and chafed and visibly dreamed of getting back into his favorite five-hundred-dollar sharkskin suit.

The reason for his farcical getup, I suddenly intuited, was sitting with one Danskin-covered hip on the edge of Marinelli's desk. Fran Panagiotis had a towel over her shoulders, and was using one end to dab her sweat-slicked face. She flashed me a demi-leer that would have melted most males into a puddle of hormones.

"Mr. Champion," rumbled Marinelli, my Minotaur, while Ariadne picked at a corn on one bare foot resting atop her opposite knee. "Glad you could make it. I like your work. I caught your lighting scheme for the

Nina Simone gig at the Gate. Friggin' brilliant! That's why I wanna offer you a job. I'll double whatever D'Lugoff is paying you. And you won't have to fix no broken windows." Marinelli winked as ponderously as a rhino rolling over. "*My* glass ain't gonna get busted."

"Mr. Marinelli, I'm flattered, really, I am. But the Gate is my home, the place where my heart and passion live. I believe in the music and our mission and the people behind it. It's authentic and true and the best thing in my life. Why would I trade all that for this plastic fake, no matter how much money was sweetening the betrayal?"

Marinelli tried to work up some outrage, but failed to be very convincing. You could tell he'd rather be ringside at the Copa watching the chorus girls shake their tailfeathers, with a martini in his hand. "Fake! This joint is genuine bohemian, the best that money can buy! Fran worked out every detail, and she's got a real feel for this stuff!" Marinelli clutched the back of Fran's neck in a grip that blended dominance and submission, love and hate. "You already seen how the marks are falling all over themselves to get in the doors. And I got Dave van Ronk playing this weekend! We're gonna put the Gate and all these other half-assed amateur joints six feet under. You just watch!"

"Mr. Marinelli, I have a counter-proposition for you. Close up now, before you lose your shirt. The Village isn't Uptown. The people here can spot insincerity and poseurs a mile away. Your place will be empty after the initial novelty wears off."

"Yeah? We'll see who goes belly-up first! Now, get outta here!"

Fran had slumped back against Marinelli, and he was kneading her shoulders. I left the happy couple and went back to report to Art.

"Fuck 'em," he said through a thick cloud of muggle. "We've got a show to put on."

* * * *

Three AM Friday night, and the Gate was officially closed. But Monk and his buddies were still woodshedding on stage. This type of scene was probably my favorite part of the job. My duties were over, and I could just blissfully groove to the supreme music.

Even the memory of Clover Sterbcow's annoying behavior that evening failed to dim my glow. After arriving with the requisite party of paying pals, she had gotten drunker than usual and been sloppy sentimental all over me.

"Oh, Nick, Nick, Nick, y'all so cruel to little old Clover. When you gonna give me a tumble?"

"When the Ninth Ward's underwater, honey."

That slur on her hometown didn't sit well, so she hissed at me, made as if to scratch out my eyes, then flounced/stumbled off. Suited me.

Behind the bar, Art was taking inventory of bottles. I sat with my feet up, sipping a Coke, grateful after standing at the board for hours.

Al Luchow was sweeping up.

The strange mute cat had proven extremely helpful over the past couple of days. Mild-mannered, eager to please, he did any small, simple chore with precision. More complex instructions, however, bypassed some essential circuitry missing from his brain. Everyone who came into contact with the guy cottoned to him. Except for Chester Kurland. The old soak didn't actually dislike his flophouse neighbor, but he seemed skittish and wary whenever they met, like the way the hens back home in Iowa used to react to anything odd placed into their coop.

But generally, Al Luchow seemed a known quantity, already an almost invisible part of the Gate's scenery, unsurprising in his range of behaviors.

But then came the Riff.

Monk suddenly played five queerly assorted notes on the keyboard, a riff sounding like some communication from the Milky Way.

Al tossed down his broom with a bang and hopped up on stage. He dashed straight to the vibraphone that Milt Hinton had been playing before he'd cut out early. Al grabbed the mallets and echoed Monk's riff.

After their initial shock at the janitor joining in, the cats on stage, highly professional all, started to comp Al, who was walloping away with his four mallets like Kali tenderizing a steak. Whoops of excitement, along with exhortations of "Go, cat, go!" filled the club. The improvised music sounded great, washing over me in dense sheets of sound.

Art came to stand beside me. "Listen to that! Who the hell knew! This guy's too talented to be sweeping up here. I think we got ourselves a new act! And for only twelve dollars a week!"

I sighed. Good news for Al. But for me—well, I could foresee I'd be picking up my own glass shards off the sidewalk again.

4. TWO BASS HIT

How Al Luchow spread his easy-going vibe—pun fully fledged, natch—and turned practically the whole Village for a short time into something resembling Big Rock Candy Mountain crossed with a Swedish May Day Free Love Festival mated with Gene Kelly's Technicolor backlot Paris from *Les Girls* is a long and convoluted tale. I know only some parts. But they're essential parts, and maybe enough to round out Al's strange biography.

And I saw firsthand how it all ended too.

That's something no one who was there will ever forget.

Am I glad Al's path intersected mine? you quaveringly quack.

Even now, years later, that much I still can't say for sure.

* * * *

After Al revealed his unsuspected talents, Art managed to convey to the enigmatic mute but grinning spade that his broom-pushing days were over, and that he had total Cartesian Blanche to play his outer-space music. Mr. Luchow and his Amazing Vibraharp would command the slow Wednesday night spot until crowds—or rather, the lack thereof—gave Art cause to change his mind.

I worked out a lighting scheme that would minimize Al Luchow's bizarre green-tinged complexion. Art rustled up an old Deagan model 'harp and the makings of a band. Thelonius Monk and crew these backing guys were not, but reasonably competent. Al spent a little over a week rehearsing with them—if you can call what they did "rehearsing." Spontaneous, uncharted woodshedding that reminded me of the more far-out stylings of that Chicago kook Sun Ra.

And then they opened.

The Gate that night filled up about halfway, and I counted that a success. Our draw had been down significantly since Marinelli's joint opened, despite my brave and defiant predictions. Never underestimate the preference of the public for fake over real. But for Al's debut I had enlisted Clover and her web of pals to flesh out the seats. And flesh out things Clover herself did. That night she wore a pink angora sweater about two sizes too small, and toreador pants to match.

"Oh, Nick," she honeydripped as she coiled around me just prior to showtime, like a rough Louisiana study for "Laocoön and His Sons," "aren't you so grateful to me? Don't we work swell together?"

I unpeeled the Dixie wench from around my person and pretended to fuss with my board. "Yeah, sure, Clover, just like Echo and Narcissus. Now if you'd let me get these settings straight…"

Clover warped into High Dudgeon. "Nick Champion, I swear! Someday you're going to find someone you want but can't have, and then you'll see how it feels!"

She stomped off to rejoin her crew, and I felt a little guilty. Like I said, Clover's not a bad sort, it's just that she's let herself get all mixed up about me.

Some straight applause interrupted my guilt trip. Al and band were taking the stage. I made with the spots.

The next half hour was a mild blast, a success but no show-stopper. The crowd seemed to dig Al's way-out sounds, and the band showed no hesitation following their wordless leader. But then, midway through a tune, Al did something totally unexpected.

While the band vamped, Al reached into a pocket of his baggy shabby suitcoat, essential part of the only outfit I had ever seen him wear, and came out with a handful of candy. He tossed it into the audience. At first people flinched. Figuring out what was going on, they relaxed and laughed. Some people unwrapped the candy and placed it in their mouths. Al threw more. Then more and even more.

Where was he getting the stuff from? I wondered briefly. His pockets hadn't been bulging to begin with, but he kept yanking out and strewing forth handfuls of the wrapped lozenges ....

A flying candy beaned me and dropped to my board. Al ceased flinging stuff and resumed playing. I heard cellophane rustling, and glimpsed people beginning to lip and tongue and mouth the candies.

Within seconds, the wigout commenced.

As wigouts go, there was nothing violent or loud or deranged about the scene. But I could sense, with the same veteran sensibilities that alerted me to a room full of cats high on muggle even when not a whiff of smoke remained behind, that some kind of altered consciousness now grew among all the crowd that had partaken of Al Luchow's candy.

People were acting like tentacles of some composite organism. They closed their eyes as one. They swayed and davened in their seats in unison, as if they were underwater plants stroked by invisible currents. The audience began to keen and moan in an almost subliminal manner, their massed voices complementing the bouncy freeform bop issuing from the band on stage.

I had never seen anything like this. Scary and alluring at once. I got a spooky sensation that while the bodies of the crowd might still be here at the Gate, their minds were gone, man, gone.

The fallen candy on my board seemed to open a sugary eye and wink at me. I picked it up, hesitated just a moment, then skinned it and popped it into the old piehole.

The taste of the strange lozenge reminded me of one part retsina to two parts aircraft dope—banana oil—to three parts rancid peanut butter. But somehow the disgusting taste did not make me want to spit the stuff out, but rather to suck harder.

Suddenly the smoky, scarred, claustrophobia-inducing confines of the Gate opened outward to infinity.

Al Luchow and his band were playing on a flower-bedecked stage under a limitless purple sky spiked with golden stars looking like Van

Gogh whorls. The audience sat on velvet rainbow cushions scattered across diamond grass. I could feel the individual spark of each soul. Apprehending my arrival, the soul sparks all swarmed around me and brought me into their groovy astral dance.

For some timeless eternity we bopped to the celestial music, all cares and differences forgotten in an omnipresent fugal pool of harmony and love.

And then, bam! New York City bringdown.

Back in the familiar confines of the Village Gate, which looked both incredibly dowdy and limited, like some dollhouse diorama, yet somehow still homey and beloved, the band had left the stage. People gazed sheepishly at each other, tentative dumbass smiles festooning their faces, as if asking, "What now, but who cares?"

Art D'Lugoff stumbled over to me where I stood week-kneed at my board. Twin trails of tears rilled his homely phizog. "Nick, Nick, what was that, man? So intense!"

Slowly, still recovering myself, I said, "That, Art, is the key to ending the fighting here in the Village, and my daily broken-glass excruciations." Then, because I am essentially a much more devious and nasty person than Art, I added, "And, it's a recipe for the bringdown of a certain Ivo Marinelli as well."

5. BYE BYE BLACKBIRD

Al's supply of cosmic candy, the Goofballs of the Gods, indeed proved limitless. Or at least large enough for our purposes. I never asked where he got the stuff, but I think maybe even then I suspected. A suspicion about to be mostly confirmed by one certain private moment between me and Al. Yeah, yeah, I'll tell all, you greedy sickos, and we'll be just like schoolyard wiseguys pawing over the good parts in some D. H. Lawrence novel.

But back to our campaign to remake the Village: not only did Pusher Al continue to distribute his favors every Wednesday night to a growing and growing and growing, growling, grovelling crowd at the Gate, all eager for his performances, but he provided me personally, upon request, with bags of the celestial sweets. And where do you think those candies went? Why, out among the great unwashed of the Village scene.

We—and by "we" I mean mainly Clover Sterbcow, Bird bless her, and her crowd of Luchow-converted acolytes—handed out the stuff to every A-Trainer, Bircher, militant pansy, Bronx Bagel Baby and Minor Mafia thug we could connect with. And the effect was immediate and radical.

Peace and harmony dropped down upon our Village—yea, verily, like unto ye Holy Night in Bethlehem. Cats were getting into each other's bags like no tomorrow. Squares loved the hipsters, chicks dug rival chicks with whom formerly they had engaged in hair-pulling, eye-scratching fights, and tightass cops could be seen breaking bread with blissful winos. Peaceable Kingdom, NYC-style. The Omphalos of something new and holy.

The newspapers ultimately got their hands on the story and played it up fairly big:

MASS MELLOWING OF GREENWICH RIVALRIES

VILLAGE SQUABBLES HIT ALL-TIME LOW OUT-BREAK OF BOHEMIAN CO-EXISTENCE

The reporters couldn't quite track down the reason for the change—or if they did, they thought it was too fantastical to include in the record, or smacked too much of endorsing drug use. But who cared what the establishment perceived? We were all high on the sci-fi, Sputnik visions sent to us by Al Luchow.

All of us except a certain Ivo Marinelli.

Custom at Marinelli's joint had plumetted, with the popularity of the Gate as the nexus of the new vibe. I had heard through the grapevine that Marinelli was boiling over at this turn of events—mainly due to the constant goading from Fran Panagiotis, whose terpsichorean exhibitions played to scanter and scanter seats.

I wanted to bring Marinelli over to our side, before he decided to do the Gate some real harm through his underworld connections. But I let him stew a few weeks before I had Art issue an invitation for him to come hear Al's show next Wednesday.

Marinelli and Panagiotis bulled in just minutes before showtime with a couple of goons flanking. Tonight, as if to reassert his power and status, Marinelli had reverted to fashion type, sporting an Italian suit that would have given Liberace's tailor the screaming meemies.

I performed the introductions among Ivo, Fran and Art.

"Listen, you punks," Marinelli said, "I'm only here to laugh at your amateur hour. Next week I'm bringing in the heavy artillery. I booked Mitch Miller and his Orchestra, and you guys will be history. And if that don't work—well, I got other irons in the fire, if you get my drift."

I could see Art bristling, ready to lay into Marinelli, but I calmed everyone down and got them all seated at a table close by my board. Then I had one of the waitresses bring them the "special" round of complimentary drinks, while I watched.

Prior testing showed me that Al Luchow's mind candy dissolved readily in alcohol, and worked just fine. Godawful taste, though. But I had the girl announce that these were genuine "absinthe" drinks, and that impressed Marinelli.

Elbowing Art slyly, Marinelli said, "I see you got nothing against a little bit of illegal hooch. Anything to turn a dime, that's the way to do it! Well, here's looking atcha!"

He chugged his cocktail just as Al and the band took the stage. Fran Panagiotis sipped hers with distaste, but then Ivo forced her to down it all. "Whatsamatta with you, you got no class?"

Minutes into the first song, Marinelli and his girlfriend were plainly cruising with Captain Video and his Video Rangers, syncopating and swaying with the rest of the galactic groovesters in the club. I stayed straight.

When the drug finally wore off, Marinelli got shakily to his feet, with Fran using him as a scaffolding to pull herself upright.

"I—I—" Whatever he wanted to tell us wouldn't come out. Finally he blurted, "I gotta go see someone," and staggered out.

The rest you probably heard. How Ivo Marinelli left the nightclub racket for good and founded a firm to make and sell spaghetti sauce: his mother's recipe, Mama Marinelli's Marinara. He got even richer than before his epiphany, but without any of the hardnosed gangster stuff.

And Fran? Last I heard, she had shaved her head and was sitting at the feet of Alan Watts.

* * * *

So that was that. Everything copacetic. Happy weeks passed. The whole Village resembled an easygoing Eden, the Gate was raking in the crowds and their cover charges, and my own life had become carefree and streamlined, like the tailfins on a Chrysler Imperial.

We all thought it would go on forever.

But then Al Luchow's friends came to collect him.

I should have known something was up that Wednesday. No one had seen Al Luchow all day, and he usually made a point of jamming beforehand.

A worried Art corralled me.

"Nick, you gotta track Al down and make sure nothing's wrong with him. People will riot tonight if he's a no-show, and they are stiffed of their happy pills and the kicky tunes."

"Too true. I'll get right on it."

So knight errant Nick Champion set out on his quest.

I checked the most obvious place first: Al's room above the club.

The grim sweat-redolent flophouse held no sign of Al. His possessionless cubicle could have been vacant for days.

I bumped into my old pal Chester Kurland in the dark cabbagey corridor. He grabbed my shirt and stuck his rummy face close to mine.

"Nicky, they're coming! They're coming from far away, but right around the corner! Two more of them!"

I unclamped Chester's grip. "Okay, okay, Chester, calm down. Always room for two more at this big happy shindig."

I left the bum muttering, and went out onto the streets.

Al was nowheresville.

Then something impelled me down to the Gate's basement.

I found him there in the room where he had first materialized. He was huddled over the grating in the floor, making unintelligible noises, the first time I had ever heard any sounds issue from him since the day of his discovery.

As I kneeled down beside Al, he jerked erect and began to sob.

I put my arms around him. "Hey, now...."

And then we were kissing.

It felt so right. I hadn't touched a man in over a year, since I left Iowa. Sixteen months, three weeks and five days, to be precise. Celibate Sam, that was me. Kill the perverse urges, while running through my skull on an infinite loop was the voice of my mother telling the lousy faggot who was once her son to get out and never show his face in her house again.

Al Luchow's mouth tasted just like the happy pills: retsina, banana oil, bad peanut butter. I figured he did so much of the nameless drug it was just part of his system.

I was half right.

We somehow ended up on a pile of flattened cardboard boxes. My senses were spinning, and I never saw Al get out his clothes. But in some strange manner they had disappeared. I fumbled my own off, and then we were making it. Everywhere my tongue went, it met with the same taste. And then I knew.

Al Luchow *was* the drug.

We met naked on that other world, and made forever love. I wanted for us never to part, always to be here in Martian paradise.

And that, my sicko friends, is all the details you will ever get.

Inevitably, though, we ended up back on Earth. Al seemed calmed by our lovemaking. I got up and turned away from his naked form in order to reclaim my own scattered clothes. When I had gathered them up, he was already dressed.

"You'll play tonight, Al?"

He nodded, mutely, and we left the cellar together.

* * * *

Al and the band were just taking the stage in front of a packed house, when a tide of excited whispers rose from near the entrance and moved inward, along with two late arrivals to the club.

The source of the hubbub soon revealed itself as these eminences.

Threading majestically and with catlike grace through the labyrinth of tables came Miles Davis and John Coltrane. Unmistakeable.

Although when they passed by a forty-watt bulb near the bar, I thought to detect the same green undertone to their complexions that Al exhibited.

Miles and Trane ascended the stage, the one so compact and feral, the other burly and powerful. Al Luchow hung his head in embarrassment, like a kid caught with his mitt in the cookie jar. But his pals laid a hand apiece upon his shoulders, and Al Luchow raised his face and tentatively smiled.

Miles made a peremptory gesture, and the stunned sessions players passed over a trumpet and a sax.

The new cats began to play.

All the flames on all the candles stuck in all the chianti bottles flared up like torches for a moment before subsiding.

As Miles launched the impeccable, unimpeachable riffs of "So What," all the others musicians joined in. The hypnotic, seductive, looping sonorousities climbed into our laps and whispered into our ears, and even without any drugs, we all went voyaging among the stars.

On that nameless, placeless world, the eight minutes of the tune stretched out to eight eons, and we could have gone for eight more. On that foreign, exotic stage, beneath a canopy of polychromatic solar gems, Miles, Trane and Al pounded out the whimpered, weighty, wispy notes, riding us their listeners like exhausted horses.

And then, silence, and a sad return.

Al, Trane and Miles were gone from the stage, leaving behind their stunned backup players. A ghostly note from Al's vibraphones seemed to hover, then evaporate.

I collapsed onto a stool at my board. Then Art D'Lugoff was beside me, hopefully frantic.

"It all changed, Nick. Everything."

"Sure, Art, sure. But now we've got to keep going all alone."

ABOUT SPECTER-BOMBING THE BEER GOGGLES

When you write a story that is going to appear under the auspices of MIT, the pressure to be scientifically innovate and accurate and insightful is on! No hand-waving or elves allowed! I think I met the high standards of Hard SF, though I am hardly an expert in that sub-genre. In any case, employing a humorous tone, I think, defused some of the awesome responsibility.

This is one of my favorite stories to read before an audience. It always seems to go over well.

SPECTER-BOMBING THE BEER GOGGLES

Firpo Manzello was looking to get lucky. He hadn't had sex in three weeks, and was beginning to fear he never would again. Yotta-toxic, serkku!

Part of the carnal drought involved Firpo's job. He worked for the city of Cambridge, Massachusetts, in their Public Works Department, Sewer Division, Rogue Transgenic Squad. Firpo's job involved descending into the subterranean labyrinth of utility tunnels with his team each morning and cleaning up whatever escaped the filters and traps of the numerous biotech plants in the city. Most days, the team's quarry was nothing more challenging than some errant slime mold or motile vat-cortex. But from time to time, more complex organisms got loose. Firpo still bore crosshatched scars on his ankles and calves from tangling with a pride of anomalocaris. Believe me, serkku, those things could bite! What the hell had the fabbers been thinking when they endowed the monster shrimps with that pincer equipment? Lots of good eating there in the grabbers, but still—

Firpo's job description itself wasn't the actual problem. Some women actually found his duties sexy. Great White Hunter/Urban Superhero Guardian and all that. No, the hard nut was how Firpo smelled after a day at work. Heavy aromatics in those sewers! Even industrial-strength odor-remediation ribozymes from TraumaTech failed to eliminate every molecule of stench. Hard to get close to a babe when you reeked even faintly of seaweed-fermenting yeast strains.

But a liberal dose of Hack's Bodyspray could generally mask Firpo's signature smell at least long enough for him to make a love connection. The other, greater part of his problem was his erotic selectivity.

Firpo had developed a kink, hardwired now in his neurons by way, way too much gameplay in the online universe of ElfQuest. (A geezer at age twenty-eight, Firpo had prefered the old-fashioned platform over the augmented reality live-action version.) SAD, the experts called Firpo's kink. Sympathetic Avatar Dysmorphia, brought on by excessive somatic identification with one's virtual self and peers. Although he managed to kick his gamer addiction, he could only get turned on by women who looked like elves. Needless to say, such real-life women were a tiny minority on the dating scene. True, there was a small community of modded and cosplay elves at MIT. But Firpo had kinda aged out of that scene, and dramatically burned some bridges.

That left him only one choice really if he wanted to get laid.

He was going to have to download the Beer Goggles app.

The Beer Goggles app was a piece of augmented reality software that ran on your memtax. It changed the user's visual perception of other humans, overlaying onto them whatever physical parameters the user dictated. Beer Goggles would allow Firpo to perceive every woman as an elf. Or so he had been assured by the vendor's sales pitch. He had not actually used the app yet. Before today, the thought of downloading it into his phone felt too much like defeat, giving in to his neurosis and carrying around a talisman of his deviance. He kept telling himself that he could beat his kink and get normal. But three celibate weeks had proved he was too weak to defeat his kink.

So, eager to be loved again, Firpo took the decisive step.

First he popped in a new pair of memtax. The brief interval when his naked eyes beheld the world, when unmediated photons struck his rods and cones, seemed weird and incomplete, as if he had been stripped of one of his senses.

Memtax were living contact lenses built out of jellyfish proteins laced with graphene circuitry and an RGB chromatophore micromatrix. They subsisted by drinking the wearer's tears, lasted forty-eight hours, and a year's supply came free with most annual phone contracts. Possessing only minimal memory and processing power (about as much as a turn of the century PC), they had just one function: painting the user's retinas with high-res realtime imagery. Oh, yeah: their outward-facing side replicated the user's iris and pupil—or any other image the user chose.

The memtax were übertoothed to Firpo's phone, which in turn rode the cognitive E3 cellular network to the vast global cloud.

After losing his expensive smartphone several times in the sewers, even when secured in a supposedly failsafe holster, Firpo had invested in a wearable phone, now strapped to his wrist. The size of a sports watch, the phone ran on a thermopile that converted Firpo's excess bodyheat to electricity. It also served as a bodymonitor with continuous transdermal monitoring, sending telemetry back to the squad's HQ while Firpo squelched through the sewers, wearing his memtax, übertoothed earbuds and a piezoelectric conduction mic strung on an innocuous locket around Firpo's throat.

Firpo's haptic bling—a smartring on each finger—completed his toolkit.

The memtax settled into place and booted up. The Apple-Asustek app store icon hovered in the upper left corner of Firpo's field of vision, seemingly as real as the rest of his kitchen. He spread the icon open with a two-fingered gesture, his Haptic User Interface rings providing the tactile sensation of cutting a trough in a bowl of porridge. He quickly found Beer Goggles, and, for €3.99, downloaded it.

He started the little augie program running and directed it to the ElfQuest MMORPG site for its templates. The game had ten million players, over half of whom were women with distinct avatars. With that many images to choose from, the AI in Beer Goggles would certainly be able to overlay all the women Firpo could possibly meet in his lifetime with non-repeating masks.

The neat thing about Beer Googles was that it only came online when the user got drunk, as determined by his phone's measurement of the ethanol levels in his sweat. The app said it was operative now, but of course Firpo wasn't drunk. Yet he wanted to test it, so he overrode its defaults to bring it immediately online. Then he looked outside.

Rents were too high in Cambridge for Firpo to afford living there, and the city did not demand residence within its borders as a term of his employment, so he lived in a cheap neighborhood in Charlestown. His quarters were a leaky, drafty houseboat moored at a louche marina protruding practically from the base of the Bunker Hill Monument. Connected to the hungry sea, the rising waters of the Charles and Mystic Rivers had reached partway up Breed's Hill, drowning the old street-level neighborhood. The repurposed district had a certain gritty charm. Firpo always enjoyed watching the scuba divers below his boat, circulating through the drowned tenements in search of archaeological tidbits.

A Duck Tour was offloading a group of sightseers at an adjacent commercial dock. Judging by the snatches of excited conversation that drifted to him through his open window and by the appearance of the men, Firpo suspected the tourists hailed from Singapore or Malaysia. But judging by the women—old, young, fat, lithe, tall, short—the group hailed from Abode, exotic world of two moons, Wolfriders and Sun Folk. Long pointy ears, big slanted lantern eyes, golden skin, heart-shaped delicate faces.

Firpo hurriedly dropped the shade on his, his sudden arousal painfully pressing against his pants. He took Beer Goggles offline, and then brought up the active lifestreams of three of his posse from the Rogue Transgenic Squad, teleking them and arranging to meet them at the Cantab that evening.

Plenty of time to elven-ify the female world when he reached the bar.

* * * *

The house band at the Cantab Lounge, Jasmine Mofongo, pounded out their bhangra-bachata so loud that Firpo had to recalibrate his earbuds to filter out most of the music before he could hear his friends talk. Illumined like a cross between a hospital ward and a Victorian opium den, the Cantab was old, grotty and cramped, its staff rude and capricious, but the place felt like home to Firpo and his squad mates. They often came here straight from the showers after work, and had never once been called out for being a tad whiffy. The patrons were simply grateful for the protection from roaming sewer shoggoths, a popular urban legend. (One excessively wasted female patron claimed to have been attacked once by a pseudopod emerging from the Cantab toilets.)

Being a Saturday inching toward midnight, the joint was jamming. Firpo and his three friends had been lucky to get stools at the long scarred bar. A score of booty-shakers thronged the small dance floor. Balky heat pumps chuffed to chill the place, to little effect. The early June temps had averaged high nineties all week, and now the heat was baked into the building's old skeleton, mere prelude to August torture.

Firpo was drinking a cocktail called "Important Intangible Cultural Property Number 86-1," whose main component was the South Korean liquor munbaeju. The stuff was potent, and this was his second one. But he knew he wasn't clinically drunk yet, because Beer Goggles had not kicked in one hundred percent. But the app's stealthy oncoming seepage, an unadvertised surprise feature to Firpo, was tantalizing.

The app was using morphing algorithms to bring every woman closer to divine elfdom by degrees, the drunker Firpo got. Right now, all the females in the place looked like sixty-forty hybrids, with a preponderance of fey. Imbibing a third "Important Intangible Cultural Property Number 86-1," should provide the tipping point.

Glancing to his right at Ellie Salo, Firpo jumped a hair to see how his co-worker had been transformed. Uncanny, serkku! Her familiar pleasantly wide mouth, squarish chin and broad nose seemed to have been shaved down and resculpted by an invisible plastic surgeon, and her olive skin was assuming amber tones. The upper curve of her ear was trending Spock-wise.

Sight of the partially elven-ified Ellie left Firpo feeling confused. He didn't want to hit on Ellie, or even consider her as an erotic object. Sex with co-workers was generally a bad idea—imagine having a lover's spat in the stenchy subterranean dark while some unknown critter was stalking you—and he knew Ellie too well to harbor any romantic notions. But if her transformation continued, he'd be unable to keep his hands off her. And more alarmingly, she might not object to his attentions.

Firpo said, "Scuse me a minute," and got up to head to the john. Once there, he opened the Beer Goggles app's preferences. Much to his relief, he found a blacklist option and entered Ellie's phone number. He returned to his stool and gave a small sigh to find Ellie looking completely like her baseline self. He downed another gulp of cocktail, and was rewarded with an intensification of estrogen elvishness everywhere else.

"So like I was saying," Ellie continued, "I hear that Celexion has brought a tankful of space squids online."

On the far side of Ellie hunkered Ismail Bazzy, a nervous scarecrow in Carhartt coveralls trimmed with nutria-fur accents. Ismail lived on the edge of constant worry and collapse, but this very hair-trigger, tripwire state had saved their bacon more than once.

"Oh, great," Ismail said. "Now we can expect to encounter krakens. I'm putting in for a raise."

From Firpo's left, Alun Lovat spoke up. An unflappable and dapper British ex-pat out of demi-drowned Liverpool, Alun seemed the antimatter counterpart to Ismail. And yet his sangfroid had proven equally valuable in the trenches. "Oh, come now, Izzy, they're only small chaps."

"Yeah, sure, now they are. But once they escape into that devil's broth—and you know damn well they will—then you just wait and see—"

"What's Celexion doing with the squids anyhow?" Firpo asked, while he tried to ignore the increasing allure of the bevy of pub-crawling, beer-swigging, gyrating Galadriels circulating all around.

Ellie answered. "They're extracting some kind of useful lipids from their synaptic vesicles. The cosmic-ray-induced mutations did something really weird to those orbital cephalopods."

Firpo's third drink had arrived, and he downed a slug.

That was all it took. Within seconds, every woman in the Cantab went full-bore elf. The effect was like when black-and-white Kansas turned to Technicolor Oz.

Firpo slid jerkily off his stool like an untrained robot fresh from the factory. Ellie looked quizzical. "You okay?"

"Uh, yeah, fine, swell. It's just—I think I see somebody I know over there and I wanna say hello."

Firpo wasn't lying. The woman he saw across the room was a creature he had long been familiar with from his dreams. He began to make a beeline in her direction.

Alun chuckled. "Do nothing not in my playbook, my lad." Ismail said, "Be careful!" Ellie, sounding slightly disappointed, said, "We'll see you before we leave."

Firpo just nodded absentmindedly. Jasmine Mofongo launched into their big hit, "Mi Dulce de Hyderabad," a song Firpo always loved, but he never heard a note.

* * * *

The space between Firpo and the elf woman he had singled out disappeared without his conscious volition. Standing with her female pals, nursing a drink, she had watched Firpo approach with a wry and knowing amusement. Now within her intoxicating personal space, he found himself momentarily unable to utter a sound.

Although her squad of buddies all exhibited elvish allure in differing proportions, the Beer Goggles had created something special in this one woman, perhaps having had a superior baseline body to map onto. But there also existed something authentically vibrant in her stance and attitude, the way she comported herself. Facially, she looked exactly like Leetah of the Sun Folk: masses of wavy red hair through which poked enormous lynx-like ears; pool-like canted eyes, their green-painted lids echoing their emerald depths; arrowhead chin and complexion of buttery copper.

"Um," Firpo stumbled. "Can I buy you a drink?"

"Got one."

"Okay. Wanna dance?"

"Sure."

Leetah handed off her glass to a pal, who sniffed discourteously (or was she whiffing Firpo's *eau de cloaca*?), and they squished themselves into the sardine-thick dance floor pack.

Jasmine Mofongo segued into "You Say Somosa, I Say Pastelito," perfect tune for a slow dance. Firpo took Leetah into his arms. He longed to stroke her impossibly tall and curvaceous ears, to see how well the haptic feedback matched the visuals, but he refrained.

After a few moments of sweaty shuffling more or less in place, Leetah said, "I'm just curious—what are you seeing when you look at me?"

Busted! Could he deny—?

"Don't try to fool me. I saw from across the room how you went all googly when some kind of app kicked in. What is it?"

Why'd he have to pick a sharp, smart elf? Firpo resigned himself to starting over again, with some lesser goddess. But before he ditched her, he owed Leetah an answer, so he explained.

"Hmmm, well that's not as icky as what I imagined."

Firpo untensed. Maybe this could still go somewhere. "What about you? What are you seeing when you look at me?"

"The real you."

"Not likely."

"Fosho. I don't do Ay-Are. No memtax."

This perverse luddite revelation shocked Firpo more than getting caught out using Beer Goggles. Did he really want to get involved with such a modern primitive?

Undecided, and the song ending just then, he let Leetah lead him to a relatively quiet pocket in the room, near the entrance.

"No Ay-Are? How do you function?"

"Oh, I manage. But sometimes it is inconvenient. Like right now, for instance, you could save me a few steps if you order me another drink."

Firpo teleked the Cantab's bartender, and soon they had fresh cold glasses in hand via the Boston Dynamics servebot. Just in time, for Leetah was reverting gradually to human. Firpo boosted his blood alcohol, and she popped back to Rivendell.

"Hey, by the way, I'm Firpo Manzello."

"Vicky Licorice."

"Fosho?"

"It's my pen name, but I've gotten to like it."

"Would I have seen any of your stuff?"

"Only if you have a pre-schooler at home. *Little Lost Dino Escapes the Vat*? *Little Lost Dino in Manhattan*? *Little Lost Dino Saves the Great Barrier Reef*?"

"Sorry."

"That's okay. I can hardly stand to read them myself once they're published."

An hour or so of amiable, intermittently teasing conversation ensued—although hearing a beautiful elf discourse about Cambridge city politics was slightly disconcerting—and around midnight Firpo felt ready to try for a kiss.

Unfortunately, that was the exact moment when all hell broke loose.

Days later, crowdsourced and media reports had comprehensively pinned down the nature of the event, which came to be labeled "Apparition Eve."

A coalition of monkeywrenchers—everyone from The Universal Grammar of Hate to Tragedians of the Commons—had hacked into augiespace with specter-bombing malware. Insidiously, their strikes arrived not all at once, but in a timed cascade where each new incident fed on prior confusion and chaos.

And one of the first, smaller assaults was against Firpo's new app, Beer Googles.

Leaning forward boozily to kiss a receptive Vicky Licorice, Firpo experienced instant yotta-terror as a gunshot boomed in his ears and he watched Vicky's head disintegrate in a bloody mist. He even had haptic feedback of a spasming body.

Firpo screamed like a pitchforked pig. For an infinite span of nauseous seconds, he was utterly convinced someone had randomly assassinated the woman in his arms.

But the non-reaction of the immediate bystanders—as well as Vicky's own confused exclamations, issuing from the ruins of her face—alerted him otherwise. However realisitic, it had all happened only in AR.

Elsewhere around the bar, other apparent Beer Goggles users—not all of them males—were showing similar distress.

An augie intruder popped up in Firpo's vision. The badass female warrior-type said, "Happy date-rape, bastard! Beer Goggles promotes violence to women! This has been a message from The Sisters of Lysistrata."

The specter dissolved in a spray of unicorn sparkles, but Vicky's ruined countenance remained. Firpo couldn't stand the horrible sight. Even as he awkwardly thumbed out his memtax, cursing, he found space to wonder how blowing up the heads of women could serve as the best possible anti-violence message.

The actual Vicky of course looked nothing like Leetah. A concerned expression filled a charming Latina face.

"What the fuck was that all about?"

His pulse slowing, Firpo told her. The other victims were calming down as well, and reconnecting with those they had seen killed.

Then the next attack struck.

A subset of the crowd shrieked and reared back from something invisible and threatening in the center of the Cantab. One woman screamed, "It's hell! Hell's opening up!" Another person yelled, "The teeth, the teeth!"

The shrieking of the damned filled Firpo's earbuds, and he plucked those out too. Now he felt truly insensate. Without his own connection to augiespace, Firpo had no notion of what the horrified patrons were seeing or why they had been selected out of the crowd. He felt bewildered and helpless.

People were beginning to surge toward the narrow exit. A stampede seemed imminent.

Vicky took charge. She grabbed Firpo's hand and pulled him outside.

The hot night air hit Firpo like a wool-padded sledgehammer. "My friends! They're still in there!"

Firpo attempted to re-enter the Cantab, but the sound of exploding stacks of amplifiers stopped him. Specters must have tricked Jasmine Mofongo into some kind of "turn it to 11" mistake with their equipment. Suddenly a copious outflow of other fleeing patrons carried Firpo and Vicky out onto Massachusetts Avenue.

Dodging wild-eyed pedestrians, they regained the curb just in time. The orderly, scant flow of late-night vehicular traffic was disintegrating. Whatever specters the passing drivers were experiencing—children in the road, sudden sinkholes, giant kaiju, their dashboard telemetry red-lining—were causing them to swerve wildly and crash into lamposts, buildings and unfortunate pedestrians. The din was terrific: bending metal, fleshy impacts, sirens and screams.

Vicky pulled Firpo into the doorway of a shuttered store. "Your friends will have to manage on their own. The first responders will be here soon. We can't do anything. We've got to get someplace safe. Where do you live?"

"Charlestown."

"You're closer. I'm way out in Waltham. Let's go."

Regaining a little more composure, Firpo took a step out from their sheltering niche, then stopped.

"What's the matter?" Vicky said.

"I have no idea how to get home. I always followed the augie trail here."

Vicky took some kind of antique handheld device out of her purse.

"What's that?"

"GPS unit."

"That must be fifty years old! It still works?"

"No memtax, you get creative. C'mon!"

They did not dare use the subway. The sound of titanic crashes emanating from underfoot was persuasion to stay aboveground. Even as cautious pedestrians, they ran into plenty of dangers. One of the worst was plummeting bodies, as baffled, specter-tormented victims were led to step from high windows and off rooftops that must have appeared to them as safe paths. Smokey fires contributed to the Dante's Inferno atmosphere of a city in upheaval. Were other places under attack as well? Firpo had no way of knowing.

But eventually, after a few hours, Vicky and Firpo reached the relative safety of his houseboat and collapsed wearily into bed. After a few mumbled endearments, they both fell asleep.

And in the morning light, amidst the humbled wreckage of the city, augmented and physical, even without Beer Goggles, using just his naked eyes, a grateful Firpo discovered that Vicky looked plenty beautiful enough to drive all thoughts of Leetah and her kin forever from his mind.

ABOUT SWEET SPOTS

I have a gripe with the universe. It's constructed so that it's much easier to screw up than to succeed. I guess it has something to do with entropy. But humans exist in little pockets of negentropy. You would think we would have developed some kind of intuition about "making the right move" in all situations. Well, here's the story of one fellow who did—and it's that darned teenaged protagonist again!

SWEET SPOTS

"Officials were trying to determine on Monday how a man who walked through the wrong door on Sunday afternoon turned the busiest terminal at Newark Liberty International Airport into a human traffic jam on one of the busiest travel days of the year."

—James Barron,
"Security Investigation Begins at Newark Airport,"
The New York Times, January 4, 2010.

*

The way Arpad Stroll discovered his unique ability to identify and utilize universal sweet spots involved the unlikely confluence of his unrequited love for Veronica Kingslake, Mrs. Christelli's physics class, the apelike antics of Willy Squidgeon, half a raisin bagel, an errant shaft of sunlight, a colored marker, a pair of cheap shoes, and a host of other unqualifiable factors, many of which were unknown to Arpad himself—at least on the conscious level.

Arpad's desk in Mrs. Christelli's class occupied the front row, and stood nearest the door. Thus the teen had, if he so chose, an unrestricted view of one of the corridors of Edward Lorenz High School through the wire-gridded glass panels of the classroom's exit door.

Now, generally speaking, Arp enjoyed Mrs. Christelli's physics lectures, and paid close attention. Science was cool, and offered a lot to occupy Arpad's ingenious, busy mind.

But on this grey, changeable, mostly overcast day, his mind was elsewhere. He had absorbed this section on entropy already, reading the textbook at home. The concepts of thermodynamics, intriguing as they were, held no mysteries for him.

So, slumped in his seat, he was daydreaming about Veronica Kingslake—her long glossy blonde hair, her lush shape, her hypnotic, ass-switching walk, her light-hearted laughter—in short, all the assorted physical and tempermental characteristics which, conjoined into one exotic package, made her so alluring to Arp and to practically every other straight male at the school. How, Arp wondered, could he ever vault to the front of the pack of Veronica's wannabe boyfriends—

At that very moment, while dumpling-shaped Mrs. Christelli lectured with her back to the class while scrawling equations on the whiteboard, Arp chanced to look to his right and spotted Veronica herself ambling down the corridor.

Arp straightened up magnetically, drawn to his beloved. If only he could escape this class and join her on whatever lone errand she pursued! Separated from the clique that normally accompanied Veronica everywhere, he might attain some new relationship with her that transcended mere indifferent tolerance.

But Mrs. Christelli handed out lavatory passes with a parsimony approaching zero tolerance, especially in these waning minutes of class. If he couldn't escape within the next few seconds, all was lost.

What inspired Arp's next move, he could not say, then or ever. There was no conscious thought, no deliberation or reasoned chain of logic. No calculating assessment of circumstances and possibilities and potentials. Whatever obscure engine of parsing and action that took command dwelled deep below even his subconscious, and transmitted its impulses directly to his muscles.

Arp turned his head back to the class and caught the eye of Willy Squidgeon, fidgeting and bored.

Willy was the class clown. It was a role he cherished and seemed positively born to. He resembled a good-natured, shaggy, red-haired Neanderthal with a face of malleable rubber. Once, Willy had legendarily climbed semi-naked to the top of the school's cupola on a dare, substituting his boxer shorts for the state flag.

Arp made the silent archetypical suite of chimp gestures—armpit scrabbling with curved hands, pop-eyed duckface hooting—and that was all it took.

This shorthand semiotic challenge invariably provoked a vivid display of imitation Cheetah behavior from Willy. There was no possibility he would decline a performance if triggered. Even in the midst of memorial services for car-crash senior-prom fatalities, Willy would respond.

Now he leaped to his feet, scrabbled atop his desk, and began to cavort noisily and exuberantly, with simian grace.

Everything else fell into place almost simultaneously.

Of course, the class went wild.

Mrs. Christelli turned away from the whiteboard, marker in hand, to chastise Willy.

At the back of the room, Ludmilla Duda instantly choked on the piece of bagel she was surrepetitiously eating. Her frantic, panicky gasping for breath distracted the teacher's reprimand, causing Mrs. Christelli to pivot uncertainly between harmless Willy and the direly choking girl.

The clouds outside parted just then in a perfectly configured slit, and a blazing hot beam of sunlight, made all the more dazzling by the circumambient gloom, drove down from the heavens to strike square upon Mrs. Christelli's face. Momentarily blinded, the teacher shuffled awkwardly in place like a tango dancer encountering a banana skin while trying to partner a horse. One shoe of her cheap, overstressed pair of Payless pumps chose that moment to exhibit a structural weakness, and its heel snapped off.

The hefty Mrs. Christelli went down like a felled sequoia, but not before she launched the whiteboard marker in her hand directly at Arp.

The marker struck Arp weakly on the forehead, but without a moment's surprise or hesitation he spontaneously clapped both hands to his left eye, bellowed wordlessly, and dashed from the room, yelling, "Nurse Miller, Nurse Miller, help!"

Out in the corridor Arp slowed, lowered his arms, tugged his T-shirt into place, tried to assume a look of nonchalance, and caught up with Veronica.

"Hi, Ron, what's up?"

Veronica, in all her Abercrombie & Fitch finery, bestowed a look upon Arp which, under the most charitable interpretation, might be deemed one of charitably suppressed pity mingled with innate repugnance.

"Hey, Stroll. Going home early. Severe cramps and wicked PMS. See ya."

This intimate datum so disconcerted Arp, engendering a wild welter of stunning mental visuals, that he ground to a halt, mouth open like the bell of a tuba, and let Veronica depart.

Opportunity blown.

But—opportunity at least initially secured.

The stunning reality of his providential escape from Mrs. Christelli's class suddenly hit him.

How in hell had all that unlikely stuff come together so perfectly?

* * * *

Jason Wardlaw, Arp's best friend, enjoyed a curious pastime of his own invention, which he had dubbed "urbex skateboarding." Disdaining professional skateparks as lame, and even turning up his nose at forbidden, police-patrolled municipal venues such as plazas, staircases and promenades, Jason would employ his battered Toy Machine Devil Cat deck only in ruined and abandoned industrial facilities, where dangling wires, cables and chains; rotting planks, detritus-laden floors and roofs;

as well as teetering girders, ramps and towers offered the largest challenges to his art.

Luckily, living in Detroit afforded Jay innumerable such sites.

This afternoon, Arp was watching Jay shred inside the old Fisher Body Plant Number 21 at Piquette and St. Antoine. As Arp sipped his Orange Mango frappuccino amidst the somber decay, Jay executed some truly sick moves involving several fifty-five-gallon drums, a handtruck, a seventy-foot-long conveyer belt, and a stack of empty doorframes.

Observing his friend's maneuvers, Arp, who had no skills whatsoever involving skateboards, became possessed of a curious yet adamant knowledge amounting to a certainty. If Jay were only to *twist* like so at this point, and *leap* like so at this other point, while *landing* just so at the finale, his generally dismal GPA would rise by some twenty-five percent.

The absurd certitude of this unrequested intuition unsettled Arp, and recalled to him the weird sequence of events that had freed him from physics class yesterday. What could such sensations mean? Was he going crazy, having a brain meltdown? If his incitement of Willy had not led precisely to the desired yet utterly unforeseeable outcome, Arp would have been sure he was going nuts. He wished he could test this new skateboard-generated revelation by having Jay perform as he envisioned, and then wait till next report card. But the moment was already over, Jay having ground to a halt amidst a pile of metal shavings.

Arp noisily sucked down the dregs of his drink and walked over to his friend's side. At lease he could share his experiences with Jay and perhaps get some reassurance.

"Jay, listen to what happened to me yesterday…."

Like a good pal, Jay paid attentive heed, even while he fussed with the trucks of his deck, picking out aluminum flinders. Arp finished his account with the epiphany that had just struck him.

Jay remained silent for an interval, and then said, "Follow me."

Arp trailed Jay over to a spot in the vast pillared space where a storage firm had stacked a giant mound of cartons before going bankrupt. Weatherbeaten and decaying, the listing cartons contained hundreds of thousands of big rough glass marbles that served as feedstock in fiberglass production.

Jay stood by one corner of the mound and said, "Watch this." He surveyed the setup intently, and then, with both hands, peeled away the lower half of one shoddy carton.

Immediately, all the marbles began to avalanche noisily out of the ripped carton, spilling accrosss the floor like frightened mice. As that carton deflated, the ones above it and around it began also to tip and burst, releasing their contents. Ultimately, a flood of marbles caused the boys to dance backward. The avalanche finally ceased of its own volition when a new equilibrium in the pile of cartons had been reached.

Jay gestured to the sea of marbles. "Okay, show me the moves you would make to get them all back to where they were."

Arp snorted. "That's impossible!"

"Of course it is. And you know why as well as I do. It's entropy. The whole universe is rigged for chaos. Mankind is fucked from the start. There are so many more crummy states of being than good ones, that the odds are stacked against us doing anything useful or desirable. Chances are that whatever move we make will result in a lousy outcome. That's how a single person can cause so much grief with so little effort. I don't care whether it's a pile of marbles or sand or snow, or some kind of human system, like a computer program or a democracy. Chances are, you stick your oar in, you just churn up a shitstorm. One little wrong twist of your car's steering wheel, and you've got a mile-long fatal pileup involving a hundred other people. Not some kind of spontaneous Shriners parade."

Arp nodded thoughtfully. "It's all true. Entropy rules, and that sucks. You and I have talked about this before. Murphy's Law is a bitch. But you don't understand exactly what I'm getting at. First off, we know that humans are negentropy agents. Even if only temporarily, we can push chaos back. But that's not even what I'm theorizing here. It's more like, more like—"

"Yeah, more like what? I'm waiting."

The perfect analogy from science struck Arp like a dodgeball taking out a nerd in the gymnasium of his mind. "It's like the Butterfly Effect!"

"Butterfly wags its wings in Brazil, you get a blizzard in Chicago?"

"Yes! By being in just the right place and doing just the right thing, a small action can launch a major result. It's called, um, sensible impedance—"

"'Sensitive dependence on initial conditions,' jerkface!" Jason pondered where the discussion was leading. "And you're saying you can suddenly see just what the butterfly has to do for something specific to happen?"

"Yeah, exactly! It's not something I can verbalize, and if I tried to pass on the knowledge to anyone else, the moment would have slipped away. And you obviously can't achieve every possible outcome from any given starting point in time and space. You'd be limited to the network of cause and effect radiating out from that particular moment in spacetime. But I can do it, I know! I did it in class!"

"How come all of a sudden?"

"How the hell do I know? My body's changing! Maybe I was bitten by a radioactive butterfly!"

Jason punched Arp in the shoulder. "Did it feel anything like that?"

Arp punched back, and the two tussled for a few seconds. Breaking out of a clinch, Jason ran a hand through his flyaway hair and said, "Arp, my buddy, we need to experiment with this new skill of yours. And I've got just the goal to shoot for."

* * * *

Arp and Jason meadered through the GM Ren Cen. On this Saturday, the mall was packed with families and packs of teens, squads of power-walking elderly and alert security guards.

"You seen any invisible hooks yet?" asked Jason.

"I don't think of them as hooks," said Arp. "That analogy just doesn't work somehow. It's not anything that reaches out and grabs me. It's more like—"

"Sweet spots! That's what you're seeing. The Nexus of All Realities, like where Man-Thing lives! Except there's millions of them everywhere! Millions of little nex-eyes!"

"Yeah, right. No, that's not exactly it either."

"Or maybe it's more like the universe's clit! Tickle it just right, and everything explodes. You should know, the way you always score with Ronnie K!"

"Shut the fuck up!"

Seething at his friend's crude yet cutting joke, Arp surged ahead, entering the food court on Level A. Jason caught up with him, genuinely apologetic.

"Aw, c'mon, did you forget I was a lowlife ballbuster? Look, I'll buy you a couple of dogs at Coney Town, okay?"

Mollified, yet feeling slightly bummed that he had not yet encountered the sweet spot he was searching for at Jason's behest, Arp agreed to the offer.

Seated at a table with their food, Arp and Jason ate and surveyed the passing scene.

In the middle of the food court, employees were setting up an inflatable bounce house for the enjoyment of the kiddies. The muted roar of the fan designed to keep the structure erect and bouncy suddenly sounded, as the blower underwent a test activation. Then the fan was shut off and disconnected from the flattened bounce house for examination of its workings.

And that's when Arp saw the desired sweet spot, pure and potent and invisible to anyone but him.

He only had time briefly to advise Jason—"Watch!"—before the moment demanded his action.

Arp threw his half-eaten hotdog at a nearby trashcan, deliberately undershooting so that the food waste landed on the floor.

One of the ever-circulating food court cleaning staff, armed with broom and dustpan, saw the defiantly messy gesture and spun around indignantly to confront and chastise Arp.

The handle of the guy's horizontally held, lance-like, fast-moving broom caught a geezer right in his stomach, causing him to *oof* and stumble against his geezer wife. The woman lurched forward, catapulting her many bursting bags of purchases directly under the feet of one particular passerby.

This important passerby, a brown-clad UPS delivery fellow, was pushing his heavily laden flatbed at top speed across the polished floor. He tripped over the strewn consumer goods and went down, releasing his grip on his cart, altering its vector and even imparting a slightly greater impetus to it.

The cart barreled toward the kneeling bounce house worker inspecting the fan. He activated the blower just as the cart took him out and glancingly hit the fan.

The roaring untethered fan swivelled around on its wheels and caught a new group in its blast.

Entering the food court at that exact moment, the heretofore-unseen shoppers who became the target of the rogue blower consisted of a pack of insouciant and attitudinous Bad Girls. These adolescent Snooki-lookalikes wore crop tops emblazoned with legends such as FUTURE MILF and GUESS WHERE I'M PIERCED. They also sported incredibly abbreviated skirts over bare legs.

Whomped by the blast from the high-powered fan, the shrieking girls felt their fluttering minuscule skirts being blown skyward. They fought at first to tug down their garments, but then a pedestal table bearing a highly breakable sugar shaker crashed into the path of the whirlwind, and their eyes were filled with flying sucrose, forcing them to abandon decorum. Now their various styles of risque undergarments, barely concealing a catalogue of tramp stamps, were on shameful display.

As various Good Samaritans and mall employees raced to the aid of the Bad Girls, Jason turned to Arp with awe suffusing his face.

Arp said coolly, "You asked me to provide...?"

"Girls in their underwear standing around in the mall. Sweet bleeding Jesus!"

* * * *

The next several days after the stirringly and reassuringly confirmational mall incident, Arp faced nearly continuous uncertainty about how to proceed with his new powers. The aching dilemma occupied his mind almost every minute. A pure case of "new superhero" angst. The whole "With great power…" thing.

Should he proceed selfishly, as unconflicted Jason counseled, employing his gifts solely for personal satisfaction?

Or should he embark on a course of selfless altruism, seeking to right a worldful of wrongs?

Didn't he have an obligation to function as a counteragent to all the entropic fuckups accidentally sowing pain and disorder everywhere? Walking through airport security the wrong way and immobilizing thousands? Tapping into oil pipelines and causing massive conflagrations? Speeding down a freeway and racking up scores of crashed vehicles?

But on the other hand, how could he know just what goals would best reverberate to mankind's advantage?

Suppose he pushed at a sweet spot to force the discovery of a brand new mega-barrel oil field in the Gulf of Mexico? He had actually half-sensed just such a sweet spot lurking at the periphery of his consciousness. It was over in Chicago somewhere, a not unreasonable distance to cover, given the payoff. Sure, doing so would make a lot of rich people richer and even help some middle-class schlubs and the general economy. But what would the long-term effects be? More pollution, a swifter plummet into Greenhouse Earth? How could he, sixteen-year-old average teenager Arpad Stroll, make such decisions wisely? Wouldn't he be better off just going for little things that would mean a lot to him alone? But what a waste of his gifts!

The circular labyrinth of reasoning and worrying preoccupied Arp for a week during which, despite Jason's imploring, he did not employ his powers again. And, to add insult to injury, he had to deal with an old problem as well.

Blueberry Chefafa.

Blueberry Chefafa was in love with Arpad Stroll, and the feeling was not mutual. Just as he pined for Ronnie Kingslake, so Blue longed for him.

Really, there was no solid reason for Arp's lack of interest in the pretty girl. Granted, Blue was not a knockout like Veronica, but her distinctive looks, derived from a blend of African-American and Greco-American genes, attracted many a male glance. There was, admittedly, the matter of her, ah, somewhat robust build to contend with. No petite princess, Blue captained the female wrestling squad at Edward Lorenz High. To report that the team was undefeated was to convey something of Blueberry's possibly intimidating physicality. Arp knew from experience that she could beat him at arm-wrestling. But her muscles were packed along attractive curves, and she certainly sported a more impressive rack than slim and WASPy Ronnie. And Blue's academic record matched her sporting accomplishments: sharp and quick, she excelled in the classes she shared with Arp.

No, there was no reason not to have the hots for Blue, other than the sheer mysteries of the heart.

But would the girl give up in the face of Arp's deliberate cold shoulder? Never! She pestered Arp ceaselessly, doing him unrequested favors, finding reasons to be wherever he was, casting meaningful glances his way in crowds, getting her friends to go to bat for her. It was enough to give a guy the jitters.

The week of Arp's special befuddlement, Blueberry exhibited extra attentiveness toward the object of her affection, as if she could detect that something potent was troubling Arp. She even showed up at his house, ostensibly bringing news of a homework assignment she thought he had missed hearing about. It took him half an hour to ditch her.

And now here she was, in Mrs. Christelli's class, auditing it for extra credit during her study period, she claimed, and seated right next to Arp. Her foot had strayed more than once into his personal space, and she kept fluffing her abundant dark hair to waft the scents of her floral shampoo his way. What a pain in the ass!

Mrs. Christelli, fully recovered from her spill of a week past, finished cabling her laptop to the big flatscreen at the front of the room. "Today, class, we are going to watch the most recent episode of NOVA. The topic is earth-grazing asteroids, how to detect them and what might be done to stop one from impacting the planet. I'm sure you will all find it extremely interesting."

The lights went down, giving Blueberry a chance to inch closer, and the screen came alive with solar system vistas and the narrator's placid yet somehow alarmist voice.

"Always at risk for another celestial impact event such as the one during the Permian-Triassic era that killed ninety percent of life on Earth, our planet dodges many near-misses each year. In fact, scientists at the University of Arizona's Spacewatch mission currently have their telescopes focused on one newly observed and fast-moving asteroid, dubbed Perses after the destructive Titan of Greek mythology. The experts are nearly certain that the hurtling rock will miss our world, but the projected clearance is the smallest ever recorded…"

Blueberry took that cue to utter a gasp of exaggerated fright and grab Arp's arm. That was when he lost it.

The two sweet spots which Arp had heretofore poked had resulted in a cascade of macroscopic events. But somehow, this time, he knew he was tapping into something more subtle.

Instead of casting off Blue's hand, as he wanted to, he took it in both of his own and squeezed. He could feel her pulse accelerate and a hot blood rush beneath her skin. Metabolic and cellular processes began to churn within the girl. At the same time, Arp put his head closer to hers, but then forced a sneeze out directly at her, spraying her with his personal blend of microbes.

"Oh, dude, sorry," Arp said unctuously.

Blueberry took no offense. "Don't worry," she whispered.

"Class, quiet, please!" Mrs Christelli admonished.

Arp continued to squeeze Blue's hand, even massaging a pressure point on the underside of her wrist. Blue practically purred. He listened for a rustling of paper. Sure enough, under cover of darkness Ludmilla Duda was unwrapping a sandwich. The odor of a highly spiced Middle Eastern shawarma filled the room.

Blue began to fidget. She withdrew her hand. "I—I don't feel so good. My stomach—" She began to retch and jumped awkwardly to her feet. Gagging wholeheartedly, she dashed from the room amidst unsympathetic laughter, and Arp sat back with a feeling of relief, accomplishment, and, if truth be told, a smidgen of guilt and remorse.

But overall, it felt sweet.

* * * *

Jason and Arp came to call the sequence of events triggered by poking a sweet spot "okiegoes" or "rubes," after the elaborate Rube Goldberg device depicted in OK Go's video for "This Too Shall Pass." Witnessing the perfectly sequenced cascades of improbable events—at least the parts that fell under their immediate point of view—began to assume an allure almost as great as obtaining the desired outcome.

Not that Arp turned his nose up at getting things he wanted for almost no effort.

The incident with Blueberry Chefafa had tipped Arp's mind over into the "for profit" side of the moral equation. After many months of trying to discourage Blue's unwanted attentions, he had disposed of her in ninety seconds. The aftermath of contracting a flukey and short-lived stomach virus, coincidental with Arp responding to her overtures, had weirded Blueberry out. Although not actually repulsed by his presence when their paths crossed, Blue reacted like a startled fawn, jerking up short and leaping back an inch or so, while regarding Arp with puzzlement as to his intentions or exact nature. She seemed to regard him nowadays as something other than human.

Every time she jumped so, Arp winced a bit inside.

But on the whole, he was satisfied with what he had accomplished.

Rewarded instantly, his brain demanded more. Forgotten or buried were all thoughts of embarking on a do-gooder's career.

For nearly a month now, Arp had indulged his every idle wish. Or at least those for which local sweet spots availed themselves. None of his desires reeked of megalomania, cruelty or excessive greed. But they were all self-centered. Except for those which he activated for Jason's sake.

A partial catalogue of Arp's conquests—or, viewed another way, presents from the obliging universe—included: a thousand-dollar gift card at the Dearborn branch of Marshall Field's; the grade of A-plus on his latest civics paper, composed in half an hour with copious use of the internet; a promotion for his Mom in her job at the Detroit Metro Airport; the public humiliation of a crooked city councilman who had taken away a local park by eminent domain for his own profit; and the infusion of an unexpected federal grant into the cafeteria at Edward Lorenz High, ensuring that Arp's favorite lunch of steak tips, asparagus and French fries appeared on the menu with increased frequency.

As for buddy Jason, the cynical slacker now sported a sick new Bump-brand deck, a closet full of Neff t-shirts and hats, and six new pairs of Vans kicks, all obtained at no cost to him, thanks to his unwarranted but uncontested inclusion on a list of professional skateboarders.

After tapping so many sweet spots, Arp had begun to understand them better and better on some deep, non-verbal level. He began to intuit where they could be found and what kind led where. He just hoped that his extra-normal senses were not developing along the lines experienced by the hyperacute hero of *The Man with the X-Ray Eyes*, a movie which had scared the pants off him a few years ago, when he had streamed it off his Mom's Netflix. But so far as he could tell, his sanity remained solid.

One thing Arp had learned: not every goal was obtainable in every location. In computer networking terms, Arp realized, sweet spots featured only a "partially connected mesh topology." Some sweet spots persisted, while others were highly evanescent. And some required more physical input on his part than others. For instance, to obtain the thousand-dollar gift card, he had been forced to wade out into the yucky River Rouge, with Jason acting as spotter and lookout, dive to the bottom, and push a shopping cart exactly one foot deeper into the muck. Not exactly easy.

But taken all in all, the employment of sweet spots for personal gain offered immense payoffs for very little input.

Having gained confidence in his new talents, Arp decided he could proceed with his ultimate goal: to get Veronica Kingslake to fall in love with him. After that, what more could he possibly ask for?

Arp would have prefered to poke one of the multiple relevant sweet spots when he was alone with Ronnie. But since that never happened, he had to do it at school.

Under the lackadaisical and inattentive guidance of Mr. Mollusk, who as a former youthful track star had no real interest in any sporting activity other than sprints, mixed phys-ed class generally devolved into groups of girls standing around gossiping and bunches of guys horsing around the equipment. Today was no different.

Arp was chilling with Jason and a few other dudes, while they shot baskets in a half-assed fashion. He participated with one eye on Ronnie where she stood across the gym with her friends, near an exterior wall. He hardly heard the banter of his pals until something Armando Zavala said made him take notice.

"Hey, who's ready to die?"

Arp got nervous. His formless intuition regarding the effects of the sweet spot he was about to employ revealed potential for some collateral danger. But he felt he had to risk it.

"Whatta ya mean?" Arp asked.

"Aren't you following news about that Percy asteroid? Seems like it might've hit something out in space and gotten aimed our way. The scientists aren't so sure it's gonna miss us anymore."

Jason commented drily, "The margin for error in their predictions is plus or minus fifteen percent. Not exactly betting odds."

Arp was going to reply, but then the basketball was passed to him, and his moment to poke the sweet spot had arrived.

Arp heaved the ball high and wide of the basket. It soared through the air and struck a small frosted window fifteen feet up the wall near where Veronica stood.

Held in place only loosely by an invisibly deteriorated seal, the glass popped outward. The rest of the okiegoes cascade was not immediately visible, but Arp heard the unmistakeable indignant yawp of a disturbed crow, the frantic cursing of what was presumably a passing pedestrian, and the screech of car tires. Even while everyone was laughing at him for his failed throw, he was running toward Veronica and the other girls.

With a tremendous crash, accompanied by female screams and shrieks, the forequarters of a huge SUV thrust through the wall, blasting bricks everywhere even as it lost momentum amidst the wreckage. Several girls, including Ronnie, had fallen to the floor, but no one seemed really hurt. Arp spared a microsecond to give thanks, but kept racing forward.

Once securely attached to the destroyed wall, an accordian-style folding room divider tall as the gym began to peel off and fall directly toward Ronnie. Wailing, she made a scrabbling attempt to rise, but seemed to have forgotten how to work her limbs.

Almost without seeing it, Arp encountered the pommel horse he had been aiming for, braced his hands against the device, and began to push. Only some hundred and twenty pounds, the device slid easily, especially under Arp's adrenalin-powered urgency.

The pommel horse stopped precisely alongside Ronnie, and Arp dropped down to further shield her fetally recumbent form just as the detached assemblage of aluminum and vinyl crashed down onto the sturdy support—and no further.

An eerie silence reigned for a moment, before shouts erupted. But Arp hardly heard anything.

Ronnie's beautiful tear-streaked face loomed inches from his, her lips parted invitingly, albeit unromantically slicked with snot, and a look of absolute adoration bloomed across her features, betokening her heart as forever his.

At his moment of triumph, doubt suddenly besieged Arp.

He sure hoped Veronica was worth it.

* * * *

"Aw, c'mon, Arp, just one little rube, please! Winter'll be here soon, and I really need that new snowboard and a plane ticket to Aspen."

"No! I told you, no more sweet spots!"

This Saturday morning the two friends were hanging out on the old Thornhill Place Bridge, where Jason had been practicing his moves on the crumbling bridge railing, despite risking a fifteen-foot drop to the greenway below. Some three weeks had passed since Arp's staged heroics in the gym, and this was the first time he and Jason had been able to chill together.

Veronica had fallen for her factitious savior more deeply than Arp could have predicted. She was inseparable from him, and much of their time together was spent in lusty clinches that stopped just short of sex. (Ambitious Mom and Pop Kingslake had plans for Veronica that did not include any chances at teenage pregnancy, and she had internalized their goals completely.) Arp found himself chafing under his new role and responsiblities. He felt like a total fake. He had gotten precisely what he wanted, but it was proving less—or rather, more—than he had envisioned. In short, Ronnie was cramping his style and freedom, and making him feel continuously guilty of fraud.

And besides, the disturbing fallout from that last sweet spot still bothered him. People had gotten hurt! Several of the other girls had suffered contusions and even a fracture or three. All as the result of Arp's selfish actions. The thought of unintended consequences accompanying future use of sweet spots plagued him. Sure, he got what he wanted every time, but at what ancillary cost, seen or unseen?

And now douchebag Jason was bugging him for a frigging snowboard and plane ticket, of all things!

Arp got ready to tell his friend off, but Jason spoke first.

"Aw, fuck it! What's the point of pretending we'll ever even see another winter anyhow? This planet is totally doomed."

The two teens automatically cast their eyes heavenward, though of course no sign of the killer asteroid dubbed Perses showed in the bright daytime sky.

"You really figure it's gonna hit us, Jay?"

"I don't think anybody figures otherwise anymore. Even Glenn Beck and Bill O'Reilly caved in. But everybody's just too stunned to argue or give a fuck anymore."

Arp recognized this much to be true. Under the imminent threat of inescapable planetary catastrophe, the global population was proving remarkably calm. Maybe because no one could really envision the catastrophe. Oh, sure, there had been isolated riots and protests. The loss of the Taj Mahal, the Kremlin, the Vatican, and Lubbock, Texas, still stung. But on the whole, there had been no scenes of contagious mass hysteria. Something about the certitude of the non-human-engineered destruction and its mutual nature, as well as a tiny smidgen of hope, had forestalled utter panic. There was no place to run or hide, no one exempt or special. Everyone was in it together, and so a sense of ostrich-head-in-the-sand resignation and willful cognitive dissonance prevailed.

Arp had reacted much the same as everyone else. With one small difference.

He had a nagging, half-unadmitted intuition that he could save the world.

Being alone now with Jason for the first time in weeks, he finally felt compelled to spill his guts.

"Jay, what would you say if I told you I saw a sweet spot that could stop the asteroid?"

Jason grabbed Arp by both shoulders, his face beaming, and shook his friend. "I knew it! I knew it! I told Blueberry you could do it!"

Arp jerked away. "What! You told Blueberry! How does she even know anything about sweet spots?"

Jason had the grace to look sheepish for once. "Aw, Arp, you didn't have to see her and listen to her these past few weeks. You know I like to hang with Blue, but she was getting to be a royal pain. She was so bummed about you and Ronnie hooking up. But at the same time she was all like, 'Oh, what a hero he is! How could I have ever doubted him? He's so good and noble. Yada yada yada!' I just couldn't take it anymore. So I had to set her straight."

Arp pondered this development. "So now what does she think of me?"

"She thinks you're a total jerkwad, and she loves you more than ever." Jason snorted. "Girls!"

A strange hot sensation suffused Arp. He knew that if Ronnie ever found out the truth about him, she would turn on him in an instant and despise him forever. As she probably well should. Yet Blueberry Chefafa knew the whole story, and still loved him.

Suddenly the world seemed to invert like an old sock, and Arp saw everything differently.

"Let's go find Blue and talk all this over with her."

"Righteous!"

The boys found Blueberry home alone, so they could discuss everything without pretense or secrecy.

"So it's like that," concluded Arp. "The sweet spot's somewhere in Chicago, but I can't pin it down at this distance. It seems to shift back and forth across a small area. Plus, it looks like it will involve some major input to trigger the rube. And it's the, um, densest one of I've ever seen. Totally gnarly with connectivity. I don't really understand the complexity of it. Some of the links seem to go down to the subatomic level. All those factors are why I just didn't rush in and trigger it. Of course I want to save the planet. But who knows if I wouldn't be causing something even worse?"

Her gaze earnest and wise, Blue cut to the heart of the matter. "Exactly what could be worse, Arp? You plunge the planet into the sun? Not likely, I say. No, you've got to take the chance."

Arp felt truly heroic at last. "All right, I will!" He instantly deflated. "But how can we get to Chicago?"

"Just look around," Jay said. "There's got to be a useful sweet spot right under your nose."

With Jason driving, it still took Arp two whole hours into the five-hour trip to Chicago to master all the dashboard controls of the stolen Lexus LX570, Blue offering helpful advice from the back seat. They didn't feel rushed or nervous—at least in terms of the police; the threat of Armageddon was another matter entirely—since the decisive suicide note found along with the car keys on the seat of the unlocked vehicle indicated that the owner would not be reporting the theft anytime soon.

Around hour four, as they got into the city proper, everyone quieted down to let Arp focus his powers. Eyes closed, he began to issue directions based on his sweet spot GPS, until finally he called, "Stop!"

Opening his eyes, Arp found himself at an iconic spot.

The street at the base of the Sears Tower, once the world's tallest building, and, coincident with its loss of that stature, redubbed the Willis Tower.

"Where now?" asked Jason.

"Up."

The car-owner's wallet afforded them the fifty dollars needed for three Skydeck passes. They rode to the 103rd floor in silence.

At the point of exiting the elevator, Blueberry suddenly balked, letting the other visitors stream past. Jason held the door open.

"No, Arpad, I don't feel good about this. Something tells me there's danger ahead. Let's turn back. It's ridiculous to think you can do anything here to change the fate of a whole planet."

Arp felt himself in the grip of dreamlike forces larger than himself. Vistas of luminous cosmic webs full of shining nodes of action swam before his eyes. "No, we've come this far. I have to try now."

Arp existed the elevator, followed by Jason and Blue, and headed straight for one wall.

Attached to the wall at intervals, glass boxes projected outward a few feet, so that visitors could step inside and have the illusion of standing unsupported in midair. As a family of tourists emptied out of one, Arp and his friends crowded in. The whole panorama stretched away below them like a Lego cityscape.

"It's right out there," said Arp. "The sweet spot to deflect the asteroid and save the planet."

Jason squinted. "Where?"

"About five feet ahead at the level of my chest."

"How can you possibly use it, Arp?" Blue asked plaintively.

Arp pressed his face to the glass separating him from saving the planet. "I *know* I can trigger it if I can reach it. But reaching it—"

Arp suddenly paused. "Of course! I just need to use *this* rube right here. A sweet spot whose function is to give me access to the other sweet spot!"

At once Arp knew why Blue had to be present. "Give me your bag!"

Blue's bag in hand, he rummaged inside and found what he was looking for: Blue's geeky science-girl laser pointer.

He turned back to the window and shone the little intense laser out and up at a precisely intuited angle.

Seconds later, a small plummeting object appeared in the sky.

Information flooded Arp's brain, as if the sweet spot were talking to him.

The object consisted of a chunk of blue airplane toilet ice, discharged from a United Express flight. But more importantly, frozen in the middle of the chunk was a worker's forgotten steel alloy wrench.

Arp yelled, "Get back!" He shoved Jason and Blue away from the observation box.

The glass shattered into a million fragments and rained downward to the street and inside the Skydeck. Freed from its icy casing upon impact, the wrench bounced along the floor until it hit the elevator door, wedging itself between the panels so that the elevator could not be easily opened to permit the arrival of any interfering authorities.

Arp stepped forward to where cold clean air gusted in. He could sense the floating sweet spot even more vividly now, since access had become unimpeded. It called to him. He couldn't fathom the entire long and braided cascade of events connected with it, but he knew with a certainty that triggering the okiego would save the planet.

"What now?" said Blueberry.

"I jump!"

Jason was shedding atypical tears. "Do it, dude, do it! We believe!"

"Kiss me, Arp!"

Arp hesitated. His timing had to be perfect. Was a kiss allowed?

Intuition told him to go for it.

He hugged Blueberry and kissed her for what seemed forever. And at the same time, further illumination flooded his mind.

A few stories above the Skydeck, having duplicated the 1999 feat of daredevil Alain Robert, who had ascended the Sears Tower's exterior human-fly-style by hand and foot alone, an illegal BASE jumper named Burnett Kershaw, resting on a ledge, was preparing to leap off, ripcord of his chute firmly in hand.

The very last part of the first stage of the rube fell into place as a TV station's helicopter arrived.

Arp broke off his kiss, smiled, ran toward the empty window, and hurled himself into space, eyes tightly shut, praying wordlessly.

Something told him to tuck and roll.

He felt himself passing perfectly through the sweet spot, activating the rube.

He untucked at just at the right moment to intersect an extremely startled Burnett Kershaw in his descent. Arp clamped his arms around the guy's torso, then burst out laughing.

And a quarter of a million miles distant in space, an asteroid named Perses began to shiver.

ABOUT SPLASH

I don't even really remember now what part of this story—the largest round-robin I have ever participated in—I wrote! That is the kind of major hallucinatory effect that Don Webb has on anyone who strolls innnocently into his personal sphere of juju. Suffice it to say that I think everyone involved enjoyed the hell out of this process. And that's good, because I think we each got about $39.00 when the story was published.

SPLASH

[WRITTEN WITH DON WEBB, RICHARD LUPOFF, SCOTT CUPP, MICHAEL KURLAND, MICHAEL MALLORY AND JIM KELLY]

When the Human Culture Council reintroduced *reading* sixty odd years ago, humans rediscovered the cliché. Many Treaty Beings, like myself, published memoirs. Amusingly one of them had parts that originally belonged with my human base set. Getting these notes published may be hard given my current home, but they may be popular because I have a happy ending, and happy endings *sell*. The critics will love me because I avoid three clichés.

Cliché number one. I identify with humans. With the human cause and the human way of life. Nope, I haven't identified with the human way of life for a long time (although some would say that I now have found a sort of heaven). Before the First Galactic War, "I" was 100% human. A dashing one with ebony skin, bright silver hair and standing at 2.1 meters. After the first treaty I was 50% human and 50% Free Machine. My life and struggles, like other Treaty Beings spawned new arts and religions and sciences among human and Free Machines. Sixty years later after the Second Galactic War I was 25% human, 25% Free Machine and 50% Siirian. My life and struggles spawned – you get the gestalt. Then after the Third Galactic War I was 12.5% human, 12.5 % Free Machine, 25% Siirian and 50% V'rrr. Mainly I identify with the V'rrr except that I prefer not to live on thousand kilometer long fungi in dark matter nebulae. As a Treaty Being I am property, humans own me – so I keep my body pruned into a more-or-less human shape.

Cliché number two. I mourn Old Earth. Nope. I was on the deck of the *Narcissus* when Humbert Chang gave the order to blow up the planet. It hadn't been a fit place to live for centuries despite what blind poets sing at spaceways for spare credits.

Cliché number three. I am old and weary. True I am old for a human, but V'rrr don't ever die (technically speaking). I have no more nor any less space-weariness than any composite being.

I was visiting Chagnaur IV for a little vacation. It is a nice warm planet that humans need to pick up some new lungs for because of the cyanide in the atmosphere. You weigh a little more than Old Earth standard, and unless you love exo-archeology there isn't much to do. My human component had been brought up on New Mars, so I loved exo-archaeology, and I try to take all of my vacations on planets with ruins. The one small continent is covered in purple neo-grass and silvery forests. It is a wet world, over eighty percent covered by water. I was lying on a beach of a vast inland lake when it happened.

I had pruned my purple and gold wings off in the morning, and spent a few hours in ecstatic communion with the V'rrr One and the V'rrr Three. I decided to sleep in the suns and see the ruins after nightfall, I oiled my black and green exposed flesh and lay down to be warmed by the suns, when I felt the planet sentience net go down. For those of you who have never known silence, it is scary. Suddenly data didn't rush into thoughts, and I knew the workings of my body were not being monitored. If I died my back-up wouldn't be current. My mechanical parts began looking for the field generators at the poles, when I heard a loud splash. I didn't see her fall into the lake. I can't over-emphasize that point. There were no vehicles overhead, no tall trees or nicely overhanging cliffs. But there was a huge splash. My radar detected a warm body in the water, and my eyes saw what might have been a human woman thrashing about in the middle of the lake. Two things caught my eye. She was without clothes. She didn't know how to swim.

I plunged in. Both as a human and a Siirian I had been a strong swimmer. It took only seconds to get to her. Rescuing her was another matter. She thrashed with pure panic and as I tried to grab her, she struggled. I punched her out, so that I could drag her body to shore. She was pretty with brown skin and blue-black hair. I pulled off two vermilion leeches that had decided she was a good host. I tossed them in the air where two local butterflies with wings the color of beaten copper caught them in their beaks.

I laid her on my blanket and covered her blue furred reproductive parts, which are taboo in some human societies. She moaned awhile and then regained consciousness.

"Why the shit did you hit me?" she asked.

"I was afraid that you were going to pull me into the water."

"Well thanks. Have you sent for a medico?"

"Planet's down."

Her eyes widened. She seemed to listen.

"No shit," she said, "I've heard about this, but I never actually though I would be in it." She looked over at the weathered basalt towers of the so-called Temple City. The "birds" – big flying plants were flocking to the large somewhat phallic tower – were making it appear to be the giant member of some jolly green giant. One of the watermills on a nearby river still turned, a tribute to the ten thousand year old engineering skills of the Chagnaurians. She looked at the dual suns, smelled the acrid air, and listened to the songs of the butterflies.

"I am called T'eela." She said.

"My human component was called Radiant Heat Monopoly Schabaco. My friends call me 'Radiant'." That line had actually impressed potential sex partners before the First Galactic War. Maybe cliché three isn't off the mark.

She pointed toward the green tower. "What's that?"

"Most exo-archeologists believe it was a primitive observatory. The Chagnaurians were religiously obsessed with the second moon – offering it their first sproutings. They were more-or-less a walking (or rather gliding) fern."

"No." She said, "I mean what planet are we on?"

"Chaug—" Suddenly, to my surprise, I started gonadically stimulating. But as things stood, what with the planetary sentience net down and all, I had other things to think about than copulation. Still, it was something to bear in mind for later reconsideration.

"Okay," I flurmed. "This happens to be Chagnaur IV. But what are you doing here if you don't know where you are? What is your mission? Where are you estivating while you're on-planet?"

"Estivating?" she asked, opening her eyes wide with curiosity. As she did so I noticed for the first time that she was not really a down-to-the-subcellular-level, real, live, one hundred percent human being. Of course the fact that she had more than one head should have been a clue, but when you meet as many different species and mixes as I do in my business, you sometimes fail to notice such little things.

What caught my attention was the fact that her eyes weren't organic. At least, the ones in the head that had been carrying on her dialog with me were clearly bits of technology rather than biology. Two of her other heads were engaged in a heated debate in a language unfamiliar to me, and that in itself was pretty remarkable. I don't mean to brag, but in the recent Rosetta-Gutenberg Interspecies Linguistics Cup competition I came in a strong second by performing simultaneous real-time multilingual translations in no fewer than 31,000 distinct languages and dialects.

I would have won if the judging hadn't been fixed to give the cup to a F'neerian sentient forest. The F'neerian topped out at barely over 11,000 languages. I not only beat the daylights out of the F'neerian, I totally left it (him, her, them, take your pick) in the dust. But the judges ruled that the languages of the Snool Nebula, in which I am totally fluent, could not be counted as the Snools refused to apply for membership in the All-Sentient Species Federation.

Hey, not my fault! What could I do? To quote an ancient cultural artifact that I came across on an expedition to Sol VII. "I don't make the rules, you know." Well, I didn't make that rule about the Snools but I had to live with it as they say. Then I stopped myself. "Wait a skurbo. Why don't you know what planet you're on?"

She shook her heads. Under different circumstances I would have found the gesture charming, even erotic.

Without warning T'eela reached into her belly pouch and... What belly pouch? You ask. And rightly you should. That's another feature that some of those odd bio-creatures have. Lactating mothers carry their young in their belly pouches, where they are protected and nourished until they are able to leave home and fend for themselves. Before the Second Galactic War the marsupial-look was a major fashion trend. I think it's sort of sexy.

Clearly T'eela was not a lactating mother so she used her belly pouch as a convenient repository for small useful items.

Where was I?

Oh, right: T'eela reached into her belly pouch and extracted a small, metallic disk. She held it up to one of her mechanical eyes and a ray shot from the eye to the disk.

Then she tossed the disk at me.

It landed on one of my V'rrr chelae with a metallic clang. Other than its slight impact, I felt nothing. At first.

Then without warning my weight seemed to increase dramatically. I weighed twice my normal 257.4 zarns, then twice as much again. I felt my muscles straining to keep me upright. I felt them start to snap – a bicep here, a tricep there, a latissimus dorsi here, a sartorius there. Then my metal parts began to bend. I was growing heavier and heavier. I sank to the ground. I lay spread like a flat diagram of myself, then felt myself sinking into the ground.

Within a few glions I had burrowed involuntarily to the water table, then to bedrock. All around me was pitch black. The pressure was growing ever more intense as my weight continued to increase. I was being crushed to powder by my own huge weight and the immense pressure around me.

After what seemed an eternity – I later realized it was only about 47.983 glions – the agony grew less. I knew that I was dying. All of me, of course, except for the V'rrr portion, which was transitioning into its mnmbv state.

Now the process reversed. I could feel my powdered molecules reassembling themselves, my metal rods and gears regaining their proper shape and connectivity, my muscles growing back together.

The immense weight that I had experienced slowly faded away and I regained my normal condition.

Of course I was still far beneath the surface. I had to dig my way back through layers of rock, swim to the surface of a swift-flowing underground steam, then climb out of a deep hole with steep sides.

T'eela smiled at me. At least, half a dozen of her heads did. She reached forward and removed the little disk from my chelae. She looked at it, a bright ray shot from her pseudo-eye to the disk, and she dropped it back into her belly pouch.

"That was for the punch," she said sweetly. "Heroes rescuing maidens in distress by knocking them out and hauling them to safety like sacks of grudderns are out of fashion, or didn't you realize that?"

Before I could frame an answer she once again shook her heads. "To get back to your last question, the last I knew I was on my home world. I was attending a glorification rite for my eldest bud-mate."

"What is your home world?" I asked.

"Aphrodite IV," she said. "It's actually a captured asteroid, now a moon in orbit around Aphrodite, an uninhabitable planet of Xarch."

I shook my head, feeling grossly inadequate for having only one head to shake. I decided that I'd look into the cost of some additional ones when I had a chance. "Never heard of a planet called Aphrodite or a star called Xarch," I told her.

"Well," she resumed as if I had not said anything, "there I was, immersed in a bottomless vermilion pleasure tank, singing the virtues of my eldest bud-mate, when something very big and very scary looking swam up from the bottom of the tank and—"

"Didn't you just say it was a bottomless vermilion pleasure tank?"

T'eela looked as if she was going to cry. "Don't interrupt, will you? Of course I said it was bottomless. And this – this – this *creature* came swarming up from the bottom of the tank and grabbed me by the legs and lifted me out of the tank and flung me bodily into the air. It was one amazing fling that the thing flung, too, because the next thing I knew I was here on – what did you say this place was?"

"Chagnaur IV."

"*She is lying, you know,*" came the voice into my mind. "*She knows exactly where she is and is hoping to prey on some vague sexual attraction to get you to drop your natural defenses.*"

"*Who are you?*" I thought to myself, not knowing how to address the speaker. "*And how do you know these things?*"

"*I am part of the being who has identified itself as T'eela. I am the other head that you do not see. T'eela is a multidimensional being and I am in the sixth dimension. Which you cannot comprehend, therefore I am not visible to you here, because I am not ... here.*"

I shook the one head I had while keeping my three eyes on whoever or whatever T'eela was.

"*So, if you are a part of her, why tell me about this? Does T'eela know you are doing this?*"

T'eela, I saw, was still talking about the bottomless vermilion plea-sure tank. I smiled to indicate I was following her story and enjoying it.

The voice returned. "*T'eela knows I am here and that I do not agree with her actions. She is from this world of Chaugnar IV and hates it here. She wants to go elsewhere in the universe but cannot do so. It is her hope that you will want to replicate with her and that she can then implant enough of herself into you that you'll cease to exist and she can use your body with the V'rrrian genetics and the mnmbv adaptations to build a new T'eela to escape this prison planet.*"

"No one ever said Chagnaur IV was a prison planet. It's nice, warm, two suns. Admittedly, the cyanide atmosphere can be rough on some spe-cies. Why not just go to the spaceport, hook up with a freighter, a krxxl miner, or a Grandisiian pleasure barge and go elsewhere?"

"*T'eela's body has an attachment to the planet so that it will not allow her to leave. If she attempts, she dematerializes from the site and rematerializes somewhere unpleasant and has to reconstruct. That's what just happened. She snuck on the pleasure barge and wound up in the water, unable to swim. She would not have drowned or died, but it would have taken a long time to walk the lake bottom until we got out, particularly if she did not choose the correct direction.*"

I paid some attention to the T'eela I was facing. "So, if you were on Aphrodite IV, how could you get here? It has to be a long way away, if I have never heard of it. I mean, xeno-planetology, astronomy and linguistics are all a major hobby of mine."

She began to relate her sob story again this time with wilder gesticu-lations involving her arms and all her (visible) heads.

I began talking to the other dimensional mind again. "*So, why are you telling me her plans? If you are part of her and this is a prison planet for your species (and what species is that?) why aren't you helping her escape?*"

"*T'eela is a Nyarlathian construct from Symzonia VII. I was from the Z'ccarphian empire. I chanced upon her while traveling and was absorbed into her being. I am not in favor of her plans for escape. We did the crimes so we should pay the time. After all there are only 17,843*" *more Chaugnarian years to go. A mere pittance of time. T'eela does not agree. I have waited a long time to find that right combination of V'rrr, human, and Siirian to be able to communicate with. She has been waiting for the planet systems to fail as they inevitably must. We have been here 17,157 years waiting for it to happen,. If she finds out that I have told you of her plans, well, that will just be grrxly."*

I nodded in agreement which must have been the wrong thing to do. The physical T'eela grabbed me by the chelae and began to shake me in five directions all at once.

"You brxtrachian traitor!" she screamed, apparently to herself. "I am going to use him to get out of here and you can rot away in the freaking sixth dimension for all I care! I'm getting out of here and doing it now!"

She reached inside that belly pouch and pulled out a wicked looking Nalbondian sabre (which I thought were illegal and only in museums) and began to run the blade along the teeth of two heads. The rasping sound of the blade sharpening was earsplitting. She ran a long prehensile tongue along the teeth cleaning the filings away. Her smile was grisly.

This could end badly. I cowered. I shuddered. I cringed. I wet myself through three different orifices. I was afraid. I was very afraid. But was I afraid enough? I sure felt like I was—but something deep inside of me evidently disagreed. It would take more.

"Are you threatening me?" I wheezed.

Her eyes widened. Her eyes narrowed. Her eyes bulged. Her eyes closed. I don't know what the eyes on her other heads did—they were looking somewhere else. She set the tiny drill heads at each of the Nalbondian sabre's dozen kill-points spinning with an ear-splitting whine.

"Threatening you?" she screeched over the whine. "I'm about to kill you. Do you find that threatening?"

I cowered in her grasp. Her hands around my throat were surprisingly strong. "How," I squeeked, "will that help you?"

She grinned a tight-lipped grin with three of her mouths. "I'm hungry," she said.

Fear would be my savior. Fear was, oddly, my only hope. Was I afraid enough now? Apparently not.

"Further intercourse with you is a waste of air," she said, lifting the sabre over her head. "My race has a motto: 'Those who are not with us are not around any more.'"

"So," I said, doing my best to sound indignant rather than merely frightened enough to molt out of season, "what your sixth-dimensional body part told me is true—you were planning to use me and cast me aside."

"Actually I was planning to join with you and cast *me* aside," she said. "Once inside your body, this would become a mere lifeless hulk."

"*Lifeless?!*" Came the angry thought from the sixth dimension. "*What do you mean lifeless, you pink, purple-dotted fur ball?*"

"Pink?" I wondered. "Purple dotted?"

"*In the sixth dimension she is,*" the voice said. "*Not only that, but she's—*"

"*IF YOU DON'T SHUT UP,*" she screamed, "I'll amputate those disgusting appendages you use for copulation!"

There was a silence from the sixth dimension.

She turned all of her various attentions back to me. "If I can't join you," she said, exposing some of her more interesting teeth and shifting the sabre into striking position, "then I'll cut you apart!"

When the sabre reached full striking position it would strike on its own, unaided, swift and deadly. Its target—me—would be reduced to myriad thumb-sized cubes within microseconds. Bloody fleshy boney gorey thumb-sized cubes. I was microseconds away from a horrible, excruciatingly painful death. Was I finally sufficiently afraid?

Evidently I finally was.

My Nik-O-Time Hydro-Cortical Save-Ur-Self® Stimulator (Patent Pending on 2,347 planets, Defended by Right of Duel or Joust on 13, & Expressively Prohibited on 9) went into action. Finally, and just in the advertised nik-o-time.

The universe, or at any rate those parts of it near me, slowed down to a crawl while my own awareness and reflexes increased by a power of twelve. T'eela, or whatever her real name was—T'eela was probably a Symzonian curse word of unimaginable filth—was frozen in killing position, her hands that weren't around my neck holding the Nalbondian sabre above her head. The sabre's tiny drill heads were barely turning. Everything glowed a lovely ruby red as the photons were shifted by the time dilation effect of the Stimulator.

I eased my neck out from T'eela's grasp and fell backwards—gravity was evidently not impressed by the effects of the Nik-O-Time. I accomplished a sloppy back roll on the mauve grass and stumbled to my feet. What to do? I had perhaps half a skurbo, Nik-O-Time time, to incapacitate T'eela before the effects of the Stimulator ceased. I wrenched the sabre out of her hands and found the kill (you should excuse the expression) switch and turned the thing off. I briefly contemplated using the sabre on her, but rejected the idea. The idea of killing a fellow sentient being, even a dangerous and threatening sentient being, in such a horrible way was repugnant to me, and besides the Nik-O-time was for defense only and might cut off if I tried to kill her while she was helpless. I pulled the charge cell out of the sabre and threw it wayfar into the water.

I took off my sash and tied most of her hands behind her back. Then I looped one end of my belt around a neck, stretched the belt down her back, and fastened the other end to a foot, pulling it up so that if she tried to straighten out she'd strangle. I could only hope that this was one of her more important heads.

The effects of the Nik-O-Time wore off with a lurch that made me want to throw up everything I'd eaten for the past decade. I sat down in front of T'eela and tried to look grim. There was little point in running— if she could get loose she could catch me. And besides, without her sabre, we were probably a pretty even match. No—the thing to do was to sit in front of her and glare at her confidently. Treaty Beings are well trained in glaring, pouting, growling, and divination. Just last night I had read my Schwll leaves and told myself, "You will meet an attractive stranger with dimensional irregularities."

"What the hell—" she said, jerking her heads around to look in all possible directions. "What just happened? How did you— Where is—" she tried to sit up and yelped as my belt tightened. I was in luck—it seemed to be around one of her more important necks.

"I am a peaceable man," I told her, improvising wildly. "I don't like being forced to use my powers, but—"

"I DETECT," a powerful voice telepathically impinged on my brain, *"A DISTURBANCE IN THE FARCE. A SLIGHT, PIDDLING DISTURBANCE, BUT A DISTURBANCE NONETHELESS."*

"Oh by the seven cursed gifts!" T'eela swore, ducking all of her heads and rolling into as tight a ball as she could manage with my belt around her neck and leg. "It's She." I could sense the capital "S."

"She?"

"She who trapped me here. She who said I was disturbing 'the Farce'. She, who made me frantic enough to try to kill you. *She who must be obeyed!*"

"The Farce?"

"She finds life amusing. She also finds the absence of life amusing." T'eela screwed up several of her faces into grotesque frowns. "In order to thwart my paltry attempt to chastise you, you have alerted a truly dangerous being and given her an itch to scratch."

"SILENCE!"

The power of that shout nearly exploded my brain into microdust, and since my brain is a component of my human 12.5 percent, it remains one of my most vulnerable parts. The source of the voice was not apparent, cloaked, even, from my radar. What I heard next was a form of language that even I would not translate. "I cannot understand you," I said.

"*YOU BOAST OF FLUENCY IN 31,000 LANGUAGES, YET FARCI IS BEYOND YOUR GRASP?*" the voice taunted in the language of V'rrr, and while it was both within and without my head, it at least no longer shattered my consciousness. My human component would liken the voice to "chewing on tin foil" while "listening to Beethoven backward." Realizing my eyes were closed; I dared to crack them open. T'eela was curled and cowering, but now she had only one head, which was the way she appeared when I first saw her. I wanted to reiterate *I do not understand*, but the response to that came before I could articulate the words.

"*SHE WHO GIVETH HEADS CAN TAKE THEM AWAY.*" As though to underscore that point, I felt an eruption in the cortruxe region of my body and experienced a sensation akin to separating. A moment later I was looking at my own head from a second, identical one. Before I could blink at myself, the second head was reabsorbed into my body.

I spun around in a confused circle. "Who…what…are you?"

"She is She who must be obeyed," T'eela whimpered. "She is—"

"*I NEED NO SENTINAL TO ANNOUNCE ME,*" the voice roared. Then in much softer, almost seductive tones, which resonated all around me, She said: "*You wish to know who I am? I will tell you: I am you. You are I. I am her, too—*" the reference to T'eela was spoken with disdain— "*and she is me, also, more's the pity.*"

"Release me, then," T'eela said, her previous defiance now reduced to a pleading whimper. "Let me leave this planet."

I now realized T'eela's true situation: like me, she must be the property of another. But unlike me, whose possessors were human, T'eela must be the property of She who must be obeyed.

"*ONLY IN THE MOST ALL-ENCOMPASSING SENSE,*" the voice replied, once more reading my thoughts. "*You are proving to be an arresting presence, Radiant,*" she said silkily, startling me by using my name. "*You are a thinker, not a pest and a liar, like her.*"

"*If you like me, then,*" I thought, "*why not show yourself to me?*"

"*OH, THE CUNNING LINGUIST WISHES TO SEE ME, DOES HE?*" the voice roared in response. "*HE COMES TO A PLANET TO SEE ITS RUINS, AND WHEN HE STUMBLES UPON THE ANSWER TO ALL QUESTIONS, ENCOMPASSING ALL DIMENSIONS, HE MUST SEE IT WITH HIS OWN EYES AS WELL.*" There was another time-confusing pause, followed by a rumbling chuckle. "*How human of him,*" She who must be obeyed purred. "*But since I like him, why not?*"

In less than a nanoinstant, I was looking at myself as though through the eyes of another. It was as if my entire being had been lifted out and separated from my body. I could also see T'eela, crouched and quaking by the lake, from a vantage point high overhead. I appeared to be flying—soaring—rocketing…and not through the power of my wings. I was being drawn back through space as a separate entity, far, far, far back. Chagnaur IV was now a ball beneath two suns, surrounded by other flashing and beautiful orbs!

Further, further, further back; the suns were the center of an atom… more atoms now; more suns; more circling orbs; a cluster of atoms forming a molecule, creating galactic tissue; tens of galaxies congealing into a cell; a hundred, a thousands, a million-billion-trillion cells forming a finger…

…back…back…back…no sense of velocity, no sense of feeling, no sense at all; instead visual bombardment. An overall form was now coming into view, a mass constructed of infinite galaxy-cells, made up of more than infinite solar system-atoms…

…further back…further back…further back…until a figure became apparent, set against a void of nothingness, self-illuminated by innumerable stars. It took the form of a female, though whether I was recognizing that by visual data, or whether I simply somehow *knew* it, I could not tell. An approximation of a mouth opening, quintillions of light-years across, moved and I heard She's voice pronounce: "*I AM AUL.*"

Then the universe figure winked at me.

In the next nanoinstant, I was back on Chagnaur IV, disoriented and reeling, wondering if I was still sane, and questioning whether I ever had been.

"*ARE YOU SORRY YOU ASKED TO SEE ME?*" Aul inquired.

"Yes…no…I don't know," I managed to utter. "I would like to go back to my homeplace."

"*NOT BEFORE THE AMUSEMENT BEGINS.*"

"What amusement?" T'eela asked, raising her techno-optic beams from the ground for the first time since Aul's arrival.

"*SEPARATELY, YOU TWO ARE DISTURBANCES IN THE FARCE—ANNOYING, BUT NOT UNIQUE. TOGETHER, HOWEVER, YOU HOLD THE PROMISE OF BECOMING MORE THAN A SIMPLE ANNOYANCE. THAT I CANNOT PERMIT.*"

"What do you plan to do with us?" I asked.

"*MAKE YOU ENTERTAIN ME.*"

"How?" T'eela cried apprehensively.

The ground suddenly shook, making the sound of deadly laughter. "*THROUGH CLICHÉ NUMBER FOUR,*" Aul pronounced, mocking my earlier thoughts. "*YOU SHALL FIGHT TO THE DEATH, AND THE VICTOR SHALL BE ALLOWED TO LEAVE THIS PLANET.*"

"That is insanity!" I shouted. Then my senses opened to the truth. *This* was the Farce! The First Galactic War; the Second Galactic War; the third Galactic War—*all were aspects of the Farce*. All had been performed for the amusement of She who must be obeyed.

"SINCE ONE OF YOU HAS POWERS NOT YET REVEALED TO THE OTHER, THIS SHOULD MAKE FOR A FINE DIVERSION," Aul thundered. *"NOW COMMENCE FIGHTING, OR DIE REFUSING."*

T'eela's now-solitary head betrayed an array of contradictory expressions: terror, excitement, dread and determination.

I had been manufactured as well as born and hatched and grafted together for peace. Not only do I have healthy desire for self-preservation, which is why I spent vast sums for my Nik-o-Time; but I driven to make peace. Some men might say they would cut off their left testicle for peace; I have actually done so.

Chaotic, cloaca-loosening fear, I suddenly realized, would never reveal the answer to my mortal plight. Only immense sanity and coolness of thought would prevail. I had been praised as a Thinker by Aul. To have this one trait of mine singled out must mean something. Unless the perfidious She Soul of the All Farce had been deliberately trying to misdirect me down fruitless paths…? No, my empathic Nodes of Emobeeber were still functioning, and I had read utter sincerity in her offhanded, shouted compliment. So, linear rationalism, with a judicious admixture of lateral thinking, would be my lifeline.

Get busy, multiple heterogenous brains of my hybrid lineage! In concert, my white, green, grey and puce matter had to come up with a solution before Aul lost patience—or before T'eela made a hasty move to disembowel me and consume my most vital catalytic sacs.

Activating my Nik-O-Time implant in full mode again was impossible, as my onboard capacitors had not had time yet to recharge their quantum dots. But it was just barely possible to invoke a small, short-lived zone of hypertime around my thinking parts alone. Unfortunately, this would have the effect of isolating my brains from contact with my bodily functions. And while robust autonomic subsystems would insure that my lungs and spiracles would continue to breathe the delightful cyanide atmosphere of Chagnaur IV and that my heart and vascular muscle clumps would continue to pump blood and ur-chyle through my veins, arteries and contra-conduits, I would suffer from certain embarrassing side effects. My mouth would slacken and rainbow drool would pour forth; my other orifices would contribute a symphony of fluids and particulates; my limbs would experience an alarming storm of epileptic fits; my oculars would fluctuate ultraviolently across the entire spectrum; and I would emit noises like the Grunting Ducks of Mucklestone Minor. For a fellow convinced of his own suaveness and proud of the public impression of dapper congeniality that he conveyed, especially among potential intercoursal partners, this condition would be almost a fate worse than death.

But not quite.

So, bang on, Nik-O-Time!

I went instantly senseless, and consequently could not feel myself fall to the ground as a quivering mass of puking jello. I only hoped that T'eela and Aul would not interpret this as some kind of obscene attack, and consequently hold back from exterminating me.

Meanwhile, my manifold brains began humming like a Vortigernian volvox.

How does one defeat another in any contest?

By being superior to the opponent.

But by definition, nothing was superior to Aul. She had shown me that she was manifest in the entire substrate of creation. Even if there were room for a second such entity in this universe, it would be only identical and equal to Aul, and consequently unable to defeat her.

Yet she had said that T'eela and I, combined, would manifest some threat to Aul. How could that be?

"Because, my friend, there are more universes than one!"

Thus spoke the Z'ccarphian, that sixth-dimensional rider within/outside/abaft of T'eela.

"Tell me more," I begged silently.

And the Z'ccarphian did.

It seems that all of infinite creation that stretched out from Chagn-aur IV, the myriad, myriad galaxies that comprised Aul, were contained merely on one brane amongst the metacosmic stack of all branes. Even Dimension Six where the Z'ccarphian lived was part of our brane's construction. But from his peculiar vantage, the Z'ccarphian could sense how to reach the adjacent branes.

"On each of these countless universes you have a doppelganger. If you could assemble all of them into one mega-Radiant, you would be invincible!"

"But how!"

"I can thrust your quantum consciousness up one level. After you unite with your counterpart there, you two together will have the trick and be able to instantaneously agglomerate all your infinite brothers."

"Do it then!"

"Gladly! But I cannot reach you so long as you remain outside T'eela. Her corporeal defenses prevent me from acting upon anything in your realm."

"How can I attain your presence?"

"You must let her envaginate you. Once you are inside her, we can connect. But I warn you, it won't be pleasant."

The Z'ccarphian sent me a mental picture, and I shuddered. *"Well, if that's the only way—"*

"It is. Now, here is the formula for the pheromones you must emit during your battle to provoke her envagination response."

"I have them. Let us commence."

I brought down the interior cerebral Nik-O-Time zone, and was instantly back in my foul form.

Climbing slowly to my feet, I registered T'eela's disgust. It might not be so easy to provoke an envagination response as the Z'ccarphian imagined.

"That was just a small ritual my kind performs before going into battle and facing death," I extemporized.

"YES," shouted Aul, *"I COULD SEE HOW EVEN DEATH WOULD BE PREFERABLE TO THAT PITIFUL CONDITION! NOW, FIGHT!"*

Already I was brewing the necessary long-chain molecules within my ribozymatic factories. While they cooked, I launched myself through the air at T'eela!

From around her midriff erupted a bevy of whip-like scaly tentacles, previously concealed on interior take-up spools. They lashed around me, halting my trajectory in mid-air. Painful acids oozed from their pores! A daunting maneuver—to one who had not fought in and survived three Galactic Wars! My conformable integument erupted in millions of oscillating micro-razors that severed T'eela's tendrils into a zillion squirming pieces!

She screamed like a wounded Sea Tiger from Satan's Closet. I dropped to the ground, landing in a fighter's stance. T'eela and I circled each other warily, feinting, testing, neither wishing to incur another injury.

Then my mind registered a ping from my busy internal factories, just like the bleat from a gamma-ray oven signalling that one's dinner of Bruxtian mold chops had been sufficiently warmed.

Without further ado, wondering only what polite yet intimate form of address would suffice for hailing my extra-brane doppelganger, I blasted out the provocative pheromones from my axillary glands.

To me they smelled of the bilge of a certain Grandisiian pleasure barge of my intimate acquaintance, or perhaps the scat of a herd of swamp dragons, but within scant skurbos they had stopped T'eela in her tracks. A look of transcendent lust crossed the features of her remaining head, and a thin gruel of snot began to leak from her nostrils.

"If only I had known," she murmured. It seemed to me that she was growing larger, perhaps engorged with lust. "Why didn't you say something?" Where before she had held her body taut and ready to spring at the flick of a malacash, now her limbs took on fluidity. The curves of her torso swelled until they seemed more like geography than anatomy. There could be little doubt now that she was bigger than she had been, or at least she was bigger than I was, although I could scarcely comprehend how she could have acquired mass so precipitously. Was my Z'ccarphian ally making an interdimensional transfer?

"WHAT IS THIS?" roared AUL. *"I SAID FIGHT, NOT MATE!"*

"And the difference is?" T'eela closed the space between us and with a swipe of her mighty hand, lifted me off my feet. As I dangled in her grip like a pleasure bot caught in an electromagnetic pulse, I realized the awful truth. She was not growing – I was shrinking.

"RADIANT, PULL YOURSELF TOGETHER. YOU ARE SPOILING THE FUN!"

"You!" I screamed, simultaneously into Chagnaur IV's charged cyanide atmosphere and into a mocking sixth-dimensional silence. *"You tricked me, Z'ccarphian!"*

"Perhaps," it admitted, *"or perhaps I am helping you to become your best self, and in the process to start life afresh."*

While I had no idea how T'eela was doing what she was doing, I was pitifully aware of exactly *what* she was doing to me. She was flensing me of 87.5% of my being—Free Machine, Siirian and V'rrr—and leaving me with just the 12.5% that was human. As I reduced from my normal strapping self to a mere homunculus, I began to comprehend my peril.

"Pardon me," I squeaked, my voice now as small as my manhood, "but I think we ought to discuss this before we do something we both might regret in the morning."

"WHO ARE YOU TALKING TO?" A raft of toxic cumulonimbus clouds had gathered above us. Aul flung bowling balls of lightning at the weathered basalt towers of Temple City to get our attention.

"Us," said T'eela and tucked me into her fetid pouch.

At this point, as you might imagine, I was utterly lacking in agency. I was a dust in a tornado, wheat in a thresher, choat in vinegar. I am not proud of what happened next, but then neither am I responsible for the instincts which overcame me, marsupial as they may have been. The skin of T'eela's belly was undeniably warm and inviting and the taut skin of the pouch caressed me hard against it. I cannot say for certain how many teats she had; all I know is that each of them promised a fulfillment unlike any I had enjoyed since before the First Galactic War. In the darkness I lowered my mouth greedily onto one after another and slaked a thirst I had never known I'd had. And still my transformation continued unabated. As I diminished into a near fetal state, one of the last conscious thoughts I had was that someone was shouting awfully loud, although the sound was muffled by the layers of T'eela's skin.

"*STOP!*" I think, or perhaps it was "*SWAP!*" And then,"*NO!*"

Or was it "*KNOW?*"

Thus I have no memory of what happened next and have only T'eela's account of the hazardous journey I made southward from her pouch toward my ultimate envagination. I count this as a mercy; there are some things man is not meant to know. And of I can scarcely describe my next conscious thought, because it was not only mine but that of all the Radiant Heat Monopoly Schabacos across all the myriad possible universes, and in that instant all my conjoined selves suffered a common pang of existential incoherence—

What the fuck?

—a mighty flock of puzzled cognition wheeled and turned on the Aul, beating at it with wings of confusion, pecking at it with razor-sharp beaks of ontological angst,. Aul was popcorn to the gulls of my myriad myriads, Aul was pollen to the winds of Radiant wonder, Aul was a pair of dice rolling snake eyes in Monopoly's infinite hands, Aul was nothing in the chorus of everything Schabacos. My selves as Self saved me from Aul, and in this are theologies corrected. As Aul fell into the fragments of each and every, my Self unfolded itself into me and me and me and…

And then I was alone.

Well, not alone exactly, since I was still within T'eela, which is where I remain to this day. We have struck a pact to live together in her body until such time as we can find the means to part ways. Of course, this would necessitate obtaining a host body for me but the fact is that I am in no hurry to reassert my individuality. T'eela is happy at becoming Aul-like to me, and I have the comfort that I lost when I was chosen at age six to become a Treaty Being. Mother and father and my sociopathic brother and my valentine-sweet sister are all reborn as the marsupial momma-lover-whore. I am happy as 12.5% of a man belonging to one and not many, and my happiness reflects through all the worlds to count-less little Radiants. I have seen Aul of the possible worlds, and I am truly in the best.

I came, as I said, to Chagnaur IV for a little vacation. There is, as I have discovered here, more than one way to leave one's troubles behind.

ABOUT LET'S ALL SING
LIKE THE BIRDIES SING

I hate Twitter. There, I've said it. Let the chips fall where they may. I think it's juvenile, destructive, moronic, degrading, inutile and a waste of precious time. I can't wait till it goes extinct—so long as it's not super- seded by something worse. Feeling this way, I had to let out the emotions in fiction. And so a unique artifact, of whatever debatable but measur- able lasting value, got created.

And all because I wasn't wasting my energy tweeting.

Old fogies will get the allusion in the title. The refrain of the ditty referenced is "Tweet, tweet tweet, tweet tweet."

LET'S ALL SING LIKE THE BIRDIES SING

Nearly all biohackers agree on one thing concerning the infamous Twaddle virus: it was elegantly scripted. Contagious via mere touch or aerosol dispersal (a sneeze, a cough), the synthetic infection was able to cross the blood-brain barrier within hours of contact with a human host. A retrovirus, it wrote itself ineradicably into the victim's cortical genome, forever altering the sufferer's neurochemistry. As a final insult, the parasite caused the mocking signature logo of its unknown maker to appear upon the brow of each victim, scribed in colorful active OLED nanopixels: a GIF of an obese cartoon duck waddling across a barnyard: what soon came to be known as "the Twaddle duck."

Of course, the well-known primary effect of hosting the virus was something else entirely, and rather more severe and debilitating.

The Twaddle virus caused in each host a continuous logorrhea, a stream-of-consciousness dump, uncontrollable and omnidirectional. The victims resembled Tourette's sufferers, and experts speculated that the Twaddle designer had learned how to tweak that same neural circuitry. But an additional wrinkle obtained: the insidious hacker had built an automatic shuffle function into the bug. The victim's oral spew jumped in unpredictable scattershot fashion among any and all topics available to his or her mind, at such a rate that the Twaddler's pronouncements— "blurts"—were all clipped and relatively short.

The Patient Zero of the Twaddle plague is generally deemed to be one Durst Jacksy, a young Berlin-based musician with a small following in the underground "grey goo" scene. Some have speculated that Jacksy was Twaddle's actual designer. Others, that he merely represented an unfortunate first host to the accidentally escaped or deliberately released virus. In either case, data-mining research across the entire internet has definitely pegged Jacksy as the original locus of the disease.

The patrons of the Kurfürstendamm café known as Durchfall's were alarmed to see a wild-eyed, panting Jacksy burst into the establishment one autumn morning, spouting a stream of unprovoked non-sequiturs. One patron recorded the historic incident with her smartphone, and a rough transcription (into English) of Jacksy's historic first blurts is attached here:

"What a sunrise! Can't wait for *Harry Potter Meets the Incredibles*. Have you seen the price of guitar strings lately? Where's my car keys, I've got an appointment. Elections don't change a damn thing. Mom always loved Uther best. I need new shoes. That sex with Adette was fantastic! Ginger cookies and milk remind me of school days. These pants are my favorite ones. Cancer took my uncle first, then his wife. I wish Lady Gaga hadn't married the American president. Kittens are cute until about a month old. Have yourself a merry little Christmas!"

The video continues to show all of Jacksy's concerned friends clustering around him, trying to calm him down and help. (Of course, they were immediately infected, thereby launching the plague across the city, and thence the world.) "Is he on drugs?" someone asks. A despairing Jacksy covers his mouth with both hands, muffling his speech but not stopping it. The spectators recoil in horror when the Twaddle duck emerges on his forehead. Eventually, an ambulance crew arrives and takes Jacksy away. But much, much too late to halt the plague.

The subsequent few weeks followed the standard pattern of all twenty-first-century epidemics: confusion, panic, official reassurances, recognition of the vector, quarantine, analysis of the infectious agent, and, ultimately and to much global relief, the creation of a reliable vaccine. But all those developments took nine months, and by then nearly one hundred million people worldwide had been infected. What was worse, they were incurable. The vaccine only protected against initial infections.

The accomodation by society to one hundred million thought-broadcasting beacons in its midst was disparate, to say the least, varying from one country to the next, from one city to the next, and even from one neighborhood to the next.

In some places, the Twaddlers were shunned and ostracized, even subject to disgusting acts of violence. In other places they actually acquired "followers," cultish or stylishly ironic acolytes who trailed the victims, treating every blurt as a kind of Delphic utterance, annotating them, trading them, parodying them. Criminals preyed on Twaddlers, looking for leaks of blackmail-ready disclosures, stock tips, and other valuable information. Polite, liberal sympathizers walked a middle path, pretending nothing was wrong when they had to interact with a Twaddler and actually attempting to respond conversationally to any halfway relevant blurt. Once the threat of contagion was removed, Twaddlers became the easy butt of late-night comedians, and the repurposing of the old Marx Brothers "Why a Duck" routine led to the meteoric rise of one lucky stand-up fellow. The catchphrase "I can hear myself think!" was everywhere for a time.

Many Twaddlers sought the comfort of their own kind, congregating in Twaddle ghettos, where their affliction passed for the new norm. The noisy neighborhoods resembled rookeries or sea-lion colonies, and had to be surrounded by noise-abating walls. Scientists, politicians and marketing experts were frequent visitors to these "blurt barrios," where they attempted a kind of crowd-sourcing, polling the massed blurts in search of some signs of psychic premonitions from the collective mind of the Twaddlers. But other Twaddlers could not so easily forsake their old lives, and they resorted to various coping mechanisms to fit into society at large. Surgical mutism was by far the most common and effective treatment. Literally silenced, the Twaddlers could continue their old existences almost innocuously, even acquiring valuable government-sponsored disability compensations. Various types of ball-gags became fashionable. Noise-cancelling mechanisms from Bose, worn on halters, proved effective. Of course, the non-afflicted could always opt for conventional earplugs. The living tattoo of the Twaddle duck proved ineradicable, but simple makeup or certain hairstyles afforded concealment. Most people did not mind knowing a Twaddler was living and working among them, so long as they did not have to listen to a steady stream of simple-minded blurts.

And so, as it always does, the adaptable old world quickly absorbed this new class of harmless freaks, and returned to its own mindless chatter.

ABOUT LUMINOUS FISH
SCANALYZE MY NAME

Damien Broderick and I have never met IRL. Nonetheless, we have developed an affinity for each other's minds and tastes and whims, leading to a couple of jointly authored stories, and to one whole book: Science Fiction: The 101 Best Novels 1985-2010. *With Damien residing in Texas (far from his native Australia), and me in Rhode Island, our relationship echoes the famous connection between Robert E. Howard and H. P. Lovecraft. I hope no shoggoths intervene.*

This particular jape resulted from a shared love of Michael Moorcock's work—as the dedication at the end informs you.

LUMINOUS FISH SCANALYZE MY NAME

[WRITTEN WITH DAMIEN BRODERICK]

From: The Beadle Monger
To: Local Secundus
Subject: Brane Breakthrough
    Let's get this effort on the road. The team has been futzing about far too long. The Faith Gambit pissed itself up against a wall for 3000 local years, and the Science Trope has just about done for them far more quickly. I need a Brane Breakthrough, and I want it now. I suggest you take a closer look at candidate Jeremiah ("Jay") Cornelius, Registered Earth Sentient 2744692043.

* * * *

From: Local Secundus
To: Lord Beadle Monger
Subject: Brane Breakthrough
    Your Eminence, the department has developed a plan for your consideration. Please see Attachment 5338.

* * * *

From: The Beadle Monger
To: Local Secundus
Subject: Cornelius Brain
    Very droll. A pun in their native language, quant suff! Proceed at pace. I want to see a working Messiah before the Galactic Ginnungagap Event closes the Brane Potential Portal and we lose that universe.

* * * *

Jay made a beast of himself during dinner. Nobody there except Tim had the faintest interest in the tedious horrors of toiling in the bowels of Henry McKinley's disgusting empire. Least interested of all: long-suffering wife Jessie.

If you don't like working there, man, get another job, she thought but did not say. God knows, she was complicit. They needed the money, and it wasn't going to come from her PhD scholarship. Jessie gazed remotely at her plate, moving a fragment of gristle about the rim. After a time she began to polish her serrated steak knife with a paper napkin. A sort of rough dandruff floated from the napkin to the tablecloth. Annie's glance snared her drifting, absent soul. With a start, Jessie put the knife aside, pushed back her chair, took herself away to the bathroom for a quarter of an hour. Jay, more than half-drunk on Chardonnay, babbled about masturbation magazines and their destruction by free pr0n on the internet.

On the Metra home (at least he hadn't attempted to drive, although he was too mean to call a cab, justifying it by a monologue of dubious ecological reasoning), Jessie bleakly examined the ears of the brown, nodding Eastern European man across from her, next to the door between cars. At the first shrieking corner the door ratcheted, groaned, abruptly found within itself some magical lubricant and sped like a calving one-dimensional iceberg to crash back into its slot. The abrupt jolt was more psychic than physical; it bruised her. She looked at Jay, who was staring in befuddled pleasure at the smeared streetlights, their virtual reality. He failed her gaze. She stood up, pulled angrily at the door. It rolled slightly out of its slot, stuck. On the next curve it crashed fully closed. If the man with the ears had extended his foot into the doorway, Jessie thought, his bones would have been broken by the impact.

They were nothing like a beast's ears. No beast she knew of. The man's head was bald and smooth, regular as some Eastern church's dome. Mosque. At his fringes, the last of his hair was as crimped and curly as, presumably, the hair at his groin. Shit no. On his arms, then. His back. She didn't like him. His feet stuck out into the space where other people might wish to walk, could trip, tumble painfully as the tram turned a corner, might at the very least be obliged to step awkwardly. His ears were very human ears. The ears heard nothing at the moment, of course, because the man was asleep. Was that possible? Asleep on the tram. On the Metra. You can go anywhere within reason. He could easily miss his stop.

"She's certainly a very interesting woman," Jay said.

"How would you know?"

"Know what, precisely?"

Oh, Jessie saw in his mind, you're in one of your moods, are you? One of your incomprehensible, incalculable, unplumbable, fathomless, mysterious, womanly moods. Nothing is as it seems, nothing conveys its own transparent truth.

You prick, she thought.

If the Metra went away all the smeared reds and greens and mercury vapor shapes might be stars floating at the edge of a surging swell, salt at the back of her tongue, endless flowing steppes of grass dark and mysterious and shadowed with beasts with ears like hairy Euclidean theorems, lolling tongues, no doubt, and flowing manes, Christ; and its discontents, its woes, its nasty little mean-spirited toads.

She takes the steak knife from her bag. It has been cleaned to a certain brilliance. The door crashes open again. Jessie imagines taking a single step across the aisle. Jay is watching the night. The cry would be in no language she has ever heard. Hot and wet. Rubbery. It would come free in her hand. The man's eyes open now, staring at her, shifting his feet back under his seat. The train accelerates around a curve and back again. The door crashes and crashes.

Jessie imagines herself holding out the moist ear, a gift really. Jay would watch the man bleeding into his cupped, clawing hand.

"Well, I thought she was interesting," he'd tell her, oblivious.

* * * *

Luminous fish with rubbery lips hung from the heavens, a school of grinning, finny clown-specters. The leader squeaked like a vinyl dog toy, and said, "Jay Cornelius! I will pheromone no Eve girl!"

A dark bird of omen, sharply winged like a stealth killer drone, swooped through the dimming sky and began to gobble the squealing panicky fish with a capacious maw. Without conscious summoning of associations, Jay Cornelius knew this raptor to be an emissary of that beneficent personage known as "the Beadle Monger." Despite its predatory actions, the bird must therefore be doing good.

"I love you," cried Jay Cornelius, laughing joyously. He flung up the heavy Rasta locks from his velvet shoulders. "You are the wind beneath my wigs!"

"You fool." Stately, anfractuous Jimmy Brunner scowled. He descended a sigma sequence, a Planck egg in one hand, his swollen member in the other. "You don't even know what anfractuous means. Think, man."

Slightly embarrassed, Cornelius temporized. "You're right, but let us consider the roots. 'An-' suggests negation. 'Fract-' might be a break, a cleft, a cleavage, a...well, a fracture. So you can't be smashed?"

Now, shielded from any surveillance from the sky, the two men clung together under the bridge, smooching wetly, clasping each the other's gigantic, equine, throbbing manhood. The satisfaction of a climax seemed imminent—

"What the hell?" groaned Jay, waking. A gay Harlequin paperback dream? With babbling fish? And someone absurdly named "the Beadle Monger?" His subconscious was generally as disciplined as a Marine drill sergeant. Why this weird outburst, and why now? And who the fuck was Jimmy Brunner? Nobody he knew, had ever heard of, let alone—

His tongue and the roof of his palate were bone dry: he'd been sleeping with his damn mouth open again. These filthy allergies. His nostrils and eyes were swollen all but shut. The sensation of bristled lips pressing against his still rankled. "Oh my god. That's not me."

Half-dark still, early morning. Turning his head to find Jessie snoring faintly. Continuing to mumble his apologetic credo. "I mean, I swear to god I'm no gay basher, but for fuck's sake—" Under the sheets, he was unequivocally—albeit unequinely—erect. He nudged his wife. She replied in her sleep, "Humph?" and rolled his way. He pushed up her nightie.

"Open to me, my sister, for my need is sore great."

She woke and punched him. "I ain't nobody's sister, jerk, least of all yours. What time is it?"

"Come on, my darling, let me at you. You would not wish to connive in the sin of Onan, I trust?"

"Five minutes only," she said, and gave him a smelly après le sommeil kiss.

"Ninety seconds," he promised, "as usual on these occasions," and spat on his fingers. He returned her kiss and caressed her, lathering, heaved up beneath the autumnal covers, entered, plunged, made good his promise, fell back. "Ah my dearest girl. Later for you, I swear. No good deed shall go un..."

"Punished?" But she was falling into sleep again, her own dreams, no doubt, just as full of twisty turns and windings.

"Rewarded," said Jay Cornelius. In a minute he'd get up and check his email and google anfractuous. Where does this stuff come from? he asked himself and, remembering then some small part of the vanishing dream, groaned. Jiminy Bullard, was it? Where the hell does it come from? Jessie's damned incessant gender research, maybe.

* * * *

Laughing quietly, Jessie scans into a Word doc a passage from Edmund White's *The Beautiful Room Is Empty.*

> I had to put on a leather harness, stick a swan feather up my john's ass, and call him "Pretty Peacock" as he strutted proudly about, cocking his head from side to side like a bird while wanking off in an all too

human way. Fifty bucks for me and seventy for Lou who, after all, had organized the party.

She is up to her elbows in unlikely gender research material. These guys do seem to confuse their bodily secretions. On the morning after a rowdy party in the largely gay high rise apartment building where he was living, one New York writer reveals, the elevator floor was awash in urine.

Their own dwelling, hers and Jay's, is on the nose as well, though for less lubricious reasons. After only a week or so of fruitless emails and phone calls ("Okay, lady, she'll be right, see y' soon, sweetheart, oh sorry, look, we'll try for the next clear day, eh?") her builder Robert O'Kelly Branagan, Esq and his jobbie or rather sub contractor, a handsome hunk of bronzed expertise with a powered hydraulic nailing device, named Kyle if such a thing is credible, had appeared at the tolerable hour of 10 a.m. and tore into the roof's shoulder blades with such venom that soon the whole horrid thing lay in splinters in the concrete far below, where she stood at some risk snapping away with her nifty Nikon (as if for a forthcoming article, perhaps in the *Tribune* lifestyle supplement, on remodeling your inner city Chicago pied-à-terre), and a drafty smelly hole was revealed or created through which she cavorted bearing bulging plastic bags, happily quite light, of high thermal capacity mineral wool batts that she helped strew among the rafters, coughing and near to puking owing to quantities of dead birds, molted feathers, old dispersed nests, grime, Neanderthal men's bones and the like. Meanwhile young Kyle was nipping and tucking, sawing and hydraulicking, not a handtool in sight. Art in the age of mechanical reproduction, she thought, and laughed quietly to herself.

* * * *

The meeting that morning with Henry McKinley went poorly for Jay. Miserably, in fact. An agonizing death would be a blessing by comparison. He caught himself. Such a sentiment, he suspected, could be regarded as counterindicative of job satisfaction.

Henry McKinley ruled over the Groper Media empire like Genghis Khan over trampled Eurasia, although with less gentility. The comparison was particularly apt, given Henry's full-blooded Asian heritage—Uighur, to be specific. Adopted and rechristened at a young age by Western parents from the ruins of Urumqi after the Han Chinese had leveled the rebellious city, Henry had grown to nominal adulthood pampered and puffed-up. His native lateral intelligence allowed him to find the easiest path to any selfish goal, and to avoid hard work or any peaks of morality. He had been perfectly fitted to become a magnate in the new style of cyber-publishing. Today, Groper Media ran a passel of salacious or sensationalistic sites, such as Cunning Runts, Root and Tell, Fork Estate, and Mindlezz Pleazurez. The ad revenue from the gossipy, tawdry, eye-candy-filled venues had bought Henry a yacht (the Canoodle Canoe), a beautiful brownstone in Chicago's ritzy Lincoln Park district, a fleet of Lexuses (Lexi? wondered Jay, willy-nilly), and three mistresses, each of a different and complementary ethnicity.

Meanwhile the same enterprise had, over the last five years, provided Jay Cornelius, online editor and all-purpose whipping boy, with sixty-five thousand a year before taxes, a modest house undergoing renovations in Naperville, a monthly pass on the Metra, and wife Jessie. The continuance of all of the preceding relied, naturally, on pleasing Henry McKinley. Which today was just not happening.

Henry's fierce mustachios, cultivated precisely to engender racial memories of Mongol savagery, thus reducing subjects to a jelly-like state, quivered as he addressed Jay. "Have you gone fucking gay on me, Cornelius?"

The hyperbolic and clichéd accusation, merely one of Henry's standard taunts, resonated strangely with Jay today, after last night's disturbing dream.

"What makes you say that? I thought the layout for the Taylor Swift and Miley Cyrus spanking session was hot."

"Hot? Yeah—if you were thirteen fucking years old! Who did the photoshopping on that anyhow? A blind monkey with simian AIDS and his head up his ass?"

From the back of the room, an intern named Huddleston timorously raised his hand. "Uh, that would be me, sir…"

"You're out of here. Go to HR and collect your check."

"But, sir, I don't get paid…."

"Then just blow!"

After Huddleston slinked out, Henry turned back to Jay. The hapless editor could feel the eyes of everyone else in the room boring holes of pity, schadenfreude and terror-stoked disaffiliation into his living corpse.

"Cornelius, you're damned lucky not to be following Hudnut out that door."

Am I? thought Jay.

"You know damn fucking well that the only reason anyone visits our sites is because we continually push the envelope of good taste and libel. If we run PG-thirteen pap like this, what will that do to our Google Analytics? True, I intend to run Groper into the ground. But not quite yet, and not with lame ass posts like this. Do you understand now what's expected of you?"

"Yes, sir, I do."

"Well, say it then! What's our fucking cri de coeur, man? Our god-damn pole star!"

Jay found the puerile words as unpalatable as fetid garbage, but was forced to utter them anyhow. "Tell it—tell it like it's jizz."

"Fucking ay! Now, get back to work. And get fifty percent more nip slip and camel toe in there!"

Back in his upholstered veal-fattening pen, Jay Cornelius laid his head upon his desk and silently wept for precisely thirty indulgent seconds. Luckily, his back was to the shared aisle and any passersby. When he raised his reddened eyes, the first thing he saw was a picture of Jessie. So he returned to work, ordering a re-shoot of the simulated celebrity catfight with fifty percent more of the mandated lascivious ingredients.

* * * *

His spirits revived, briefly and somewhat guiltily, on the Metra train home that evening. Usually Jay drowsed, stunned into stupidity and re-sentment by the day's grotesque demands. Now he opened his weary eyes as a strange rustle went through the car, murmurs and one squeal. A gust of perfume galvanized his allergy-stricken nostrils, and someone dropped into the seat beside him. Jay glanced sidelong, blinked, felt his jaw loosen, looked away, looked back. The young woman ignored his glance. She was fantastically gorgeous. Jay felt his reason totter. Impos-sible! On an evening Metra route? Wait a minute. It had to be a photo shoot. Vox pop video, something viral for YouTube. He didn't want to be filmed as the sort of idiot who stands behind a celebrity holding up rabbit ear fingers behind her head, so instead he let his eyes shuttle back and forth in search of the AV devices. Doing that he probably looked just as dorkish, he thought in self-reproof. But he couldn't hold his incredulous curiosity back a moment longer. He was a journalist, after all. Sort of. He turned, feeling a fatuous grin on his face, unable to block it, and said, "Excuse me, aren't you—"

"Girly D'joan," the pop diva said wearily. Her voice was electrify-ing. "Don't tell me your name, bozo, I'm not interested. Frankly, I'm bushed. You want to know why I'm on the Metra instead of coddled with a limousine, but this badge I'm wearing on my left breast which you are far too bourgeois and inhibited to look at declares my allegiance to the principle of Carbon Frugality, which I trust answers your ques-tion. Also that guy on the other side of the aisle who looks like a gorilla on steroids is my bodyguard, Slim Harry, and he's packing a taser. Just saying. Have a nice rest of the day." All this canned diatribe, which was surely rehearsed, came at him without a single glance from her famously dazzling icicle eyes. Something slammed into the window. Jay jumped.

"Jesus!"

A smear of dark blood. More thuds. Birds were tumbling from the sky, dozens of them, plummeting in the faded light, hundreds, maybe thousands.

Ms. D'joan gazed impassively past him. "Another avian toxic death event," she murmured to Slim Harry, who'd instantly loomed at her side, protective and immense. "Good thing we took the Metra instead of driving." Multitudes of birds were still flinging themselves at the ground, clanging against steel roof and sides, splattering blood. A window cracked but failed to shatter.

Ahead of the train, rattled by the same suicidal flock, one Sal Travett, behind the wheel of a ten-year-old Kia, tried to slip under the closed gates at a grade crossing and got stuck in the path of Jay's train. The Metra locomotive made short work of Sal and his Kia, but an undetected weak spot in one of the buckling rails caused the car containing Jay, Girly, Slim Harry and a score of other riders to jackknife, punching a metal-edged folding tray completely through Jay's midriff, nearly severing him in two.

* * * *

The Beadle Monger cradled Jay Cornelius's head in its infinitely large, infinitely soft lap, while Jimmy Brunner caressed Jay's fevered brow. "There, there," whispered Jimmy, "it's not as bad as all that. Just take it easy, and you'll soon be whole again."

Jay raised his head up tentatively and looked down upon himself. He was saddened but not surprised to find that he had no body below the neatly truncated waist. He tried to express his feelings about this, but could not speak.

Brunner began softly to sing. "Oh, it's no feat to beat the heat. All reet! All reet! So jeet your seet, be fleet, be fleet—cool and discreet, Honey..."

The warbled lyrics soothed Jay, and he began to relax—until Jimmy saw fit to administer a cure. The male nurse clutched what appeared to be a grinning moray eel, large around as Jay's forearm. Now he tried to feed it head first down Jay's throat.

Gagging as the eel's snout passed his lips, struggling for breath, Jay rebelled, thrashing futilely without legs, like a character out of a Tod Browning film.

"Cool and discreet, Honey," sang Brunner, as he impossibly threaded the eel down Jay's throat—

"Please sit down, Mrs. Cornelius," said the doctor, grave face sun-lamp-tanned. "This gentleman is Dr. Hare, our Ethics Officer. Let me offer you—" He pressed an open box of Kleenex toward her side of the desk. Jessie took one, swallowed, blew her nose.

"Ms. Kanavan," she said. "Call me Jessie, Dr. Wu. I want to see Jay. Why won't the bastards let me?"

"Jessie, you do understand that your husband was in the very gravest condition when we began the surgery three days ago. Please let me be blunt. We were obliged to perform what is called a craniectomy—" He broke off, coughed. "Your husband's lower torso was severed almost entirely just below the ribs. Very fortunately, we had a compatible donor, who suffered a massive internal brain injury in the same train accident and whose—"

"God damn it, why didn't you let him just die?" She was weeping again. Bent over, clutching her own belly. It felt torn open.

"Well, you must understand, Ms. Kana—Jessie," the Ethics Officer told her, offended. "The Hippocratic oath. This facility's top surgical team has been preparing for another incident of this kind for five months. Your husband will receive the best—"

"My husband the guinea pig! You're telling me you stitched him onto some dead woman's lower body."

Wu regarded her. "This was a far more serious and complex procedure, Mrs.... Jessie. Fortunately, recent outstanding work with stem cells allows us to anticipate fully functional regrowth of anastomozed neurological structures subserving the—"

"What? What are you babbling about?"

"We originally planned to graft his head to the neck of the donor. That proved infeasible for a number of— In lay persons' terms, Jessie, we transplanted his brain."

She sank back in her chair, faint, ill with horror.

"You fucking shits," she shouted at him. "You've given him a woman's body? What makes you think he'll want to live like this?"

"A rather sexist objection, don't you think, Ms. Kanavan?" said the Ethics advisor.

Jessie was on her feet, enraged, hands extended and clawed, making sounds even she did not recognize as words. Dr. Wu rose, too, made shushing motions with his expert surgical hands. "We have many months of recuperation ahead of us," he said. "You will both adjust. It is a sort of miracle, you know. If this terrible accident had happened anywhere else, your husband would indeed have died within minutes, hours at best. We brought him back from the brink. And that poor woman's death—

"Such a generous donor family!" said Dr. Hare.

"—is not entirely in vain, not now."

* * * *

REPORTER: So what's that shiny thing sticking out of the top of Girly's head? Looks like someone left half a hatchet stuck there.

DR. WU: His head. The patient is Mr. Jay Cornelius. His identity is unchanged. Ms. D'joan is deceased. Let me remind you that the donor's identity is strictly embargoed. It will not be puCorneliused, and there will be no photographs! You have all signed—

REPORTER: Hey, come on, he's got tits. Great tits.

REPORTER: So've you, Billy. Time to cut back on the Quarterpounders.

(Laughter)

REPORTER: Yeah, but Girly's are better. What a waste.

DR. WU: Gentlemen! And ladies! Please, some decorum. This is a patient who has recently undergone an immensely stressful operation, as the videos you've just viewed demonstrated. Now the fellow from the Post asked about the microwave reflector inserted into the cranium between the two halves of Mr. Cornelius's brain.

REPORTER: It's a Space Age Mohawk!

(Laughter)

DR. WU: What you see is the outer portion of a steel microwave reflector that has been positioned with exacting care to avoid damaging the corpus callosum, which joins the twin hemi—

REPORTER: Keep it simple, doc. We're not all from The New York Times.

(Laughter)

DR. WU: Very well. Let me explain. In simple terms, we had to open the top of the skull to allow the traumatized brain to expand, as it does after injury. In order to effect the transfer without further deterioration, the patient's brain had to be cooled to nearly freezing point, as was explained in the video for those of you who kept up. Now, the stainless steel plate acts as a heat sink and a reflector for the 4GHz microwave—that's 7.5

cm—as well as a temperature control device. Following the Gregory Jones cranial protocol, the microwave beam is collimated with a simple catadioptric collimator, and we use the reflected pi-phase-synchronized microwaves from the central plate to interfere destructively at the center of the brain with the incoming non-reflected beam—

(Noisy hubbub)

MEDICAL DIARY OF PATIENT 005: ENTRY #17

Magritte is the prophet of my life. The shards of his broken window, each shattered portion of burst pane thick with the paint strokes of sky, trees, grass, the world; everything ordinary broken yet nothing lost, everything refracted and held, ruined, beneath the raped window. Holograms of indecipherable meaning.

Magritte is the prophet. His bland civil servants falling in eerie quiet through the sweet, undubious sky, bowlered and umbrella'd. Filthy Magritte in his own business suit and the oiled tip of his brush.

The "corporeal face." Do you know that terrible painting, that piercing painting? My portrait. The hair like some damned socialite's winter coat, framing and tumbling about the Face, the Face, the round blind breasts staring back at me below the brow of the shoulders, the unscented nostrils of the navel, that pubic beard with its pursed, hidden mouth, its toothless lacking mouth… Let's see Jessie cite her fave psychiatrist Lacan when she reads this.

I broke the mirror with my small bloodied fists. They brought the mirror to my room last night and left it here. They told me the time had come to get used to reality. Enough denial. Life is better than death in a ruinous accident. How ungrateful I was to turn my face away from the world to which I had been retrieved with all the surgical skill of wonderful hands cutting open my wrecked cranium and cupping my bloody brain and slopping it into an impossibly handy histocompatible corpse. But nothing is improbable once it's happened. Break down these walls of denial! Implosion therapy, it's called. Beyond a certain point, they implied, coddling has a bad track record. One of their early triumphs, the whispering rumors tell me, found a nail file in her handbag and before they got to her almost had her penis sawed off. Oh God, shit. The fucking feckless bastards.

At least they've taken out the famous "Space Age Mohawk" and screwed my skull back together. Her skull. Nobody mentions her name but I know that face, even with the bandages. Sitting right beside me, poor bitch. Skull itches like a bastard.

Jessie leaves messages every day, comes in two or three times a week. Of course I refuse to see her. Your wife called, they tell me. Your wife. I'd like you to meet Mrs. Jessie Kanavan Cornelius and her wife, Mrs. Jay Girly Cornelius.

The mirrored glass didn't stay on the carpet long enough for me to put any of its slivers into my filthy new body. Clean orderlies. They watch everything through cameras which they make absolutely no attempt to hide. Implosion therapy. Panopticon therapy, Jessie would call it. That damned Frog Foucault. Undoubtedly they'll be pawing through these notes the moment they give me my injection. They'll love that line about filthy new bodies. Stick the injection in. Sleepytime, Jay. Shut eyes. There's a good girl.

* * * *

From: The Beadle Monger
To: All Employees
Subject: Jay Cornelius

I am not pleased. Not pleased at all. You are not trying hard enough. Not by a long shot. I have plans for this one. Large and extensive plans. We all know the drill. A new Messiah is called for upon my favorite test planet, and I am convinced Cornelius has the makings. A certain mundane and self-centered insanity. A perverse genius for creating disturbing new parables of existential unease, longing and dread. A new hybrid physiology. (Very important! Take note!) Wide semiotic bandwidth. Look at him/her, people! What better raw material could I give you to work with!?! It took a hell of a long time for me to set up the plausible concatenation of circumstances, the cascade of bad luck, the woman on the train, the dead birds, all the shit that would make this possible. And you guys are blowing it! Cornelius is slipping away into a funk of self-pity and mordant despair. What happened to the guy who chortled at the luminous fish, and passionately embraced the Brunner eidolon? We need that fellow back in harness!

Let's get that dreamscape romance going again! Fast!

And don't tell me that Unknown Kadath wasn't built in a day!

* * * *

The new drug the nurses gave Jay Cornelius during the second week of his/her post-op mental struggles was one of the recently developed ultrapotent anti-depressives, an acetylcholine uptake enhancer. Irrational and bitter, he/she struggled womanfully against the injection, unfamiliar undermuscled arms flailing, breasts getting in the way, but was unable to thwart the burly orderlies. The drug was intended to induce a kind of passive state of mental beneficence, but had the unforeseen effect on Jay of rendering him/her utterly flatline, heart as pulseless as a stone, starving cells screaming shrilly.

While the hospital staff rushed about madly with defibrillators and oxygen tanks, and the clinic's spokesperson hastily prepared a worst-case speech, Jay was very busy elsewhere.

* * * *

Polychromatic water glistened and heaved like billows of luscious, nigh-edible acrylics: goldenrod, magenta, periwinkle. A sun like the Google Chrome logo blazed in the sky. The big luminous fish, hefty as barracuda, were swarming ashore to breed, and the human harvesters of L'Almadrava cove were waiting, spears poised.

Several feet offshore, skirt pulled up and tied between her bare, wet, bronzed legs, white blouse pasted to her nubile breasts, her toes gripping the shifting, sucking sands, Jayne hefted her own pole nervously. Her first harvest. She was only sixteen. Would she comport herself well? The future prosperity of the village rested partially on her shoulders.

A rough male hand dropped upon one of those very shoulders now. As if reading her mind, Jaime Brunelli said, "Your stance is bold, little one. But the angle of your spear lacks a certain, ah, utility. I predict impalement of your own delicate foot upon the first thrust. Here, let me adjust your cast."

Big hairy arms enveloped her, along with the musk of male sweat. Jayne trembled. Jaime Brunelli was one of L'Almadrava's most handsome and desirable bachelors. The fiery way he had danced at the last festival— Jayne found the sea-engendered wetness between her legs taking on new hormonal qualities.

But before she could respond either coquettishly or haughtily to Brunelli's suggestive help, the first battalion of luminous fish were upon them. With a bull-like battle cry, Brunelli disengaged, and Jayne was left on her own.

The first rainbow fish that reached her began to plead for its life, as was the wont of these creatures. It employed a human tongue, but to produce gibberish.

"Beep me the be-bop downlow, sister! Raster the roster! It's a treat to beat my milt on the Missus's eggy strand! Oh, no, don't pierce my male maidenhead!"

Ignoring the siren tones of the fish, using both hands on her hard shaft, Jayne plunged her razored spearhead down and into the fish's back, at just the designated point to sever its spine. Her blow was fine and forceful, and the fish ceased its spasmodic mating dance, beginning a prolonged expiration at her feet like some war captive at the feet of a Roman princess.

"Ai, bonita! I flounder! The word for the world is tuna! Monkey see, sea monkey do!"

Jayne disregarded the pathetic gasps and inane drivel, and continued to stab and slice. Soon, a mound of fishy carcasses surrounded her, putting other victims beyond her reach. Thin fishy sparkling blood threaded the waters in an abattoir's aquarelle. She tried to clamber over the bodies, but only collapsed wearily upon the scaly pile, unaware of time's passing until familiar hands cupped her under her arms (and against her breasts!) and raised her up, totally out of the water.

"My little goddess! Victory is thine! You shined like Venus. No, like Bellona! Your ancestors are grinning in heaven!"

Jayne was suddenly shivering, despite the heat of the day. Instinctively, she wrapped her lithe legs around Brunelli's treetrunk torso and hugged him to her.

He whispered in her ear. "You were made a hunter today, but I will make you a woman tonight!"

It seemed the interval between the end of the catch and the village celebration in the plaza passed in mere seconds, and when Jayne found herself in the fragrant shadow of a lime tree, kissing Jaime Brunelli with fervid languor, she could sense her destiny unfolding. When he raised her fine skirts and stuck two rough fingers up her wet vagina, she came close to fainting. And when he followed that invasion with the whole rushed length of his thick penis, leaping unleashed from his own gaily decorated trews, she finally did indeed lose consciousness of her whole world.

* * * *

Jay Cornelius's latest dream had left him/her somewhat gentled, filled with an odd combination of waning remorse, waxing resignation and acceptance, dwindling suicidal impulses, and a barely germinating interest in and excitement about her/his personal future, an emotion tender and crushable as the first pale sprout of a maidenhair fern. Additionally, the brute compulsion of a healing, nicely toned body supplemented the blossoming good spirits.

Lying in bed, she/he poked at the still-vivid memory of life in the fishing village, Jayne's piscine conquests and arboreal defloration. Some sense of eternal recurrence lingered, a lineage larger than himself. Life had gone on in such a fashion since the dawn of human history, for men and women alike, each grappling gender playing their part. Who was Jay Cornelius to fight such immemorial rituals? Just because he had involuntarily switched sides in the old competition, he had no solid right to complain. Happened to a limited number of citizens all the time, at their own instigation. Nip and tuck, fold and invert, extrude and stretch, plump and polish....

Of course he spent some time exploring his new body, as the nerve attachments to his brain strengthened, clarified their renewed identity, pulsed from numbness to dulled medicated aches and twinges and at last into a palette of prods, pinches, strokes, soothing, fondlings. Of course his fingers caressed those fabulous boobs, swept down to touch, titillate, enter the exciting, terrifying complex emptiness where his brain gibbered that his penis should be. But it wasn't like the dream of fervent lusty girlhood. Yes, there were some of those sensations he'd tried to turn into market fodder for the Groper Media empire and his odious boss McKinley, but mostly it was like trying to tickle yourself. His brain literally didn't know if he was coming or going. If he was Arthur or Martha. He took his fingers away from his vagina and sighed.

At that moment, Jay decided firmly and spontaneously on one simple thing, easily within his/her limited grasp. Pronouns. At least she could be a she. Simplify, simplify, for accuracy's sake and ease of conversation. After all, what mattered more, the meaty mass of corpore or the smaller quantity of mens? Even that organic, formerly male brain was now awash in the female chemicals and hormones this body pumped out, laved by a luteal lake.

And so Jay determinedly became Jayne herself. A certain straining tension immediately evanesced.

Over the next few days her concerned handlers, noting the "progress," let up on the meds and allowed more privileges.

Such as getting attired in loose grey sweats and sitting up in this cheerful, sunny lounge, to receive her first real visitor.

Henry McKinley, togged out even more pavoninely than usual, as if in deference to some imagined girlish heart-flutter susceptibility of his interviewee (Jayne admitted the publisher did carry clothes well), brazened into the lounge with his usual air of bestrider-of-worlds. But Jayne thought to detect, beneath the macho bluster, a layer of nervous uncertainty and ego-failure. Had Henry always radiated this self-denying put-down-ability, or was it something new, engendered by Jayne's unique circumstances?

Oh. My. God. Was this insight a case of feminine intuition coming into play? Faintly suspect. No evident logic. Impossible to spreadsheet. Could be useful, though...

McKinley thrust out something he had carried behind his back. An enormously expensive box of Godiva chocolates. "Take it! Jessie said they were your favorites, even before this titanic fuck-up."

Jayne felt her mouth watering. Nice to see Jayne's body's tastes conformed to Jay's.

This body. The stranger's eyes she hid behind. Who had the donor really been, in her short extravagant life, her legacy of accomplishments and relatives and friends, of dreams and hopes? For the first time since their mutual tragedy, Jayne resolved to think at least a little less about herself and more about the famous young woman she inhabited.

Henry pulled up a chair and sat down, his knees almost touching hers. He leaned forward, intruding into her personal space. What an obvious boor! Still, his interest was flattering.

"So you've been talking to Jessie?"

"Damn straight! Couldn't talk to you, could I, lost in that self-pitying fugue. My god, Jay—"

"Jayne."

"Whatever. Don't you realize what you almost threw away by vegging out and indulging in Britney-Spears-magnitude hissy-fits like that? You are the number one media sensation of the millennium! Or at least of this year. All the other freaks like you who survived—sorry, I mean 'lucky beneficiaries of modern medical wizardry'—have proven hideously unsuitable for inspiring the semi-grossed-out adulation by Joe Sixpack and Jane Soccer Mom. Either the bodies were less than optimally hot, or the brains belonged to rat bastards, or both. The worst case was that embezzling bigamist transplanted into the trailer-park mother of seven. Eeeyeuw! But look at you! A smart, sane guy in a smokin' bod!" Henry paused a moment and looked quizzically at Jayne. "You are still sane, aren't you? No, don't answer that! We can work around anything! Where was I? Oh, yeah, so here you are, with the gifts of the fucking gods in your lap—ha, your lap, that's rich!—and you're like, 'Oh, no, woe is me, I don't have a dick anymore, I miss the old sub-average third leg which I never used anyhow except to dip into the stale wifey once a week tops.'"

Jayne felt a surge of anger at this rude characterization of both her quondam private member and the uses to which it had been put. But then, miraculously, some kind of estrogen-based counter-surge of tolerance and humor overcame the anger, and she smiled.

"Okay, bossman, so I'm incredibly lucky. What about it?"

Henry McKinley held his head as if to prevent it from exploding. "What about it?!? What about it!?! Haven't you been working for me for five years? What did I teach you? Didn't you absorb even a gnat's ass's worth of savvy from me? You are going to assign to Groper Media all representation of you and your incredibly sexy-sad story, and we are going to ride this to fame and fortune and megastar-fuckability. I can say that to you, can't I? You're still Jay Cornelius inside that pretty little head, aren't you?"

"Mostly. But why should I necessarily pick Groper to handle my story? Shouldn't I start a bidding war? Man, this is the body of Girly D'joan! And I'm right here. Talk about an inside scoop!"

Henry seemed genuinely taken aback. "Jayne, do you really think there's anyone out there with more sleaze-marketing expertise than yours truly? This is the story I was born to ride!"

Jayne pondered this honest and unsparing self-assessment. She realized that she no longer hated Henry, but only pitied him. Fuller comprehension of his drives and character had brought tolerance.

"Let me hear some of your marketing plans," said Jayne. "And don't spare the dirt."

* * * *

From: The Beadle Monger
To: All Employees
Subject: Jayne Cornelius
  I am highly pleased, highly pleased indeed! Operation Androgyne Messiah is back on track! Big kudos to all relevant departments: creative, fieldwork, grok-meld, scanalytics, sevagram programming and astral bookkeeping. Bonuses to be dispersed according to seniority, with highest senior grades receiving no less than one hundred quanta of karmic fluxion.
  Please keep up the good work as we move ahead into the next stages of our campaign of enforced enlightenment.

* * * *

Jayne felt like a hundred million dollars, which was appropriate given yesterday's judicial verdict confirming her sole ownership of all her donor's worldly possessions. This still struck her as an insane decision, but she wasn't complaining. All the usual biometrics declared that she was, indeed, beyond question, Girly D'joan, alive and well and almost fully recovered, her fingerprints and retinal scans and DNA genomic profile unaltered by the dreadful accident. Yes, she now had a different brain, but then similarly, too, all those other transplant patients had grafted kidneys or hearts, and nobody expected them to waive their legal rights of full possession and enjoyment thereof. Henry McKinley had spared no expense in hiring the best law firm and suborning the most pliable judge in Chicago.

But thoughts of wealth and borrowed fame were a distraction. Jayne Cornelius rolled out her Pilates mat, dropped into position, and allowed the energy of oxygen to pass into her blood and tissues. And they were hers now, every cell and corpuscle. Calm, calm. Concentration. Control. Center. Flow. Precision. And the soothing, energizing pulse of breath.

"Jay. Jayne. Christ, sorry, should have knocked." In the doorway, Jessie gazed down at her former husband raised full length from the mat in a Shoulder Bridge, right foot squarely on the floor, perfect left leg raised perfectly in alignment through her elevated torso and hip, left toes pointed like a ballerina's. "My god, Jayne," she said in a tone of confusion, "you're hot, man."

A raw sexual jolt went through Jayne's vagina, roared up her spine, clobbered her diaphragm and lungs en route, brought her to the floor with a crunch. This was nothing like her abortive attempts to touch herself. This was that dream, brought to life—Jaime Brunelli of L'Almadrava. But not a rough, beautiful man from a fantasy. Her wife. Jessie. She felt…wet.

"Come here, you," she said, and rolled to her feet, lithe and poised with the body of a 22 year old diva. They fell upon each other with hot mouths. After a long raging moment Jessie batted away her hand.

"This is wrong, Jay! You're a girl!"

"I thought you were the expert in gender confusion," Jayne said, withdrawing, pouting despite herself, chagrined. "And what's the probability of that, anyway?"

"It's a popular course," Jessie said. She backed away, found a chair, sat primly, watched her husband, her wife, in that sparkling sequined leotard cut in a lewd slash from her sharp hips all the way down to—"Your lawyer called. Congratulations on the decision."

"Thank you. Jessie, I want you to know that—"

"None of it is mine," she said bitterly. "Yes, your Miss Priss made it very clear. Since you are still legally Ms. D'joan, we're not married and never were. So under the settlement laws of Illinois and indeed everywhere else on the entire planet, I can expect nothing, not a penny."

"Hey, hey, baby." Jay surged up inside Jayne. "You'll have everything you need, and more. This… my donor, she was loaded. Is loaded. If I never sing another song for her, she'll be rich until we both die."

"She's already dead. Or you are, whatever."

"You and me, I meant. I told Jesus to write you a check for a million and a half and have it ready for you at the office. Didn't you—"

"Who's Jesus?"

"Jesus Saves." She pronounced it in the Hispanic fashion, Hay-soos Sah-vays. In a happy moment, like the past of their marriage instantly recovered, Jessie blinked and her eyes rolled.

"You're shitting me. You have a money manager named Jesus Saves?" Anglo pronunciation.

Jayne burst out laughing, and felt the tension fall away from her tensed shoulders. The Pilate mat was calling to her. "Right. Right. Man, it's just one crazy coincidence after another."

She found a chair and kicked it closer to her wife. Ex-wife. Widow. Whatever. She reached out both hands and after a moment's pause Jessie took them. "Babe, this is too crazy. But I'm taking steps right away to deal with one issue." Jayne took a deep breath, let the dreams flood through her. Something was trying to tell her something, that was sure as shit. Jay no more. Cornelius no more, either. Time to roll the dice and start over. "I'm changing my name."

"You already changed your name." Now Jessie was stroking her right hand as if it were a small child's, or perhaps a kitten. "Let me guess. Um. Darby N. D'joan?"

"Ha ha." Some old movie they'd seen together? No, an 18th century poem Jessie had studied in her gender crimes course, wasn't it? The weather beaten old couple who'd stayed together through thick and thin. "Sorry, not any longer, sweetheart. This thing that's happened to me, I tell you, someone up there either likes me or hates me, and I don't know which it is, yet. But I got stuck here in this gorgeous bod for a reason, Jessie. Maybe I'm some kind of message to the world."

"Oh shit, Jay." Her widow dropped her hand. "Don't tell me you've got religion. It was an accident, and then a bunch of medical ghouls used you for an experiment. I know, sorry, that was uncalled for, you've recovered beautifully, but…" She trailed off. After a moment she said, "So what's the new name?"

"Jayne Brunner." The person in Girly D'joan's living corpse stood up, squared her shoulders, felt the still-unfamiliar weight of her breasts as they shifted under the lycra.

"Well, whatever. So are you now Mrs. Brunner or Ms. Brunner, Jay?"

"Neither." She offered her widow a vulpine display of teeth, and led her toward the door. "I'm an old-fashioned girl, it seems. Call me Miss Brunner."

* * * *

Somewhere behind the multiverse, the Beadle Monger experienced a small frisson. *The Eidolon Lure had been taken.*

A Glaroon nodded in satisfaction. "*Now to nudge the human's Messiah Complex into overdrive, Beads.*"

"*Yes indeed. 'Miss Brunner',*" *they muttered to itselves.* "*Now that sounds…quite promising.*"

[for Mike Moorcock]

ABOUT A PALAZZO IN THE STARS

Here is another story specifically commissioned to commemorate a conference appearance, this time at Sticon in Italy. My local publisher Armando Corridore at Elara, did this up as a beautiful chapbook that was handed out with purchases at the con.

I love writing steampunk, of course, a category this story belongs to. But I am a little sick of setting stories in the USA and the UK. The Victorian era encompassed the whole world, after all—and beyond, as we see here!

A PALAZZO IN THE STARS

1. A CURIOUS OFFER OF SELECTIVE EMPLOYMENT

Camped out in the middle of Saint Mark's Square with their new-fangled Austrian folding-seat walking sticks, the three brash young Americans attracted every native eye as they cut some carefree capers amidst their more serious artistic endeavors. They winked and smiled at all the passing women, young and old, beautiful and homely. They swigged heroic draughts of Chianti straight from straw-buffered bottles. They enjoyed a steady service of foodstuffs delivered to them from the Café Florian by scurrying waiters whom they had cajoled with largesse. They made gestures of over-obsequious deference to the suspicious patrolling carabinieri. They blew airy kisses to nuns and priests. And, of course, they sketched up a positive storm.

The past turbulent decade-and-a-half in Italy, including the country's proud but bloody Unification, had diminished the number of timid, pleasure-seeking foreign visitors to the newborn Kingdom, and these three travelers were appreciated much as returning birds in spring, their presence regarded as a possible herald of increased patronage by Northerners reinstating Italy to the Grand Tour. An influx of highly useful dollars and pounds and francs and marks looked likely—unless of course the recent collapse in this year of 1877 of the corrupt government of Prime Minister Agostino Depretis resulted in further chaos—unfortunately, an Italian speciality, and hence one of the more dreaded outcomes.

Under a beneficient June sun as mellow as the expression on the face of Titian's Madonna di Ca' Pesaro in the Basilica di Santa Maria Gloriosa dei Frari (a sight which had just this morning inspired the three men), the trio of visitors continued to sketch, while flocks of rock doves, wheeled, landed, then soared aloft again. With narrow, lithe, linen-clad buttocks firmly ensconced on their small canework ovals atop hinged tripods, and well-used scuffed boots planted firmly on the pavement, they employed long, narrow, landscape-favoring sketchbooks featuring covers in mossgreen, oxblood and jonquil, as well as an assortment of pencils and charcoals, to capture some of the vibrant scene about them.

One fellow exhibited a long narrow face with a slightly bent nose, hair in two wings across his brow, radiating from a central parting, and a lush mustache. His technique as he sought to render the famed Doges Palace quite obviously partook of the new vogue of impressionism.

The second sketcher boasted a more-oval face, hair already thinning across his crown, but compensated for by enormous bushy eyebrows above piercing optics. His nascent depiction of the Campanile (he had shifted his pad ninety degrees for that assignment) exhibited a sturdier realism.

The last artist possessed a somewhat plump face adorned with a small neat strip of mustache. But his thick untidy thatch of wheat-colored hair needed a trim. An aggressive chin dominated the lower portion of his physiognamy. The intensity of his concentration on the page seemed somehow, even to strangers, self-evidently a habitual part of his demeanor. Few if any smile lines had graven themselves onto his youthful but weary countenance.

This man sketched not any portion of the delightful, soul-stirring architecture of the Piazza San Marco, but rather the passing show of souls. He employed a technique midway between the naturalism of one friend and the impressionism of the other. But today at least, his style featured a certain soupçon of the fantastic. The characters on his page were not rendered as they had been born, but rather sported in a subtle fashion, emerging from their garments in a manner at first almost imperceivable, tails and wings, horns and claws, fangs and abnormal, disturbing growths.

The trio of artists continued with their antics—the japes of the fantasist rang a bit hollow compared with those of his genuinely enthusiastic pals—and with their drawing, until finally the impressionist had cause to look over and regard the page which the wheat-haired man was fanatically belaboring.

"Good lord, Frank! Those are absolute monsters! One would think you were sitting in Bosch's *Garden* rather than here in this lovely Mediterranean clime. What's gotten into you, chum? Do you feel all right?"

Frank clapped his sketchbook shut and slid it into a scratched leather satchel by his side. He managed to look both rueful and maligned. "Oh, damn it all, John, I don't know what's the matter with me. Nothing physical, if that's what you mean. Just some kind of black dog at my heels. I had imagined this trip would rid me of the beast, but no such luck. And I can't really plan my future intelligently with that mean mongrel nipping at my britches."

John, the youngest of the trio by several years, seemed genuinely sympathetic and respectful of Frank's dilemma, but only up to a point. "Well, I'm sure a path will present itself to someone of your sterling talents. And just consider, you have a rock-solid foundation to build on. After that knockout show in Boston—"

Frank vented his irritation on his friend. "Oh, to hell with that Boston show! It was two years ago after all, and the load of praise rode in on the years-long coattails of insults and studied obliviousness. What a preening bunch of hypocrites, to admire the work they had slighted for so long. And all because it came from the son of a poor immigrant kraut laborer, an upstart boy who had to learn his trade decorating churches! No academy for me or rich patrons meant no respect. I still can't forgive the bastards."

The third man, sitting slightly removed from his comrades, now put down his own work and stepped over to see what the fuss was all about.

"Here, here, Frank, come off it. Get down off that high horse! What's given you the vapors? We're here to enjoy ourselves, in a land of beauty and delight, with plenty of lira in our pockets, no duties, and the winning charms of three young demiurges! Now, show me what you've been drawing that's caused so much turmoil."

Frank reluctantly took his pad out of his satchel. "Oh, all right, William, if you must see."

Holding the book in his lap, Frank flipped through its pages, the weird illustrations of that afternoon's composition eliciting exclamations and sage or joshing commentary from his appreciative, art-besotted bretheren. Frank began to feel somewhat less downtrodden and downhearted. Surely capturing these phantoms of his imagination in graphite had rendered them harmless to further disturb him.

So intent were the trio on examining Frank's sketches that they failed to note that a new observer had joined them. Their attention was diverted from the pages only by a sonorous voice proclaiming in charmingly accented English, "Wonder of wonders! You are the very man I have been seeking!"

Frank looked up to confront a patrician figure. A rail-thin elderly gent with facial hair and a poet's locks, both of the most startling Cremnitz White, as found in the Winsor & Newton palette. The man's old-fashioned suit, though shabby, bespoke elegant tailoring. He carried a cane whose silver grip mimicked a dragon's head.

"Whatever can you mean, sir?" asked Frank.

"Let us have introductions all around first, before I explain. I am the Duke of Fossombrone. Here is my card."

The Duke tendered a neatly engraved card apiece to the artists. In turn, Frank gave their names.

"I'm Frank Duveneck. And these two roarers are John Henry Twacht-man and William Merritt Chase."

"And what brings you all here to the Queen of the Adriatic, my friends? I can't credit that it was simply to meet my needs."

"We've been studying art in Munich for some time now," Frank said. "I've reached the point where I'm thinking I might even open up my own school there. But after so much hard labor we grew tired of that city, and sought to experience something completely different and relaxing."

"Well, you have come to the antipodes, so far as that dour German culture is concerned. I'm sure you will all benefit from your stay here. And I know I will."

"What do you allude to again with this cryptic assertion?"

"Only that I have been looking for an artist who might be able to chronicle an expedition I plan to undertake soon, and I believe you are that man."

Frank felt compelled to speak up for his pals. "But my friends have as much talent as I. Why not one of them, or perhaps all three of us?"

The Duke said, "Allow me to see your work, gentlemen."

John and William complied with the request. After examining their portfolios, the Duke said, "Very accomplished and stirring, sirs. But your work lacks that resonance with ineffable mystery that I detect in Signore Duveneck's. So it is to him alone that I will tender my offer of employment."

His curiosity piqued, Frank asked, "Exactly what are the terms and nature of this employment?"

Duke Fossombrone smiled with some small underlying sadness attendant. "It is all too complicated to explain in the middle of the Piazza under a wilting sun. Please do me the honor, all three of you, of sharing dinner with me at my home tonight. Simply ask anyone for directions to the Ca' d'Oro, and try to arrive by nine. Please bring neither wine nor flowers nor sweets, as I have a cellar, a garden and a baker, all of superlative caliber. I'll see you then, gentlemen."

The Duke of Fossombrone walked away with a slight limp, but seemed rather too proud to employ his stick as fully as another man might have done to maximize its benefits.

2. THE *JOLIE LAIDE* AND THE LEGLESS MAN

The gondola ferrying the three American artists to the Ca' d'Oro rocked precipitously as John and William stood at its prow, supporting each other tipsily whilst trying to harmonize with their propulsive steersman at the rear on some native barcarole whose foreign lyrics they had adapted to an indecent English doggerel. The sun had just set, empurpling the gently sloshing Grand Canal and its dreaming houses, and allowing a few eager bright stars to appear above. Civic gas lights vied with oil lanterns to oasis the dark streets of the marshy city.

Slouched comfortably low down in the boat on cushions, Frank smiled at the antics of his comrades. At the moment he felt constitutionally incapable of joining them, but he admired their high spirited roistering nonetheless. To surround oneself with boisterous chums when one was feeling grim was sound medicine, albeit of limited efficacy.

Frank's thoughts turned to the mysterious proposition tendered by Duke Fossombrone. To take on the mantle of evidentiary artist for some daring expedition into uncharted realms sounded jim-dandy to Frank at the moment, with or without compensation. So far, Italy had not proven sufficiently remote or distracting enough to alleviate his anxieties. If to attain peace of mind he had to emulate Pierre de Brazza, currently engaged in charting the upper reaches of the Ogowe River in Africa with nothing more than a bale of trade fabrics, then so be it!

The gondola began now to arrow toward the shore. The two crooners ceased their caterwauling and substituted whistles and exclamations.

"Is that really where skinny old Saint Nick lives?"

"What a manse! Look at all that gilt. Her lines ain't so bad neither! Though she ain't no Jefferson Market Courthouse!"

"Frank, you snagged yourself a rich fish, boy!"

Sitting up, Frank took in the ornate, filgreed, columned façade of the alabaster palazzo. The elegant building radiated the worn dignity of an elderly widow.

"I'm not so sure about his wealth, boys. I'm pretty certain he's just renting the place. The House of Gold's been on and off the market for decades, ever since Marie Taglioni gave it up."

"Not that hussy of a ballerina who started the craze for short skirts? She lived here?"

"Indeed. While you boys were out liquoring up, I made a few inquiries. Duke Fossombrone came to town only a year ago, with his son and daughter. They don't socialize hardly at all, and no one seemed to know much about them."

"Daughter!" said John. "Now you're talking! Bill and I will tickle her while you and the Duke are picking sand fleas outta your trousers in Outer Mongolia."

The gondola bumped the slanted, partly submerged, algae-slick stone steps of Ca' d'Oro; the riders disembarked, paid the boatman, and found a big, shadowed wooden door with a large knocker that they loudly employed.

The door swung inward after only a few seconds delay to reveal a young woman, dressed not as a servant, but in a fashionable ensemble of dove grey and mauve.

Bill and John doffed their hats immediately, but Frank was a laggard. He was too poleaxed by her appearance to respond.

Duke Fossombrone's daughter, if such she were, demonstrated the type of woman dubbed by the French *jolie laide*, or "beautiful-ugly." Her thick black eyebrows were paralleled by a sparse and downy but undeniable mustache. Her oversized nose and mouth were out of all proportion to her face. Her figure was good, but her hands were too big. Her eyes resembled those of startled, intelligent doe. The overall impression she radiated was chimeric, that of the hybrid offspring of a human mother and some satyr or troll.

To Frank, she seemed beauty incarnate, some Mona Lisa that Goya might have limned in a twilight moment.

After what seemed an eternity of contemplation, Frank too removed his hat. The woman smiled then, said *"Buona sera, signori."* She indicated by gesture that they should enter.

The artists were conducted to a cool inner garden with high walls which had been arranged to host their meal. Capacious terracotta pots overflowed with tropical greenery. A large trestle table draped with a plain white cloth held a bounty of enticing food: steaming plates of vegetables and chicken; bowls of macaroni in tomato sauce; cheeses and fruit; baskets of rolls; as well as pitchers of water and wine. Tall footed free-standing candelabra illuminated the repast.

Standing to welcome them was the Duke. He laid his hand on the shoulder of a seated young man, presumably his son. The handsome lad, perhaps twenty-seven or so, wore a brave look compounded of equal parts hope, despair and physical exhaustion.

"Welcome, gentlemen, welcome! Allow me to introduce my family to you. My daughter, Restituta, you have met at the door. Her English, I fear, is minimal."

Restituta curtsied in the manner of a large bird settling from the skies onto a tree limb, an awkward signature mode that Frank found only enhanced her peculiar charm.

"And this is my son, Ludovico."

"I would stand, sirs, but cannot do so very easily, and so beg your indulgence."

Frank noticed then two artificial limbs, with wool-padded cupped tops and dangling leather straps, resting on the floor near some crutches that leaned against Ludovico's chair.

"My son lost both legs at the Battle of Villa Glori, some ten years ago, fighting to unite our motherland. He has been struggling back to health all the time since, but I fear he has his defeats as well as his victories."

Ludovico smiled bravely. "I was proud to make the sacrifice for our glorious Kingdom."

Duke Fossombrone continued: "Now, gentlemen, I'm sure you have a thousand questions. But our rapidly cooling meal beckons, and I for one am famished. Let us dine, and then you'll hear all."

Living as they had been on a limited budget, the hungry artists needed no second invitation to commence. Selecting linen napkins and piling high their plates—more like salvers, really—Bill and John took up seats on either side of the Duke's son (inexplicably disdaining his alluring sister) and soon had the lad reminiscing vivaciously about his martial prowess. The Duke watched approvingly, while doing more drinking of the potent red wine than actual eating.

Restituta first made up a plate for her brother, then assembled one for herself. After she found a chair, Frank brought his own meal over to sit beside her. Unable to pass more than a few words in each other's language between them, they contented themselves with enjoying the food and exchanging smiles and nods of appreciation from time to time.

Frank was pleased to see that the young woman had a hearty appetite and no timidity about indulging it in front of strangers.

Finally, once all were sated, Duke Fossombrone got to his feet, a tad unsteadily due to his imbibing.

"Mr. Chase and Mr. Twachtman, I am sharing this secret with you, although I choose not to avail myself of your services, out of respect for your camaraderie with Mr. Duveneck, whom I definitely do wish to employ. I enjoin you to keep this knowledge *sub rosa*, or you might scotch the whole affair. For you see, I have had many narrow-minded auditors of my dream, men whom I relied on for friendship and support, react with sneering incredulity and even threats of incarceration, as if I were a dangerous madman. Simply because the expedition for which I need Mr. Duveneck's talents is no common earthly one.

"I am going to the Moon!"

3. VISIONS OF A LUNAR EMPYREAN

"Let me get this straight," said Frank for the fifth time.

The hour was well past midnight, and several candles had already guttered out and been replaced. John and Bill, wearying of the infinite parsing of what they were already calling "Fossombrone's Folly," had departed boozily for their lodgings in the cheap pensione where all three artists shared a room. Ludovico, wan and exhausted from the small normal efforts of eating and socializing, had been helped to bed by his sister, clomping out of the garden on his unnatural legs like some amateur, untrained stiltwalker. But Restituta had returned swiftly after seeing to her brother's comfort. The long table had been cleared of food by a quiet and efficient servant, and on the board now was spread an expansive sheet of paper whose quasi-mechanical diagrams reminded Frank of Leonardo's sketches.

"This mystery substance which you have access to," Frank continued, "possesses the power to cancel out gravity? How can that be?"

Duke Fossombrone sighed. "I have no idea how it works, young man, I know only that it does. As I told you, it is a unique element, possibly stellar in origin, discovered by the Rae-Richardson Polar Expedition nearly thirty years ago. One huge chunk of ore was mined in the Arctic and brought back to civilization, where it sat in a warehouse as a useless enigma for decades, until my chance discovery of its true nature and potential."

Duke Fossombrone had disclosed to Frank that he was a respected naturalist with connections to the Academy of Sciences at Bologna, and well-versed in experimentalism.

"And now you own this miraculous stuff, and plan to use it to travel to the Moon."

"Finally you comprehend!"

"Oh, I savvy all right—I just don't believe any of it!"

Duke Fossombrone sighed. "Given the lateness of the hour, I had hoped to forego a demonstration until the morning. But I can see I will not gain your participation without proof. Restituta!"

The Duke addressed his daughter in their native language, and she hastened dutifully off. Fagged from the busy day and the incredible assertions of the Duke, Frank blurted out an impolite question.

"What's the story behind your daughter's odd name?"

"She is named after Saint Restituta, patron saint of Ischia where she was conceived. My wife and I had long been barren, but upon a recreational visit to that charming isle we found ourselves granted our fondest wish. Unfortunately, Restituta's mother perished in giving birth to her, but that in no way dimished my wife's dying allegiance to the saint, nor my living pledge. And in fact the name has proven peculiarly apt, since Restituta's main miracle was to cross the waters to Ischia not in any conventional craft, but riding upon a millstone! A voyage no more nor less wonderful than the one I intend to make to the Moon."

Restituta returned, pushing a wooden trolley. On the trolley sat a bulky box, with wires extending that ran into and out of some intermediary device. Frank did not recognize the apparatus at all, and Fossombrone sensed his puzzlement.

"This is nothing more than a Plante-Faure lead-acid cell, a storage mechanism for electricity, with a Wheatstone rheostat as part of the circuit. That latter device allows proper modulation of the current. All common as the pox. But here—here is the real marvel."

The Duke picked up what appeared to be a small thin sheet of hammered copper.

"Here is a small piece of the worked ore, Mr. Duveneck. I have named the substance 'cavourite,' after our beloved patriot, Camillo Paolo Filippo Giulio Benso, Count of Cavour. Now, Frank—if I may be so bold as to employ your Christian name—please donate a small object of your own so you will know I have not prearranged a hoax."

Frank found a bottle of ink in his pocket and handed it over. The Duke wrapped the bottle in the foil, then stuck the leads from the lead-acid cell onto the assemblage with a pinch of putty. He set the wrapped bottle down on the table.

"Now, watch closely, as I regulate the voltage flowing through the wires, starting from nil. I have to use a delicate touch, and my hand is unsteady at this hour, which is one reason I had hoped to postpone the demonstration."

Manipulating the rheostat with a slight tremble, the Duke radiated an expectancy which communicated itself to Frank.

The artist kept his gaze fixed on the bottle, but a corner of his vision allowed him to note that Restituta was similarly entranced.

Was that a hairsbreadth of space showing between the bottle and the tabletop? Yes, it was! The bottle was floating!

As the Duke adjusted the rhetostat the bottle wrapped in cavourite lifted higher and higher till it halted at eye-level, floating as innocently as a dandelion clock. Frank passed his hands through the sphere of air all around the bottle, looking for invisible threads, and found naught.

"But—but this is incredible!"

"Yes, it is, isn't it? You see, the metal is inert until an electrical current of the proper type is passed through it. Then, pure levitation." Pursing his lips, the Duke blew upon the weightless object and it drifted away in reaction. "And that is how one can maneuver in space. With breath, of a special sort." The Duke cut the current, and the bottle fell with a solid thunk to the table.

The steed of Frank's excitement, racing at a fever pitch, experienced a sudden reining in. "But why the Moon, of all places? This invention has so many earthly uses. Flying carriages, for one! You could become rich, or change society. Why go haring off to another world? What's waiting for you there? What's so special about the Moon?"

"Ah, Frank, that's where my daughter comes in. Ever since birth, perhaps because of the special blessed circumstances of her conception, she has had visions. Vision of otherworldly scenes and personages. Even communications from them, which I have come to trust without reserve. And her visions have told her that on the Moon dwell beings who can help us. Specifically, they can restore her brother's legs. And that is the thing my darling girl most desires."

Frank stood flabbergasted. "But—but such creatures would have to be angels!"

Restituta understood something of Frank's declaration. She grabbed both his hands and transfixed him with her large, dark eyes, like some lamia out of Keats. "*Si, si, signore! Vedo gli angeli!*"

4. PREPARATIONS AND FLIGHT

Frank saw little of John and William these days: he was much too busy getting ready to fly to the Moon.

Once dawn had broken after the incredible demonstration of the levitating ink pot, he had hastened across the city, woken his pals, and informed them of his intention to move out of the pensione. His chums regarded him as a man possessed, but did not seek to dissuade him. Rather, they sleepily and bemusedly wished him luck in his quixotic pursuits. Frank accepted their endorsement, gathered up his small belongings, and returned to the Ca' d'Oro. Shown by the lone servant to the room that would be his, he laid his head down on a pillow for just a moment and woke up twelve hours later.

Finding his way down the the main dining room, he discovered the Fossombrone family already seated at table.

"Ah, Frank," the Duke said, "you have left the realm of dreams at last. Join us now, for we have much to plan and discuss. Sit with Ludovico between yourself and Restituta, and my son will translate anything you wish to say to my daughter, and also of course whatever she replies."

So began the daily, hourly makeshift translation routine by which Frank would begin to know better the fascinating Restituta, supplemented by his gradual acquisition of a smattering of Italian, and her growing mastery of English. Ludovico proved to be so mild and obliging a linguist, one whose fondness for his sister made light all chores regarding her happiness, that at times Frank almost forgot the young man was even present. It seemed as if Frank's expressions of meaning went straight to Restituta's consciousness, and vice versa.

When Frank did suddenly take cognizance at intervals of Ludovico's presence, he had to smile, for the situation reminded him of the famous quandary Cyrano de Bergerac had gotten himself involved in. And was not Cyrano also author of *The Other World: The States and Empires of the Moon*?

In any case, that second meal in the Ca' d'Oro marked the beginning of a growing friendly intimacy between Frank and the *jolie laide*. And what he discovered over that and subsequent days—many hours of which were spent sketching Restituta—was a creature composed of paradoxical qualities. Shy in most matters, yet bold in detailing and affirming her angelic visions. Free from personal agendas, except for her bulldog tenacity in wishing to secure Ludovico his legs. Innocent of the ways of the world, yet able to see through any sham or pretense of human behavior. Intensely religious, and yet with a passion for mortal life and its sensual pleasures. Not coquettish, like so many other young women Frank knew, and yet harboring a smoldering allure. All these yoked antinomies of her character and nature made Frank regard her as a marvel, and soon, without intending to, he found himself in love with Restituta Fossombrone.

He broached his feelings just once to her, and received this reply:

"All my energies and attentions are devoted now to Ludovico's healing, Signore Duveneck. But after we succeed, I would not look cruelly away from your kindly face."

Frank had to content himself with that nebulous gesture of future attention. And although in other courtships he had been perhaps impatient and overbold, he found himself charmed to a new placidity.

But really, there was hardly time to play Romeo, for Frank was kept busy much of each day with the preparations for the trip to the Moon.

First, he had been ordered by the Duke to begin sketching angels. This he did by channelling Restituta's verbal descriptions of the creations she had seen (or just imagined?) into lines on the page. This portion of his job (for which he was getting room and board and the promise of a sizable payment in dollars when they returned from the Moon) was very pleasant naturally, for, with Ludovico's help he was able to chat amiably while he sketched. After a week or so, Frank had compiled a large portfolio depicting strange beings—gaunt, attenuated, winged like bats, with faces like holy horses, creatures adapted from Doré's oeuvre—which he presented to the Duke.

"Wonderful! These are brilliant patterns of the vague ghosts I had flitting in my mind from my daughter's accounts. Vivid renderings will be immensely helpful, for we must be able to recognize Restituta's patrons when we arrive on the Moon, to distinguish them from any other races we might encounter."

But aside from employing Frank's artistic skills, Duke Fossombrone also put him to work with a task involving some skilled artisinal labor.

"You will have noticed," said the Duke, "that many hired men are busy about the palazzo, performing certain tasks of construction."

"Indeed," said Frank, who had, to his puzzlement, witnessed a sizable gang of laborers outside the palazzo each day, from dawn to dusk. They appeared to be entrenching around the foundation of the building, as if fashioning a moat, while simultaneously encasing the building in a sturdy frame of timbers anchored to the structural elements of the Ca' d'Oro.

"Perhaps you would care to see an interior modification they have embarked on just this very hour."

"Lead on, Duke."

In one of the big upper-storey loggia that looked out on the Grand Canal, men were curtaining the ornate portals with thick panes of glass, whose seams they sealed with generous stroppings of India rubber. They were also applying the viscous latex substance to all the other joints in the room's ancient construction. Moreover, at either entrance to the loggia, small anterooms were being constructed.

"Looks like you're anticipating a Vermont mud season with those makeshift wardrobes there, Duke."

"Ah, not at all, Frank. We are merely guarding against the intrusion of nothing. Now, come along with me to see some machinery, please."

Perplexed but game, Frank followed the old savant.

A mass of newly delivered wooden crates awaited downstairs. The Duke itemized their contents.

"Here we have a phalanx of Planté lead-acid batteries to store the electrical current generated by these Gramme Dynamos. The Dynamos are hand-cranked, which is another task you can assist at, Frank, as can Ludovico, who possesses very strong arms, as you might have noticed, from shifting his crippled frame about. These two components insure that we will have plenty of voltaic resources to impel the cavourite, and also to power some lighting fixtures. One of my peers, Sir Joseph Swan, has graciously consented to loan me some of his prototype 'incandescents,' as he dubs them And then there is a third use for the electrical current. It will fractionate water into its moieties of oxygen and hydrogen. The oxygen will be released into our sealed loggia as necessary, to replenish what we breathe, while the hydrogen will be compressed and stored in tanks situated around the perimeter of the palazzo. And from these tanks will protrude directional jets.

"All of this invaluable equipment will be situated in the loggia, except for the peripheral holding tanks, of course, which will be controlled from the loggia via very reliable electro-mechanical linkages. Additionally, we will lay in plenty of foodstuffs and beverages, extra garments and bedclothes, a few pistols and some tools. Do these preparations begin to hint at anything to you, Frank? And have you any suggestions to make?"

Frank stared silently at the Duke for a few moments, before breaking into a huge grin. "Well, damn my soul! If you don't put old Columbus in the shade, Duke, I don't know who does! My hat's off to you! I won't even dare to say what I think you have up your sleeve, but if you can pull it off, the world will hail you as a hero."

The Duke grinned modestly, and bowed his head. "A father will dare much for his progeny. And if some new knowledge of the cosmos accrues along with the patriarchal deeds, so much the better."

"I would suggest one thing, though. Heat."

The Duke cogitated. "Hmm, the transmissive properties of the aether, and its density, are unknown quantities. I had thought solar flux might be enough for comfort... But certainly we could add some extra insurance. Very well, I'll write to Sir Swan immediately and see what he can provide! Now, as to your task, which requires a delicacy I cannot demand of the common laborers—"

Down to the lowest level of the palazzo the men went. There Frank saw many bundles of cuprous plates, along with kegs of hide glue.

"Here is all the cavourite in the world, hammered out to its thinnest dimensions consistent with lifting strength. I need you to affix it all evenly to the stone interior walls and and columns, beams and ceiling."

"Not the floor too?"

"No, the floor is extraneous. But elsewhere, the plates must be tightly secured. Can you do this?"

"Why, sure, it's just like sloshing rabbit-skin glue onto a canvas. Let me at it!"

True to his boast, Frank found the process of tiling the basement of the Ca' d'Oro with cavourite to be a trivial, albeit hot and messy one. Shirtless, with heated pots of glue bubbling, he laid down one metal square after another, conforming the pliable sheets to arches and columns alike. As the days progressed, with other work continuing in parallel, the basement of the palazzo came to resemble Peter the Great's famed "Amber Room," a shining sun-colored box.

Restituta came demurely to visit at regular intervals, bringing refreshments and conversation in her improving English. She seemed neither repelled nor distracted by Frank's bare manly chest, rather regarding it as a mere natural phenomenon.

When all the cavourite was in place, a single wire was run from the basement plates (their contiguous conductive surface needed only one point of electrical contact) to the batteries and rheostat controls in the loggia.

And then came the day they had all been working toward: departure for the Moon.

The voyagers had waited deliberately until darkness had descended, bringing with it the anticipated full silvery pockmarked orb high in the heavens, for which they could aim.

The loggia, illuminated by Shaw's incandescents as if a carnival scene, was replete with supplies and equipment and furniture, but still relatively spacious. Even the big tuns of water did not loom too oppressively. Through the glass wall, the gay night life of Venice continued in its immemorial fashion, with passing watercraft arrowing lazily through the canals.

Restituta attended to the electrolysis device that was fractionating the water into useful gases. Seated, Ludovic cranked the handle of a generator to top off the batteries. Duke Fossombrone stood at the master controls. The household's lone servant had been sent away on a contrived errand. A subliminal but real vibration of excitement and expectancy infused the chamber.

"Testing the propulsive jets for the final time now." Muted hissing penetrated the loggia from various points around the palazzo. "All operational. I will now begin to enliven the cavourite."

The Duke slid the rheostat control, and the Ca' d'Oro began to shift and creak, as if in a windstorm. He advanced the control further, and new and louder popping and ripping noises mounted. Still further, and a cataclysmic tumult battered their ears, as the ancient and now weightless palazzo, reinforced by its cage of timbers, but suddenly lacking a bottom to the otherwise intact Amber Room, tore completely loose from terra firma and rose gently into the sky, like a drifting feather in reverse.

The Duke halted their ascent at the height of about forty feet. Despite his expectations, Frank was astonished, his heart beating like a race horse's at the end of the newly inaugurated Kentucky Derby. He looked down at the light-pricked city and, despite the darkness he could see the spot vacated by the Ca' d'Oro filling with water. Astonished gondoliers were falling into the Canal, and bellowing pedestrians pointing upward.

"Goodbye, City of Bridges!" proclaimed the Duke. "We go to build the *ponte di stelle!*"

5. TO THE MOON, AND WHAT AWAITED

The unforeseen nullity of gravity once Earth had been left behind proved merely distracting and awkward for the Duke and Frank. Luckily, they had brought along extensive coils of stout rope of varying gauges. Using some of the lesser-strength stuff, Frank was able to arrange a spider's web of lines that allowed one to maneuver about the loggia with ease, and to anchor oneself at a desired spot. (Of the embarrassingly messy and counter-intuitive chamberpot arrangements, conducted behind a floating folding screen, the less said the better.) Thus Duke Fossombrone could handle the propulsion controls of the flying palazzo without fear of drifting away at a crucial moment, and Frank could tether himself before the windows in order to fulfill his mandate to sketch their voyage.

Not that he needed any lure of wages to make him hasten to fill his pad, pencilling madly and furiously enhancing with pastel colors for hours at a stretch, till he had to be coerced to sleep or eat. What an opportunity this was, one for which any artist would have gladly given his non-facile arm. Had any painter ever been presented with such magnificent vistas before? These incredible and colorful pastures of the heavens, strewn with stars and planets and planetesimals and polychromatic nebulae as thick as daisies, made the subject matter of the vaunted Hudson River School look like a ditch full of rainwater. Not even Thomas Cole had ever achieved such grandeur. If only John and Bill had been able to come along— But they hadn't, and when Frank returned to Earth it was his name alone that would be made. All uncertainty about his future, all world-weariness had vanished amidst these celestial splendors.

But if the lack of weight had proven simply a bit of "weather" for Fossombrone and Duveneck, an irksome aspect of the foreign environment, for Ludovico and Restituta the new condition had proven, respectively, inebriating and estranging.

For Ludovico, the lack of weight endowed him with perfect freedom of movement for the first time since he had sustained his wounds and loss. As if granted wings, he soared about the loggia, laughing and shouting.

"Sister, look at me! I fly like an eagle! Already your perfect faith has blessed me! Even if our mission does not secure me new legs, I will always have had these hours of bliss!"

Thus addressed, Restituta, huddling miserably in a floating chair that threatened to dislodge her with every stray breeze, looking like a scared rabbit in a corner of its warren, and clutching a needlepoint cushion to her bosom, tried to make a suitably positive reply.

"I am so glad, brother. You deserve such release."

Her smile was wan and forced, as if she were trying to manufacture cheer despite some internal upheaval that commanded her true attentions.

Frank had not initially given much concern to Restituta's grim mien, chalking it up simply to natural female timidity and anxiety. But as the trip proceeded with no cause for alarm, and she still refused to brighten up despite all cajoling, he became alarmed for her. Catching her alone in a far corner of the loggia, he spoke frankly to the *jolie laide*, for whom he still retained the largest of affections and hopes.

"Restituta, *cara mio*, what ails you? Aren't you happy that things are going so swimmingly? Thanks to your father's foresight and inventiveness, we are as safe as bugs in a rug while we journey where no man has gone before."

Restituta's large eyes brimmed with tears, but did not quite overspill. Frank thought she had never looked lovelier.

"Yes, Frank, I am proud of father. And of you too. You have both exerted yourself beyond compare in fulfillment of my implausible dreams. But it is those dreams themselves that trouble me. *Le voci degli angeli*— the voices of the angels, which I heard only as a murmur on Earth, have become a swelling chorus in my brain. There is not a minute now when they do not chatter to me. And some of the things they say are—disturbing."

Frank sought to minimize Restituta's worries. In truth, he only half-believed in her angels, placing his faith more in the Duke's natural philosophy. Granting credence to this tale of supernatural beings living on the Moon and able to confer new limbs on Ludovico had been, he was certain, merely a necessary pretext to motivate a more practical and rational venture.

"Don't worry, my darling. I'm sure the angels are just excited finally to have a chance to meet you. If they are indeed angels, then their intentions must be only for our good."

Restituta spoke haltingly. "Yes...yes, I continue to believe that. But it is only that what angels deem good is so much larger and more complex than what mortals understand of that realm. And that infinitude frightens me."

Frank spontaneously clutched the young woman to him in an embrace that sent them both pinwheeling away across the loggia. Ludovico looked up from his cranking of the Gramme Dynamos to smile. The Duke was napping, sending gentle elderly snores into the room.

Frank stole a kiss and whispered, "Have faith, Restituta. This will be a bold tale to tell our children once we are safely home, doddering elders in our seats by the hearthside."

"I would like to believe that, Frank. Truly, I would."

Over subsequent days, Frank continued to hover for most of his waking hours near the windows. The swelling bulk of the Moon provided endless inspiration—to the Duke as well, who employed a telescope upon its silvery face. The limiting factor on Frank's sketching was the intense cold radiating inward from the glass. Despite positioning one of Shaw's electrical heating mechanisms close to him and wrapping himself in a blanket, his hand would often chill and cramp.

The Duke acknowledged Frank's stamina, saying, "What a blessing you hit upon those heaters, son! And to think I was going to put our water supply outside the loggia to save room, and pipe it in. It would have frozen solid, and then where would we have been?"

Frank pictured the rest of the rooms of the Ca' d'Oro, outside their tiny, fragile nest of warmth and air. The ghostly mansion must be a dark and frigid and spectral domain, like Dante's lowest Hell, or some spell-locked castle from a Gothic novel. He shivered at the forceful image.

The Duke had regularly to make steady adjustments in their course, puffing hydrogen this way and that, always seeking to catch up with the Moon not where it currently appeared, but where it would be in its orbit upon their arrival in that region. He relied more on dead reckoning than mathematics. Luckily their supply of hydrogen gas seemed equal to the task.

At last came the day when just a tiny slice of the satellite filled their view, and they hung motionless with respect to the orb.

"Daughter, where shall I land us?"

Restituta was supine, if such a term could apply in the absence of up and down, with her eyes closed and a cold wet cloth laid across her brow and held in place with a limp forearm. Her voice when she spoke was haunted, of a timbre unheard before.

"Move the palazzo slowly around the lunar globe, and I will direct you."

Before too long, Restituta signalled that they hovered over the exact landing spot prefered by the angels. The Duke changed the orientation of the flying mansion, and suddenly for the first time the Moon seemed *below* rather than *ahead*. They began their controlled descent.

The return of some small fraction of their terrestrial weight was accompanied by a soft *crump* of the palazzo settling to the lunar soil. Outside the windows, a cloud of fine argent dust from their landing arose in eerie slow motion unlike any such event on Earth. Light spilling forth from the mansion illuminated a small wedge of pockmarked ground.

Duke Fossombrone uttered the first words of mankind upon another world. "All praise to Isaac Newton, Garibaldi, and the Pope."

Frank swore. "Holy Christ! What I'd give to be outside so I could sketch the sight of a Venetian palace smack dab in the middle of all this starkness. It's more fabulous than anything out of Lane's *One Thousand and One Nights*."

Restituta had joined them mechanically. Dragging himself forward easily along the ropes with leg stubs trailing, Ludovico arrived at the windows also, completeing the quartet. "Lift me up, please, Frank, so I may better see." Frank turned a fallen chair upright and hoisted the cripple into it.

"Your angels, sister! The ones who will help me. Where are they?"

Restituta's voice sounded resigned. "Right before us, brother. Can you not see them?"

Frank said, "But there is nothing—"

And then an unearthly city appeared, as if a painted curtain of false lunar scenery had been instantly whisked away.

Needle-shaped crystal spires of all sizes, warty with random ex-crescenses, thrust toward the black, star-riddled sky. Portions of the structures seemed to spin, and wink into and out of existence. Twinkling pinlights of all hues glimmered from within the towers, as if signalling a convocation of fairies. And outside among the spires the angels cavorted, looking just as Frank had drawn them, employing their big bat wings to dip and curvet, swoop and glide, in whatever strange Selenic atmosphere existed. Their emaciated equine muzzles opened and closed in silent ex-altation.

"The angels want to see me," said Restituta mournfully. "I need to go to them."

The Duke began, "But my dear, please consider—"

Frank said, "Forget it!"

Ludovico said, "Is that truly necessary, sister?"

Ignoring the men, Restituta moved toward one of the capped exit doors. Frank raised a hand to halt her—

—and found himself frozen! Straining with all his might, he still could not budge.

Restituta opened the inner door of the little "mudroom," as full of air as the loggia. She entered the chamber, then closed the door. She must have unlatched the outer door leading into the cold, dark precincts of the palazzo, for an audible *whoosh* of air reverberated through the panels of the mudroom.

Unable even to vent his rage and impotence, Frank felt himself going mad. Then, just at the nadir of his frustration, he lurched forward, released. He took a step or two after Restituta, then was brought up short by the Duke's exclamation of "Look!"

Outside the window, Restituta walked serenely across the lunar soil, the hem of her long skirts stirring up the dust. A transparent nimbus seemed to cloak her. She moved steadily toward the angelic city, and then disappeared within its precincts.

"I'm going after her," said Frank.

"No, my son! You do not know if you could even survive the lunar conditions."

"She did!"

"But," Ludovico said with a mixture of sorrow and fraternal pride, "my sister was always favored of the celestials."

Frank felt he had to do something. "I can't just stand here!"

"Let me pump some air into the portal then."

The Duke did so, and Frank hurried to the exit chamber. He entered, and latched the inner door. Then he opened the outer one.

The air gusting instantly out into the vacuum swept Frank off his feet and carried him willy-nilly to bang his head against the wooden arm of a sofa. He felt hot and cold at once, and struggled to rise. His eyeballs seemed as dry as the dust in an Egyptian tomb. Impossible to think—

Frank awoke lying on a pallet of blankets. He opened his eyes and saw the Duke and Ludovico bending solicitously over him. He tried to speak, but his throat was so raw he could only croak. The Duke gave him a drink of fiery grappa.

"What—what happened?"

"Ludovico was just a second or so behind you. The air pressure inside the loggia, acting against the chamber door with naught but vacuum on the far side, made it incredibly hard to open. But together, we did so. My son was sucked through, and I let the door slam. Apparently, he was able to retain his sensibilities long enough to crawl to you and drag you back. Thank the Lord you had not fallen even further away! Then he even managed to pull the outer door shut before losing his own consciousness, whereupon I could introduce fresh air into the portal. Then I hauled both of you unfortunates inside."

Frank regarded Ludovico, and saw that the young man's face was a map of vacuum-blistered blood vessels. He supposed his own mug looked the same. He gripped Ludovico's mighty bicep with one hand and said, "I owe you my life, brother."

"I learned in battle that one's comrades are as dear as one's self."

Frank got painfully to his feet. "What of Restituta and the angels?"

"Nothing. And yet I—"

Without warning, silent speech filled every niche of Frank's mind. He could tell the others were undergoing identical communications. This must have been what Restituta had experienced unrelentingly throughout the voyage.

"You may leave now," said the majestic voice of an angel. "The one you call Restituta is safe with us, back once more where she belongs."

"No!" shouted Frank. "Duke, pick this place up and drop it on them! We'll rescue her somehow!"

Restituta spoke now in their minds, in a relaxed and gentle tone. "No, Frank, there is no return for me. You can only do yourself harm to cling to what I was. Please, go back to Earth safely now, while you still can. Just remember me in your heart."

Frank lunged toward the controls that would send them aloft and hurtling suicidally into the crystal towers—

The Moon was suddenly below them, and then in the next eyeblink had shrunk to where it filled only a single pane in the array of loggia windows.

The angels had hurled them at least halfway back to Earth.

Frank howled, then started batting the floating objects around him. But all his massless punches could not assuage his grief.

By the time the Earth loomed large, the three men had all reached an emotional and spiritual accomodation, one way or another, with what had happened. Frank had even found it within himself somehow to do a number of sketches of the angelic lunar city, several of which featured Restituta striding toward it like some numinous pilgrim.

But all joy and pride in his drawings had evaporated with the loss of the woman he had loved. (And could he ever love that intensely again?) He knew he would never display his artwork from this incredible voyage, or otherwise advertise his trip. And he suspected the Duke and Ludovico felt the same. The Ca' d'Oro would settle down onto its former foundations and be reintegrated with the city. The scaffolding would come down, the inert cavourite be warehoused, and people would soon forget the day a palazzo had taken off for the stars.

Then they were in the upper atmosphere of Earth, with the Duke at the controls, searching visually for the motherland of Italy where it lay waiting below.

Ludovico had ceased cranking the no-longer-necessary Gramme Dynamos and was scratching at the tied-off ends of his trousers.

"What's the matter?" asked Frank.

"I don't know, but there is a confounded itching on my stumps."

Frank felt bad. "You must have sustained damage there while rescuing me. Probably frostbite or abrasions. And we never checked. Let me look."

Frank unknotted one fabric leg and skinned it back.

Ludovico's stump was no longer a mass of scars and dead cells. The skin gleamed pink and alive, and from the growing surface five perfect embryonic toes poked forth.

ABOUT KAREN COXSWAIN

This was my first story whose initial appearance happened inside an original audiobook, no print incarnation at all (till a subsequent sale). Weird publishing times, man. I even got to visit a professional recording studio and tape an oral introduction to my piece—which I have subsequently never dared to listen to.

I am enamored of the "afterlife fantasy" sub-genre, but had never attempted one before. Recalling Mark Twain's ventures along those lines, and being instructed to start my story with a famous first line of literature, the not totally unxpected results of me channelling Twain's voice occurred.

KAREN COXSWAIN

OR, DEATH AS SHE IS TRULY LIVED

You don't know about me without you have read a book by the name of *The Adventures of Tom Sawyer*; but that ain't no matter. But of course I ain't talking about that pile of YA puke we all got shoved at us in middle school back on Earth, sometime between our first boyband crush and our first sloppy blowjob. The sappy, cornfed book that old Mark wrote in 1876. No, the *Adventures* I'm holding up as a not-totally-authentic introduction to my current life—afterlife, really—is the second one that Mark wrote—here in Hell, just a few years back.

You see, at that time, I had taken a lover onboard the *Ship of Shadows*, my first infernal beau, and after our brief honeymoon our carryings-on soon escalated to such hysterical, fucked-up, window-smashing, curses-bellowing, biting, screaming, flailing, lowblow-throwing melees, followed by makeup sex nearly as destructive and outrageous, that I began to acquire a certain seamy reputation in all the cities we regularly visited, from Beetleburg to Crotchrot. Just imagine, said all the righteously and proudly damned infernal citizens: that nice Karen Coxswain, Captain of the *Shadows*, previously such a respectable gal, consorting with a low-life yeti from Tibet, one who had been moreover the righthand man and mystical advisor to none other than bloody Kublai Khan hisself, and who was plainly now such a bad influence on the previously serene and pleasant Captain. (Khan hisself doesn't actually figure into my story, since he was then living in the city of Scuzzy Ashenhole about forty thousand miles away downriver, far from my stomping grounds.)

What those scandalized citizens didn't realize, however, was that I had never really been anything like a good girl, back when I was alive. Really, if they had thought about it for even a minute, why else would I've ended up in Hell? I had only appeared docile and meek and mild-mannered for the past ten years, since I had been taking that amount of time to more or less mentally adjust to my death and to process my feelings about my new role in the afterlife, the job of ferrying folks from one side of the Styx to t'other, and up and down its blasted, cindery, jizz-bespattered shores.

I'll never forget my entry interview with the Marquis Decarabia, when the stinking old goat (and he was at least half goat, for along with his naked, brick-red, totally ripped human upper half, big as a Cadillac Escalade SUV, went an actual billygoat-style bottom half, and he stunk of garlic, curry powder, lanolin and Axe body spray) discovered that when I had been alive I used to work on a shrimper running out of my hometown, Apalachicola, Florida, often taking the wheel when the Captain got loaded. The *Virgin Berth*, that woulda been, under Skipper Israel Shuby, a fine man, but with a weakness for Jägermeister.

"Why, this is more than splendid!" boomed the Marquis, then belched like a thousand underwater gator-frightening swampgas farts in the deepest Everglades. "Sorry, just had a heavy lunch of banker entrails. Where was I? Oh, yes, your past maritime experience! We're right this minute in need of a cross-Styx pilot, and with the first name of Karen, you're practically destined from birth! We'll get you your 'papers' and you'll be on the water—if you can call that toxic sludge water—before a devil can shake his dick!"

And then, just to illustrate matters, he peed all over me and disposed of the last few droplets across my wet face with a vigorous waggle of his pointy goat member. Luckily, the demon piss tasted just like Kool-Aid. Unluckily, it was the world's worst flavor, Kickin' Kiwi-Lime, endless pitchers of which had been forced on me as a child by a cruel Mama Maybellene at the Home, before the Kool Aid honchos came to their senses and discontinued the raunchy flavor.

So that's how I found myself in my new Hellish job. As I say, it took some getting used to the notion that I was stuck here for all eternity, cruising these cursed waters under a smoldering sky or canopy or cavern roof that looked exactly like that kind of grey Corrections Department toilet paper made from one-hundred-percent re-re-recycled older toilet paper, which had then been used to clean up the butts of one million pureed-spinach-and-mashed-bananas-fed babies. But by the time I finally met my yeti man, I was pretty well accomodated to my new position, and ready to have me some fun.

Did I mention yet that the old horny, hot-headed 'bominable called hisself Tom Sawyer? Yup, that he did. Turns out he had met up with Twain a century ago and become good friends with the writer, glomming onto all Twain's books like Holy Scripture. Apparently, there was some kinda simpatico link between Twain's brand of humor and the typical yeti way of looking at life. So whatever my hairy boyfriend's original furriner Tibetan-Mongol name had been, he was now called Tom. And when I met up with him he used all his borrowed downhome American wit and humor to sweep me plumb off my feet.

And so as that beatup old steamer, *Ship of Shadows*, with its boilers fired by the catalyzed and condensed screams of succubi, plied its slow way up and down its few thousand assigned miles of the Styx, delivering its motley passengers to such stops as Rat's Alley, Bone Palace, Migraine Gulch, Toadlick, Culo de Sciacallo, Twitterville, Clayface, Vuht, and Hernia House, Tom and I conducted our intense bunk-busting affair that veered all over the emotional map, from whispered sweet-nothings to black eyes and bunged-up heads. When we weren't easing along like two Junebugs riding a leaf, all goofy smiles and hand-holding, we just grated on each other like Democrats and Republicans, or weeds and Roundup. I acknowledge I was wound pretty tight and could be kinda demanding, a go-getter with ambitions—whatever that entailed in Hell. Whereas Tom was an easy-going slacker, interested mostly in getting plenty to eat (mostly stray dockside cats, watermelons, Twizzlers and Rusty Humphries Ol' Southern Style Beef Jerky, which I had introduced him to) and scratching his grapefruit-sized balls en route to a long nap. No way we coulda made a longterm go of our mutual thing, and I guess I knew it all along. If that sugar-tongued, Muppet-furred bastard hadn't featured a bone inside his furry ten-inch cock, I woulda ditched him a year sooner than I eventually did.

But by the time we did finally split, our shennanigans, as I hinted at, had become somewhat notorious along both banks of my route, and somewhat inland, toward the Debatable Territories and the Impossible Zone. And that's when Twain decided to put the two of us, thinly disguised and grossly misrepresented, inside his new *Adventures of Tom Sawyer*. (And why the guy half of the romantic duo should've gotten star billing in the novel, I leave up to you to figure out. Men! If they didn't hang together, we could hang them all separately!)

Mark later confessed to me, half apologetically and all puppy-dog-eyed, that he had been in a bind. He was under contract to Hades House to turn in a new novel in less than a month (having frittered away over the course of the past year his advance of 100,000 chancres, mostly on hookers, cigars and gambling at billiards), and he was just plumb dry of ideas. That's when he hit upon fictionalizing the relationship between Tom and me. I must admit, he did a good job, however sensationalized and gossipy it turned out, and he got a bestseller out of the novel, even making enough to gift me a few thousand chancres out of guilt when I needed the dough. (And I mostly always needed the dough.)

So, long story short, that's why I say you probably haven't ever made my acquaintance personally outside the pages of some lurid book. But at the same time, my portrait in those steamy pages being so reality-show, it hardly counts even if you read the thing.

Of course, another way you mighta gotten to know me actually is if you've ridden my scow. But out of all the trillions of creatures in Hell, that number amounts to the tiniest fraction of souls. There's just so many beings in the infernal regions that the chances of any two bumping up against each other is smaller than the odds of me jilling off and cumming just at the exact second a meteor destroys Earth by landing precisely in my busy lap.

Which is why you coulda knocked me over with a feather off the Angel Jegudiel's wings the day I stood at the head of the *Shadows'* boarding plank and saw my big bruiser of an ex-husband, Jad Greenlees, strolling onboard, handsome as a dragon and twice as surly. (And I should know dragons, having had a one-night stand with a Jap one named Uwibami, on the sorrowful rebound from Tom.)

Now, last time I had seen Jad was just about three days before I died. And he had been slightly instrumental in me buying the farm. Maybe even more than slightly. Not that I held it against him anymore, having come to the realization that the fault was truly all mine. Knowing Jad as well as I did back when I was mortal, I shoulda been more careful.

The way it happened was like this.

The *Virgin Berth* was in port for a week, and I had wanted to make a little extra money. My eye was snagged by the Facebook announcement for a Demolition Derby up in Pensacola, at the Five Flags Speedway, just three hours or so down Route 98. I had done Demo Derbies before, and, if I say so, was pretty damn good at them. I figured I had a good shot at taking one of the prizes.

But right that moment, I had no suitable vehicle to enter. So I resolved to get Jad to let me take his old beefed-up Dodge Charger to compete with. It was the least he could do, seeing as how it was my earnings that had paid to kit out the car in the first place. Letting him have the souped-up beater after our divorce had been pure niceness on my part. And I knew he wasn't using it for anything anymore, since he had made some real money and bought hisself a cherry-clean 1985 IROC-Z. So over to Jad's I went.

Standing on the beatup shady porch of Jad's shack, I could hear a lot of instant frantic rustling around inside, in response to my knocking. Not wanting Jad to flush all his merchandise and then blame me, I hollered out through the ripped screen door, "Hey, shithead, it's just me!" The scrabbling and shuffling stopped, there was a whispered conversation featuring a female voice I didn't recognize and a male one I knew too well, and then my former hubby appeared on the far side of the floppy copper mesh.

Jad looked kinda like Magnum, PI—one reason I had first fallen for him—except for considerable extra inches around his middle, a chewed-up ear from a particularly evil bar fight—the same brawl what left a scar kinda like Harry Potter's birthmark on his brow—and a trademark expression of baffled confusion, irritation and suspicion arising from a far-less-than-Advanced-Placement level of intelligence.

Now he scowled. "So it's you."

"Generally I follow mighty close behind my voice, jerkoff."

"Whatta ya want? I'm busy."

"Yeah, I bet. Cutting your coke, no doubt. You're not still using that de-worming shit you stole from the vet, I hope."

Jad had the grace to look embarrassed. "Not since I lost myself several dead customers, no. Made the skin fall right offen them in hunks."

Jad's ramped-up involvement with drug dealing had been the primary reason for our splitting up. I just couldn't reconcile even my sketchy set of ethics with the stuff he was pushing. It had been all right when we first married, and he was only selling grass and Scooby Snacks. But I drew the line when he moved into bath salts and all that other deadly junk.

But all that was in the past, and any hurt or loss I felt for what we had had and thrown away was moderated by an equal sense of relief and freedom at being single again.

I explained my errand to Jad, and he brightened up, obviously relieved that I didn't want any weightier favor. For a moment I could see the fun-loving, easy-going, carefree, considerate guy I had married. Then the woman's voice called out to him to hurry up, and his attitude changed to worry and haste, pissed-offedness and anxiety. I recognized the voice.

"Is that Scamp the Tramp O'Dell in there?"

"So what if it is?"

I shook my head. "Man, Jad, I thought you had more sense and good taste than that. She is ten kinds of nasty layered on top of a heap of meanness. What can you possibly see in her?"

Jad leered. "She fucks like a cageful of tigers getting their first meat after a week's worth of carrots. And she helps me in my job."

There was nothing I could say to that, except to offer up that they truly deserved each other. Jad took it as a compliment. Then he scooted past the door, opening it just slightly as if afraid I might try to sneak inside. But nothing coulda been further from my desires.

We went out to the side yard where the Charger sat on its cinderblock-chocked trailer, covered in leaves and bird poop. I insisted on spraying the car somewhat clean with the garden hose before I took it.

"What's become of you, Jad? You used to love that car and take good care of it. Don't you give a shit about anything anymore except selling drugs?"

"That and pussy. Except not yours. Now, c'mon and hurry. I got things to do."

Burning mad and biting my tongue, I backed my old Ford Ranger up to the trailer and let Jad hitch them up without even getting out of the cab.

And that was my fatal mistake. I shoulda inspected what Jad had done.

Jad fucked up installing the safety chains. First off, they were too heavy a gauge for the load. Then he secured them not to the rig but to the frigging Charger itself! So a few days later, when I was barrelling down Route 98 and the trailer coupling separated from the ball mount on my truck after hitting a bad bump, I suddenly found myself connected to a loose, airborne automobile—the Charger—that had leaped off its runaway trailer, shredding all four tires when it landed. The drag caused my Ranger to career from lane to lane, sideswipe the Jersey barrier, roll over, hit the pillar of a billboard, and explode in a fiery Hellball, sending me straight to my new job as Captain of the *Ship of Shadows*.

For a time I would ask myself if Jad had rigged the setup deliberately to cause my death. But ultimately I figured, Naw, it was just bad luck and circumstances. That trailer was hauling fine till we hit the bump, and there was no way Jad coulda predicted that. It was just sheer hurried incompetence on his part, and lazy inattention on mine. My death had been just fallout from his lameass haste.

So before too long into my infinite stay in these realms, I forgave Jad Greenlees for my death, and even managed to ressurect a few—very few—happy memories of our time together to comfort me occasionally in my daily rounds.

Which is not to say I did not have some mighty conflicted feelings churning inside me as I watched the big bastard climb that gangplank!

For once Jad was not swaggering. In fact, he seemed kinda bummed and stomped-down, looking like a dog what had got its boner knot caught between two fence slats. He wasn't dressed in the usual High Ghetto style he favored. In fact, I recognized the suit he wore as the kinda cheap secondhand clothes Hell handed out to newcomers, sorta like the suit prisoners got back on Earth when they were released. His head hung down and he looked only at his shuffling feet. He didn't even do a doubletake when Humbuzz, my purser, took his ticket. And if you're a human who doesn't jump when you first encounter one of the Bee People of Venus (far as I know, they lived about umpty-ump millions of years before humans even existed), then you're some kinda superman, and Jad was never that.

Once onboard Jad started to head for the ladder down to steerage, so I knew two things: he was traveling some distance, and he truly had no chancres. Nobody rides steerage if they can help it, it's so dismal and stinking, full of screaming ogre babies and their bone-gnawing parents and ignorant Neolithic shitkickers. And most passengers just crossing from one shore to the next like to stay up top and enjoy the hot, clammy, coal- and sulfur-scented breezes, for whatever relief they offer.

I felt so sorry for the boy I stepped right into his path to halt him. He bumped into me, muttered an apology, and tried to sidestep me. But I hailed him by saying, "Hey, Scarface, dontcha have any time for old friends?"

Jad looked up and, with no small effort, his expression changed from grim and glum to bogusly boastful. I almost regretted making myself known. But if he was riding any distance, we woulda come face to face sooner or later anyhow.

Jad's voice sounded rough, as if maybe he had spent the past month of Sundays crying in his beer. "Well, sweetcakes, fancy meeting you here! I thought for sure that your holy ass woulda brung you straight to the Other Place."

"Holy ass only next to *your* sinful carcass. How'd you end up here anyhow?"

"My meth lab blew up."

That figured. Jad had trouble remembering not to nuke his tinfoil-wrapped leftovers. Putting potentially explosive chemicals in his hands was asking for disaster.

"Anybody else screw the pooch with you?"

Jad got crestfallen again. "Just Scamp."

"Oh? How come she's not lovingly by your side right now?"

Now Jad looked mad. "One of these high and mighty demons done stole her from me!"

I got the story from Jad in confused bits and pieces. Seemed like he was still in that period of disorientation and disbelief that hits everyone when they first arrive in Hell, and only evaporates when the damned soul has fully reconciled itself to its fate.

Upon their flindersization, Jad and Scamp's joint entry interview had been conducted by Supreme President and Earl Rampant Glasya-Labolas, one of the mightier potentates of Hell, who outranked my own mentor Marquis Decarabia by about several hundred thousand ass-kissings and ritual face-in-the-mud abasements. Glasya-Labolas' form was that of a giant coondog with rainbow griffin's wings, and he loomed 'bout as big as your average Redneck Riviera McMansion.

Turns out that the Earl Rampant had taken a shine to Scamp the Tramp as new meat, and she had no doubt encouraged the demon in her slutty fashion, once she saw which side of the Hell waffle had the molasses. Glasya-Labolas had done the dirty deed with Scamp right then and there in front of her outraged boyfriend. (Don't ask how a sewer-pipe-sized dog dick fits into a normal-sized human pussy; physics is mighty variable in Hell, not to mention biology.) Jad had been so enraged he had very foolishly attacked Glasya-Labolas, all to no avail of course. Except that Jad had ended up on the demonic shit list.

Glasya-Labolas had flown away with Scamp on his back, to his castle known as Dark Epcot, about nine thousand miles downriver from where the *Shadows* was now docked. And when Jad had recovered himself and tried to fit into the Hell economy the only way he knew how, by drug-dealing, he had discovered that the only job any of the established drug lords would give him was the low-paying one of lookout or mule—quite a comedown from his mortal rank. A few months of that treatment and he had got to feeling lower and lower until about the only thing he could think to do was to voyage to Dark Epcot and apologize to Glasya-Labolas and ask to be forgiven.

This was why had had booked steerage passage on my ship.

Telling his story seemed to alleviate some of Jad's funk, as sharing troubles mostly will, even in Hell. In fact, he began to act like his old cocky self and presume on our prior connection.

"Christ, Karen, you're looking extra damn hot, like some kinda Hollywood *Pirates of the Caribbean* bitch."

I hadn't even thought twice about my outfit, but I realized after Jad commented that it was indeed pretty piratically smoking. I wore a paisley scarf tied around my hair like Little Steven on tour with Bruce. My boobs were covered with a lurex tube top in red, over which I featured an unbuttoned denim vest. My Daisy Dukes left nothing to the imagination, and I wore Vivienne Westwood ankle-high pirate boots. (A girl's got to splurge now and then.)

"Why, I guess that's about as much of a gentlemanly compliment as I could ever expect from you."

I made the mistake of smiling at Jad then, and so he felt obligated or entitled to grab my ass.

That's when I let him have it in the face with my tail.

You should picture about four feet of thick scarlet scaly garden hose, normally coiled up tight to my butt, that ends in an arrow-shaped knob of flesh about as dense as Mike Tyson's fist. I can unfurl that sucker and whip it around faster than a snake. My tail constituted those "papers" Marquis Decarabia had said he was gonna give me as token of my new job.

Jad flew back about ten feet and landed on his ass against a bulkhead. Several of my crewmembers came running. And most of them, even the humans, looked scarier than Humbuzz. They helped Jad up but kept his arms pinned. He looked dazed as a manatee in a marina.

"Humbuzz," I said, "how far does his ticket take him?"

"Fishgrunt only."

I turned to Jad. "That's not even halfway to Dark Epcot. How'd you plan on getting the rest of the way?"

Jad acted properly humble, though I knew he'd be burning up underneath. "I dunno... Work at something, I guess..."

"Well, how'd you like a job as stoker on this ship? Join the Black Gang and work your passage off. I need someone, and the experience might do you good. It's manual labor, but it's not too hard or dirty. And you get to bunk with the crew."

Jad was too dumb to be suspicious of my offer. He musta thought I was just all full of womanly pity.

"Well, okay, I suppose. Gee, thanks, Karen, that's mighty white of you."

"All right then. The boys will take you down and show you the ropes."

As Jad walked off, nursing his jaw, I had to smile again.

The boiler of the *Shadows* ran on condensed succubi screams that came in the form of gleaming silver bricks slick to the touch. Handling one brick was enough to give any male an instant hardon—and stiffen the clit of many a female too. By the end of each shift, after handling hundreds of those bricks, Jad would ache like somebody was amputating his balls with a butterknife.

His only likely partners in relieving his needs, those willing Neolithic and ogre gals in steerage, were going to have no end of Greenlees loving on this voyage.

With Jad squared away, I turned my attention to my duties. We were docked at Scrope, and due to cast off in the next half hour or so, heading cross-Styx for Halfhead. As you can imagine, schedules drift pretty regularly in Hell—demons ain't concerned with making no trains run on time—and ferry passengers come to resign themselves to reaching their destinations at any old hour, happy and satisfied with the service if arrival occurs on the same day promised.

Now, every ferry on the Styx ran a shoelace pattern: scoot diagonally across the murky waters from one settlement or town, shack or city, to the opposite bank's destination, unload and load, then angle off toward a downriver or upriver dock on the shore you had set off from just prior. Every straight mile of travel up or down the Styx was attained only by multiple miles of cross-river churning. The necessity to serve every community, however small, in this zigzag fashion meant a leisurely pace.

But that was fine with me. No pressure, no rush, just piloting *Shadows* lazily under the dirty furnace skies, thinking my thoughts, however elevated or gutter-drenched, watching for snags in the form of behemoth corpses or floating war debris, blowing the big horn to alert smaller craft, steering clear of larger ones, aware all the while that at any moment some subaquatic leviathan outta one mythology or another, flashing six heads, each sporting a mouthful of fangs big as my leg, could breach and threaten to swamp us. Every day brought news of one ferry or another stove in and capsized with greater or lesser loss of life. (Where did the dead and damned go when they died? You *really* don't want to know!) But that's why the *Shadows* boasted some sweet honking deck artillery fore and aft. That, and dealing with local Illustrissimos and Dominions who might've gotten a little too big for their goat bottoms and decided to levy some unfair taxes or kumshaw or fees. My patents from Marquis Decarabia were, document-wise, as powerful as my tail. But some small-pond jokers were just too bag-of-hammers dumb to know when to kowtow without a few hundred 50mm shells from a chaingun upside their heads.

So before much longer we were underway, sluicing through the small floating corpses and frothy fecal scum, plastic soda bottles and slicks of glowing chemicals, maneuvering just like a bottom-heavy mechanical swan paddling through a tub full of acid-wash and tie-dye colors and jeans.

Darkness never really falls in Hell, but most creatures operate on some kinda wake-and-sleep cycle that approximates Earthly days and nights. So by the time we had gone from Scrope to Halfhead, and then back across to Shriektown, it was getting on toward the end of my working day. I gave the orders to tie up for the night, made sure a watch was posted, checked that our new cargo of Trojans, gin, pineapples and roofing nails was secured, and retreated to my cabin.

On the way to my rest, I thought I heard wild yowls betokening sexual release of a mixed appreciative and flinching nature wafting up from steerage. Among the grunts and bellows and hollerings was a certain species of mating call I had come to know intimately, from being pressed beneath their source back in Apalachicola. I think my grin lit up a circle of deck planks around me.

Lying in bed on my belly (I do miss sleeping on my backside), I thought how much fun I could have accompanying Jad all the way down to Dark Epcot and witnessing his meeting with Supreme President and Earl Rampant Glasya-Labolas. My usual run of the Styx didn't extend so far, but us Captains were always swapping routes just to liven up infinity a bit, and I had no doubt I could bring the *Shadows* all the way to Dark Epcot. As sleep overtook me, I made the decision to do it.

So the next day I announced my new plans to the crew, and got a variety of reactions ranging from plain old "who-gives-a-fuck-why-are-you-even-bothering-to-tell-me-this?" to "way-awesome-dude!" None of the swabbies objected, since one quiet spot in Hell for their labors was as good as any other to them, they being mostly rootless, non-family types who had chosen this way of life precisely for its permanent migratory nature. And in fact, two thousand of the nine thousand miles to Dark Epcot were familiar territory, my last regular stop being Saliva Tree Hill.

The river beyond that, natch, was an unknown quantity to me. But how different could it be? I thought.

Jad of course stood assembled with the other hands to hear the message, and, having had one taste of my double-edged "favors," mustered up enough wits to look dubious at this large-hearted gesture. He hung back when the crew dispersed, so's he could pester me with his questions. He kept rubbing his crotch like some hip-hop star, and I almost took offense until I realized it was an unconscious reaction to being sore.

"So, uh, Karen, why the change in plans? You figure maybe that once I'm on the good side of that pissant demon canary-dog I can repay you somehow? Is that it?"

"That's exactly it, Jad." Some evil whim shaped my next words—not too uncommon a perverse happening here in Hell. "But I'm actually holding out for even more. I think you can kick Glasya-Labolas' butt and take his place."

This was exactly the kind of impossible ego-boosting bullshit Jad was primed to accept at face value. After all, his default inclination was to picture himself as the magnificent, alpha-dog center of the universe wherever he happened to be, on Earth or in Hell. That notion had just taken a little posthumous beatdown, but it was plainly bubbling under, ready to be stroked and revived.

"You really think so?" The agreeable idea took hold of Jad's whole brain, which was a process like a rising creek spilling over into a shallow ditch. "Yeah, what's that Glassy-assed Labia Lips got that I ain't got! After I learn the ropes here a little more, I can beat him at his own game, and get Scamp back. Gee, thanks, Karen, you showed me the light."

Jad limped off for his stint in the Black Gang, and I shook my head in amazement and took my own place in the pilothouse.

The next several months went by in regular, business-like fashion, as the *Shadows* slipped greasily down the Styx, from one steamy, heaving, maggot-mound burg to another. Pinchbottom, Gallbreath, Cracked Moon, Furnace Heart, Zezao, Outcast Flats, Gringo Guts, Bloody Albion, Sidereal City, Nopalgarth....

Pardon me if I get downright poetic for a minute. The lack of any kind of weather or heavenly bodies (ha!) contributed to a timeless and uniform existence, filled with an endless cycle of deeds and thoughts, just variable enough to foster some sense of living. The routine daily rituals of piloting. The steady stream of embarking and disembarking weird chittering, crawling, gesticulating passengers, so that the gangplank seemed at times like a conveyor belt with its source in some crazy deity's fevered brain and its outlet in some universal maw of destruction—which pretty much described matters as they actually stood. The occasional bouts of shore leave, when me and my crew gambled, got drunk, got laid and lost all our chancres, not necessarily in that order. The continuous transhipment of stuff, stuff, stuff, so that sometime it seemed like the hold of the *Shadows* held merely X number of stationary pallets whose transient contents morphed like a mirage.

Such was life in Hell, a hazy, lazy, crazy, dazed damnation.

About the most you can reliably say is, shit happened.

So before you knew it we were down to the outpost at the end of my usual reach, Saliva Tree Hill. About the only incident that really stood out in my memory of that time was when we carried two bounty hunters for a few hundred miles, until they caught up with their quarry.

At the dock at Cornhole two beings came on board and sought me out to present their credentials. They called themselves Coffin Ed and Grave Digger Jones, after two human detectives outta some books by a guy named Hymie or something. Coffin Ed was pretty much a crayfish as big as a man with some kinda helper seaweed and clams attached all over him. He walked upright on his tail somehow. I didn't care to look too closely. Grave Digger Jones looked like some critters I saw in a comic book my nephew Cooter showed me once: stone men from outer space, fighting that long-haired guy with the hammer. Grave Digger did the talking cuz I'm not sure Coffin Ed could.

"Captain Karen, your gentleness, we are seeking a miscreant named Brian Passwater. We have reason to believe he is hiding downriver from Cornhole. Travel by your vessel will allow us to search for him circumspectly and relatively swiftly, as opposed to making arduous and flashy quarry-alerting peregrinations by land, up one shore only. Will you accept payment for our indefinite passage?"

"Well, lemme think a minute. How long you gonna take in each port? I can't screw up my schedule too-too much."

"No time at all, practically speaking. Coffin Ed has very acute and instant remote sensory abilities."

The big crayfish bowed toward me and waggled his antennas significantly.

"Well, okay, I guess. But I can't change my circuit to bring this perp back up here to Cornhole for justice, once you catch him."

"Do not trouble yourself over justice, Captain Karen. We are equipped and authorized to dispense it *in situ.*"

Coffin Ed clacked his big serrated claws like castanets. Probably a lotta good eating in those grabbers, I thought, but I for one did not intend to get near enough to learn for sure.

So for a week or three the two bounty hunters stood like some kinda figureheads at the prow of the *Shadows,* a half circle of deferential private space always surrounding them, no matter how crowded the ship got, silent and unmoving until we approached land. Then Coffin Ed's antennas would start thrumming and vibrating like Butch Robins' banjo strings. Once or twice they got an interesting reading and went ashore while I waited, but they always came back empty-handed. Until we hit the metropolis of Crocodile Crater. Then, with Coffin Ed's crayfish deelyboppers vibrating too fast to see they raced off into the twisty rubbish streets of the city before the gangplank was even firmly lashed down.

They returned just as I was getting ready to leave them behind, and in fact they were done with my services and only wanted to say thank you and goodbye. In his big pebbly paw, Grave Digger Jones was carrying a double-layered paper shopping bag that showed the store logo for the Hell branch of Whole Foods: a radioactively glowing tomacco fruit. The bag was dripping, and one of Coffin Ed's lethal pinchers was smeared the same color as the drippage.

"Captain Karen, we wish to inform you of the success of our venture, and hope that the unutilized chancre-redeemable portion of our tickets will serve as sufficient emblem of our gratitude."

"Uh, sure, right, boys… Happy hunting!"

I never did learn what crime poor Brian Passwater was guilty of. Probably not something really major, like offending one of the Lords of Hell. That would've brought a more vicious supernatural punishment. He musta just got on the wrong side of some powerful Hell citizen, one probably involved in some less savory line of business.

Like I say, that was pretty much the most exciting thing that happened in two thousand miles of travel. And as we pulled into Saliva Tree Hill, I wondered if the rest of the journey would be as boring. But we wouldn't begin to find out until tomorrow, because we had to wait for the arrival of Captain Nance Piebald and his ferry, *Satan's Inglorious Rapture*, in order to swap routes.

That night I had a confab with Jad. I had to say I was mighty impressed, despite our past track record of mutual hostility and incomprehension, with his new look and attitude. Work in the Black Gang had trimmed off all his excess poundage and muscled him up plenty. He seemed more self-assured and even a whit more considerate of others. I was guessing that maybe some ogre gal had objected to aspects of his callous and selfish lovemaking and undertaken to teach him some manners and perhaps even the meaning of the word "foreplay." In fact, I detected a hickey on his neck exhibiting the unique tusk patterns of that species of female. Half of my objections to Jad as a husband had been to his egotism and unthinking brute ways, and those seem to have been smoothed off, making him a halfway attractive prospect again. Of course, as I soon learned, there had been no alteration in his intelligence or tastes, which were fixed solid as the Mason-Dixon line.

"So, Jad, we've come two thousand miles so far, with another seven to go. You had any change of heart during all that time? Maybe fancy sticking on as a member of my crew? It's not a bad ol' life, is it? Why not give up Scamp and the notion of hitting back at Glasya-Labolas?"

"Nuh-huh! That jumped-up cocker spaniel has it coming to him, and I'm just the bangtail roarer to hand him his head on a platter!"

I pondered telling Jad about some of the more excruciating tortures that the Lords of Hell reserved for upstarts like him, but his next words decided me against handing out such sensible advice.

"Besides, I want Scamp in my arms again. She is the only woman for me. She's always stood by me, and she is the best piece of tail on Earth or in Hell. That girl could peel the skin off a cucumber with that educated pussy of hers."

I blew up. "Stood by you! She ran off with the first demon she saw!"

"I been thinking hard on that. I'm sure she did it just to protect me. After all, the Earl Rampant musta known from my Earthly career how threatening I was gonna be to him, once I got my feet on the ground here. She sensed I was in danger, and so she sacrificed herself to divert him, and now she's just waiting for me to come rescue her."

I threw my hands up into the air. "You're just impossible! Go back to your green-skinned bilge trolls, you asshole!"

Jad grinned. "Sounds to me like somebody's not getting laid regular. Maybe you can get your hands on some incubi ingots."

He left laughing and I went fuming to bed.

Nance Piebald and I had met once before, but his appearance always knocked me out. A pure African black dude from some vanished kingdom called Opar, a smidgen over seven feet tall, he suffered from that disease what Michael Jackson always claimed he had, where his skin was patchy all over, fishbelly against coal. He proudly wore his native costume, which left most of his appaloosa acreage exposed, so's you could hardly miss his condition.

We shook hands at a grog shop named Ginza Joe's right on the dock at Saliva Tree Hill. Over a regular Johnstown Flood of Mount Etna Lava shots with Black Ram Ale chasers, we caught each other up on our respective beats.

"You'll want to be careful downriver from Dumpster Town," said Nance. "Prince Malphas and Queen Onoskelis are at war again."

I shuddered at that. The domains of Malphas and Onoskelis sat directly opposite each other on the Styx, and the rulers were given to lobbing bundles of flaming typhoid victims and other less pleasant material at each other's burgs, whenever they got their Irish up. Getting past them intact would be a bitch.

"Well," I said, "just have to try some of my best broken-field sailing under a flag of truce."

"Perhaps they will have ceased hostilities by the time you arrive. They are over three thousand miles away from here, after all."

"Anything else I should know?"

"There have been several incidents involving Typhon and Echidna near Hooftscarrow. It is believed the pair were mating on the river bottom—or perhaps just shifting in their sleep. Several ferries lost."

"Oh, well, we all gotta go sometime."

Nance and I clinked glasses, and then parted to assume each other's routes.

Now, to be sure, I'd like to fill up the rest of my story with all the many scary and funny and creepy and boring stuff that happened to me and the *Shadows* on our seven-thousand-mile journey downriver. But truth be told, none of it was very exceptional or interesting, at least by Hell standards. The voyage had that same kinda not-all-there quality I described earlier, like a dream of a dream. And if I've learned one thing from my friendship with Mark Twain, it's to cut to the chase.

So we steamed past Malphas and Onoskelis with no worse damage than a busted smokestack that intercepted a missile of frozen demon shit, and rode the tsunami caused by Typhon's buggery of Echidna for a quick thousand mile surfer's shortcut, and dealt with a hundred-hundred other happenings, morbid, dumb and funny. And before you knew it, we were tieing up at Dark Epcot.

Glasya-Labolas had been particularly taken with the philosophizing of Walt Disney when they met, and so had remodeled his domain along the lines of Disney's theme park. But whereas the Earthly Epcot featured pint-sized models of famous landmarks, Dark Epcot boasted recreations of famous Hell landmarks that were even *bigger* than the originals, to testify to the President Supreme's exalted status and cheese off his rivals.

Paimon's Pit of Perverted Passions. The Ninety-Nine Gibbets of Ninurta. Haagenti's Mansion of Horrors. Trump Palace. Stolos' Kitchen. Furfur's Arcade of Screaming Souls. Ziminiar's Car Wash. Okay, I know that last one might not sound so deserving of being immortalized, but take my word for it: the original was one *Hell* of a car wash!

With an enormous frontage, the domain stretched for hundreds of miles backwards from the Styx, like some kind of demonic Washington, DC: all monuments, all the time, with thousands of citizens being screwed every minute.

Jad and I walked up to one of the gates of Dark Epcot. I had instructed my second-in-command, Cheb Moussa, to leave with the *Shadows* if I didn't come back in 24 hours. I figured my chances as a simple observer of escaping the shit that was gonna fall on Jad's head were slightly better than even. Jad's odds for survival I pegged at about a trillion to one.

My ex carried one of the smaller pieces of artillery from the ferry in his arms, looking like some kinda Redneck Rambo. He kept tripping over the dangling ammunition belt, and eventually I just picked up the end of the sucker and carried it like the train of a bridal gown.

"You sure you wanna go ahead with this now?"

Sweat covered Jad's brow like brine on a freshly netted shrimp. I had to give him points for courage. If only he weren't so damn stupid and self-centered.

"I'm totally sure. What's left for me in Hell if I can't get Scamp and my pride back?"

"Okay, then, it's your second funeral."

I banged on the big riveted iron door, tall as two Nance Piebalds, one atop the other. In less than a second it swung open, and we marched in.

We were met by the most metrosexual demon I have ever seen. He wore Topsiders, skinny-leg designer jeans and a pink polo shirt that musta cost about seven hundred chancres together. He had even threaded his eyebrows, an elegant look that was marred only by the enormous pus-filled carbuncles covering every inch of his face and neck.

"Welcome to Dark Epcot. My name is Andras, but just call me Andy. You're expected, so if you'll be so good as to just follow me… Oh, you can check your weapon with Shary over there."

A smiling human woman stood behind the counter of a large open booth. Behind her were scores of cubbies, mostly empty but some stuffed with weapons.

"Better do what he says, Jad."

Kinda flustered by this pleasant reception, Jad stowed his gun with Shary and got a claim ticket in return. Shary hoisted the huge weapon with one hand, and I was glad we hadn't messed with her.

Andy walked off at a guide's measured pace, leaving us to follow. The streets of Dark Epcot were filled with bustling minions, imps and elementals, as well as smiling tourist families. We strolled past one ginormous structure after another. I only recognized a few, chief of which was Vassago's Chamber of Excruciations. Man, you have never *seen* so many Stairmasters in one place!

Eventually we got to what could only be Glasya-Labolas' personal castle, judging by the number of spiked head adorning its walls. Many of the trophies were still talking and weeping, bitching about their fate.

Andy brought us right inside, past all the minor Lords and guards and attendants and plain-clothes security types, and before you could say "The pain of his reign stays mainly in the brain," we were left unaccompanied in the Throne Room.

Glasya-Labolas' Throne Room was about as big as Tropicana Field in St. Pete, where the Devil Rays played. At the center of it loomed the President Supreme and Earl Rampant's mighty chair, a seat made all outta bones and sinews. I could suss out Glasya-Labolas, sitting down with his big griffin's wings enfolding him like a cloak.

Gulping down our scanty spit, Jad and I walked forward.

When we had gotten to within an easy field goal's distance of the Throne, Glasya-Labolas unfolded his wings and stood up, rearing what seemed like miles high above us, and I wondered how he'd gotten so big.

Except it wasn't Glasya-Labolas, it was Scamp!

Now I have to admit, all hatred and jealousy aside, back on Earth Scamp the Tramp O'Dell had been one hot mess. Big rack, skinny waist, long legs. Hair black as a crow, heart-shaped face. Eyes that were always daring men to come after her, and challenging women to outclass her. She'd try anything once, then a few more times just to be sure she had the knack of the trick. When I knew her, she was intent on climbing to the top of any heap she happened to find herself in.

Occupying Glasya-Labolas' Throne, a jaybird-naked Scamp at fifty times her standard size looked pretty much the same as she had on Earth.

Except that her knobbly skin was a dozen shades of putrid green, like something you'd find at the back of your fridge, and her nipples had eyes. She sported a mouthful of giant fangs, long thick claws on fingers and toes, a tail that put mine to shame, and gnarly bat wings with the span of what you'd expect on a 747.

When she talked it nearly made my ears bleed.

"JAD! YOU LAZY FUCKER! WHAT TOOK YOU SO LONG?"

Jad's jawbone was clacking against his collarbone, and a string of drool crept out one corner of his mouth.

"Uh, I came fast as I could, Scamp. Where—where's Gla-gla-Gla-sya…?"

Scamp's shriek of laughter made the dome of the Throne Room rain down cement dust.

"OH, I KEEP HIM CLOSE BY SINCE I TOOK OVER! LEMME SHOW YOU!"

I don't get grossed out that easy. But when Scamp reached down into her furry crotch and pulled Glasya-Labolas outta her twat like a tampon, I came nigh to puking.

Scamp swung the soggy comatose demon by his tail like a pendulum.

"COME JOIN ME, JAD! I GOT AN OPENING JUST FOR YOU!"

It's plumb amazing what tricks an abused memory can play on a person. How we got back to the *Shadows* I cannot say, right up to this day. I was bloody, covered with welts and scratches, and had lost most of my clothes. But I was still alive. Or after-alive.

And there was Jad beside me, in a similar condition.

I guess Scamp really couldn't be bothered with such small fry as us, given her new exalted rank.

After we had partially recovered our wits and gotten cleaned up and launched the ferry away from Dark Epcot, with Cheb Moussa at the helm, Jad and I sat on two deck chairs partaking of some well-deserved drinks.

"What next?" asked Jad.

"The Styx is a mighty big river, dude. Let's just see what's round the bend."

ABOUT PORTRAIT OF THE ARTIST AS A YOUNG CHIMERA

This story is short enough that I can try something a little different in this volume with it. First I am going to present the original draft, and then the published version, after editorial changes. I can see why the changes were made, especially after my kindly editor stated his reasons very clearly and explicitly. But I still think my verion is a better story!
Your feedback solicited.

PORTRAIT OF THE ARTIST
AS A YOUNG CHIMERA

For a number of reasons, I felt nervous going into my interview with Stephanie Leduke, the social worker from the Chimera Reassignment Bureau (a branch of the Chimera Welfare Agency, which was a branch of the federal Department of Health and Sophont Services). Both my stomachs were rumbling like the Yellowstone Supervolcano just before it blew.

First, like every chimera on the Island of Misfit Toys, I was facing the scary prospect of manumission and full citizenship. How I would live up to the responsibilities and privileges of this exalted new status were all unknown. I had been mere property for all my short life till now—and abandoned property at that!

Second, I was hyperconscious of my appearance. When it had been just us chimeras on the island, weird was the norm. But as soon as the humans showed up—we had never seen them on a regular basis before, with airdrops of supplies being the rule—I instantly realized how far my looks deviated from the baseline of humanity. Even among my fellows, I was a bit of a freak.

My face, furred in an attractive palomino like the rest of me, featured eyes proportionately as big as those of a tarsier. Lots of the remaining facial real estate was dominated by a prehensile snout like a tapir's. I sported enormous fangs, even though I was a herbivore. Tall ears like a jackrabbit's erupted from my noggin. (One had a sexy fold at the tip—or so the crumple had been deemed by my last lover.) My very expressive tail forked three-quarters of the way along its hyperarticulated length. But my worst feature, in light of my fanciful career ambitions, were my hands. They were just big mitten-like paws resembling a leopard's, no more capable of delicate manipulations than the pincers of an ore-crushing robot.

Seated now in the former recreational facility of the island, with many of my fellow products tailored by irresponsible DIY synthbio hackers, I despaired of being understood, admired, or of ever being able to attain my dreams.

My black funk was broken by a small bot calling my name and ushering me into Ms. Leduke's office (the former boardgame storage closet). In the tight quarters I could smell my own musky odor. But young and pretty Ms. Leduke, bless her, made no notice of it, not even a wrinkled nose, but instead stood up with a big smile on her face and shook my hand.

"Nibbles," she said, "I'm here to inform you of your new rights and duties, and to enroll you in various governmental and charitable programs designed to help you make the transition to productive citizenship."

She read me the full text of the Presidential Chimera Emancipation Proclamation—which of course I had practically already memorized—pinch-poked and swiped through several AR presentations with me, and then, finally, asked the question I had been dreading.

"So, Nibbles—um, you do know that you may legally change your name now too?—what type of career do you envsion for yourself, given your aptitudes?"

"Ms. Leduke, I want to be a painter!"

"A house painter? Well, that's mostly a job for bots—"

"No, an artist! Like Picasso or Wyeth or Schorr! I know I can do it! It's something in my neural biobricks. I see the paintings in my head, all day and all night! Such colors, such compositions! I've studied art history for so long, it's all that interests me. But then, there's these!"

I held up my clumsy blunt paws.

Ms. Leduke looked dubious, but not without hope. "Well, there *is* a program for surgical modifications of pre-existing detrimental conditions…. Let's get a workup on your physiology and genome first."

I left her office so happy. But when the report came back after I saw Dr. Stoltz and his team, all my dreams crumbled.

Ms. Leduke was angry and appalled. "Nibbles, according to this, you shouldn't even be alive! Your cells exhibit about six different suites of synthetic amino acids, arrayed in triple-helix form, with a dozen different encoding and transcription systems. Your ribosomes are twice as complex as baseline ones, and you have not one, not two, but three enteric nervous systems, as well as distributed ganglia galore! The experts say that any kind of standard hand transplant would be rejected immediately."

"There's no hope then," I moaned, venting a loud honk through my snout.

Ms. Leduke's face assumed the steely-eyed, determined expression of the lead soldier in Frederic Remington's "The Cavalry Charge."

"Don't give up so fast, Nibbles! If we can track down your geppetto…"

"But he cast me off soon after he made me and tired of me! I don't even know his name!"

"That's all right. We have forensic experts who can follow the tiniest clue you can recall."

So I went to work with the CSI people, and they fanned out into the big wide world, looking for my maker. Finally, when I was the last chimera left on the Island of Misfit Toys, and just about to abandon all hopes, they found him! His name was Samnang Yim, and he lived in Bandung, Indonesia, where his respectable dayjob was engineering mycoplasmic logic circuits. But his dodgy nighttime hobby was creating creatures like me.

Our reunion took place in the NIH Clinical Center in Maryland. I went in shaking and scared, but swiftly became angry. Samnang Yim had no guilt or remorse for making me. All he did was size me up with a cool look, then say, "Those ears! What could I have been thinking! I do still like the paws, though. Shame they have to go. But yeah, sure, I can swap them out for hands."

His guards conducted Samnang Yim away before I could conjure up a comeback. But my anger soon dissipated. I was going to have hands!

I woke up after the surgery to find that my new hands blended nicely with the rest of my heterogenous appearance. Not precisely human—I think they were modeled on raccoon paws—but delicate enough to hold a brush and palette!

Now, on the eve of my first solo show at the LeVine Gallery in New York, under the proudly retained name of Nibbles, I look back at those uncertain days with almost a kind of fondness. Who could have guessed then that Ms. LeDuke—dearest Stephanie—would ever have consented to pose for my acclaimed fanciful portrait, "Naked Maja—With Horns," already sold before the premiere for more than Samnang Yim makes in a year!

ABOUT MODIFIED IS
THE NEW NORMAL

And now, redacted for your consideration.

MODIFIED IS THE NEW NORMAL

HOW I TRANSCENDED THE BASELINE FOR ART'S SAKE.

I was on edge going into my interview with the social worker from the Chimera Reassignment Bureau (a branch of the Chimera Welfare Agency, in turn a branch of the Department of Health and Sophont Services). Like every chimera on the Island of Enhanced Sapiens, I now faced the prospect of manumission and full citizenship. Unknown was how I would live up to my new responsibilities and privileges, considering I had been property (by law) my entire life—abandoned property at that.

I was hyperconscious of my appearance, especially around the normals. When it had been just us chimeras on the island, it was the normals who we would have seen as weird. But as soon as they showed up—we rarely saw them before, with supplies dropped in by parachute—I realized how far my looks deviated from the baseline. Even among my fellows, in all their variety, I was unusual.

My face, covered in fur, like the rest of me, featured eyes proportionately as wide and alert as those of a tarsier, with enhanced night vision, by intentional geno-pheno design. Much of the remaining facial area was dominated by a prehensile snout as pointy as a tapir's. I sported fangs, even though I was a herbivore, also by design. Tall supersensitive omnidirectional ears like a jackrabbit's sprouted from somewhere above my eyes. My expressive tail forked three-quarters of the way along its hyperarticulated length, the better to dangle from tree limbs when picking fruit, also by design. However, by far my most distinctive (and problematic) feature, in light of my personal ambition, were my hands, which were really just big paws, like a leopard's, no more capable of delicate manipulation than the pincers of one of the mindless bots crushing ore in the pits on the island.

Seated now in the island's former recreational facility, surrounded by fellow "enhanced" sapiens, all clearly rendered by undisciplined bio synth hackers, despite their professional certification, I despaired of ever being understood or achieving my dream of producing art on canvas through a brush or on screen through code.

My funk was lifted a bit by the sound of a small springy one-wheeled bot calling my name and ushering me into an office. In the tight quarters I could smell my own musk, despite it being bioengineered to overcome any potential social revulsion, especially among the normals. The social worker took no notice, not even a wrinkled nose, standing instead to shake my hands, such as they were.

"Nibbles," she said, "I'm here to spell out your new rights and responsibilities and enroll you in the programs that will help you transition to productive citizenship among the normal population." That is, they'll ignore you, I thought, mercifully.

She read me the text of the National Chimera Emancipation Act—I had read it myself a hundred times already—pinch-poked and swiped through several AR presentations with me, then, finally, asked the question I had been dreading:

"So, Nibbles, what type of career and gainful employment do you see for yourself, given your aptitudes?"

"I want to be a painter," I said firmly.

"You mean houses?," she said, "but that's a job for bots—"

"No, like a real artist, like Picasso or Wyeth or Schorr. It's already programmed into my synthetic neural circuits, awaiting activation all this time. I *see* the image *before* brush touches canvas. Such colors, such compositions. But, there are these…" I held up my paws.

She looked dubious though not without hope. "Well, under law, we do provide surgical modification of pre-existing conditions. But first let's analyze your genome and physiology."

Some hours later, seeing the Department's report, my dreams crumbled.

"According to the report," the social worker announced, "you shouldn't even be alive. Your cells exhibit six different suites of synthetic amino acids, arrayed in triple-helix form, with a dozen encoding and transcription systems. Your ribosomes are twice as complex as baseline standards, and you have not one but three enteric nervous systems, not to mention multiple distributed ganglia. The geneticists say any kind of hand transplant would be rejected, no matter what kind of immunosuppressive therapy you might use."

"There's no hope then?" I said, venting a modest honk from my sniffling snout.

Her face assumed the determined expression of the lead soldier in Frederic Remington's "The Cavalry Charge." "Not so fast, Nibbles. Perhaps we can track down your original bioengineer…"

"But," I said, "he lost interest in me the moment he consigned me to the administrators. I don't even know his name."

"Leave it to the forensic analysts," she said. "They're quite capable of following any bio or neurological clue, even those in your deepest synthetic unconscious."

* * * *

Some weeks later, they located him at his day job creating mycoplasmic logic circuits for the mycoplasma genome. However, his hobby was and always would be creating synths like me.

Our reunion was in the island's Clinical Center where my fear turned to anger. He showed no remorse for making me the way he did or for sending me away. He said only, "Those ears. What could I have been thinking? I do like the paws, though. Shame they have to go."

But, but… that means I can have hands.

I woke after the surgery to find my new ones blending nicely with the rest of my cobbled appearance. Not quite human—a raccoon would be proud—but refined enough to hold a brush and palette, of proper scale.

Now, on the eve of my first solo show, I, humble Nibbles, view my early despair with mixed feelings. Who would have guessed the social worker would consent to pose for my now-acclaimed portrait, "Naked Maja—With Horns," already sold for more than my own peripatetic bioengineer makes even in a good year.

ABOUT THE MOOD ROOM

And here is my third conference-inspired tale, created for the marvelous Fractal festival in Colombia, to which I was invited by the super-creative organizers, Hernan Ortiz and Vivi Trujillo. (Later, I would insert both of them into a story written after my trip. But not this one, created before we had ever met.) Again, I got to present it live, was taped, and later went on to precisely zero internet fame.

THE MOOD ROOM

Hello! Come right on in! Yes, I'm Val Hallogren, only human within two AUs in all directions. Thanks for dropping by. Nice to see some folks in the flesh for a change—baseline or otherwise! Just leave your suits by the vacuum brane. Oh, they don't come off? Permanently bonded? That's a new one on me. Guess I've been out of the noetic cloud for longer then I realized. What, you don't even call it the "noetic cloud" anymore? It's the "emergent heliotect?" So things are changing even faster than when I was young, way back in the first quarter of the 21st century.

Let me just tweak the room parms to make things a little more Earth-like for you. Not everyone appreciates "Propane Rain on Titan."

Man, I love these baseline surf sounds and the ocean smells and the August sunlight! But I don't use them too often. I could find myself all too easily living exclusively in the past. There, feeling comfortable? The effect's a little too twentieth-century unmediated? You feel naked to the "killersphere?" Let me dial it back a bit. How's that? Fine! Let's talk!

You told me you wanted to hear some of my recollections face to face, focusing on one incident in particular. I suppose it concerns my work at Disney-MIT. That was really the apex of my career. I was part of the team that designed and built the first Mood Room, way back in 2021, nearly seventy-five years ago. You won't find my name on any of the patents or in the media coverage—I was just a programmer. But I like to think that my work contributed a lot to the success of the project.

Of course, one bug in my code did nearly lead to a real disaster. I almost killed our two core visionaries before we could even launch our product! That would have sucked, wasting years of my life. But we escaped by the hairs on two bare asses—literally—and no lasting harm was done.

This all happened of course before Disney-MIT bought us out. After they took over, we had all the glitch-hunting software we could use, more debugging power than a Monsanto-backed agronomist fighting superlocusts. But the original project was very much a garage-band, *Maker*-style affair, just five or seven of us in an old repurposed Kodak factory in Rochester, New York. We called our startup Total Immersive Environments, or TIE, and our goal was to build an artificial-reality chamber responsive to the user's thoughts. Kinda like Bradbury's "The Veldt," right? You don't know Bradbury? They burnt all his books? Ha! You had me going there for a minute.

Okay, massive chutzpah on our part, right? But that was our dream, and we thought we had success well within our sights.

Let's look at the two halves of the whole equation we had to solve.

The mind-reading tech was basically off-the-shelf stuff, jazzed-up a bit. Just your standard XfMRI kit, the same rig that Stephen Hawking used at the time to control his personal exoskeleton. How's he doing these days, by the way? Eternal Distributed King of the Kuiper Belt? Good for him! But back to our primitive mind-reading rig.

The XfMRI equipment could not, of course, interpret actual stream-of-consciousness-type thoughtforms. There was no way at that point that you could get it to scan your neural activity and verbalize what you were thinking. "Man, what a great steak!" or "Wow, what a hot babe!" or "I wish I didn't have to get up so early." No, all it could do was identify with pretty good accuracy the broader brainwave patterns that indicated, say, "Make a fist" or "Lift right leg." That's how Hawking used it to drive his mecha.

But our gang had tweaked the kit to register moods and emotions as well, with some keen discernment. Those wordless states proved to be very consistently readable across all humans.

So, that was half of our Total Immersive Environment, the less radical half. The really cool part was the room itself—the Mood Room, as it came to be called.

Picture a big tough flexible sphere suspended in a cradle of omni-directional actuators, kinda like a ball being massaged by hundreds of robot arms and fingertips that could push and pull and shake and stretch and tilt and rock and spin the held object. Neat, huh? The spherical outer sheath was an inert weave of spidersilk and Kevlar, infinitely deformable. But the inner surface of the hollow ball—the Mood Room itself—was revolutionary. It was a proprietary substance we called Active Living Display.

The substrate for the ALD was an animal epidermal culture gridded with Organic Light-Emitting Diodes, PolyVinylidene Fluoride speaker patches, Electro-Active Polymer haptics and artificial ommatidia for vision. So the stuff's full designation was the alphabetic mouthful "ALD-OLED-PVDF-EAP," but we just called it ALD. It was powered by integrated Microbial Fuel Cells that ran off Karo corn syrup. Additionally, controllable micropores arrayed throughout the skin accessed embedded reservoirs of various volatiles.

Every point on the ALD gave and received haptic feedback, and was also addressible as a luminescent pixel. The micropore system catered to the olfactory spectrum. We had the whole sensory range covered. Best of all, none of this tech was perceptible to humans when inactive. In its offline mode, the ALD just looked like beige leather, warm to the touch.

These two essential components of the Mood Room—the mind-reading rig and the ALD—were the inventions, respectively, of TIE's two youthful genius partners, Harmon Stroeve and Amaranth Bayless. You need to know some background about them to appreciate my story.

Harmon was a guy, in charge of the XfMRI gear. Amaranth was a gal, creator of the ALD. Both brilliant, they were so much alike that they were total opposites. Or were they one and the same, precisely because they were so different from each other? Anyhow, they disliked each other so intensely they were fated to mate. (That's when disaster almost struck.) I know, it's all paradoxical, but I can't think how to say it otherwise.

Harmon was completely self-taught. He had built his first 3-D printer out of cannibalised parts when he was twelve. Apprenticing himself to various brilliant mentors, both corporate and rogue, he had totally avoided higher education, for which he had a great disdain. He lived on the bleeding edge of poverty.

Amaranth came from Long Island money. A bit older than Harmon, she had gotten her doctorate from the Department of Cell and Molecular Biology at Uppsala University in Sweden, where she had enriched the university's endowment by several patents, not the least of which blueprinted an artificial leaf.

It was always a temptation, upon first meeting the inventors and seeing their interpersonal dynamic, to label Harmon hard-edged, a physicist, an engineer, and Amaranth a soft and squishy biologist. But Harmon's main concern these days was with the human brain and emotions, the ultimate amorphous discipline. And Amaranth treated organic cellular mechanisms like gears and circuits, plugging them together in different combinations like a plumber. That's part of what I mean about them being so dissimilar, yet so simpatico.

The two had met at the Fractal 2020 conference, and, despite some initial high-watt sparkage, had begun to discuss their dream projects, which swiftly dovetailed into the ambitious Mood Room. Amaranth had easily secured venture capital through her high-class social network, and TIE was born.

In such a small nascent company and in such tight quarters, TIE's founding parents Harmon and Amaranth had necessarily to work intimately together. The resulting storm of melodrama when their attitudes and outlooks clashed frequently left us feeling like typhoon survivors.

One day after a particularly intense battle, feeling a need for relief, I retreated inside the Mood Room, ostensibly to test some new subroutines I had installed, but really just to get some peace and quiet.

The door into the Mood Room sphere was a small round latched portal meant to maximize structural integrity. It always oriented itself at the equator when the Mood Room was inactive. Once you crawled inside past the swung-aside actuators, however, there was plenty of room to stand up. Sensing a user, the interior of the Mood Room would automatically suffuse with a warm white light from every inch of the ALD.

Inside the Mood Room, you were automatically subject to the mind-reading rig. But the gear did not begin acting on your thoughts automatically. You had to transmit a certain mental command, one that I had selected. Trying to be a little too cute, and to choose a unique trigger not likely to be accidentally employed, I had settled on the mental waveform that synced with clenching your Kegel muscles. You know, the pubococcygeus muscles of the pelvic floor that are exercised to strengthen bladder control. Everyone knew how to clench them, but it was not something one generally did unintentionally.

So I made the clenching gesture and said, "Let's run." Besides the XfMRI mood reader, our device also employed conventional voice-recognition with some mild AI as backup.

Immediately the interior of the Mood Room transformed into an ultra-realistic 360-degree environment replicating a portion of the trails at Presidio Park in San Francisco. Hot sunlight laved me, the cry of seagulls sounded, I smelled the ocean, a breeze stroked my cheek, and then I took off. In reality, the Mood Room was spinning like a hamster ball. But for me, it was as if I were jogging outdoors on a beautiful day. I even felt gravel track beneath my shoeless feet, not soft ALD, thanks to the haptics. I mostly forgot about my headaches at work, although when I momentarily recalled some collateral insults I had received from Harmon and Amaranth, the Mood Room caused clouds to pass across the sun, and the air to chill.

Eventually I worked off my tension and slowed my pace, the Mood Room reacting accordingly. I did the Kegel maneuver and mentally instructed the machine to shutdown. I exited, finished the work day, and went home.

That night, the bad thing happened.

Amaranth and Harmon both decided to work past midnight. The atmosphere was somewhat triumphant and celebratory, since their baby was so close to perfection. Apparently, liquid intoxicants—just some beers—entered the picture. One thing led to another, all competitive interdisciplinary barriers were breached, serious snogging ensued, and an impulsive decision to seal their new empathy with sexual congress was made. (Years later, when Hollywood released the biopic about Harmon and Amaranth, that scene alone helped earn the film its Oscar.) The chilly, industrial, hard-surfaced factory being unconducive to their lusts, they spontaneously decided to use the Mood Room, for privacy, warmth and softness.

After hastily shedding their clothes, Harmon and Amaranth tumbled inside the sphere and continued their foreplay.

That's when all chaos erupted.

Did you know you instinctively clench your Kegel muscles at such a passionate time? Neither did I.

The Mood Room instantly began to respond to the broadcast emotions of its users.

Instantly synthesized pheromones gushed from the micropores. An audiovisual show of erotic images and sounds—many lifted from the personal social-media pages of the inventors—bombarded them. Haptic stroking and tickling assaulted the naked humans. But most dangerously of all, the actuators went wild, inventively deforming the Mood Room into some kind of peristaltically churning, bucking, massage womb that kept Harmon and Amaranth too topsy-turvy and breathless, too poked and squeezed to issue a verbal command.

The Mood Room had already humped its hapless riders into insensibility and was ready to do them to death, when a failsafe I had installed kicked in. The software sent out tweets to me whenever it attempted some new routine, and so I was awakened from sleep by my phone alarm. Once at the TIE site, I managed to shut down the Mood Room from outside, and extract its bruised and embarrassed, but still living victims.

The rest of the Mood Room's history you probably know quite well. The product rolled out and achieved market dominance faster than iPhones, iPads and iDolls combined. Me, Harmon, Amaranth and all the others got very rich, and now I have my own Mood Room XXIII habitat here, inside the remodeled asteroid, 99942 Apophis.

And nowadays, as we ease into the twenty-second century, she keeps me very happy indeed.

ABOUT YUBBA VINES

I have now co-written more stories with Rudy Rucker than with anyone else. (Although since Michael Bishop and I did two novels together, the Bishop-DiFi joint wordage is probably larger.) Working with Rudy is always a joy. He is easygoing and spontaneous, while still being a master craftsman, dedicated to his art. He takes my brain places it would never otherwise go.

Which, after all, is the whole point of reading and writing this stuff!

YUBBA VINES

[WRITTEN WITH RUDY RUCKER]

"Lifter," said Bengt, looking up from his computer tablet. "It's right near us tonight. My friend Olala has been messaging me about it. He always knows the deep underground stuff. Lifter is this unmarked transient chrome diner? It's been drifting around Boston for a few weeks. Let's run over there and eat." With a slight effort Bengt arose from the collapsed cushions of their whipped old couch.

"You're talking about a hipster food truck?" said Cammy, glancing up from her own screen at the kitchen table. "For our big evening out?" She brushed back her dark hair with one hand. It was a gesture that Bengt loved.

"Well, you know Olala," said Bengt. "He's a countercountercountercultural obscurationist. He's never even told me where he's from. Maybe Lifter is retro instead of hipster. Hearty fare for working folks who aren't afraid to say I love you."

"I'm not hearty," said Cammy, her pretty face a dusky oval in the apartment's fading light. "I'm a sarcastic social parasite, *verdad*?"

"Oh that's just your web persona," said Bengt. "Your career. But I know the real Cammy, you little slyboots. At least you *have* a career. By the way, Olala says Lifter is cheap. I figure they scour the planet for the rock-bottom ingredients. Thailand, Turkestan, Tunisia. Non-locavore and proud of it."

"I'm supposed to eat swill standing the street? The cut-rate slop spotting my sadly eager evening-wear?"

"We'll be sitting at a nice table," said Bengt. "The Lifter diner is a giant tractor-trailer truck where you go inside. Come on now, Cammy. It'll be a kick."

There wasn't anyone outside the unmarked Lifter truck. Bengt had to pound on the side of the silver trailer to get in. At the head of three folding steps, the entrance was a shiny chrome rectangle that spun on its center axis—like a rudimentary revolving door. As Cammy passed through, the door caught up with her and tapped her butt. Like it was taking her measure. Looking back from the inside, she found herself completely unable to see the lines of the door against the wall. A one-way entrance.

"Tonight specials bean pork, duck plum, or both in combo," said a chef, barely taller than the waist-high sill of the kitchen's window. "My name Barb." The woman wore a green T-shirt, a maroon apron, and a dangling twinkly necklace. Even though she looked like a aging white school-teacher, her accent was something like Filipino. Odd. "We got ice-cream too," added Barb, waving a two-tined fork. "What you preferring?"

"Falafel with mint tea?" said Cammy.

"No problemo. Mister?"

"The pork duck combo," said Bengt. "And a pistachio milkshake?"

"No problemo," repeated the cook. "Sit relax. No charge for first visit Lifter. You pay later, pay a lot." She laughed.

"Sweet," said Bengt uncertainly.

The truck's interior was dimly lit, with mirrored walls that made it hard to judge the space's size. An exit sign glowed on the far wall. The tables were reasonably sized, the chairs quite normal. The other diners were reassuringly random, some in pairs, some alone. Not down-and-outers, and not excessively hip. A few of them seemed somehow ecstatic. Slumped in their chairs.

"You think Lifter is religious?" asked Cammy as she and Bengt took their seats. "Free food is like a church shelter or a Krishna picnic."

"Could be some kind of promo," said Bengt. "I couldn't find any info about Lifter on the web at all. I just have those messages from Olala. He uses a special encryption that he and his buddies made up. Jah-code."

With an unsettling nimbleness, Barb the cook wriggled across the room, apron flapping. Bringing their plates. A thick stew for Bengt, and a very presentable pita with falafel balls for Cammy. Cammy watched as her husband tasted his meaty porridge.

"Awesome," mumpfed Bengt, mouth full. His spoon was already ladling up his second bite.

Cammy bit into her falafel. The pita dough was light and soft. The crisp fried garbanzo balls were nestled in creamy hummus, slathered with cucumbers in yogurt, and streaked with a rich red hot sauce. And the tea was a revelation. It was as if Cammy had never really had mint tea before.

They ate in silence, savoring the meal.

"Unspeakably toothsome," said Cammy when she finished. "Good call, Bengt. I'm surprised this place isn't completely full. And with a huge line around the block."

"It's hard to find Lifter," said Bengt, siphoning up the last of his pale green milkshake. "Olala says the truck moves around all the time. Very weird."

"I like being in on a secret," said Cammy. "Maybe I shouldn't even try to post about this place." She paused, considering. "But, nah. If I post, I'll be breaking fresh news. Good for my numbers. In fact—" She drew out her ever present smart phone, captured some video of the dimly glittering space, and added a few keystrokes. And then she frowned. "Damn. It uploaded, but not to the right site. It's on something called Wiggleweb? What's that supposed to—"

Just then the music started, a sweet reggae dub tape, played very loud; a bass line was running an insinuating melody over the percussive double-strums of a guitar. A seriously fat white guy hopped onto a tiny stage near the exit sign. He was pale as dough, short-haired and clean-shaven, attired in nerdly sweatshirt and khakis. He wore a dangly glowing necklace like that of Barb the cook.

Wobbling to the beat, the man began singing authentic reggae. In the break after the first song he introduced himself, delivering his words in a zestful Jamaican patois. "A man named Majek Wobble made me Churchill Breakspeare, ya know. I and I *rastafarize* you."

During the next song, Churchill stepped down from the stage and began trucking from table to table. His smoothly flowing voice had no need of a microphone. Some of the other guests seemed already to know him.

During the next break, the singer paused by Bengt. "I surely see you again. The cut of your jib so fine."

"I'm Bengt and this is Cammy. You're a great singer."

"Irie," said the doughy Churchill.

Bengt's attention was caught by Churchill's necklace. It was a loose string adorned by luminous scraps—shimmering rods, glittering lumps, patterned scrolls, tufts of threads. He'd never seen anything like it before. It was garish and...

"Hypnotic," murmured Cammy, fascinated by the necklace as well. She looked up at Churchill, almost at a loss for words. "I don't, ah, understand your business model?"

"We feed our people high and tall," said Churchill Breakspeare. "And down the line, we reap." He called out towards the corner kitchen. "Our guests want toothy treats, Sistah Barb!"

"How do you manage that accent?" asked Cammy. "It's uncanny."

"You'll learn before you know," said Churchill, patting his peculiar necklace. "Like Majek Wobble."

Barb the cook was at their table again, bubbling with equivocal laughter. The dessert plates glowed with—luminous pudding. Dark shapes lurked within.

"Living food," said Churchill. "Grow your glow." He swept little Barb into his plump arms and the two of them began skanking around the room, with Churchill's voice lilting in another island song. By now some of the other guests had left, and the remaining ones seemed zonked.

The effects of the dessert were dizzying and hard to recall. Bengt's sense of it was that he and Cammy lounged in their Lifter chairs for quite a long time, feeling ambitious, expansive and proud of themselves. At some point they decided to go home—and this wasn't entirely easy.

All of the other guests had disappeared. Churchill and Barb were huddled in the corner kitchen, perhaps preparing the next day's food. By now Cammy and Bengt didn't feel like any further interactions with their vaguely disturbing hosts.

"The exit sign," Bengt said, pointing. He and Cammy walked there holding hands—as if making their way through a frightening forest. The dim Lifter space seemed more cavernous than before. The empty tables and chairs were like toy furniture from a dollhouse. Small flittery shapes darted around the room's edges, never directly in view, visible only from the corners of one's eyes.

No actual door could be seen beneath the glowing exit sign. But when Cammy instinctively pressed herself to the wall, a narrow rectangle opened and she tumbled through—Bengt heard her cursing at her rough landing on the street.

Bengt pressed himself against the wall too, and he could feel the material beginning to thin. But at the last moment one of the room's rapid peripheral shapes sped close and nipped his left ear. He felt more than heard the sound of the punch—a juicy crunch of cartilage. He began screaming.

The wall opened up a rectangle just wide enough for Bengt to squeeze through. On his way out, he heard Churchill Breakspeare's voice echoing from within the Lifter trailer.

"Harvest party tomorrow."

Bengt and Cammy made their way home through the shady back streets of Boston and conked out on their bed without even talking. The experience had been so disorienting that Bengt didn't think to check on what had happened to his ear until the next morning. And then it was Cammy who pointed it out.

"Oh god, they tagged you. It's a yellow-green disk with weird runic symbols on it. I'd call the color chartreuse? High visibility. Like something you'd see on a wild animal from an endangered species."

Bengt fingered the oddly slick tag, took a look in the mirror. Kind of cool. Like a high-hole earring, but it didn't have a removable back. Tentatively, he tugged at it. The gaudy tag resisted, inflicting pain proportional to any pressure. He relented.

"Well, it's no weirder than half the jewelry you see on the street," he said defensively. "Urban primitive. Maybe it's like some kinda Lifter customer loyalty card? Latest tech, I bet! Favored status, bargains galore! I guess Churchill dug me."

Cammy looked at Bengt as if she were inspecting a pickled specimen at a carnival freakshow, a jar in a medical teratology museum. "Or maybe he picked up on what a pushover you are. You're the guy who gives money to those just-need-five-dollars-to-catch-a-bus-back-home street scammers. Are you saying it doesn't bother you—being microchipped like a three-toed sloth?"

"Not one whit," blathered Bengt. He still felt a little giddy from that magical pudding dessert. "Not if it means free delicious grub like we had last night. How is this any more humiliating than food stamps? Being unemployed, I've gotta cut corners, gotta manage the ol' nonexistent cash flow."

"Listen, we're getting by fine with my video blogs and sock-puppet reviews and online ads. I told you not to worry. We're married. I'll take care of you."

"Yeah, okay, but I'm ashamed. I still can't believe that my Brown University bachelor's degree in semiotics with a minor in French isn't good for anything! And meanwhile my student loans are as big as an elephant's balls, and they're not getting any smaller."

"You'll get your chance, Bengt," said Cammy, patting his cheek. "I still believe in you. But now I've got to get cranking on the edits for my new instructional video. *How To Clean Your Own Fugu Fish.*"

"You could afford a fugu?"

"I'm not using a real one. Just a sand dab. Looks the same on the video. I never did find that video I tried to upload last night, by the way. And there's no sign of a Wiggleweb. I guess that weird food made us kind of high."

"A lot of questions," said Bengt.

"Why don't you go see your pal Olala?" suggested Cammy. "A visit to his cave always cheers you up. Find out what's the deal with Lifter. And ask him about that silly tag in your ear. And while you're at it, maybe you and your old pal can do some career networking?" A giggle escaped Cammy. "He might know of a job deconstructing old issues of *Paris Match* magazine."

Bengt felt miffed by Cammy's slight upon his chosen field. "Johnny Hallyday is a king, Cammy, and don't forget it! You've heard me singing his songs. His wife Sylvie Vartan was the *Blondie* of the yé-yé era. That's too dated? How about pop philosopher Bernard-Henri Lévy, his heavily cosmeticized wife Arielle Dombasle, and his billionaire mistress Daphne Guinness? *Paris Match* has a great tag-line for Lévy. *God is dead, but my hair is perfect.* The dude puts the I in triangle, to lift a phrase."

"I and I," said Cammy gaily. "Leave me to my faux fugu, oh dog-tagged sage."

Olala Ogallala lived in a conceptual art project. He and some of his layabout computer hacker buddies had, by studying snitched blueprints, discovered a sealed-off, oddly non-Euclidean, empty windowless space in the upper reaches of a local mall. They'd covertly broken through into the concrete chamber, then furnished it by stealthily trucking in cast-off furniture via the attached parking garage. Tapping into the mall's electricity and water completed their homesteading. And waste management consisted of a reeking chemical toilet. But Olala's pals had soon tired of the inconveniently situated playroom, leaving the industrial-strength burrow to its lone eccentric tenant.

Having confirmed via jah-coded message that Olala was accepting callers, Bengt essayed the twisted path to the man's living quarters. Up oil-strewn ramps, dodging departing and arriving carloads of consumers, through toxic exhaust fumes, past the deliberately misangled video cameras, around an insulation-foam-slathered pillar. Lift aside a draped piece of tarp camouflaged to look just like the wall, and bingo-bango, home sweet home!

A man of indeterminate ethnicity and race, Olala sported a massive crop of dreads. He'd twined bits of wire into the locks, giving him the look of a dark dandelion. Olala claimed some Native-American and Romany blood, among numerous other strains. Today, as he often did, he wore filched coveralls bearing the logo of the mall's maintenance squad: useful camouflage.

Olala waved hello to Bengt without taking his eyes off his funky old laptop's screen. "Make yourself at home, ligand. Catalytic helper molecule that you are. Bind onto my magnificence. I got sorghum beer in the fridge."

Olala had picked up a learned style of discourse during his senior year at Brown with Bengt. He'd shown up, seemingly out of nowhere, and had somehow conned the university into letting him earn a BS degree in computer science during a single year, during which he'd redesigned the school's entire network for them. Olala's year of wonder had overlapped with Bengt's senior year, and the two of them had some wild times together. Bengt had always seemed to amuse his freewheeling friend.

Bengt popped the cap off an unlabeled bottle of homebrew and chugged. Tasty, but lacking some of its usual kick and savor. A patina of ghost flavors from Lifter remained on his tongue, rendering common foodstuffs bland.

"So Cammy and I went to Lifter last night," said Bengt. "I'm still a little twisted."

"Good," said Olala. "That's what we like to see. Let me push you a little further. Look at this documentary about chix and shedders." He flashed Bengt a sly smile.

"Chicks and shredders? Like the skateboard scene?"

"Way wrong, Dong Dong. The lobster industry. Chix are the youngsters, illegal to trap 'em. Shedders are the somewhat flexible soft-shelled lobsters. They're a good catch at certain times. But how do you think the fishermen filter out the chix, huh?"

Knowing Olala's penchant for high-tech gadgets, Bengt ventured, "Underwater laser interferometry tape measures?"

"Ha! They use a simple slit! All size lobsters enter the alluring trap. But only bitty ones can squeeze out the slit. Self-selecting! An elegant hack! *Feast* your eyes on these images, you tasty dude. Let your mind roam."

Olala slider-slid the video backwards and Bengt looked over his shoulder while it ran again. Why exactly was Olala showing him this?

Just to be saying something, Bengt asked, "So what happens if a lobster enters the trap at chix size, but then stays and eats so much bait it gets too fat to escape?"

"Tough titty, bro," said Olala. "It's gets all *Hotel California* weepy. The consumer is trapped by greed."

"If lobsters were smarter, it wouldn't work," said Bengt.

Olala stared pityingly at his friend. "God, you're slow, Bengt. Free food? Big box? Hard to get out?"

The penny dropped. Dizzy from the idea, Bengt collapsed into one of Olala's ragged armchairs. "The Lifter people—you're saying they're like *lobstermen*? They want to *catch* Cammy and me?"

"What it is," said Olala. "They took my brah Majek Wobble day before yesterday."

"God—I think I heard this guy Churchill saying that name last night. I'm so dizzy from that dessert they gave me. Majek is, uh—"

"Reggae musician, mon. When I went to Lifter two days ago, I took Majek with me. I met him after one of his shows at a club this weekend. Smoking spliffs, talking Jah. I took him to Lifter. And he didn't get out."

"What are you saying? They kidnapped him?"

"When you saw *Churchill* at Lifter last night," said Olala, narrowing his eyes. "Was he putting on some type of performance?"

"He was singing," said Bengt. "He has this amazing reggae voice. Even though he's totally whitebread. But he, uh, yeah, he did say he learned from Majek Wobble."

"Here's how it went. I go to Lifter two days ago to show Majek a big time. We lie around in there all day eating and smoking ganja, they don't care. We have a triple helping of the radiant pudding, and then another and then another. Everyone pigging out and feeling wavy. And then the vibe gets very tight. The truck engine starts, *varoom*. People running for the exit door. They can't get out, hardly none of them. Majek Wobble was skinny, but now he's too fat. I'm fat too, but I—well, I know how to shed."

"You sloughed off an outer layer like a shedder lobster," said Bengt, not taking this very seriously.

"Don't smile, ligand. I want you uptight. Otherwise this show's no fun. Earlier this week Churchill was singing Vegas crooner, you know. Total shit. But now he swallowed up Majek Wobble and he can sing and talk Jamaican. Proof positive. Aha!"

Bengt was weary of this mind-game. He looked around Olala's cave and shook his head. "Cammy and I had a really fun time last night. It's been awhile since things went that well. And I was glad you'd sent me there. I felt like I had a friend. And now you have to start on this weird trip about Lifter being a trap. You're bumming me out."

"It's good if you're bummed. More interesting. But I've warned you, and you'll still have a chance when you go back."

"What do you know about this tag in my ear, asshole?"

Olala gave Bengt another of his significant smiles. "I assume you, ah, didn't pick out the gewgaw yourself? No? Well—maybe it's like when the lobstermen tag an especially juicy specimen. So they can spot him when he returns."

"I want it off!" said Bengt yanking impatiently at the chartreuse disk. He saw spots and the pain made the room go dark. But he didn't let up. "Get some pliers and crush it, Olala!"

"*Calmo*," said Olala. "You want to be keeping that tag." He rooted through the rubbish at the edges of the room and returned with a craft-saw mounted onto the body of an electric drill. "I'll cut the earring-post for you."

A few minutes later, the garish tag lay on Olala's desk. Olala patched the really quite tiny puncture in Bengt's ear with scrap of tape. Relieved to be free, Bengt used his smart phone to photograph the earring from several angles. He fed the images into his web search tool. No matches.

"Shouldn't expect any," said Olala, shaking his head. "Not on the straight web. I happen to know there's a network-level filter routine to block out anything having to do with Lifter. A filter that's omnipresent malware in the Man's servers. But there *is* stuff about Lifter on the *Wiggleweb*. That's a jah-code encrypted internet relay chat thing that me and my posse use. We're making, like, a documentary."

"Nobody tells me anything."

"You're a semiotics major, man. You're lower than chix. But you'll get your chance."

"I need to go back to Lifter," said Bengt, brushing the teasing aside. He'd been suddenly sandbagged by a memory of the savory food. "Right now. For lunch. If I can find the place."

Olala gave him yet another odd, sly look. "Oh, you'll find it. But let me put an app on your phone. Why? Let's pretend that it predicts Lifter's locations based on feeds from HowSquare, WebWhere, UseeMEseeU, and ShotSpotter. Yeah, yeah, that's what I'm saying it does."

"ShotSpotter?" said Bengt uncertainly. "Isn't that the software that cops use to pinpoint open-air gunfire?"

"Would make sense. If this app was in fact what I said it was. There's been some armed assaults against the Lifter truck lately. Tasty, tasty. People losing their heads. Next of kin, embittered friends—they're like: *Lifter stole my loved one!* The anger's building to a climax. *Who killed Majek Wobble?* I can see the posters, the benefit concert, the rabid midnight mob—" Olala trailed off, busy tweaking Bengt's phone.

"I'm really not sure where you're at," said Bengt.

"Skungy Olala in his filthy cave. Into his flaky, menacing head trips. Where did Olala come from, anyway? What are his goals? Many questions. Here's your phone, ligand. Have a good time in the truck. Eat for hours and hours. And, dude, if you can—learn how to shed. It's a better ending if you do. Don't end up like Majek Wobble."

Utterly bewildered, Bengt pocketed his phone and his ear tag and left in a hurry, detouring through the mall proper to nosh on some free food-court samples. Maybe if he ate enough of that stuff he wouldn't need to go to Lifter.

But, as with Olala's beer, the tidbits of Popeye's fried chicken and Panda Express boneless ribs, usually so rewarding, failed to please. Nothing but Lifter food would do. Looking around the humdrum mall, Bengt realized that he really *did* think Olala was crazy. The Lifter truck was a soul-devouring lobster trap? Get out of here.

And okay—even if there was something sinister about the Lifter—Bengt was too sharp to trap. Why not go there, score another great meal, and get out of the place in time? He could do it.

Bengt studied the little disk of his ear tag. It was a comely object. A gift from the Lifter crew. The writing around its edge was indeed a bit like runes. Or maybe hieroglyphs. Pictograms. Would be interesting to work up a semiotic analysis of them, comparing the runes to cuneiform and to Linear B. A publishable paper in there, an entrée to grad school. That would be an answer to his job drought. Nestle into the bosom of Dame Academe.

But now, inescapably, his mind circled back to his one obsessive thought. His hunger. He pulled out his smart phone and fired up Olala's app. The app bleated, flickered, and died—leaving the phone in such a screwed-up state that Bengt had to reboot it via the on/off switch. And now the phone's server was labeled Wiggleweb. And Olala's app still wasn't doing squat.

What-fucking-ever. How to find Lifter? The ear tag! It was glowing along one edge. Like a digital compass.

Bengt left the mall, holding the ear tag flat in the palm of his hand, letting it lead him through the mazy streets of Boston. In half an hour he was back inside the Lifter truck, tucking into a massive meal. A gay banner across the crowded, bustling room read HARVEST FEST. Churchill and Barb were everywhere, Churchill singing all the while, heavy into the reggae.

When Bengt awoke from his first postprandial nap, he waddled over to the kitchen counter and asked Barb to set him up again. And again. And again.

* * * *

The sand dab had begun to stink like low tide in the Gowanus Canal. During the afternoon-long vidding of the tutorial, the hot umbrella lights had reduced the fish to the consistency of cow snot. Cammy's thoughts ran, not for the first nor the last time, down a familiar groove: how nice life must've been, back in the old, stable, pre-postmodern, un-fucked-up economy, where you punched a clock and got a weekly check for forty years of eight-hour days, two weeks of vacation every year, then a good pension. But no, she and her peers had been born into the zero-security, free entrepreneurial age of the Endless Hustle.

She wondered if the pro-tech cheerleader type bloggers ever had to confront a gloppy mound of fish guts in their daily rounds? Probably not. Would she ever reach such exalted heights? It seemed so improbable most days. Little Camila Delgado, CEO, CFO, COO, Forbes 400. Not gonna hold her breath! But at least she had her Big Papi Bengt, lovable wackjob, and they had a roof over their heads and food on the table—

Bengt? Food? Where was he anyhow? Getting dark, no call, no text. Could he have gone back to the Lifter truck on his own—summoned by the esoteric forces who'd made his ear tag, drawn in like a deer to a poisoned salt lick, a tiger to a steak-baited blind, a fly to perfumed flypaper?

Hastily shutting down her gear, Cammy whipped off a text to Bengt. Still no response. She tried a voice call. Nada. Her nerves started to thrum, like telephone pole guy-wires under hurricane assault. What appeals for help did Bengt's silence leave? Olala!

"Yeah, sure, he was here, Cam. Left hours ago. I hope he remembers to turn shedder."

"Shedder?"

"Like a soft-shelled lobster. So he can squeeze out of the Lifter truck. It's basically a giant lobster trap. They fatten us up and when we can't get out, they ship us away."

"Don't be so stoned and crazy, Olala. Help me find my husband."

"*Seguro*, I'll give you an app to find the Lifter truck, *porque no*? I gave the same app to your *hombre*. Be sure and shoot a lot of video."

Olala's use of Spanish was a habit he fell into when talking to Cammy. Normally she didn't mind it, but now it pissed her off. "*Pendejo*! You deliberately sent Bengt into a death trap?"

"Sorry, ligand. Between a man and his destiny, I interpose my carcass not. No apologies, no blame. You want my search warez? Hold the phone for a squirt of jah-juice!"

Out on the streets, Cammy turned on Olala's app—but it seemed balky, pre-beta, of no value. The only visible effect was that it changed Cammy's service provider to Wiggleweb. Early adopters get the shaft!

Shaft? She saw a sudden mental image of Bengt on a skewer running up his butt and out his mouth, her husband roasting on the spit, his skin crackling, his rendered fat dribbling into a trough of seaweed layered over steamer clams, the trough wedged between granite stones amid a seaside fire whose flames had already blackened Bengt's face and singed away his hair. His blank, boiled-solid eyes were milky white, and sinister reggae music was playing and—*No!*

Something within Cammy rose up to replace Olala's seemingly useless app. A heartlink to Bengt, a gutlink to the living Lifter dessert pudding, a global positioning system using old-school *biological* cells. At every turning, Cammy followed her instinctual twitches and tics, her heart tugs and her intestinal rumblings.

Seven-thirty PM. Streetlights—those that remained unbroken on this mingy, deserted avenue—blipping on in automatic response to daylight's demise. And there, a block away, the Lifter truck! Hulking like something awkward and out of its native element—like a boxy stranded submarine or a downed suburb of the flying city of Laputa—the truck radiated a sexy/dangerous vibe. Its edges were smooth and gently curved, its cab was sleek and wind-faired. Cammy videoed it. Somehow the truck reminded her of a love-robot Sorayama gynoid pinup calendar that Bengt and his friends had greatly admired. Boyish Bengt and his little needs.

Quietly Cammy felt along the trailer for a glossy chrome entrance rectangle that would revolve like the pivoting haunted-house bookshelves of many an *Abbott and Costello Meet Karloff* epic. But today the seamless exterior of the truck stymied her efforts.

Apparently Lifter was accepting no new patrons tonight. Full complement of overstuffed, duck-and-plum-sated victims? No spare room in the giant chrome lobster trap? Cargo hold full! And *cargo* implied a destination, mind you, a place to deliver the goods. Departure imminent, full speed to the abattoir!

Cammy wasn't about to let her Bengt be salted away. She had to add herself to the haul and rescue her temptation-trapped mate. But even now she didn't dare pound on the truck's side. She feared—who knew what from these creeps? Savage automated tridents and weighted Roman gladiator nets?

She scampered to the shiny truck cab at the front of the trailer. It was a Freightliner Century model, a thousand like it seen every day on freeways, anonymous, no painted name or logo, albeit this one had oddly sensual curves. It was a luxe sleeper model, featuring a berth behind the driver's seat. Hardly daring to hope, Cammy tested the passenger-side door.

Unlocked! In she tumbled, panting from fear more than from exertion. She scrambled through the gap between the seats to the blanket-heaped mattress in back, and drew the stained cloth curtain to shut her off from sight. The curtain's ringlets rattling seemed terribly loud. But no voice cried out.

This back part of the cabin smelled funky, but not with a pong she recognized. Zombie sweat, skin from odd hides, farts of strange esters. Cammy captured some video.

And now her hand found a heavy wrench on the floor. She clutched it greedily, like a cannibal with a thigh bone full of juicy marrow. Time seemed to stretch like a wad of Silly Putty bearing the impression of a photo, distorting the portrait of reality as it lengthened.

She heard a wild hubbub from within the Lifter trailer behind her. Footsteps hitting the pavement, two or three people escaping. Little

Barb's voice yelling after them, "You'll be back, you greedy skinny sons of bitch!" Was Bengt running with them?

No time to check, for now she heard the truck cab's door opening, with huffing fat man sounds. Churchill Breakspeare? Tuneful humming—"You Can Get It If You Really Want."

Churchill's hands beat out breaks on the truck's dash, the motor roared to life, and they moved off, Barb calling a farewell from the sidewalk.

They rolled slowly through city streets, no direction evident to cloistered Cammy. Then faster, evidently picking up the interstate. Half an hour's steady travel thereafter, before pulling off. Cammy tried to imagine a circle of likely destinations surrounding the city, but came up uncertain, there being no known facility with the sign she was imagining: *Human Feedlot And Meatpacking Center.*

Churchill Breakspeare exited the cab, still humming Marley's "Buffalo Soldier." Cammy waited a few seconds, then crept cautiously out. Inhabiting the musty bunk had left her feeling unclean. Through the truck cab's windows, she had a panoramic view of an abandoned airfield, ringed by a chainlink fence and lit by scattered security lights on tall stanchions. Now she knew where she was: a small regional airstrip, formerly used mostly by amateur pilots and an air freight company or two. It had gone bust with the bad economy. Was Lifter going to fly their human catch out of the country? Was Bengt really inside the trailer?

Cammy heard Churchill fussing with the truck's hitch, decoupling cables and such. If she exited to ground level, she'd surely be spotted. But if she could clamber above—

Cammy tucked the wrench into her waistband, slithered out the passenger side window, then up and onto the broad roof of the truck's cab. Flattened there, she spied on Churchill.

The heavyset entertainer had entirely freed the diner from its conveyance. He'd opened a hidden panel on the diner's side and was tapping various buttons in a rapid sequence. As he worked, he sang the Clash's "Armageddon Time." *A lot of people won't get no supper tonight...*

At the same time, on the flat roof of the diner, growing like mushrooms after a rain, a host of rods and antennae sprang forth—orbs and dishes, vents and baffles, vanes and widgets. Cammy videoed them. The newly sprouted equipment began to buzz and hum. The diner itself began to quiver.

Blurry howls from within, like the sounds of damned souls, and—yes—she could hear poor Bengt among them.

All four of the diner's wheels lifted, slowly but perceptibly, off the airstrip's cracked tarmac!

Without any thought or consideration, Cammy got her feet under her and sprang across the narrow, bi-level gap and onto the diner roof, quickly flattening herself there.

Churchill may or may not have heard her thump. But it was too late to do anything. The launch sequence was well underway. A glowing transparent nimbus snapped into being, enclosing the whole diner, and Cammy with it. Luckily it had formed a few inches above her head—failing to bisect her skull. Anxiously she put out her hand to feel the shining surface. It was a solid shell.

Accelerating upward, the diner headed for the sky—

—and slowed to a stop an hour later, approaching a silvery spaceship the shape of a vast disk, nearly the size of a city. Not so far below, sweet Earth gleamed like a noctilucent sea creature—Cammy could almost feel Gaia breathing. She got out her phone and captured more video. How many signal bars did low-Earth-orbit offer? Five! But only to the Wiggleweb! For a moment she forgot her worries, losing herself in the craft of her camera work. But then a pang hit her as she remembered her quiet, idle evenings at home with Bengt. Her mission was to bring that life back.

A door opened in the side of the mothership, and the diner drifted in, drawn by a tractor beam. The door closed, air hissed in, and the glassy shell around the diner dissolved. Artificial gravity reigned. Cammy slithered to the floor, awaiting an opportunity.

The lock's inner door opened to reveal—giant ants? Three-eyed lizards? Flying jellyfish? No, the ship was staffed by Cammy's fellow humans. Quislings, sell-outs, opportunistic traitors to their race. They were dressed in identical brown coveralls, the men and the women alike. And they wore those glittery fluffy cobbled-together *bricoleur*-type necklaces like Churchill and Barb. Like a death squad tricked out in aloha leis.

Cammy crouched beneath the trailer, clutching her wrench. And soon her moment came. The workers had opened the back of the Lifter van, and were herding out the wobbly captives—Cammy heard Bengt's voice again, raised as if in a querulous question. But he couldn't properly form his words. Peering through beneath the underside of the diner, she recognized Bengt's beige French designer jeans, swollen like the conical legs of the Michelin man. She videoed the legs.

At this point her plan was simple—to club down the first worker who ventured near her, to put on the worker's coveralls, to stash the unconscious victim inside the van, and to pose as one of the staff. But this was not to be. A slim, reedy-voiced man came upon Cammy from behind and seized her arms in an iron grip.

"Looky here! We got us a stowaway!"

"Too thin for the meat line," said a stern, muscular woman, trotting over. "But we can't send her back. Lock her in a cell, Earl, and we'll decide later. Maybe just take her yubba vine and pitch the rest." The rangy woman peered into Cammy's face. Her eyes had a hard, fanatical glitter. "What was your angle, kiddo? Lose a guy to our catch?"

"No, no," said Cammy. "I, I don't know what happened. I was drunk, and I fell asleep on the top of your truck and—where are we? Is this a garage?"

"That's some weak shit," said reedy-voiced Earl. "Especially with you clutching a wrench to clobber us and all."

"I'm scared!" protested Cammy, and broke into sobs. "Please don't kill me. Maybe I could be one of you? I have nowhere else to go. I'm all alone, you see. No relatives, no friends."

"She's quick with the bullshit," said the tough woman. "I like that. But lock her up for now, Earl. I gotta get to work."

"Okay, Nelda."

Holding Cammy's arms in a painful twist grip, Earl marched her inside the ship. A hellish place, like a level of Dante's Inferno. The ship's domed interior was a great, misty space, like a dimly lit underground city, with the edges fading into the distance.

As she was dragged along, Cammy noticed work stations and clusters of mad activity, with pod-like cubicles here and there. In her time, schoolchildren no longer went on slaughterhouse tours, but she'd seen exposé videos of those bleak and bustling spaces—not unlike this one, with the worst parts off in the distance.

The processing of the latest Lifter load had already begun. To make it the more diabolical, the puffed-up victims were still alive, albeit mumbling and stunned.

The captives were lined up by an oversized operating table, and Nelda, the stringy woman, was leaning over it with a glowing knife. Monomolecular fractal blade. Zen carver with the subtle stiletto. Vorpal!

One by one, the erstwhile Lifter patrons were strapped down, and Nelda leaned over them, quick with her knife as a master butcher. Cammy couldn't quite make out what the woman was doing. Extracting essential entities without mortal harm? But mortal harm aplenty awaited! After the table, the human cattle were yanked up into the air by their heels and sent slowly gliding across the ship's roof, diminishing towards a distant, barely visible nexus of assuredly deadly blades. Poor Bengt was already in transit thither, passive as a pupa.

And now Earl was shoving Cammy into one of those rounded huts. The fat door plumped shut, leaving no sign of a seam around its edges. Cammy was trapped like a seed in a pod. What might she grow into?

But all she could really picture was Bengt's excruciation. He's already suffered some kind of psychic surgery beneath the Vorpal Blade, and now he was swaying toward a more carnal demise. Grade A chops and flank steak. Her husband's childlike greed and naiveté had ruined his life and hers. If only she could have tweaked his personality somehow, willed away all his weaknesses, instilled some spine. But standard marital operating protocols stretched only so far.

Cammy's phone rang! Wiggleweb connection! She fumbled it out, dropped it harmlessly on the resilient floor, then got it up to her ear.

"*Hola, chica*! Olala *aqui*! Gonna get you out of there. Sorry for the unforeseen glitch. Unscripted's okay, but sometimes *muy* fubar. Thought you'd be way more Sigourney Weaver with that wrench. Plot stalled with our star in the hoosegow. Ratings taking an instant dip. No good for the bottom line. Renewal options off the table! But Wiggleweb has plenty of my *compañeros* surreptitiously in place among the Lifter crew. Just sit tight."

"Olala, what are the Lifters extracting before the final slice and dice! What's Bengt going to lose?"

"Oh, that's the yubba vine. Every human's got one. The yubba vine is a hidden organ network of which your Terran medical science knows *nada*. You got your circulatory system, your nervous system, your enteric system, your lymphatic nodes and—your yubba vine. It's your personality's gerbil-wheel, the circle where your mind-spark rushes round and round, making you imagine you've got a continuous self. Like when they stole Majek Wobble's, they got all his mojo plus his toasting talents too. And anyone else can wear someone's vine. Any being, any species. Glitzy, ritzy plug-in plus!"

"Is—is Bengt going to be a zombie if he loses his vine but survives?"

"Not precisely. Just kinda mentally translucent. Less solid and authentic. Insipid. You see lots of such folks around you every day right in Boston. And they still watch TV and pay taxes real fine."

"No!" Cammy began to bang against the pod's rubbery walls, but they absorbed her blows soundlessly.

"Hey, *chica*, calm down! Listen. I gotta book now."

"Wait, tell me what you really are, you *cabrón*! Ratings dip! Terran science! What the fuck is all that!"

But Olala had cut the Wiggleweb signal. No ready answers there.

The undetectable door suddenly manifested itself. Cammy rushed out and instantly collided with what her confused senses initially registered as a kindergarten class on a daytrip. Taking in the scene more coherently, out on the floor of the death arena, she found herself surrounded by a pack of three-foot-tall humans of both genders, all wearing grass skirts, their exposed flesh a gentle green, their black spiky hair like a thicket of quills. Cosmic *Slumberland* imps! Interstellar Wiggleweb elves!

The biggest elf spoke in a *sotto voce di basso profundo*. A low, grainy hum. "Quiet down, crazy lady-miss! No big scenes. We say you rogue meat going to ship's tenderizer machine. We say we want pound you like cutlet to correct anorexic skimp. But really, the Big O, he send us get you and hubby-wubby free. Dramatic *Star Wars* escape from trash compactor climax for show!"

"Show! Show! What fucking show!"

"Wiggleweb chart-topper. *Terran Self-Selecting Provender Challenge*. 'Meet the meat so sweet to eat!' 'Irresistible sophont avarice on parade!' 'Trapped by vestigial Darwinian routines!' And likewise mottos. Olala savvy PR flack, and A-number-one producer in four galactic quadrants."

Cammy felt her head might explode. "Okay, never mind. Just get me and Bengt out of this madhouse."

"Walk this way, dudette," softly rumbled the lead elf.

But before Cammy could take a step, she felt hands descend imperatively, one upon each shoulder.

Nelda stood to one side of Cammy, Earl on the other, once again having crept up Cammy unheard. Not so hard amidst the processing din.

"Now, just where you goin, little miss?" asked Earl.

Nelda squinted menacingly at Cammy. "I doubt your yubba vine is rich and ripe, but I might could harvest it anyhow."

The Wiggleweb elves' leader intervened, all seeming deference and protocol. "Bigtime orders from Chief Snickersnack! Pound the sinews of this one for refectory diet jerky! Look, we open portal straight to ship's kitchen!"

A disc of floor evanesced, revealing a shimmering gateway. Through the moiré scrim, a scene could be dimly apprehended.

Earl bent over to peer into the wormhole. "You sure you done got the right coordinates here? T'other side of this hole don't resemble no tenderizer machine. Looks to me like Prison Bay termination module Number 785, or thereabouts—"

Trusting the goodwill of the Wiggleweb elves, Cammy abruptly shoved Earl through the wormhole. And before Nelda could even shout—a fist to her gut, a leg sweep and a push sent her in Earl's wake.

The floor resumed solidity. The Wiggleweb elves bowed toward Cammy. "Most excellent Linda Hamilton style aggression! Now, the real deal!"

A new short-cut wormhole opened. Englobed like a beloved human herder by a pack of trusty miniature musk oxen vigilant against Lifter wolves, Cammy dropped through. Gravity shifted vectors, and then she was standing half a kilometer away—where Bengt dangled dispiritedly, awaiting the Kafkaesque Penal Colony Rube Goldberg machinery of filleting. He was fourth from the head. So wan and listless were the victims of the yubba-vine extraction process that they hung there as quietly as country hams.

Like macro-amoebas, the pack of Wiggleweb elves merged their substance and flowed a pseudopod around Bengt. They engulfed him, unhooked his heels, and passed him into their center, where Cammy clasped him furiously to herself. His bloated body felt semi-alien, semi-familiar.

"Oh, Bengt, you big idiot doofus glutton!"

Bengt's affect remained bland and flat and sadly diminished. "Sorry, Cammy. I screwed the hot dog, or it screwed me. Guess I'm no Takeru Kobayashi after all."

"Don't worry, B-boy, we're gonna get you home safe and sound. Everything will be super fine!"

"Super fine without my vine? How I pine and do decline. Can't refine the mind offline."

"Oh, shit! Hey, you!" Cammy addressed the general location of the head elf—who was still merged with his posse.

"Not ignorant *hey you*!" came the response. "Papa Palapa, at your rescue."

"Okay, sorry, Papa Palapa. How do I get my man's yubba vine back?"

"Oh, neato mosquito! We go check gift wrap division."

The fused mob of little people, bearing Cammy and Bengt in their metaphoric belly, dropped down another teleportal (Cammy was almost getting to enjoy these rides), and emerged at an assembly line where single-minded workers were packing up fetish-like objects into long circuit-laden homeostatic shipping boxes as big as those that might hold a dozen untrimmed South American roses. Papa Palapa whisper-boomed to Cammy: "I busy up head wrapper man, you check out vines!"

Peeling off from the pack, Papa Palapa engaged the foreman, an officious, vice-presidential candidate type, who soon assembled his team of packers to help respond to Palapa's frenetic, double-talking badinage. The yubba vines were unattended.

Very tentatively, Cammy lowered her forefinger onto one of the gnarly assemblages, a weird welter of cartilage, vertebrae, ectoplasmic tendrils, bits of bone, viscera, ganglia and dendritic microtubules.

As soon as her finger touched the vine, she was blasted with non-self memories of growing up black in Roxbury. She jerked back in surprise. Reluctantly, she began testing all the other exposed specimens, almost overwhelmed by each one's immersive sensory assault. What if Bengt's had already been disguised as a glittery lei for some—

Brown University quad on a hot spring day, tossing a Frisbee, whoa, look at that babe, gotta bone up for Derrida 101, wish I could bone her—

"Bengt! Here you are!"

Her husband lowered his face to within an inch of the funky neuro-anima web. "I think I recognize my pineal gland." He reached down and grabbed the yubba vine. Instantly the old Bengt was back! He draped the soul-chord around his neck like a scarf. And as he donned the vine, it camouflaged its grisly essence beneath a sparkling illusion of crystals, tufts, spangles and shells. "Cammy, I love you so much! I'd give you my yubba vine if you wanted it."

"It belongs on you."

The pack of Wiggleweb elves, sensing victory, shuffled Bengt and Cammy away from the gift-wrap division. And now the elf-mass subdivided into the former happy throng. Papa Palapa rejoined them.

"Okay, pards! Time now for 'Open the pod bay door, Hal!'"

Cammy felt sure they would be stopped at any minute. But another instant subquantum wormhole jaunt brought them to a collection of small shuttle vessels.

"Can't send you straight to Earth via spaghetti system," Papa Palapa intoned. "Whole planet interdicted. Must use last train to Clarksville." Only then did Cammy really take cognizance of their escape vehicle.

The flying saucer consisted of a shallow chassis approximately as big as a modest hot tub, with side and rear vanes for aerodynamic maneuvering. Half the interior space was occupied by the shielded drive mechanism. A transparent dome rested atop the passenger space. A few failsafe controls clustered around a small steering wheel. Maybe comfortable for Wiggleweb elves, but two humans could barely fit side by side on the padded bench seat, with their legs folded and knees up around their ears.

"This is all you got?"

"Lifter buggers can't be chewers! Hop in!" Papa Palapa raised the dome with a click and a whoosh of hydraulics.

Hopping was not the operative verb. Cammy let Bengt insert his unnatural bulk first, on the passenger side, before cramming herself in behind the wheel. Papa Palapa dropped the dome, which sealed claustrophobically around them with a reassuring thunk.

"Whitney Houston, we have ignition!"

The UFO trundled forward under invisible tractor beams, passed into an airlock, then was squeezed into naked space like a zit exploding.

Freedom!

Except that now they faced an enormous wormhole, big as a cathedral! Sucker-dotted tentacles the size of freight trains spilled from the hole into the raw vacuum, questing for their ship.

A hologram vidscreen on the dashboard flared into life. The three-dee monitor was filled with a writhing nest of saliva-threaded beaks and ciliated mouths, a congeries of rasping tongues and fangs. Cammy felt like puking.

The chaotic organic eating machine bellowed, "Buy one get one free offer still in effect! No rebates! You're in the offer! So get in my shopping cart, you insolent canned goods!"

Against the background of the stars, the wormhole could be seen moving like the oval of a dark anti-searchlight. The tentacles moved ever closer to the small craft with the humans inside.

Cammy shrieked, then grabbed the steering wheel and slammed a button marked FAST. She made like she was sweet sixteen—behind the wheel of Daddy's Camaro once again, all hot tequila in her veins.

The wormhole stayed on their tail for a time but somehow—after a hell of dodging and near misses—they broke into the clear, perhaps too trivial a prize for more recapture effort to be expended.

* * * *

Cammy had triumphed. Or was it Olala's behind-the-scene interventions that had achieved the thrilling climax to this episode of *Terran Self-Selecting Provender Challenge*?

As the upper edges of Earth's atmosphere began to heat the nose of their absurdly tiny craft, Olala himself appeared on the hologram display.

"Good going, kids! We're a hit again! Another season assured. And now that you're in the know, I can get loosey goosey with you. What a relief!"

Olala reached up to grip his hair and pulled off his prosthetic human disguise.

Pointing up directly from the fake shoulders of his cyborg exoskeleton sat a squat lobster head, all mandibles and feelers and beady glassy eyes. Cammy was too numb to be shocked or scared.

Bengt crowed, "Boil me scarlet and dip me in butter. Now I know why you steered clear of those annual fraternity clambakes."

"Nah, just too boring. After all, what's a little cannibalism among friends?"

DISCARD

CPSIA information can be obtained at www.ICGtesting.com
Printed in the USA
LVOW11s0839070116

469560LV00001B/173/P